First published in the UK in 2016 by Usborne Publishing Ltd., Usborne House, 83-85 Saffron Hill, London EC1N 8RT, England. www.usborne.com

p. 100 Lyric from "My Body" by Peter Alsop

p. 101 Lyric from "It's No Fun When You Gotta Eat an Onion" by Peter Alsop

p. 258 Lyric from "Go to Sleep, You Little Creep" by Peter Alsop

p. 266 Lyric from "Bored, Bored, Bored!" by Peter Alsop

For more information on Peter Alsop's songs and CDs go to www.peteralsop.com

A CIP catalogue record for this book is available from the British Library.

JFMAMJJASON / 15 03595/1

ISBN 9781409591221

Printed in the UK.

HOLLY BOURNE

HOW HARD CAN LOVE BE?

Situations that are destined to fail:

The world's most gruesome hangover

+

A ten-hour-long plane journey

+

Economy seating

+

Being five foot eleven

One

Don't be sick on the children… Don't be sick on the children…

Their little heads bobbed beneath me in the queue to get on the aeroplane. My stomach lurched again and I grabbed it. If I clutched at my guts hard enough, hopefully they'd not empty themselves over the excitable heads of the kids in front.

I couldn't be certain, but vomming over innocent kiddlywinks could possibly jeopardize my acceptance onto a long-haul flight.

Why had I done that last shot last night? Why, please? Why? WHY!?

The flight attendant in front checked another ticket and beckoned the passenger past. The line crawled forward under the brutal fluorescent lights of the departure lounge. The aeroplane waited outside the floor-to-ceiling window, looking way too small to carry all these people to America. It was white, like the horse a dashing knight would ride to rescue princesses in a fairytale. But I was no princess, and I could rescue myself thank you very much. All I needed was this aeroplane to put an ocean between me and my evil stepmother.

My stomach lurched again as I remembered how I'd said goodbye…

"Look at the state of her," my stepmother, Penny, said, loud enough for everyone in the security queue to hear. We were at that annoying bit of the airport process where everyone realizes they can't take any liquids with them so decant all their bottles into see-through plastic bags.

"I am here, you know?" I rolled my eyes because I knew it annoyed her and downed the rest of my water bottle.

She ignored me. "They won't let her on the plane."

I looked at Dad desperately for help. He held back a smile.

"Relax, Penny. Think of all the drunken stags they let onto planes to Vegas every day."

"I'm not drunk!" I protested, causing about ten separate clumps of travellers to stop and stare.

Dad laughed and pulled me into a hug. I clung onto him, nestling into his shoulder, inhaling his smell. It helped with the nausea.

"No, you're not drunk, are you, poppet? Just hungover. You had quite the leaving do. Though you do *smell* drunk." He took a deliberate whiff and pushed me away… "PHEWEE."

"I showered this morning…"

... Which I had. I'd also just happened to sweat out the previous night's sambuca shots on the drive to the airport.

Dad pulled me in for another hug. "In that case, come 'ere."

It would've been a tender moment if Penny wasn't there. But she was obsessed with always being there – like she was terrified if I got one moment alone with Dad, like, ever, that I'd make him realize what a manipulative evil bitch she was. And to be fair, I would certainly give it a go. Of course, Craig was there too – ruining the moment. Because you can't have a clichéd evil stepmother without the standardized evil stepsibling.

As if on cue, Craig looked me up and down and said, "You smell like your mum."

How dare he HOW DARE HE howdarehehowdare hehowdareHE? The crimson mist he always evokes in me descended through my hangover. I saw spots, and my foot went out instinctively and kicked him hard in the shin.

He yelped and fell down – totally, totally faking.

Penny and Dad went into utter-defence mode and the usual chaos broke out.

"AMBER. YOU SAY SORRY, YOUNG LADY."

"CRAIG, ARE YOU OKAY? DON'T CRY."

"You're crazy, just like she is," Craig added from the floor.

Dad held me away from Craig as I launched myself at him again. "Amber, no!"

I strained and struggled against Dad's arms. Penny stood protectively in front of her son – shooting me her demon glare. Like I was just attacking Craig for no reason. Like she hadn't just heard what he'd said.

People were looking. Security staff included. Dad made hush noises into my ear, stroking my hair, while I yelled, "You take that back, you take that back!"

"Amber, come on. Calm down. They really won't let you on the plane..."

I looked around. A uniformed dude was making his way over. Penny clocked him at the same time. I saw the conflict cloud her face – getting me told off versus making a scene... She chose not making a scene.

"Shh," she said – to both of us.

Craig and I glared at each other, but we both straightened up, and acted casual. The security guard stopped, examined us, then walked back to the little booth he'd come from.

I sighed. I felt *so* sick. And I'd wanted to say goodbye to Dad – just us two. I threw my empty plastic bottle into the bin provided and didn't look up.

"You apologize, young lady," Penny demanded.

I pulled my rucksack straps tighter to readjust my bag – suddenly *really* angry. With my stupid stepmother. With my stupider stepbrother. With Dad. For not telling Craig off, for never telling Craig off...

"He should apologize too, for what he said!"

"I meant it," Craig called from behind Penny. And Dad had to stop me lurching at him again.

"You know what? I can't be arsed with this." I turned and stormed off into the security queue, knowing they couldn't follow.

"Amber? AMBER!" Dad called.

I ignored him and kept walking.

"Amber, come on, say goodbye nicely."

"Goodbye nicely," I fired back over my shoulder, funnelling into the line, getting my boarding card out ready.

It was the last thing I'd say to him in six weeks.

Don't be sick on the children. Don't be sick on the children.

The two girls in front were blissfully unaware of their vomit-related danger. They swapped pink puppy cards while their parents fussed with passports, checking and re-checking they were still in the same pocket.

I was so mad at Dad. I was so mad at Dad ten million per cent of the time. What was so crappy was that airport scene wasn't even extraordinary. Just the normal everyday occurrence of me versus Craig, me versus Penny…with Dad set on keeping the peace, rather than keeping on the side of his only daughter. I was so exhausted from fighting. I was so exhausted from feeling left out.

I was so exhausted from missing Mum…

The boarding queue inched forward again and everyone moved along, dragging their bags behind them. My tummy churned, complaining about the rubbery duty-free eggs I'd eaten while crying silently in the harsh neon lighting of the airside restaurant.

If I could just not vomit…

If I could just look normal enough to be let on the plane…

Then this summer could start. I could be with Mum and figure out what went wrong and how to get her to come back and start to feel whole again.

It was the family in front's turn and the girls scurried under their parents' legs, asking the air hostesses how high the plane went, how fast, if there were Disney films on the flight… Not asking the important question: *"Is that sick-looking girl behind us going to blow chunks on our little heads?"*

They were nodded through, out of splatter range. It was my turn. I took a deep breath, scraped back my bush of hair and stepped forward to give them my passport.

Look presentable. Look presentable. Look presentable.

The air hostess had so much make-up on that I couldn't figure out what she really looked like. I focused on her foundation-caked cheeks as she took my red leather passport. She smiled and her cheek cracked.

"First time flying alone?" She used the same voice she'd used with the children.

I was scared to open my mouth so I just nodded.

"If you need anything from us, please just let me know."

"Thanks," I mumbled.

She peered at me curiously. "Are you okay? You look scared."

I'm scared of flying with the world's worst hangover…

"I'm a little scared of flying…" I came up with a genius idea. "…I get travel sick!"

"You do look peaky."

"I'm sure I'll be okay."

I'd come up with the perfect cover. Thank God.

"Let us know if there's anything we can do. Seventeen is still quite young to be flying alone."

She beamed at me, and I decided it should be illegal to be that happy so early in the morning.

The headache hit just as I'd squeezed myself into my window seat.

"Ouch," I said, out loud, startling the giant man sitting next to me. He'd struggled to fit into his seat and his knees were practically up by his face as he scrunched himself in. My own long legs already ached in the practically non-existent space. I reached into my bag for an ibuprofen, swallowed it dry, and took out my phone.

I had two messages. One from Lottie, one from Evie. I smiled for the first time that morning.

Lottie: I'M SO SORRY I GOT YOU SO DRUNK. IT WAS ALL AN EVIL PLOY TO GET YOU TO STAY HERE THIS SUMMER. ARE YOU ALIIIIIIIIIIVE?

Evie: Don't leeeeeeeeeeeeeeeeave us!!!!!!!

My smile dropped. I was going to miss them so much!

Their messages triggered a flashback to the previous night...

..."I'M GOING TO BE IN THE SKY THIS TIME TOMORROW."

We'd taken a taxi up Dovelands Hill after the pub had kicked us out. It was our hill. We'd all gone up there the night we'd first become friends. I stood up on the bench, tipped my head back and pointed into the inky blackness above me, almost falling over in the process.

Evie grabbed my arm to keep hold of me.

"Amber, get down. I'm far too tiny to catch you."

"AMERICA, HERE I COME!!!"

Lottie was dancing to no music on the sloped grass beneath us – spinning with her arms wide out.

"Amber, I'm going to miss you so much! Can I fold myself into your suitcase and come with you?" she asked, going spin, spin, spin until she fell over with a thump onto the grass and started laughing.

"Help," Evie said. "You are both too wasted for just me to look after. Amber, take my hand."

I looked up at the sky once more, then stumbled into her arms and let her guide me onto the grass. I fell next to where Lottie was lying face-up on the ground. Evie sighed and got down next to us. All our heads were together, and we all looked up.

The stars were spinning.

"One of us better not have nits," Evie said.

"Only you would think of that," Lottie replied… Which was true.

I laughed, and stared upwards, watching the universe above me turn and turn and turn…

"I can't wait to see my mum," I said, quietly. Feeling just

so…good in my stomach. "It's going to be so brilliant."

"How long has it been?" Lottie asked.

"Two years…"

Spin spin spin spin spin.

"Yikes."

"I know…"

I pushed thoughts out of my head. Thoughts like, *She didn't even invite you to her wedding*, and, *You were the one who asked to go this summer, not the other way around*, and, *Why did she have to leave you to get healthy?*

The alcohol, as always, helped me do this.

"We have six whole weeks together," I told the sky. "Six perfect weeks…"

"Careful." Evie's hair tickled my face. "Nothing is ever perfect."

"Especially if you're working in a summer camp surrounded by hyper American children," Lottie added.

"Quiet time now, oh negative ones." I closed my eyes, smiling as I pictured how Mum's face would look when we met at the airport…

The fasten-seatbelt sign wasn't even on yet, so I figured it was safe to message them back before take-off.

I'm so hungover!! What am I doing on an aeroplane?! Help me! My head hurts so much!

I closed my eyes and listened to the aeroplane noises – the intermittent beeping, the low roar of the air-conditioning, and people politely-but-not-politely organizing each other's luggage in the overhead compartments. All these people, sharing a journey with me. We'd be marooned together in a tin can flying through the sky for ten hours, then never see each other again.

Flying was weird.

My head hurt.

What *would* it be like seeing Mum again?

Was she going to, like, explain?

My head hurt.

My phone beeped. Twice.

Lottie: I can't believe you're going to be in charge of actual children! American ones too. Will they be called things like Hank?

Evie: You'll be fine! Just think, any story worth hearing starts with someone our age getting on an aeroplane.

I didn't want a story worth hearing though – I just wanted time with my mum…

I also wanted to ignore the nagging voice in my head, crowing that nothing is ever that simple when it comes to Her.

Situations that are destined to fail:

An emotional reunion

+

A mother and daughter who aren't very good with emotions

+

Two years of not seeing each other

Two

By some kind of miracle of science, I slept on the plane. Maybe my legs could only handle being so squished when unconscious, or maybe it was just my hangover knowing what was best for me. Either way, blissfully, I fell asleep after the in-flight meal of sausages that looked like the poos of constipated toddlers.

When I woke, I felt eight trillion times better. I yawned. I tried to stretch. I rubbed the sore part of my neck.

There was no headache left. No racing nausea. The children on the aeroplane of flight 105HWSF were safe from my vomit. I fiddled with my chair and got out the remote control for in-flight entertainment. I punched at it until the flight progress came up on my screen.

I felt sick again.

An ocean was now between me and virtually everyone I knew and the tiny cartoon aeroplane hovered over the north-west of America's giant expanse.

According to the real-time estimations, we'd be landing soon.

I stood up without warning, my remote ricocheting into my tall neighbour's flesh as it pinged back on its cord.

"Excuse me, sorry. I need the loo."

I practically ran to the tiny toilet cubicle and locked the door behind me. I leaned against it and took a deep breath that stank of chemical blue urine stuff. I took another one, my nose getting used to the stingy smell.

Breathe, Amber, just breathe…it's just your mum. Like, the woman who birthed you with her own body and who loves you unconditionally…despite the fact she emigrated over five thousand miles away and didn't think to take you with her.

But it wasn't her choice to move away – was it? It was stupid Bumface Kevin's with his stupid American bumchin. He knew Mum was vulnerable, and he just took her with him anyway, brainwashed her into leaving us… Plus, I mean, how unethical is it to HIT ON someone you're supposed to be treating?

I flushed the loo, and the terrifyingly-loud hissing noise jolted me out of my anger.

I had six weeks. Six weeks to undo all the damage he'd caused and make her mine again. Six weeks to figure out what had happened, what I'd done to make her go.

By the time I'd pulled myself together enough to go back to my seat, it was too late to start a movie. I dug in my bag and pulled out my sketchpad instead. The photograph of my mother and me floated out from the pages onto my lap.

I'd been copying it over the last week. I picked it up and really stared at it, the sight of her face making my intestines twist like they were playing cat's cradle. Dad had taken the photo the last time she'd come to visit me at Dad's house. We were in the garden; I recognized the rosebush in the background, and remembered the fit Penny had thrown when she'd arrived *("I don't know why I have to have THAT woman in MY house")*. We were both smiling into the lens, but I remembered how miserable I'd been that day. How I'd sobbed uncontrollably when she said "goodbye". It was the day she'd told me she was flying to California. The day when any hope Bumface Kevin wouldn't take her away from me died a gasping, desperate death.

But it's okay, she'd said. *I'll come and visit loads.*

And now two years had passed, and it was me visiting her…

… With a suitcase stuffed with factor 50 suncream, summer-camp clothes and unanswered questions.

I got out my favourite 2B pencil and did what I always did to make the thoughts go away – I drew.

The landing was bumpy. I'm usually an okay flier, but as the plane dived and jolted and essentially bellyflopped onto the runway, I found myself grabbing onto pieces of Tall Man and apologizing profusely.

"Are we dying?" I asked him, clutching spare flesh on his arm. "Why is the plane killing us?"

"It's the fog," he said, in a calm American drawl. "San Francisco is always covered in the stuff, and airplanes don't like it."

When we were safely on the tarmac, I looked out the small porthole. The weather was welcoming at least. Grey greyness was everywhere, with drizzle speckling the glass.

I turned to him. "I thought this was California!! The weather is worse here than it was in England."

He laughed. In an American accent, if that was possible. Or maybe now it was *me* who had the accent. That's the weird thing about flying, in ten hours it reverses who has the accent.

"Haven't you heard the phrase: '*I never spent a worse winter than the summer I spent in San Francisco*'?" he asked.

I didn't really understand what he'd said, but laughed politely and looked back out the window.

"At least my freckles won't erupt in this," I muttered.

Gradually the plane emptied. I said goodbye to Tall Man, thanking him for his moral support, and walked the longest way ever to baggage reclaim. Dad had warned me about the scariness of American border security so I popped into one of the hundreds of available "restrooms" to wash off any remaining trace of hangover.

Security – as predicted – was terrifying. The guy had a gun, AN ACTUAL GUN and noticed my shaking fingers as I handed over my passport. He flicked it open aggressively, like the passport had bad-mouthed his mother or something. He studied my photo and I blushed. It was SUCH a bad one. I'd taken it last year during a heatwave and my hair took up most of the frame.

"How long you staying for?" he barked.

"Er...six weeks?"

He looked up at me, his eyes angry. I actually took a step backwards.

"Why so long?"

I was too scared to be sarky and say something like, "Well, I've heard you're a real friendly country. Musta got that wrong." I looked down at his gun. Scrap that: GUNS plural. "Umm, I'm working in a summer camp?"

He narrowed his dark eyes. "Have you got your work visa?"

"No..." I said, and he went to push a red button. "Wait! I mean yes. Well, no too. I'm not working there officially, because I'm only seventeen anyway. My mum, she's married to this American guy who owns a summer camp. I'm staying with them, to visit my mum... And I'll be helping out at the camp, but not officially or anything... I've got a ninety-day visa waiver thingy. Here." I pulled out the photocopy Dad had insisted I needed.

He didn't reply, just jabbed his keyboard. Had I screwed it up? Were they going to send me back? Did I still smell of sambuca?

"Look here please." He shoved me in front of this little

black thing. It glowed red against my eyeball and made a clicking sound.

Hang on. Had they just taken a retina scan? Was that allowed? Was I in that much trouble? My heart thumped really fast. I looked around to see if everyone else was getting their eyeballs photographed. Apart from an alarming display of bumbags on show, it all seemed normal.

Just as I started freaking out, the security guy burst into a wide grin and handed over my passport.

"Welcome to America," he beamed. "I hope y'all enjoy your stay."

I wandered out into the arrivals hall, still dazed. Why did they take a photo of my eyeball? Was that a breach of my civil liberty? What were they going to do with the eyeball photo? Keep it in some database? Lottie would go mental when I told her. She was always going on about our Big Brother society and Orwell and 1984.

"Amber? Amber!"

And then, there was Mum. Running towards me. Her hair, the exact same ginger as mine, streaming behind her. And my heart, it just kind of inflated with all this air I hadn't had in me for two years.

She reached me.

"Amber," she whispered and grasped me into a hug. And I started crying. I hugged her back so hard, and smelled her smell, like roses. She still wore the same perfume. My bag was on the floor and we'd created an arrivals bottleneck but I didn't care.

Eventually we broke apart.

"Come on." Mum picked up my suitcase for me. Just seeing her walk away made my chest go all tight, even though I could follow her. Then I realized that she hadn't said, "I missed you..."

She turned back to me. "You must be knackered. I've booked us into a motel so we can have some time together before we drive up to camp. How does sightseeing in San Francisco sound?"

"It sounds...fab."

We wheeled our way to a tram that whizzed us along to a multistorey car park. The expanses of space between each thing we needed to get to were massive, especially compared to the on-top-of-each-other-ness of Heathrow airport. Mum was parked on the top floor of the car park, and I shivered in the mist when we got off the tram.

"I thought California was supposed to be, like, hot," I joked, doing up the zip of my hoody.

My mum smiled. My smile. We had the same smile. I'd forgotten. Seeing her again felt odd; I couldn't get used to her face. It jarred. Like she was a stranger. But she wasn't a stranger – she was my mum.

"It is, just not in San Fran. Wait till I get you into my mountains. It's so hot there, you'll be praying for a cold fog."

We walked between rows of cars and stopped

unexpectedly outside a huge red monster truck, with giant wheels and blacked-out windows.

Why was Mum calling it San Fran? Whoever calls it San Fran? Why was she so calm? All my intestines were knotted up with repressed emotion.

"This is us." She unlocked the doors with her beeper.

Her beeper?! In England she'd driven a beat-up Mini with a broken passenger door. When it had been her weekends to take me – the ones when she remembered and actually turned up anyway – she'd announce her arrival by honking its dilapidated horn outside Dad's house to piss off Penny. I'd had to clamber over her whenever I wanted to get in or out.

"I need a stepladder to get into this thing," I joked, hoping Mum would notice the undercurrents of judgement in my "funniness".

She didn't.

"Hey, you're as tall as me. You can hop in there just fine."

I heaved myself up into the front seat as Mum flung my stuff into the back. I dug around in my bag for the present I'd got her, and had it in my hand when she got in next to me.

She spied the gift-wrapped box.

"Is that for me?" she asked, as I held it out tentatively.

I nodded. Really nervous all of a sudden, hoping she liked it...that she understood it.

"Aww, bless you, you didn't have to get me a present."

She took it and unwrapped it carefully, not ripping any of the paper but lifting the Sellotape up delicately.

She pulled out the small jewellery box, and popped the lid. My heart thud thudded.

"Oh, wow, Amber, it's beautiful."

"It's the Deathly Hallows!" I said, unable to contain myself.

"Oh, yes, of course." She pulled the shining silver chain out and wrapped it up with her fingers to see the triangular charm. I felt so chuffed with myself – and also a little jealous I didn't have one too. I'd used all my money buying this one for her.

"I went on the Harry Potter studio tour," I explained. "It's so incredible there, I wish you could see it. Anyway, I got this in the gift shop. It's proper official. JK approved. Do you love it? Do you?"

"Oh yes. It's beautiful. I'll put it on straight away."

Which she did – but I couldn't help feeling like she wasn't excited enough… I'd literally squealed when I found it in the shop. I'd literally squealed the whole time on the tour. Mum was the one who read the books to me growing up. She'd curl up next to me in my bed, and keep me up past my bedtime, discussing all our favourite characters. Why wasn't she squealing? Why was she just starting the engine?

With a grin still plastered over my face, I tried again. "Do you remember that time you face-painted Dark Marks onto all our arms at my birthday party? And then what's-her-name's mum, Keira's mum, she went totally nuts?"

A small smile eked its way onto Mum's face, but it wasn't enough of one. Or maybe I was reading too much into it.

"I remember," she said, but she didn't add anything to

the story. Just indicated left, to steer our way out of the car park. Maybe she was just tired…that was probably it.

Soon we were cruising towards the city, on a motorway full of cars just as gigantic as ours. Mum babbled as she drove.

"I'm so excited about you coming to camp, Amber. Everyone is going to love you so much! It's all Kevin's been talking about. I can't wait for you to get to know him properly. We've got a few days before the kids arrive, and then it will be all go-go-go…"

"Mum?"

"Yes, sweetie?" She turned from the windscreen to glance at me.

"You've got an…American accent."

She touched her throat absent-mindedly. "I do?"

"You really do."

"That's weird. Everyone here always notices I'm British, right away."

"That would be the paler than pale skin and freckles, like mine." I smiled.

"No." She turned back to concentrate on her driving. "They always say '*I love your accent*'."

I didn't love her accent.

The city stretched under us, bits of it piercing through the thick layer of fog. I didn't feel sleepy or jet-lagged at all, despite it being about three in the morning my time. The nap on the plane was seeing me through. I sat up in my seat, hoping to catch a glimpse of the famous Golden Gate Bridge.

But there was just the fog, and an occasional flash of orange.

"I can't see anything," I grumbled.

"That's San Fran for you."

She'd called it San Fran again.

We got into the heart of the city and stopped chatting so Mum could focus on her driving. We rumbled over steep hills at ridiculous angles and bumped over the metal tramline tracks. I stared out the window, trying to take it all in, feeling like a complete alien. The houses were all painted the sort of colours you could order scooped up in a cone… Pistachio, cherry sorbet, lemon…

Mum pointed down a dark road to our left, all tall houses together.

"That's where I volunteer at the centre," she said. "Remember I told you?"

"Yep, I remember." It was at a centre like that she'd met the dreaded bumchin. An English branch. I wasn't likely to forget.

"We're almost there."

She indicated right and swooped down into an underground car park. Mum turned off the engine and pulled up the handbrake.

"Here!" she said, smiling brightly. "Let's get your bags into the room and go out for dinner. You must be starving after all that gross airplane food."

We rolled my stuff into the motel reception and Mum told them our names. My heart hurt a little (a lot) when she used her new surname that wasn't mine.

"Welcome to the Cow Hollow," the receptionist beamed, like she was honestly delighted we were there. "Wow, I love your accent. Are you guys from England?"

We nodded and got our keys.

Maybe jet lag was starting to creep in, because none of it felt real as we twisted through endless corridors to find our room, or when we opened the door into the biggest hotel room I'd ever seen, with beds the size of countries. I dropped myself onto one, my long body not even beginning to cover its vast expanse. Mum sat at the writing desk and smiled at me.

"You tired, hon?"

She never used to call me hon… More America.

I turned onto my stomach, sinking into the soft mattress. I suddenly felt really, really homesick. The euphoria of seeing her had peaked, and been replaced with a simmering confusion and sense of just feeling…lost.

I didn't know this woman in front of me. Not really. I didn't know this city. This country my mother had chosen over me.

"I'm okay." I reached out to pull back the curtain. The fog still lazed heavily outside, making the cars on the main road look all hazy. I couldn't hear them though, the place must have good double-glazing. "I slept on the plane."

"You hungry? I know a great place over the road. It's about as American as you can get."

I was actually more gagging for a cup of tea and some Marmite on toast, rather than a USA feast, but I didn't want to ruin our reunion by being unenthusiastic.

So I dropped the curtain, looked at the stranger's face that was half my face and forced myself to smile.

"Yummy. Sounds great."

Situations that are destined to fail:

Small talk

+

The biggest lump of meat the world has ever known

Three

"Mum, it's like someone puked up America in here."

I stepped past a glowing jukebox. The "diner" looked like the womb in which *Grease* had been incubated. The waitresses wore faux fifties hair with cute little aprons, and, wherever I looked, a framed photo of Elvis Presley stared back. Customers sat at a high white countertop, perching on shiny stools and slurping tall milkshakes adorned with glacé cherries.

Mum laughed for the first time since I'd arrived, and asked for a table for two. Our waitress led us to an actual booth and gave us menus so big they obscured both my face and my hair.

I couldn't stop sneaking glances at Mum, like she was my school crush or something. I peered over the top of my menu, while pretending to scan it. Her hair was swept nicely to one side as she considered the menu serenely, apparently not repressing a gaping well of emotion like I was. She looked so healthy. Thinner, less puff about her. Her clothes looked clean and new, which shouldn't be notable, but is when you have a mum like mine. She was even wearing a thin belt, cinching her long white shirt in... Gone were the grimy jogging bottoms she'd come and pick me up in, the stale smell hidden by cheap perfume...

"What you having, hon?"

I managed to look at the menu. "I dunno. The Pink Lady burger maybe?"

"Mmmm. Yum. You're in America now."

The waitress clopped over, like she knew we were ready to order.

"What can I get y'all?" She held up her notepad.

"We'll have a Pink Lady burger," Mum said. "And a milkshake – Amber, do you want a milkshake? The strawberry flavour is good."

I nodded dumbly.

"And I'll have the fruit salad..." She handed the menus over.

"You're only getting a fruit salad?" I asked. "I just ordered basically half a cow, and you're nibbling watermelon?"

"Oh, I don't really eat meat now. But you enjoy your food."

"What do you mean, you don't eat meat? You've always eaten meat."

Mum gave me a thin smile I didn't like.

"Well, I don't any more. Not many people do in San Fran. I wanted to take you to this raw food restaurant, but I didn't know how into it you'd be..."

She trailed off as the jukebox changed song, to that one John Travolta and Uma Thurman dance to in *Pulp Fiction.* Evie'd made us watch it for "educational purposes".

I couldn't believe Mum was a VEGETARIAN. Since when? She used to make the most amazing roast every Sunday – lamb with her special mint sauce. Well, not every Sunday. Especially not the Sundays after that day she came home from the hospital.

The food arrived and the joke I'd made about half a cow became an accurate observation. The burger towered on the plate, almost reaching my chin and swimming in an ocean of skinny fries. I took a large bite, but barely dented the meat. Mum daintily jabbed a grape with her fork, and I almost flinched. Everything was different. I hadn't been planning on everything being different.

"So you looking forward to teaching the kids art this summer?"

I nodded – because I knew she wanted me to – though I hadn't thought about it much. Bumface Kevin had said a condition of me coming to stay was to "pull my weight" and help out at the happy-clappy summer camp he'd bought right after the wedding, and art had seemed the obvious thing for me to teach. Mum had initially got me into art when I was pretty much still a toddler, and I'd clung to it like a drug, when she'd clung to…well…other things…

"Yes. Well, the children aren't like Craig, are they?"

Mum laughed sharply, and almost dropped her fork.

"No. God, no… Sorry, I shouldn't have laughed at that."

We smiled at each other conspiratorially. "Is he still...bad?" she asked.

I thought back to the comment he'd made at the airport. "He's still the worst."

Suddenly I wanted her to feel guilty – even though Craig wasn't her fault. He was Penny's fault. And Penny was Dad's fault. Because Dad swapped Mum for a Laura-Ashley-wearing, cake-baking, pearl-clutching anti-mum.

But Mum had left me with them... To suffocate in my home in a cloud of Penny's Chanel No. 5, where no one had my back any more. I used to have at least the weekends with her, now I had nothing.

Mum tactfully changed the topic, and that was new. We used to moan about the evils of Craig and Penny all the time, spending our weekends bitching and whinging, giggling like conspiratorial sisters rather than mother and daughter.

"So tell me about college. How did your summer exams go?"

"All right, I guess," I said through my mouthful of beef. "I get the results when I'm back in England. I think I did okay, but it's my portfolio that's the most important thing for art college. I'm glad I don't have to do General Studies any more too."

"What about friends? Who are you hanging out with these days?"

I swallowed and grinned. "I'm really close to these two girls, Evie and Lottie. I met them at the start of the year and we just really clicked. Evie is...well, she's tightly wound..."

I got the intense stabbing of sadness I always get when I think of Evie. She has OCD, and had a massive relapse last year. She's getting better though...whatever better means if you have OCD... "But she's hilarious, and really smart and into films. And she talks like a grandma most of the time. Seriously, she actually used the word 'yikes' at my leaving party."

"They threw you a leaving party? That's awesome."

I winced at the "awesome".

"Yeah, it was." I didn't mention how drunk I'd got. "And then there's Lottie. She's, like, a genius, but she doesn't want to be. She wants to go to Cambridge and become prime minister, but she dresses and behaves like a hippy, all lace and crochet. She's always protesting about something or other. You'd like her."

Mum took a slurp of her milkshake. "It's great that you have a friend who believes in stuff."

A warm beefy feeling spread through my belly.

"Well, actually, the three of us have formed this club. It's like a feminism club where we meet and talk about women's rights. We've campaigned for stuff too. Like, we got that horrible pop song about rape banned from being played on the college jukebox."

Mum put down her milkshake.

"Really?" The corner of her mouth twitched upwards.

"Really." The pride blew up in me. "We call ourselves the Spinster Club. We've taken the word 'spinster' and flipped its meaning."

Mum looked at me, really looked at me. She reached across the booth to take my hand.

"That makes me so proud, hon."

I bathed in the look she gave me. It felt so good to be… validated by her. Dad was a bit bemused by all my Spinster Club activity. Not a surprise really, considering he'd married Penny, who was half human, half talcum powder. I'd actually once overheard her telling Dad that my feminism was "a phase".

"So," Mum said, swallowing another grape. "Tell me then, are there any special boys back in the UK I should know about?"

I put my fork down. "Mum!"

"What?"

"I'm telling you all about my kick-ass feminist activities and you undermine it all by asking if I have a boyfriend."

She smiled. "Come on, I'm your mother. It's my job to ask."

It's also your job not to leave your child…

I put my burger down as my muscles tensed up.

Don't ruin it don't ruin it.

"Well, no, there isn't anyone. Not at the moment."

"None of them good enough for you?"

More muscles tensed in my neck.

"No, they're all babies."

I couldn't tell her, not really. That boys just…didn't fancy me. Like, ever. Especially compared to my friends. Even when Evie had her relapse, she'd still had boys following her around college. I mean, I'd rather be unfancied than have OCD...but still... It was quite a feat of fanciability. And Lottie, well, she was like bloke catnip. I knew I wasn't, like, completely ugly...just very *noticeable*. The word "intimidating" has been used multiple times by multiple people. It's like my angry feminist rants are more unattractive because I'm tall and ginger and less pretty – whereas Lottie and Evie can get away with it. And, yeah, of course I didn't want to give up all that important "me" stuff just so I could get touched up at a house party... But I still hadn't even kissed anyone, and it worried me.

I didn't want my mum to know all this. I didn't want to provide her with further evidence I was unloveable, because I was worried it might put *her* off too...

"Don't worry." She stabbed two strawberries. "There'll be plenty of boys at camp."

"I'm not here to meet boys, I'm here to spend the summer with you!"

"Well I'll be too busy, you're going to have to make friends."

Too busy? Busy?! The huge amount of meat in my stomach solidified and grew heavy. I felt dread trickle through me...it was like she was already making excuses to let me down...

No, Amber...no...don't read too much into it...

I crossed my arms. "I don't HAVE to do anything."

"Come on, Amber, don't be like that."

Like what? Myself? My bolshie normal self? The self she didn't know? Not really. Not for two years.

And yet I couldn't bear her looking at me like that. Like me being like this was the reason she left.

I forced myself to smile and took a big bite of dripping burger. It plummeted down my throat, landing with a heavy thud in my tummy.

"I can't wait to meet everyone," I lied, through my meat.

If Mum thought I'd be spending our precious summer together lusting over American boys, well, she was dead wrong.

Situations that are destined to fail:

Me

+

Warm welcomes

+

Mother-stealing bumchins

Four

From: LongTallAmber
To: EvieFilmGal, LottieIsAlwaysRight
Subject: Y'all have a good day now

So, guys, I'm here! I'm alive! I made it to San Francisco without being arrested for public drunkenness at fifty thousand feet. Are you proud?

I'm writing this in a cool-as-f*ck Internet café overlooking the bay. I'm probably within spitting distance of ten dot-com millionaires, but I'd rather write to you girls than spit on anyone right now.

How are you both? Sobbing over my departure I hope. I miss you both TONNES already. Everyone in America is SO WEIRD!

Seriously, we went sightseeing this morning and I spent most of my time goggling at Americans, rather than Alcatraz or the sea lions. Like, they all wear bumbags! Well almost all of them. And they, like, come up and talk to you!? On the boat to Alcatraz, we met this couple called Sonny and Jean *(I know, the most American names in the world, right?!)* and by the time we got to the prison *(major bummer btw)*, I knew all about their two kids, their holiday plans, what their favourite restaurant was. And THEN they just followed us around the whole thing like we were the best of friends. We even had to eat our sandwiches with them. And Mum didn't care at all. In fact, she invited them to share our crisps! You can only imagine how mad I was. You know how protective I get over my snacks.

We're about to go to a "raw food" restaurant for lunch before we drive into the mountains. I've already pre-emptively eaten some sneaky chips from a KFC I found so I don't starve to death. Seriously, Mum said the best meal at this place is *spaghetti made from raw carrot strips* – WHAT IS WRONG WITH PEOPLE? I worry Bumface Kevin has given her a brain transplant. She also keeps going on about how "cute" the boys are at camp, so prepare for horror stories about me being horrifically match-made with some redneck called "Randy".

Am I being mean? I am, aren't I?

It's not like British blokes are any better. If Guy, Ethan or Teddy are anything to go by anyway…

Please write back. I NEED YOU GUYS! Mum said there's a computer in our cabin so we can keep the Spinster Club meetings going over the summer. I will scour Mountain Hideaway camp for any traces of inequality for us to discuss. Just let me know the dates you can do, and we'll try and sort out the time difference.

Gotta go. There are some raw carrots that need eating.

Lots of love

Amber x x x

By early evening, the city was behind us and we were steering our way into the mountains.

I was shattered. Jet lag had woken me at five a.m. and I'd sat in the grey light of our motel room, listening to the steady hum of the unnecessary air con, watching my mother's sleeping body...and I'd had such a surge of memory I'd felt too sick to get back to sleep...

...I carefully pushed the door, taking a breath first so I wouldn't inhale the stale smell of inside. There was a lump in the bed.

"Mum?" I asked, scared to step in closer.

The lump turned over.

"Mum? I need you to take me to school."

The lump turned again, dislodging pockets of sweet but rancid air that caught in the back of my throat. It didn't respond.

I closed the door and rang the taxi company.

Dad had left money on the table in case it happened again.

Once we hit a certain altitude, the sun appeared – as promised. The first sun I'd seen since stepping off the aeroplane. It scorched brightly, all showing-off and *well-I-was-here-all-the-time-you-just-needed-to-find-me.* I buzzed down the window and put my arm out, and it blew behind me in the breeze. I felt awake again. Mum pushed some tortoiseshell sunglasses down onto her delicate nose.

"I told you the sun would find us," she said. "Make sure you wear your factor 50 sunblock every day at camp."

"Mum, relax. I learned by about twelve that it was impossible for me to tan. Like ever."

"Just think of the smooth wrinkle-free skin you'll have when you're older."

I brought my hand back in; it was already warm from the sun. "Hardly a consolation prize for a lifetime of ginger jokes."

She flicked her head sideways. "Kids are still making ginger jokes?"

I thought of college. "Seventeen-year-olds are still making ginger jokes."

"Well everyone will be just lovely at camp."

I kept peeking at her, watching her grip the wheel. She'd always been a confident driver, but it was odd seeing her so at home on foreign roads. Questions bubbled up my throat and I turned them over and over in my head, picking the ones I might get away with…that she might actually answer.

We stopped quickly to get bottles of iced tea to sip on the road, and after downing most of mine, I took my chance, just as we pulled out of the "Rest Stop".

"Your wedding must've been nice in this weather?" I ventured, as my opener.

The wedding I wasn't invited to.

She smiled, didn't stiffen. She hadn't caught on yet.

"It was perfect," she answered. And I didn't know if she meant the weather, or the day. And if she meant the day, that meant it was perfect without me there.

A pang, but I smiled too and delved deeper.

"Wasn't it weird being just you two?" I tried to make my voice all casual but I flaked on the "just". Mum stiffened in her seat, wiggled about. She didn't answer…not for a while. Just stared at the road like she hadn't heard me. Then, after five minutes, she turned with a giant beaming smile, wearing it like a Band-Aid, and said, "Isn't that iced tea just fantastic? I'm so addicted to it since I moved here."

Like I hadn't said anything, like I hadn't asked anything. When the flake in the "just" was so obviously a tell that I needed to ask it, and needed an answer.

The iced tea curdled in my gut.

The road gnarled its way upwards and I stared out the window. I'd never known California was so…barren. There were no trees or grass, just expanses of red dusty plains either side of the freeway, punctuated only by the odd billboard advertising Jesus. As we climbed higher into the mountains, the occasional burst of green sneaked its way into the desert, until the dust disappeared and pine trees sprouted on each side of the road.

"We're almost there." Mum's eyes didn't stray from the swerves in the road. "If you carry on straight you get to Lake Tahoe, which is just gorgeous. We're on a different lake. Still beautiful though."

My stomach twisted and dived with each bump in the tarmac. I was getting nervous. I hadn't given a huge amount of thought to camp, and fellow campers, or the art class I was supposed to be teaching, or anything really. Well, anything that wasn't backlit fantasies of Mum and me bonding together on a mountain and her promising to come home or something. I hated meeting new people. When I'm nervous I'm always…snappy with people and come across as rude, or superior… Well that's what people tell me. Lottie and Evie were the first people I'd met who liked me instantly, rather than having to warm up to me.

Even worse, I'd have to see Bumface Kevin again, and live with him. I'd not seen him since I'd screamed at him, saying he'd ruined my life. He took Mum away on a plane two days later. I bet not inviting me to the wedding was payback for that. Not that she'd tell me… Not even if I asked.

* * *

Mum indicated and we turned into this weenie gap in the trees. We passed a weathered sign: *Welcome to Mountain Hideaway Camp.* My guts clumped together like a wodge of chewing gum.

"We're home," Mum said, as we rumbled over a speed bump. I was almost too busy freaking out to notice she'd called it "home".

We hummed past tiny pathways leading into the dense woods and passed wooden signs pointing towards nightmare scenarios like *paintball* and *water sports.* I'd forgotten camp included hells such as these. Forgotten, or deliberately pushed it from my brain.

"You're about to get your first glimpse of the water."

I spotted it glittering between the pine trees and then we emerged from the canopy and saw it in all its lakey glory.

Even I could see it was beautiful. The water was so blue it was like the whole lake was made out of denim. Each ripple glistened golden as the huge honking sun hit the water. A black, weathered pier cut the water in two. It was just stunning… Well, if you ignored the banana boat, the assortment of jet skis floating about, and a few other "fun" instruments that looked like my worst nightmare realized.

"It's beautiful," I admitted, reluctantly. For a split second, I could see why she'd left grey old England behind.

We turned away from the lake and drove up a well-built road, passing a collection of giant huts. "The rec hall, the medic cabin," Mum explained. The road turned to dust again and narrowed. We stopped at the end. Bumface Kevin stood there grinning outside a cabin, and waving. I slouched lower in my seat. Then realized I should probably make an effort for Mum's sake, so I corrected myself.

He opened my car door before we'd even stopped properly.

"Amber, you made it!" He leaned in and hugged me, enveloping me with his earthy piney stench. I stiffened.

"Hi, Kevin." I was proud for omitting the "*Bumface*".

He let go and stepped out of the truck.

"Your mom has been so excited about you coming, and so have I."

He was lying – he must be lying. He was such a fake! He tried to come across all caring-carington, *I look after ickle children, and I have a counselling qualification, and I look after recovering whatnots* – when really he was all *I poach recovering whatnots from their families and move them abroad.* I concentrated on unbuckling my seatbelt and jumped as delicately as I could down from the truck.

"Wow, you've grown. I didn't even think that was possible."

Must. Resist. The. Urge. To. Pull. A. Face.

He looked just the same. Ginger too, which annoyed me, as I didn't want anyone to think he was my dad. Messy stubble. Hair too long for someone his age.

"She's five eleven now, aren't you, Amber? Just like your mom," Mum said, and hugged Kevin harder than she'd hugged me at the airport…

"Shall we show you the cabin then? You're getting the VIP treatment staying with us. The other counsellors have to bunk up and sleep with the kids. They're all having a fire by the lake this evening. You should go… After we've finished catching up with you of course."

Mum had already explained that I couldn't do certain things for legal reasons, like not being responsible for the children in their dorms, as I was under eighteen. I also wasn't allowed to be left alone in charge of them, which was just fine with me.

Kevin picked up my case and carried it down a small path lined with daisies. "Home sweet home," he said, as he opened the door to the cabin. All smug and proud of himself. There was nothing I could do but follow him and Mum into their love shack.

It was admittedly cosy inside. Wide glass windows looked out into the forest and the walls were made of corkboard. Vases of wild forest flowers stood on most available surfaces. I wondered if Bumface Kevin had arranged them, as I'd never seen Mum put anything in a vase my whole life.

"Living room," Kevin gestured towards the sofa. "Kitchen. Our bedroom is through there." He pointed to a door past the bathroom.

Our bedroom? They shared a bed and bedroom. I mean, I know that's totally obvious but it still felt so wrong. I distracted myself by looking for a photo of me in the house. I couldn't see one. There were at least eight of Mum and Kevin – boating in a raft, in front of the Hollywood Sign, in front of a campfire and surrounded by grinning campers. And, in a gold gilt frame, was their wedding photo. Just the two of them – Mum wearing a light yellow dress, clutching Kevin's hand in front of some lake somewhere. She'd emailed it over two weeks after she'd left, without even an apology for not asking me to come. I picked up the photo and put it down quickly. She'd never looked happier. No Amber in a frame though. I felt like crying.

Mum took my hand and led me past the kitchen. "Your room is through here."

She pushed open a door to reveal a box room covered with flouncy flowered wallpaper. "It's pretty small, but I promise this is luxury stuff for camp."

I stepped into my home for the next six weeks. It was simple. A single bed, a tiny cupboard, a night-table. That was it. And there, there was my photo. Of me and Mum. Framed on the bedside table that wobbled on unsteady legs as you walked towards it. It was exactly the same photo I'd been sketching on the aeroplane.

My fingers tingled.

Why was this in the guest bedroom and not her bedroom? Did Mum only come in and look at it when she was in the mood for remembering she had a daughter? When Bumface Kevin was out with his bumchin?

I blinked a lot, feeling my throat constrict.

Kevin wheeled my suitcase in behind us. "How d'ya like your room?"

"It's lovely," I said dismissively. I needed to bring up the photo. I needed to ask why it was here, and not out with the others. But I was too scared to. I didn't want her to lie to me. And I didn't want to tell her off either – because she'd never been able to handle it. So I found myself saying…

"Why wasn't I invited to your wedding?" At Kevin. Staring accusingly at his bumchin.

He stepped back, like I was a bear. "Woah, Amber. Where did that come from?"

Mum crossed her arms, and looked at him desperately.

"Amber, come on, stop being silly."

I threw my rucksack down on the bed, where it landed with a thump.

"I just saw the photo outside, that's all. And I was wondering…"

… For two years.

They shot each other a look, and it was so deep, it basically broke me. I could see the bond instantly – they were having a communication about how to handle this, how to handle *me* – using only their eyes. That's how close they were.

How close she should have been to me.

"We eloped, darling," Mum said.

"Yeah," Bumface Kevin butted in. "And we didn't have much time. We needed to get your mum a visa quickly, and—"

I interrupted him. "I wasn't talking to you, KEVIN!"

Even though I *had* asked him the question. It was easier to be mad at him than Mum.

He scratched his stubble – which grew AROUND the bumchin – and shot my mum another look. "Well, I'm answering anyway."

"Of course you are." I was so mad, so sad. I couldn't hold it back, even though I wanted to. Even though I was already sabotaging everything. I felt torn – half of me wanted it all to be perfect, but the other half was just desperate for answers. It was like my ribs were expanding to make room for the emotions that had been suddenly unearthed – emotions I didn't know how to let out without wrecking things with Mum. She wasn't looking at me, she was looking at Kevin. The faces of Mum and me on that bullshit photo stared out, watching the scene, frozen in time.

He put his hands up in a gesture I'm sure his counselling training taught him, and used a calm, soothing voice. "Hey, you only just arrived. I've got dinner planned. Let's talk about this later. Give you a chance to settle in?"

"I'm full from all that raw food in San Fran," I lied – thinking, I *need to get out, I need to get out.* Before I make things worse… Before I ruin the summer. I'd rather fling myself onto a lakeside campfire where I knew no one, than sit down for dinner with Mum and Kevin when I was feeling like this. "Plus, I don't want to miss all the staff getting to know each other."

"At least let us eat first."

I stretched my arms up, my fingers grazing the ceiling of the low cabin as I did.

"No."

"Amber!" Mum pleaded – finally looking at me.

"I'll see you later."

And ignoring their protests, I dodged my way out of the cabin into the unknown woods.

Hoping Mum might follow to check I was okay.

She didn't though.

Situations that are destined to fail:

My personality

+

A gang of Americans

Five

I didn't really know where I was going, who I was meeting. I just needed to put physical space between me and that framed photo in the wrong place.

Kevin had said the other employees were having a welcome campfire at the lake so I doubled back in the direction we'd driven. I doubted they'd be overjoyed with the bosses' sort-of daughter turning up, but screw them. I was this close to punching someone, or crying, or both. Anyway, if I made it clear I hated Kevin and his bumchinny ways they would warm to me. And I'd try and talk like the Queen so they'd think I was quaint.

She keeps your photo in the guest bedroom.

She keeps your photo in the guest bedroom.

My flip-flops filled up with dust and dirt from the forest floor. Whatever insects make that night-time buzzing noise in hot countries were ramped up and cricketing away. The steady buzz in the air calmed me, as long as I stayed in denial about all the new people I was about to meet. I saw a flickering light through the dark clumps of trees, mingled with the sound of laughter and made my way towards it. I stopped in the safety of the pines and looked out. A circle of about twenty people, all a tiny bit older than me, sat haphazardly around a pretty-decent fire. All of them looked "bonded" already as they chatted and shared beer and shoved sticks onto the burning fire between them. My heart got all pumpy, my arms stiff with nerves.

I stepped out and gulped my arrival.

The group stopped mid-laugh to look at me.

"Hullo there," I said, my voice more British than it'd ever been. "I'm, erm, Amber. Kevin said you guys would be here?" I waved, not able to make their faces out properly in the dark.

There was a brief silence then a girl stepped forward.

"Amber, hey! Wow, I love your accent! I'm Melody." She shook my hand, and, as the campfire light hit her, I saw she was a Californian goddess. All tumbling blonde hair, and glowy skin, and teeth like cosmetic dentistry adverts, and legs so far up she'd have to apply deodorant to her knee pits.

"Hi, Melody." I shook her hand, not knowing if I was doing it right as I'd never formally shaken hands with anyone before.

More people stood up, shook my hand, introducing themselves with names which I instantly forgot. They all told me they looooved my accent. A few faces stood out.

There was this one guy who looked like Jacob from the *Twilight* films, all olivey reddy skin. He looked Native American but I wasn't sure if that was the right term for it these days. One girl seemed extra excited I was there, Whinnie. She wore thick black glasses on her wide face and a Winnie the Pooh fleece. She pulled me into the circle and they all looked at me, like I should say something.

"So," I said, trying not to freak out about all the new faces staring at me. "You guys all get here yesterday?"

A few nodded. Whinnie said, "Yeah, but for most of us this is our second year here. We all—"

Melody interrupted her. "So, do you, like, live in London?" she asked me.

"Umm. Just outside London, yes," I replied.

Melody looked genuinely impressed. "Wow, have you been to, like, Buckingham Palace?"

"Er, no," I admitted.

Her face fell.

"Why not?"

I shrugged, aware of the circle focused on my every word. This one guy caught my eye and rolled his. He was so tanned I could only really see the whites of his eyes and his perfect tablety teeth shining out. I gave a small smile back. "Well, erm, English people aren't that excited about the Royal Family compared to other countries. Plus, Buckingham Palace is like, just there, you know? I could go whenever I wanted to, so I've never bothered. Like, have you guys all been to Disneyland?"

Lots shook their heads. "You see, I have been to Disneyland. The Florida one." ...*On that horrific family holiday where Mum vommed over the side of the log flume.* "But not Buckingham Palace, even though Disneyland's much further. I guess..."

Melody interrupted my babbling. "So, do you know Kate Middleton?" she demanded. "Did you, like, go to school with her?"

The eye-rolling guy caught mine again and shook his head, hanging it with mock shame. I tried not to laugh. "Umm, no. Not exactly. England's still pretty big. We don't all go to the same school."

Melody's gorgeous face fell. The excitement of meeting me was waning fast. "But, hang on," I said. "Prince Andrew came to our college and opened our new Art block. I met him."

Melody's eyes widened. "Oh my God, Prince Harry?! He is SO hot."

"Umm... No not Prince H..." I trailed off and admitted defeat. "Yes. Prince Harry. That's the one. I met him."

"You've both got red hair," she announced.

"Oh yes, I guess we do...?"

The super-tanned guy was seriously cracking up now. I kept glancing at him, and his teeth. Wondering what his face looked like in proper light. Someone plugged some portable speakers into their phone and turned some music on. Melody untangled her long limbs and announced she was getting a beer. The circle dispersed and I sighed. I'd made it through the induction, and even in my state, not been mean to anyone. It was a miracle. Whinnie scooted up closer to me and the Native American guy appeared with a huge crate of beer.

"I thought you Americans couldn't drink until you're twenty-one?" I said as he handed me a bottle. He grinned back at me and swigged from his.

"We have our ways. Just don't tell the boss, right?"

In answer, I ripped my bottle top off with my teeth like Joel, one of our metal friends at college, had taught me to do. "You're kidding, right?" I said. "The more I can do to piss off Bumface Kevin, the better."

He laughed. "Wow, you're right. I never noticed before but he does have a really big dip on his chin."

I downed half the Bud Light, savouring the sweet taste. "It's the source of all his evil powers," I said simply.

He laughed again. "I'm Russ. I bet you're struggling to remember all the new names, huh?"

"Russ," I repeated. "I'm Amber. I'm Kevin's stepdaughter, I guess. So, where you from in America?"

"You won't have heard of it." His eyes scrunched when he grinned.

I took another mouthful of my beer. "Try me."

"Taos." Then he laughed while I looked baffled.

"Is that in New York or something?"

"No. Taos is in a state called New Mexico."

"Mexico?"

Another patient laugh. "And I saw you rolling your eyes at Kyle when Melody asked you stupid questions. You're worse than her!"

I smiled. "Who's Kyle?"

"The super tanned guy who looks like he should be in an infomercial."

Ahh, the laughing guy with the teeth...

"Anyway, we have a state called New Mexico. And Taos is a small town right in the mountains. I live on a reservation there."

I'd finished my beer and risked another stupid question. "A nature reservation?"

"No, Melody-the-second. A reservation for...my people, I guess."

So he *was* like Jacob from *Twilight*...and before I could say it—

"... Like Jacob from *Twilight*," he said, reluctantly. "Before you say it."

I put my hands up. "I wasn't going to say that."

"Oh, you were."

Whinnie was kind of hopping on one foot behind him, and interrupted.

"Ignore him," she said. "He has an issue with Jacob from *Twilight*." She turned to Russ. "Dude, get over it, nobody even watches them any more." She turned back to me. "He was whining all of last summer," she explained.

"Hey," Russ said. "I'm an ethnic minority – we're allowed to whinge."

Whinnie pointed to her expansive butt. "And I'm Puerto Rican so I'm minority enough to tell you a) I get it, and b) tell it to my genetic ass."

I laughed nervously with them, not sure if I was allowed to join in. But liking them – thinking they were funny. Also highly aware that everyone was friends already.

Whinnie and Russ started chatting about their unis, or "colleges" as they called them, and I took another beer. Whinnie went to college in a place called *Albuquerque* which was the best word I'd ever heard. Apparently it was only a few hours away from Russ's reservation and they swapped favourite diner recommendations.

I was proud of how un-scared I felt. Yes, okay, so I'd now had two beers. But maybe Americans weren't so bad. I couldn't blame an entire country for taking my mum away.

I drank another beer and took everything in. Melody dancing in the sand with some jock in charge of water sports. Russ and Whinnie arguing over red chilli versus green chilli. The blackness of the lake…

And then another beer.

And then…

Two more beers later, and I was struggling not to let my inner sarcastic British bitch out. Melody was quizzing me about England again, and my eyeballs needed leashes to restrain them from rolling.

"So," Melody said, untangling the water sport guy's arm from her waist. "In England, you guys call it a pavement, right? Whereas we call it a sidewalk."

"Yes." I sounded so world-weary. "And let's not get started on the tomato thing, shall we?"

Water sport guy's eyes lit up. "Hang on? Did you just call it a to-MAR-to? That's SO English."

They all laughed and I actually closed my eyes to stop them rolling. I wished Russ and Whinnie were still here, but they were involved in some treacherous game of volleyball I'd turned down as I'm inherently allergic to "sport".

"Wait wait wait wait…" Melody interrupted. "So, like, what do you call the trash?"

I withheld another sigh.

"We call it rubbish."

She giggled with several others, repeating "rubbish" and tittering.

"… Shall we save some time here? English people call yards, gardens? And we call jelly, jam. And we call potato chips, crisps. And we call french fries, chips, and…and…" I tried desperately to get them all out the way "… And, well, Americans use 'fanny' to describe your butt, and we use the word 'fanny' to talk about OUR BIG ENGLISH VAGINAS, OKAY?"

I sat back on the log and hiccuped.

Melody and Watersports instantly stopped asking questions. I turned to look over at the volleyball game. The tanned guy, Kyle, walked over to the fire, chucking the volleyball over his head effortlessly. He'd been close enough to hear my vaginal outburst.

"Well, well, well," he said, when he arrived. He had the

most American of American accents the world has ever known. "Who'd have thought the boss's daughter would have such a dirty mouth?"

I blushed, which I hated, because Lottie says I blush ginger instead of red.

"Stepdaughter," I corrected him. I closed my eyes to stop my head spinning in the abyss of a thousand (or five) Budweiser Lights. "And you are the most American person I've ever met in my entire life."

It wasn't a reasonable thing to say…

But it was what I was thinking.

He laughed and looked down at himself. I opened my eyes a tiny bit and looked at the half of him glowing in the flickering fire. He was VERY American, to be fair. If someone had told me to sketch an American guy, I would've drawn Kyle. He was uber tall, just the right side of broad, and his arm muscles were all ripply in his T-shirt with the sleeves cut off. He even wore a backwards cap for Christ's sake. And baggy jean shorts. His skin glowed with the kind of easy tan achieved only by living in a naturally hot climate. And his face was the archetypal American face – all strong macho jawline, slightly fat head, smiling eyes.

"Who me?" he asked.

I pointed, my finger wobbling in the air. "Yes, you. Well, you're all ridiculously American here. But I think you're by far the biggest culprit."

He gestured to the empty log next to me with a gentlemanly flourish of his hands.

I nodded, and scooted up to make room. "You see, even *that's* American," I complained. "An English guy would've just grunted and sat on the log."

"I'm Kyle," he said, ignoring me. He offered out his hand.

"I know, Russ told me," I replied. "And that is the most American name I've heard today." But I shook his hand because he was the sort of good-looking that you take any opportunity to touch. "I'm Amber. I'm sorry if I'm being mean. I think I'm a bit wankered."

Kyle screwed his face up. "What's wankered?"

"Oh, bollocks." I waved my hand in the air as I tried to explain it. "It means, like, pissed. Hang on, you wouldn't get that word either. It means 'drunk'. Do you guys say drunk?" I gestured more and almost poked his eye. "Bollocks, I'm sorry. Did I get you?"

Kyle caught my dangerous hand, and held it a bit longer than necessary which might've been an American thing. I dunno. He laughed. "Well, Amber, I'm afraid that you are the most English person I've ever met. So touché! I guess we're equal."

I snorted. Always attractive, that. "Me? English?"

He raised an eyebrow. "Think back on the sentence you just said."

I did… I'd used the words: wankered, pissed and bollocks. In fact, I'd used bollocks twice.

"… And look at your English skin, and English hair, and cool English fashion, and your English freckles." I touched my hair self-consciously, not sure how I felt about all the things he'd noticed about my appearance. Cool English fashion? I was only wearing my kimono, gladiator sandals and denim shorts. It was hardly a statement. "You may be the only English person here, but you're really flying the flag for back home. Trust me."

I looked back at him. "Fair enough." We both laughed.

People had started dancing next to the water, and Melody dragged off Watersports, leaving me and Kyle alone on our log. I caught Kyle looking at Melody's legs as she strode past us, and felt that pang you feel when another girl looks better than you – even though I know thinking like that's totally toxic.

"So this is camp?" I threw my hands up to the night-time activities on the beach, the glow of the fire, the reflection of the moon off the hardly-there ripples of the lake…and to the mosquito-bite already on my leg.

"It's pretty darn American, isn't it?" Kyle said.

"Why do Americans hate their children so much that they ship them off into the mountains all summer?"

Kyle grinned, taking a sip of his beer and looking at me sideways as he did.

"Don't you British people just hire nannies to look after your children?"

I shook my head. "Only in *Mary Poppins*. Or in the aristocracy."

"Well, I guess it's sort of the same here. Well, this camp, anyway. It's a private one. There's no way my parents could afford to send my younger brother and sisters here. We just went to day camp down the road from our house."

I held my hand up. "Wait. It costs money to send your children here?"

Kyle nodded. "Hell yeah. Thousands of dollars. And I'm telling you, that money does not go much on our wages."

I shook my head, tutting. It made my brain start a tsunami of beer haze from one side to the other. "Unbelievable. They're unbelievable."

"What is it?"

"Just my mum and Kevin...they're such..." I trailed off and finished the last of my beer instead of my sentence. Such what? Phonies, I guess? Hypocrites? She and Bumface Kevin *never* told me this camp was a business. I'd assumed it was, like, a charity thing. When Kevin bought it, she emailed implying as much. I thought it was for disadvantaged kids or whoever, especially as he'd been a supervisor at Mum's rehab place. He and Mum acted like they were serving the community or something, not taking thousands of dollars so Donald-dearest could learn how to waterski ready for his summers on the French Riviera...or whatever it is rich people do. But then I remembered overhearing Dad and Penny whispering one night in the kitchen, talking about how Kevin had been forbidden from working at centres after they found out about him and Mum getting together, so maybe charity gigs were a complete no-go now.

I changed the subject to curb my anger. "So, you're the eldest?" I asked. I don't know if it was the beer, or what, but Kyle was very good-looking.

"Yep. Of four. My family all live in this podunk town in the California mountains."

I made a face. "What's podunk?"

He laughed. "Do you not have that word in England? It means small, I guess, like 'going-nowhere'."

"Podunk," I repeated it to myself. "Do you still live there?"

"Not really." Maybe he looked sad? I couldn't tell. Tans make faces look happier. "I'm at college at Brown," he said.

I blinked at him.

"It's a college. On the other side of America."

"Oh, okay." A hazy memory pinged into my fuzzy brain. "Hang on. I've heard of Brown. Isn't it one of those colleges where all the rich people go?"

He laughed. Again. I seemed to make Americans laugh a lot. "It's Ivy League, I guess. Yeah."

"So your town can't be too poo-dank if you're attending an Ivy League school?"

Kyle scratched his neck and didn't correct me. "I got a scholarship."

"A football one or something? Like Forrest Gump?"

More laughter. "No, just a regular smart one."

I sat back on the log and wobbled. "Wow. You must be REALLY smart." I pointed at him again. And almost took his eye out again.

He shrugged, all modest. "They offer one in my old high school per year group. It's, like, the only way to get out of my *poo-dank* town." He smiled, his teeth reflecting all the moonlight. "So I studied really hard..." He paused, took another sip of beer. "That said, I am on Brown's college basketball team."

I snorted. "Basketball team? Who even plays basketball? What are you, the captain or something?"

He nodded, grinned uncomfortably. "You got it."

I pushed his arm playfully because beer had made me brave.

"You really are, categorically, the most American guy in the universe," I said. "Next you'll be telling me you were Prom King. And you drive a red pick-up truck."

He pushed my arm back. "Prom King *and* Homecoming King. And my jeep is parked in the camp parking lot."

I rolled my eyes. "Yeah right..." I started. Then I looked at him. He wasn't laughing. "... Wait, you're not kidding?" I dropped my mouth open, so much I probably ate double my daily protein recommendation in bugs. "You were a Prom King? I'm sitting next to an all American actual real-life Prom King."

He shrugged, like it was nothing. NOTHING. But hello!?! Prom King?! All my life I've been watching movies about Prom Kings. I never thought they were real, and not Zac Efron.

For some reason, I stood up, swaying a little. This information bothered me but I was full of too many conflicting emotions and digesting too many new experiences to understand why. Suddenly I felt lost and homesick. And really bloody sad.

"Where you going?" he asked.

I swayed and adjusted my feet so I didn't fall over.

"It was lovely meeting you." I could hear myself slurring my words. "But I'm going to go to bed now. I'm scared that if I stay sitting next to you much longer, I may start sweating out apple pie and guns."

He looked confused. "What?"

Just as I was trying to explain what I meant, even though I didn't really know myself, Russ and Whinnie walked up. The volleyball game had finished.

"Hey, what's up?" Russ asked. His olive skin was all shiny with sweat.

Kyle gestured to me. "Amber's wigging out about being in America."

I huffed and crossed my arms. "Only because you are too American. Like genetically modified American or something," I argued.

"She can't believe I was a Prom King," Kyle said.

Russ pulled a face. "Dude, you were?"

"You were?" Whinnie echoed. "Ha ha. You've kept that quiet."

"Yeah, you did. Ha. Can't say I'm surprised though." Russ steadied me as I was in the process of falling over. "Amber? You all right? How many beers have you had?"

"Hey!" I straightened myself out and got ready to point again. "I am British. BRITISH! And there's one thing I'll have you know about British people. We're very good at drinking and very good at holding our drink. You don't have to worry about me."

And that's when I fell over the log.

Situations that are destined to fail:

Creeping into a cabin of squeaky floorboards

+

Drunk

+

A mother waiting up for you

Six

Kyle offered to walk me home.

By "home", I mean the cabin of doom where my photograph is kept in the guest bedroom.

"Bye, Amber." Russ slapped my hand in a high-five way – another American thing I needed to catch up with. "It was great meeting you. I hope you feel okay at training tomorrow."

Training. All day tomorrow. Shite…

I hugged Whinnie goodbye, already feeling like we were the best of friends. "I love your Winnie the Pooh fleece," I told her honestly.

She beamed back at me. "So lovely to meet you, Amber. I can't wait to hang out tomorrow."

"I still don't see why I can't take myself home," I grumbled, as Kyle and I left the fire behind us.

"Just wait until we get into the trees," he said.

"So? Trees are trees." I shrugged and stumbled.

But, as we stepped under the canopy, the moonlight was swallowed whole and I couldn't see a thing.

"Kyle, I don't like it in here."

He laughed and put his arm around my shoulder. Not in a creepy way, in a protective-American way.

"LUMOS," I yelled, pointing my arm into the air. "EXPECTO PATRONUMMMMMM."

"Umm, you know Harry Potter isn't real, right?" Kyle said, as I looked disappointedly at the lack of my magical ability.

"Mudblood," I muttered, and he laughed again.

"Are all British girls as funny as you?" he asked, steering me in what I supposed was the right direction.

"I'm funny?"

I felt him nod in the dark. "You are. The way you pulled faces when Melody asked you all that dumb stuff."

"I wasn't pulling faces." I'd been trying *so* hard not to anyway. "That's just what my face is like."

He laughed again. "See, hilarious! Sometimes people here piss me off so much. Like, how can they not know more than one member of the British Royal Family?"

I thought about it. "To be fair," I said, "I didn't even know we had a Prince Andrew until he turned up at our college. Lots of people in England are ignorant too. There's this one bloke, in my Art class, who said he had a photogenic memory."

More laughing. "Maybe your cute accent makes you sound more intellectual?"

I stopped in the darkness. "Did you just sexualize an accent?"

Kyle stopped beside me. "Oh, because girls don't do that?" he asked, and he put on a high squeaky voice. "*Oooo, I just lurrrve the Italian accent on men. It's so sexy.*"

"I've had too much beer to argue with you right now."

"That means I'm right."

"No, that means I'm drunk and tired. It's like midday tomorrow my time."

"I still think that means I'm right."

I smiled, knowing it was too dark for him to see.

It wasn't just dark actually, it was jet black – like the plug had been pulled on the world. Without Kyle, I would've ended up lost and eaten by coyotes. Whatever coyotes are…

"How do you know your way in the dark?" I asked. "I can't see anything."

"I told you, I grew up in the middle of nowhere. I'm used to it, that's all."

When slivers of moonlight started sneaking their way through the overhead layer of trees, I guessed we were nearly back. I hoped the door wasn't locked. It wasn't like Mum would be waiting up for me.

She'd never once waited up for me…

… I dragged my duvet down to the sofa, tucking its edges around me to stop the cold sneaking onto my skin. Dad sat wearily in his chair, his finished newspaper

wilting on his armrest, his reading glasses slipping down his face.

"What are you doing down here, poppet?" he asked. "You should be asleep."

"I want to wait up for Mum too." I paused and fiddled with a loose thread on my duvet. "Dad, she is coming back, isn't she?"

All sorts of expressions crossed his face before he replied – expressions children shouldn't see on their parents' faces if they can possibly help it.

"Of course she's coming back," he said. Even then, aged twelve, I could tell in his voice he wasn't sure. "She's just out with friends, that's all, having fun. Your mum's allowed to have fun, you know?"

I turned over and used the armrest as a pillow, knocking Dad's paper to the floor.

"She's always out with friends," I grumbled.

The cold air from the front door woke me. Someone had left it open.

Oh, and the shouting. The shouting woke me too.

Kyle and I emerged into the clearing, blinking at the light of the cabin. The kitchen light was still on, so bright it burned into my retinas, making me see fuzzy purple shapes.

"I'm so jealous you're in a proper cabin," he whispered, so as not to wake the Bumface lurking inside. "You should see the state of mine. All bunks, a chemical toilet, and in two days it will be full of hyper children."

I kicked my foot in the dust of the forest floor.

"Yeah, but at least you don't have to share a house with your boss."

"That's a point."

We stood, awkwardly, both drawing spirals in the dropped pine-needles with our feet. I realized I didn't know this guy. I didn't really know anyone here. Not even the woman inside who shared half my DNA. The sadness hit my guts – I was sobering up.

"Thanks for walking me back." I was suddenly too nervous to look him in the eye. Further proof I was sobering up. "It was very gentlemanly and American of you."

He shrugged. "Hey, it was nothing. And it was cool meeting you. You'll get used to camp. And America too, I'm sure. I've always wanted to come to England, so I'll bombard you with questions tomorrow as payback..." He saw the look on my face "... Don't worry, I know the basics already. There is more to England than London and you don't all hang out with the Queen."

I grinned and made myself make eye-contact.

"Only on Sundays. She's busy the rest of the week – saying 'one' a lot and mainlining cucumber sandwiches."

He laughed so loud I had to shh him.

"You all right getting back to the party?" I asked.

"I'm all good. Podunk night vision, remember?"

"I'm so confused by your words."

He stood a moment more, then softly punched my shoulder, like I've seen fraternity brothers do in movies.

"Night, Amber."

"Night."

Only when he was fully submerged in the darkness did I let myself smile…

Maybe Americans weren't so bad after all.

Maybe this summer would be fun.

I carefully nudged the front door open.

Maybe Bumface Kevin will get a tick in his bumchin and have to go to hospital so Mum and I will be left to look after the whole camp together.

Maybe…

Mum sat on the couch in the living room and I jumped out of my freckled skin.

"Mum? What are you still doing up?"

She put down the magazine she'd been reading – *Mind and Spirit* – and pointed to the closed bedroom door. She made a "shh" face.

"Amber, have you been drinking?" she whispered.

I shook my head, closing my mouth so she couldn't smell my breath.

"You look all sweaty."

"I'm in California, and I'm ginger. Sweat is what happens."

She patted a bit of the sofa next to her and I hesitated. I stank of beer, I was sure of it. Maybe if I talked with my mouth closed?

I gingerly perched next to her and, without warning,

she pulled me in for a hug. I sank into her body and let the feeling it gave me fill up my gut.

"So, was everyone friendly?" She kissed the top of my head.

I nodded into her. "Yep, Americans are known for that though, aren't they?"

She pulled away as abruptly as she'd hugged me. "You need to apologize to Kevin. I can't believe you just stormed out like that. He was pretty upset, Amber; he's really been looking forward to you coming."

The feeling in my tummy deflated. Why wasn't *she* upset? Why just him? He wasn't anything to me, and I wasn't anything to him. I was just the annoying "extra" he had to put up with to stay with the love of his life. He was just the jerk who seduced my mother at the most vulnerable time in her life and shipped her back to his country. Mum was my mum, and I was her daughter – yet Kevin was the one who was upset?

I sighed, not saying what I was thinking. Never really saying what I was thinking. "I'm here to work, aren't I? I needed to meet all my co-workers."

"He'd cooked you a nice welcome dinner! And you just came bursting out with that ridiculous wedding question."

It wasn't ridiculous...

I shrugged. "You could've followed me and told me this then...but you didn't." It was the closest I could get to saying how I felt.

"He was too upset to follow you."

Kevin was upset...Kevin... Not her.

I stood up.

"Whatever. I'm going to bed."

Mum sat still for a moment and I waited for her to say something – anything. To answer my questions about the wedding. Or maybe just to ask if I was okay. Because I so obviously wasn't okay. She just picked up her magazine and started reading again. My eyes stung and I told myself it was from campfire smoke.

Just as I opened the door to my pokey guest room, she said: "I can smell beer on you. I can't believe you've been drinking."

I stopped. "Are you going to tell Kevin?" He'd love that – any reason to put me on a plane back home again so he could keep Mum all to himself...

She shook her head. "No. But don't do it again, Amber. You're here to work."

A thousand replies ran through my head.

You'd know all about drinking, wouldn't you, Mum?

I'm not here to work, I'm here to see you.

I stretched my arms up, not wanting a fight – just wanting us to feel okay, like I'd imagined it on the flight over. I was ruining it...but maybe she was too.

"I only had one," I lied. "And it was a light beer, anyway. Whatever the hell that means."

Mum smiled a little.

"Well, still, be careful...you know..." She trailed off and her eyes glazed over with sadness.

"I know..."

Situations that are destined to fail:

Hangovers

+

First-aid training

Seven

With a hangover, I found Melody even more annoying.

"Ooo, no, not my boobs, stupid," she squealed, as Watersports openly groped her chest.

I had a headache. It was over twenty-eight degrees, though everyone kept talking in Fahrenheit. And Melody had volunteered herself as a model for artificial resuscitation, despite the TOTALLY AVAILABLE PURPOSE-BUILT DOLL the camp had for this activity. It hadn't helped that she'd spent the last twenty minutes, telling anyone who would listen about the time she'd "totally kissed some girls" at cheer camp.

Watersports boy faux apologized and pumped Melody's ribs.

"Like this?" he called to Kevin, who was using an actual doll with the other half of the group.

Kevin turned and laughed.

"Melody, you don't have to do that. That's what resuscitation Annie is for."

"Yeah, but it's much better to practise with a real body, don't you think?" she giggled.

Watersports certainly seemed to agree.

I scuffed my shoe in the dusty grass, and focused, yet again, on not being sick. All twenty of us were on our compulsory first-aid part of training day. In the already strong sunshine, it seemed we'd be the ones who needed first aid for heat exhaustion...or maybe that was just hungover me.

Whinnie sidled up next to me. "You okay, Amber? You look a little...green."

I nodded, concentrating on getting through the wave of nausea.

"Was I bad last night?" I whispered. I'd only just met her, but she seemed like the safest, nicest, person to ask. When she made a cooing reassuring sound I knew I was right.

"You were fine," she said. "Everyone got pretty wasted after you left anyway. Melody and some of the others ended up skinny-dipping."

That wasn't a surprise. I'd only met Melody yesterday and it wasn't a surprise.

"Really?" I asked. "Who else did it?"

"Umm, a few of the girls...like Bryony. Did you meet her? The jock guys..." As she was talking, Kyle and Russ came up behind us. Whinnie turned to them. "You didn't, did you, Russ?"

Russ shook his head. "Skinny-dip? Nope." He punched Kyle's shoulder. "I didn't want to make all the other guys jealous. Especially Kyle here."

Kyle thumped him back. "Dude, we share a shower. I've seen it all."

"Yeah, and you cried afterwards."

Whinnie gave me a "boys" look. I smiled and returned it, distracting myself from my headache for a short moment.

"Did you do it?" I asked Kyle. And annoyingly I felt myself blushing at the thought of him naked.

He stretched his arms up and nodded, like it was nothing. "I grew up in the middle of nowhere mountains. Skinny-dipping was the only thing we had to do at the weekend. Why, you don't do it in the UK?"

I blushed harder as I wondered if he was now thinking of me naked, as I was him. I shook my head. "If you skinny-dipped in England, you'd get frostbite of the dangly bits."

They all cracked up, and my face got even redder.

"I don't even want to know how you know that," Kyle said.

"I don't know it for sure!" I protested. "It's just a theory. I've never had any dangly bits to test it on…" I needed to stop talking. All three of them were laughing uncontrollably now, so much so we attracted the attention of Kevin and his bumchin.

"Guys!" he said, clapping his hands to startle us out of it. "This isn't a playground. This training could save someone's life. Come on, Amber. Let's teach everyone how to put someone in the recovery position."

Melody and Watersports were standing up now, and Kevin jutted his hand out, to pull me to the centre.

"Now, Amber, let's have you demonstrate. Lie down on the ground here."

He smiled, like he was doing me a massive favour by putting everyone's attention on me. I happily – despite him – lolled onto the earth and closed my eyes. It felt nice. It calmed my churning stomach.

"Who wants to help? Kyle? You wanna put Amber into the recovery position?"

"Be careful of her dangly bits," Whinnie said, only loud enough so I could hear her, and I giggled with my eyes shut.

I felt my face get cast into shadow as Kyle stepped forward to follow Kevin's instructions.

"Now, Kyle, if you just kneel next to Amber, and gently put the arm nearest to you up at a right angle…"

I felt his fingers touch my skin and I almost jolted away at the shock of it. His hands were warm, his skin a little rough. He picked up my hand and put it back onto the earth. I breathed in as deeply as I could. I realized this was the first time a guy had ever held my hand…and he was putting me into the recovery position. I was pathetic.

"That's good…now pick up her other hand and place it onto her cheek. The side of her face that's nearest to you."

I braced myself for the physical contact this time, but it still felt stupidly nice as he touched me again.

"You all right there, patient?" Kyle asked softly. I opened one eye up at him, hardly able to see him against the sun.

"This is really helping my hangover," I whispered, and he laughed.

Kevin tutted. "Come on, Amber, you're supposed to be unconscious."

I closed my eyes again and let his words flow over me, making myself floppy so Kyle could manoeuvre me easily.

I didn't need to be taught how to do the recovery position.

I'd had to do it myself, on my mum. When I was thirteen and Dad dared to go away for the weekend and leave us. She'd passed out on the kitchen floor and I was worried she'd choke on her vomit. I'd had to Google it, and follow the directions of a YouTube video.

I never told Dad what happened though… In case this was the thing that tipped him over the edge. The thing that made him leave.

Didn't matter. He left anyway. Less than a year later. Wrenching me with him.

Later I'd figured out he'd been with Penny that weekend.

Situations that are destined to fail:

A webcam

+

My sunburn

+

The slowest internet connection EVER

Eight

Evie and Lottie waved madly at me – Lottie jumping up and down with excitement.

"Hello, traveller," they called. "We are here from Planet Skype, to serve your insatiable need for sarcasm."

I wanted to reach into the computer monitor and yank them both through the screen, dragging them into America with me. I was sitting in the corner of Kevin's cabin, sweating into my vest-top and feeling so far away from them. It had been a HORRID day of training. Horrid mainly due to my honking hangover combined with lectures on pus and blisters and blood. I'd given myself a break – for aftersun application, and much-needed girlie catch-up time.

"I miss you guys so much!" I yelled, jumping in my chair, high off seeing them.

Lottie and Evie beamed back. Their faces were all pixelated and smudgy. Lottie's eyes were just two black holes.

The slow connection obviously couldn't adequately process her copious amounts of eyeliner.

"We miss you too." Lottie's voice warped in the high pitch of her squeal. "Though your face scares me. I want to courier an industrial vat of aftersun over to you."

I touched my burned red face sheepishly. I could feel the heat from it on the back of my hand.

"I promise, on all of the Buddhas, that I used factor 50. I just didn't realize I'd have to apply it every ten minutes."

Lottie burst out laughing.

"Hey, it's not funny. It hurts!"

"Oh, but it is."

"You still look beautiful," Evie said. "… It matches your hair."

"HEY!"

They both giggled themselves into a frenzy and I had to sigh and wait it out.

"So how ARE you?" Lottie demanded, after she'd recovered. Her hair was all scooped up on top of her head and she pushed her kohl-covered eyes right up into the webcam. "What the blazes is happening over there in America? You having fun?"

I nodded. Shook my head, then nodded again.

"Uh oh," Lottie said. "Tell me everything."

This was why I loved them – their constant ability to know when something was up. "No, it's great," I said semi-honestly. "It's so pretty here, and all the other counsellors are okay. REALLY American, but friendly and stuff. I've had basic training all day. In the sun, as you can see… The children aren't arriving until tomorrow…"

Evie pushed towards the screen. "How about things with your mum?" she asked quietly.

I did my nod-shake thing again.

"Okay. Well, not really. But not bad, it's so weird…" I trailed off. "Is it okay if we don't talk about it?"

They looked at each other and nodded.

I changed the subject. "Did I tell you they made me get resuscitated by people? With a hangover! I thought I was going to die. Last night there was this welcome campfire party and I drank too much. A headache in altitude is, like, worse than listening to Joel's band with a migraine."

They laughed. Joel's this guy from back home, the boyfriend of Evie's old best friend, Jane. He's in the world's worst band ever – death metal, with added lack of talent.

"So…" Lottie's head loomed close again. "Have you met any American HUNKS?"

I rolled my eyes.

"I hope you saw that eye-roll. It is destined for you. Never has an eye-roll been so destined for you."

Lottie pretended to catch it, like it was a blown kiss. "What? I'm only asking."

"Well, yes. There are American guys here. Some could be classified as 'hunks', I guess…" Water sports guy would definitely qualify. Maybe Kyle. Though we'd spent all of training today talking about how he loved reading biographies – that wasn't typically "hunky".

"I want a hunk!" Lottie said. "I'm getting on a plane now."

My stomach dropped, even though I knew she was joking. If Lottie was here, all the "hunks" would've swarmed to her – like bees to a honeypot made of the juice of a thousand genetically-modified rose petals.

Evie interrupted, with reason as always.

"Amber's not there to go boy hunting though, is she? She's there to see her mum." Evie sighed. "Anyway, aren't we supposed to be having a Spinster Club meeting? Isn't objectifying men as 'hunks' slightly counterproductive?"

Lottie and I smiled at each other through the webcam.

"Right you are, Evie," I said. "What's the topic of discussion for today? It has to be quick. They're threatening another campfire later."

Evie's head ducked down and reappeared with some notes. "I thought I'd choose a transatlantic theme." She coughed, in a fake announcement. "*Ladies: America or England – which is the most sexist country?*"

I grinned and Lottie gasped. "You can't do that, Evie!"

"Why not?" Evie asked.

"Because America and England aren't allowed to battle each other. We're, like, proper mates. We watch the same TV and fought together in World War Two."

"That's why I picked it," Evie said. "Because we think we're so similar. It would be too easy a fight if we compared England to, say, I dunno, a super repressed country where women can't go to school or vote, or drive or whatever."

I nodded. "Makes sense to me."

Lottie shrugged. "Okay, then. Fine. Break the special relationship."

"I will." Evie shuffled her cards. "So, Amber, as you're over there, you have to argue America's corner. Lottie, you can defend the UK. And I'll flit about in the middle of the debate being Switzerland."

Lottie put her hand up, like she was in school. "Okay okay okay, I've got the perfect start. The UK is better at feminism because we've had a female prime minister."

I wrinkled my nose. "Does Margaret Thatcher count? She hated the word 'feminist' and had only men on her cabinet."

"At least she had the right junk," Lottie argued.

"Is that what we're calling genitalia now? Junk?"

"Okay, she HAD A MASSIVE VAGINA." And we all crumpled into laughter. Just as I was about to point out that gender is so much more than biology, I heard the door of the cabin slam. I jumped.

"Why are you always screaming the word 'vagina'?"

It was Kyle's voice. I whipped around. Him, Russ and Whinnie stood in the doorway – looking equally perplexed and amused.

"Oh my God, guys. I'm...erm...I'm online speaking to my friends back home."

Lottie's face was immediately right up on the screen.

"LET ME MEET YOU, AMERICAN ONES," she yelled.

I beckoned them in. "Come on, they're umm...a bit excited. We're having a meeting."

Kyle raised an eyebrow. "A meeting?"

"A VAGINA MEETING," Lottie cackled.

"Lottie, shut up!" I stage-whispered.

The Americans stepped nervously into the sitting room, looking around. I guessed it was weird for them, being in their bosses' house.

"HELLO, HANDSOME," Lottie's voice boomed from the speakers. She'd clocked both Russ and Kyle as they stepped into view of the camera.

I covered the camera with my hand. "Ignore her...she's... erm...drunk..."

"I'M NOT DRUNK."

"Girls," I hissed into the computer's ancient microphone. "I need to go do camp stuff."

"Noooooo," I heard Lottie yell, but I waved bye and turned off the computer as quickly as I could.

"They your friends?" Kyle nodded towards the now-blank screen.

"Yeah, we were just...umm...what are you guys doing here, anyway?"

Russ was already picking stuff up off the table, reading Mum's *Mind and Spirit* magazine upside-down and pulling a face.

Whinnie answered.

"You're in our group. For the welcome show tonight. We all have to put on a little performance for everyone."

I closed my eyes slowly. Performing... I hated performing. "Really? Do I have to?"

Kyle smiled as he nodded. "We all have to." He didn't look bothered at all. "Now, are you going to explain why your computer was yelling rude words?"

I sighed, cursing Lottie.

"Let me get my stuff, then I'll fill you in."

I put on some flip-flops, and rubbed more suncream in, then followed Kyle and Russ into the forest. They said there was a clearing outside their cabins which would make a good place to practise.

"Practise what?" Whinnie asked. "We don't know what we're going to do yet."

"How about a silent protest?" I suggested. They ignored me.

I still wasn't used to the heat and just the walk there was tough. I could feel my hair expanding to three times its normal volume.

"So when you going to explain to us, Amber?" Kyle teased.

I shot him a look. "My friends and I back home, we… well… We have this like women's rights group. And we were having a meeting using modern technology."

I pushed past some ferns and scratched my leg.

"You're in a women's rights group?" Russ asked.

"Yes. It's awesome. You should join one."

"I think I'm okay, thanks."

"What was your meeting about?" Whinnie walked right beside me, and she seemed genuinely interested rather than taking the piss.

"We were chatting about America actually. They wanted us to argue over who has the best women's rights – England, or you guys."

"Are you kidding?" Whinnie's eyes went all big behind her glasses. "It's totally your country. Do you, like, know what they're doing with abortion law over here?"

I shook my head. "Not good?"

She shook her head. "Muchly not good."

"Well, I'll let them know. And, jeez, I'm sorry."

She gave me a huge grin. "It's okay. We're protesting about it on college campus. We won't let them win."

I found myself high-fiving her – America was already rubbing off on me.

"You all right, Kyle?" I asked. He'd gone all quiet on the walk.

"Yeah...fine..." He trailed off. I hoped he wasn't a secret chauvinist.

We stepped out into a clearing framed by two cabins. They were both so sweet, it looked like a scene out of a fairy tale.

"Welcome to Casa Awesome," Russ said.

Whinnie and I shared a look, and I knew we both had the same idea at the same time. We ran into the sunshine, past a circle of stones, and flung open one of the doors.

"Stop them," Russ yelled, but it was too late.

"Eww," Whinnie said, as she stood next to me in the doorway.

"That. Is. Disgusting," I agreed.

The inside was a mess. Smelly boy clothes were flung all

over the empty bunks, a half-eaten packet of crisps (or potato chips) was scattered over the sheets. It stank of stale boy stench…

"Oi," Russ said, catching up with us. "It's not fair that you're snooping."

I turned to face him. "Russ? Seriously? You've only been here a few days! How is it so gross? And how are you going to tidy it before the children get here?"

He looked suitably ashamed of himself.

"Kyle said he's going to help me."

Kyle arrived at the door. "Well, that's not true, is it? I said I'd keep you company while you tidy."

Russ's face darkened. "Well, some of us aren't anally neat like you."

"Kyle's…tidy?" I asked.

Whinnie caught my eye and we shared another thought in unison.

"Let's see!" she yelled, and we both ran into the other cabin – the boys flinging themselves after us.

We burst through the door of the other cabin, just as Kyle caught me by pulling on the back of my T-shirt.

I stopped in my tracks.

"Wow, your cabin is like crazy tidy," I said. "What the hell happened to make you so *neat?*"

Kyle had made up all the beds to military precision. His belongings were aligned in perfect angles around his bunk. There was even a plastic cup filled with flowers on the window sill. It was almost as tidy as Evie's room back home

– though Evie's tidiness didn't have much to do with her OCD. She was just neat, and thought I was a slob…

He tried not to look embarrassed but his blush gave him away.

"Duuuude," Russ said. "My mum would want to adopt you. How do you keep it so clean?"

He shrugged. "I have a lot of siblings. If we were all messy back home, we'd live in utter squalor."

I walked further into the cabin, liking how it smelled. All clean and fresh with an underhint of mint. From Kyle's bodywash, I guessed.

"How are you going to cope when the kids turn up and trash the place?" Whinnie asked.

"I'm trying not to think about that."

A thick biography of Vincent van Gogh caught my attention – laid out adorably on Kyle's pillow. My heart lurched and I picked up the book. I opened the pages, fanning them out, turning to the section of the book that showed all the colour photos and paintings.

"You like Van Gogh?"

Kyle exuded a shrug. "I'm really into reading biographies, and I'm only halfway through that one. But I'm liking it so far. Van Gogh seems like a dude…"

A dude…

One of the greatest painters and visionaries to ever grace this fair planet…a dude.

"Isn't that the guy who cut his own ear off?" Whinnie asked.

I withheld a sigh. "He did do that yes, but..."

But he did *so* much more. With his oils, with his lines, with the mood he could create using only an easel, paints and his fingers...but that was art stuff, and only I seemed interested.

Russ stretched his arms up, bored. "Can you stop poking around our stuff so we can discuss what the hell we're doing this evening?"

We left Kyle's tidy cabin and stepped into the harsh sunlight of the clearing. I sat on a log and fanned my face. It was even hotter, if possible. The air was so dry, like someone had sucked all the moistness out with a Hoover. I remembered Mum telling me I'd miss the fog of San Francisco. She was right.

Sometimes she was right.

Sometimes...

My arms were already crossed just thinking about the upcoming evening. I hated people looking at me. A lifetime of being too tall meant I was too used to it.

Kyle lay back in the dust and kicked his legs up. "So what do we do, guys?"

Russ sat down, then stood up with inspiration.

"I know," he said. "We've got Amber in our group. We should do something British!"

I rolled my eyes. "Well, that's not obvious."

Russ looked confused. "What do you mean? It's pretty obvious?"

Kyle grinned at me. "Amber's being sarcastic," he explained.

"Contrary to popular belief, we Yanks do understand sarcasm. Though, yes, maybe we're not all such cynics."

"I'm not a cynic," I protested. "I'm a terminal pessimist with an edge of angry realism."

"That's quite a mouthful." He smiled again.

I smiled back. "It's true. What are you anyway, Prom King? An *if-you-wanna-see-rainbows-you-gotta-put-up-with-the-rain* person? Do you, like, post motivational quotes on a blog somewhere?"

He grinned wider. "And what's wrong with rainbows?"

"Enough enough enough!" Russ waved his arms against the blue sky, interrupting us. "We're losing time. What British things do you know, Amber?"

I wracked my brain and looked at Whinnie. "Erm, Winnie the Pooh?"

"I'm not doing Winnie the Pooh," Russ said.

"You'll only violate his values anyway," Whinnie said.

"Why don't we just sing American campfire songs with morals in them?" I asked. "Isn't that what campfires are for?" I got a sudden memory of a CD collection Mum brought on one of my childhood holidays to America. We'd played it over and over. "How about Peter Alsop?" I asked, fumbling for the name in my head. "It's perfect for a campfire, surely?"

Whinnie and Russ pulled a *huh-what?* face. "Who?" they asked, just as Kyle said: "You're kidding me. You know Peter Alsop?" His face lit from within, making his tan more golden. "I swear NOBODY knows him."

"Yeah, I know him. I thought everyone in America knew him? In England no one has heard of him. My friends always thought I was weird when I played his CDs at my birthday parties."

"Who the hell is Peter Alsop?" Russ asked. "Is he, like, in a band?"

Kyle and I grinned at each other, with that shared positive energy from finding someone who knows the same obscure thing you do.

I thought about how to explain him. "Peter Alsop is a children's singer."

"But he's also a child psychologist," Kyle added. "And a hippy, I think. He writes all these songs for kids, teaching them important life lessons and stuff."

I jumped up off the log and started to sing. "My body's nobody's body but mine. You run your own body, let me run mine!"

Kyle jumped up too. "Ahh, yes! Oh my God, the please-don't-touch-me song. I never got that as a kid. Do you remember 'Where will I go when I'm dead and gone'?"

"That one that teaches you about death? Yes!"

Russ and Whinnie looked totally bewildered but we ignored them, high off the reminiscing. "What's your favourite?"

Kyle beamed at me again. "Easy. It has to be 'I am a Pizza'."

I AM A PIZZA. THIS GUY KNEW "I AM A PIZZA".

"I can't believe you just said the words 'I am a Pizza' to me. That makes me so happy inside."

"And then there's 'You Get a Little Extra When You

Watch TV'. And 'It's No Fun When Ya Gotta Eat an Onion'."
Kyle practically jumped up and down with excitement.

"Onnnnnnniion," I sang, remembering the old lyrics instantly.

Whinnie and Russ just stared at us, their mouths open.

"You two are weird," Russ stated. "I think that needs to be acknowledged."

I sat down on the log with a thump, a smile stretching to the widest cracks of my mouth. "You would understand if you had Peter Alsop in your childhood too."

Russ actually waved his hands to make us shut up.

"Guys, guys. We have a show to put on! And Whinnie and I don't understand your weird psychobabble singer. I still think we should do something British. Amber, you're useless, especially as you're actually English. Kyle, any ideas?"

Kyle's face had transformed in the short interval I'd not been looking at him. His wide grin gone, he nibbled at a hangnail and stared into the dust. He gave a big boy shrug. "I don't know," he said, all personality-transplanty. "Whatever."

Whinnie and I exchanged another look.

"How about Monty Python?" she then suggested. "Surely we all know that?"

"Monty Python," I repeated. Dad was obsessed with the Python people and forced me to watch the films all through my childhood. I'd loved the weird animations in them that broke up random scenes. They were so delicately drawn, so perfectly painted – yet all that effort for utter nonsense.

"Monty Python could work," Russ said. Kyle said nothing, but nodded into the dust.

I sighed with resignation. "I'm in."

Situations that are destined to fail:

Americans

+

Attempts at British accents

+

Vodka

Nine

I had an obligatory "family" dinner to get through before the obligatory campfire humiliation.

Bumchin Kevin had made fajitas. I think to try and make peace after the previous night's row. He kept saying the word all high-pitched: "Fa-HEE-taz". It was like torture – so much so that if you recorded it and played it back to me on a loop, I'd tell you all the secret information I held about my country.

I felt a bit sick anyway – from leftover hungoverness, sunstroke, and the thought of all the children arriving tomorrow.

"Here they are," he said, carrying a sizzling plate of chargrilled vegetables over to the tiny dilapidated dining table. "Fa-HEE-taz. Tuck in everyone." He carefully put everything into the middle.

Mum acted like he was a caveman who'd just dragged in a mammoth he'd killed with his bare hands. "Kevin, these look INCREDIBLE. Don't they, Amber?"

I nodded, wishing there was meat in them. Wishing I could be eating in the rec hall like everyone else.

"Don't they look lovely, Amber?" she pressed again.

I nodded again. "That's why I nodded."

"You could say thank you to Kevin too."

Kevin waved his hands. "Don't be silly, it's my pleasure." But Mum gave me a "look" over the steam of the burning onions.

"Thank you, Kevin." My voice sickly sweet.

I jumped when Kevin thumped his glass down on the table.

"Don't talk to me like that in my own house."

"What?" My heart thumped from the shock of him banging the glass down. "I said thank you."

"I'm not an idiot, Amber!"

"I…I…"

I didn't know what to say. I'd broken through Kevin's fakery, within a day. I was half pissed off, half quite impressed that he wasn't pretending any more.

"Well, they look great. Just great," Mum repeated, trying to cut through the tension, taking plates and dolloping on piles of veg before passing them round.

We ate in an anything-but-contented silence. I stared at Kevin's beer bottle for a long time. He slurped from it occasionally, tipping his head back, dribbling some into his bumchin.

Dad never used to drink in front of Mum. I wondered how she could stand it. But she seemed not to notice as she sipped at her iced tea.

"So, Amber." Kevin downed more beer. "You looking forward to the kids arriving tomorrow?" He said it sternly, daring me to be rude again.

"I guess."

"I can't wait for them to try out your new art class. We've never done art here before." His voice was falsely enthusiastic, but with threat underneath.

"Hmm."

I hadn't exactly planned my "art classes" yet – though technically I was supposed to have created my own syllabus. In fact, I hadn't really thought about the fact that loads f American children were rocking up the next day and I was supposed to look after them. All I'd thought about was Mum. I was jolted by another memory…

Of one of the good weekends I occasionally got before she went into the centre. Of us sprawled on the carpet of her dank flat, Sellotaping paper together to make one giant sheet, like we were both children.

"Mum, I'm supposed to be doing my art homework."

"You can do that later." She waved her hand in the air, a thick felt tip clasped in her fingers. "Creativity is about fun. Okay, let's try and draw every single Harry Potter character."

And my homework hadn't got done, and Dad had yelled, and Mum had forgotten to pick me up the next weekend, and I'd ripped our giant picture up and dramatically tried to set it on fire in the garden and Penny had flipped out, and Dad had tried to explain, and it was all a mess.

I felt angry suddenly as I looked at her – angry about the way she sipped her iced tea, angry about how she chewed delicately on her fajita, angry about how she seemed like a washed-out version of the mother I used to know, like she'd been put through the laundry too many times. Old Mum wasn't a vegetarian – we'd have rib-eating competitions at the shitty cowboy themed restaurant in town. Old Mum wasn't "wholesome" – she was loud, and brash, and all over the place – and yes, sometimes it was embarrassing and she wouldn't remember and would never say sorry – but it was energy, it was real. Old Mum definitely didn't wear gingham. And definitely didn't follow men around like a lovesick puppy… She never looked at Dad the way she looks at Kevin.

After two years of yearning and wanting and missing, now suddenly all I had was bitterness and resentment and confusion. Was the Mum I knew even still in there? She wasn't…bad any more. But, since I'd arrived, she also wasn't…good?

Yet, when she pulled me in for a hug before we left for the campfire, I clung onto her like a limpet covered with superglue. She laughed and stroked my back.

"I saw you laughing with Whinnie at training today. It's nice to see you're making friends."

I just kept hugging her.

"I knew you'd love Whinnie, she's so unique, isn't she?

And I thought it would be interesting for you to get to know Russ, he lives on a pueblo, did you know? Who else is in your group tonight?"

"Kyle."

Mum heard it in my voice, before I even knew there was anything there. She pulled away, gave me this hard look, and said, "Don't go falling in love with him now. I had enough of that last year." She wagged her finger.

"What? What are you talking about?" I protested. But I sort of knew what she meant…he was very good-looking… and genuinely, well, very nice too.

She studied my face quietly. "He worked here last summer, and I swear my job became less manager and more The-Kyle-Recovery-Centre. Every other minute some girl would come up to me, crying that he'd rebuffed them when they were so sure they shared a connection."

So sure they shared a connection…

I thought of Peter Alsop, Kyle walking me back in the dark, his Van Gogh book…

"Be careful," Mum warned, in an uncharacteristic bout of motherly advice. "Guys like him seem to make connections with lots of people, without even meaning to…"

I instantly felt so stupid.

I was in the middle of The Spirit Circle.

The vodka felt warm in my belly. My face felt warm in my head. My everything felt warm from the fire behind us.

… So I didn't mind so much that I had a tea towel on my head and was yelling, "We are the knights who say NIIIIII."

"NIII," Whinnie shrieked, also bedecked with a tea towel.

"NI."

"NI."

Kyle stared at me, a tinfoil crown we'd made atop his head. "You're the prom king, you play King Arthur," Russ had said. Kyle's lips trembled as he struggled not to laugh. The audience weren't struggling at all. I could hear their howls behind me.

"Bring me a SHRUBBERY," I demanded. "A nice one. Not too big." Just as the audience was on the cusp of hysteria, I threw in an extra "NI" for good measure. Whinnie joined in and everyone dissolved around us. Even Russ and Kyle were bent over now, their hands on their knees, shaking. Bumchin Kevin's donkey laugh hee-hawed louder than everyone else's.

I felt quite proud of myself.

Proud, and a little pissed.

Russ had passed around a hip flask before our performance to "give us comedic courage".

It had worked.

I was drunk. Again.

We stumbled our way to the end of the scene, stopping regularly to let the laughter calm down. Finally, we took our bows. The four of us stood in a line and dropped our heads. Everyone got to their feet and applauded hard. I looked up for Mum in the crowd. She was standing on top of a log, whistling using two fingers. I waved and she gave me such a watery look of pride that I had to bow again, using gravity to stop the tears rolling down my cheeks.

Kyle pulled me into a big hug.

"You were incredible, Miss England," he said.

I couldn't reply. His touch had done something to me. Mum's advice came back to me.

Lots of girls think they have a connection with Kyle.

I stiffened as my defence mechanisms kicked in.

"It was good, wasn't it?" My accent had never sounded so plummy and cold and unfriendly British.

Kyle stiffened too and released the hug. He coughed, looked down, and then pulled Whinnie in for one. "You did great, Pooh Bear," he told her. I instantly felt jealous that Whinnie was hugging him, and not me.

Russ high-fived us and we returned to our seating area. The Spirit Circle was in a large natural clearing, with space enough for a bonfire right in the centre. The Opening Ceremony night wasn't going as bad as I'd thought. Kevin had started things off by dragging out his acoustic guitar and making us sing campfire songs I didn't know about cowboys. Then we'd played some team building games before The Show, seeing who could build the highest human pyramid. Everyone was drinking and Mum and Bumface were either pretending not to realize, or really just didn't realize. Now we were sitting around the crackling flames, watching each group perform their skit. There'd been a makeshift Shakespeare, some ill-advised raps – our Monty

Python was definitely winning so far. I settled back onto my log and tried not to sense Kyle sitting next to me.

Kevin made his way to the front, still applauding.

"That was great, guys, just great." He gave me a thumbs up in front of everyone and I ducked behind my hair. He was so cringe, overcompensating for losing it over dinner. "Now, we've only got one group left to perform. Melody? You said you needed these?" He pulled out an old iPod and some big portable speakers.

Melody leaped up in her bare feet. "Thanks," she said, and called to the rest of her group. "Come on, girls."

They got up less gracefully behind her. Her group was all female, and none of them were wearing many clothes. A pocket of dread blodged into my belly about what might happen next. Melody wore just a bikini top with a tiny pair of denim hot pants. I stared enviously at her body as the girls got into a dance formation. Her tummy was so flat, a Malteser would stay perfectly still on it and not roll off if she lay on her back. Her bum cheeks didn't merge into her thighs like mine did. Even her feet looked thinner than mine. We waited for the music to start and I turned my face away, accidentally catching Kyle's eye. He gave me this weird smile.

The beat started. I recognized it instantly and held back a groan.

The Pussycat Dolls. "Don't Cha Wish Your Girlfriend Was Hot Like Me?"

Melody and her mates clumped together, touching each other's limbs provocatively then grinding down to the floor.

All the guys started cheering, and Melody did this self-satisfied smile that made me hate her. The clump broke apart at the chorus and they shimmied into a series of synchronized moves. The cheers got louder. Everyone started clapping in time to the music. I gave Whinnie a desperate look, wishing so much that Evie and Lottie were here to tell me everything I thought was right. But Whinnie obliged by sticking her tongue out and pointing to the back of her throat.

I reluctantly clapped along. I didn't dare look at Kyle and Russ – not wanting to tarnish our fledgling friendship by seeing them drooling.

The chorus hit and Melody and the others strutted forward. Melody made a beeline right for us.

Not us, Kyle.

I saw his face as he twigged what was going on. He gave me the tiniest look, or maybe I imagined it, then broke into a grin. Melody pointed at him and he gestured down at his torso all overdramatically, like, *Who me?* She flicked her hair, nodded and plucked him from beside me, dragging him into the middle. Well, "dragging" implies a lack of willingness. Kyle didn't look like he lacked anything right then. The rest of the dance posse pulled in three other guys, including Watersports.

It's weird when emotions take over, with no rhyme or reason at all. But that's what happened as I watched Melody twirl Kyle under her arm before nestling into him. Everything slowed, like the world really wanted to rub this in my face as much as possible. I blinked a lot… They just looked so…good together, as they danced. He was grinning, all not-taking-it-seriously, but when she smiled back at him a tiny something of intimacy crossed their faces. I watched his tanned arms stroke up her body, jokingly, but still with the confidence of a guy that had stroked girls before. She wiggled back, jokingly, but with the confidence of a girl who had wiggled against a guy's crotch before.

I'd never been to an American high school. But now I felt like all those kids in the movies – the ones who stand watching from the bleachers as Prom Kings and cheerleaders have the time of their lives.

I'd never even kissed anyone. Seventeen – and no one's lips had ever pressed against mine. I was five foot eleven, ginger, and every boy at school only seemed interested in midget, wannabe pole dancers. I kept hoping they'd grow out of it, or grow into me, or maybe it was just a British boys' thing… Yet the rules of life were exactly the same, no matter what side of the Atlantic Ocean you were on. All the good feeling from our Monty Python skit evaporated.

I couldn't look any more so I budged up closer to Whinnie on the log and whispered to her.

"I've thought of another thing that makes America worse at feminism than the UK." She looked up at me expectantly through her big bottle glasses. "… Cheerleaders."

Whinnie nodded. "Cheerleaders were the curse of my life for a long time." She pointed to her Winnie the Pooh T-shirt, her glasses, her ponytail. "You think someone like me had an okay time at high school?"

I pointed to my freckles, my ginger hair, and stretched out my long legs in front of me.

"You think I did?"

We both giggled and Russ shushed us, before craning forward again.

It was the final chorus and Melody now stood bent over against Kyle, pushing her bottom into him.

I turned away once more.

"What is it with you and Winnie the Pooh then?" I asked, looking closer at her red Disney T-shirt. "Is it just your name?"

Whinnie's face looked so lovely lit from the campfire, all warm and open. "Winnie the Pooh is the answer to happiness," she answered simply.

"And, can I say, 'huh'?"

"He is the living embodiment of Taoism."

"Whatism?" I asked.

"Taoism. It's this philosophy thing," Whinnie said, stroking the Pooh on her jumper. "Taoists believe human beings overcomplicate life by over-thinking everything all the time, and this makes us unhappy. If you read the Winnie the Pooh books, you'll see that Pooh is always happy, because he sees things in a simple way. He's actually on a higher philosophical plane than most of us."

"So this is far more interesting than Melody proving to an entire campfire of people that she's sexually attractive," I whispered. "Tell me more."

Whinnie's lips twitched with laughter. "Well, look at the

other characters in Winnie the Pooh. They all actually demonstrate that Pooh is the most mentally balanced. There's Tigger, I mean, that tiger just can't stay in the moment and enjoy it. He's too much of a hedonist; he always wants the next adventure. That's not healthy, he'll burn out."

I started properly laughing. "And what about Eeyore?"

"Well he's a depressive, isn't he? If Eeyore walked into my doctor's office he'd be prescribed with a lifetime supply of antidepressants. And not just because US doctors dole them out like candy canes at Christmas."

The music stopped and I found myself clapping without even looking.

"But Pooh?"

"Pooh lives in the moment. He doesn't fret about the past, or freak about the future. He's an expert at mindfulness."

Kyle walked back to us, smiling, all breathless.

Russ high-fived him. "You lucky bastard." Kyle sat next to me on the log. I could feel the heat from his body, but it didn't bother me any more. I was thinking how much Lottie and Evie would love Whinnie.

"Mindfulness is supposed to be the secret to happiness, isn't it?" I asked her. "One of my friends back home, she has, like, umm, OCD stuff, and they're sending her away on a mindfulness weekend to help her with her anxiety."

Whinnie looked triumphant. "You see! And think how long Pooh has been around. He knew the secret to happiness before we did."

"What you guys talking about?" Kyle asked.

Russ replied. "Don't ask, man, don't ask. They were laughing about freakin' Eeyore all the way through the best part of the night."

I spun round to face them, my hair flicking into my face. "If you call 'that'" – I gave Kyle a dirty look – "the best part of the night, then I feel very sorry for you."

Russ threw up his arms. "What can I say? I'm an obvious guy."

Whinnie whispered in my ear. "And Melody was making it abundantly clear she was obviously a girl."

I giggled. "I almost forgot she had boobs, I'm so glad she stroked them to remind me."

Whinnie wiggled her eyebrows madly. "And I almost forgot she had such a tight ass. It really was very kind of her to rub it up against men so it didn't fade into obscurity."

"That would've been such a shame." I nodded. "Nobody with an arse like that wants to have only a cult following. Arses like Melody's deserve to be mainstream..." I trailed off and pretended to look into the distance. "If only Melody knew that."

We both dissolved into snorts of bitchy laughter. I knew it probably wasn't strictly feminist, to bond with one girl by bitching about another... I'm sure Lottie would have some kind of academic term for it. But seeing Melody dance with Kyle had made me feel oddly weak.

Pathetic? Of course. But feelings always are.

The applause died down and Bumface Kevin picked his way to the front. He cleared his throat loudly and we all fell quiet. Kyle, who'd heard our whole bitchy interchange, gave me a quick look. There was no smile in his eyes. I couldn't tell if he was angry at me, or embarrassed at himself.

"Guys, that was incredible," Kevin said. "You are ALL INCREDIBLE. We are going to have such an awesome time together. I can't wait for the kids to arrive tomorrow so we can get this summer started." Everyone cheered and whooped. Whinnie and I rolled our eyes at each other.

"And now..." Kevin picked up a small wooden drum by his feet. "As is camp tradition, we will welcome in the summer with a drum circle."

I turned to Kyle. "What the heck is a drum circle?"

He gave a small smile back. "It's the best bit, come on."

Kevin started hitting the drum and Kyle pulled me back into the middle of the circle, next to the fire. Drums appeared everywhere and people started bashing them, forming an infectious beat. I crossed my arms, feeling exposed.

"What do we do?" I asked, though my feet were already step-tapping to the beat.

"We dance," he said simply. He gently took my hand.

The people who weren't hitting the drums poured into the circle, joining us, their feet also instantly sacrificing themselves to the rhythm. Whinnie and Russ grabbed some maracas and wiggled their way into the circle, shaking in time with the others.

I tensed up. "I umm... Girls as tall as me...we don't tend to dance. It looks like I'm the maypole on May Day."

Kyle was already waving my hands over my head.

"Don't be stupid. And what's a maypole?"

The combination of his touch, the thud of the drums, and the flicker of the fire, just kind of filled me up. I grabbed his hands tighter and spun with him, my body surrendering to the music.

Everything sort of faded away as Kyle and I moved. He never let go of my fingers, and whenever I looked at him he looked straight back, the corners of his eyes crinkling. It wasn't dancing like the way he danced with Melody – and I'm sure that's because just one of my butt cheeks is the size of both of hers. But we were still proper dancing, our bodies in tune, all this heat building in me, rising from my chest. I looked over at Mum and she was staring right at me, hitting a drum. She nodded her head towards Kyle and raised one eyebrow…

… Reminding me…

"Every girl thinks they have some kind of connection with Kyle." I.e. don't be a statistic, Amber. A Kyle-support-group statistic.

I froze up.

"Umm," I stumbled, not sure what on earth I was feeling. "Umm…" Our dancing ground to a halt.

"You okay?" he asked, his face sweaty.

"Umm," I mumbled again.

And I was saved by Whinnie. She jumped between us and grabbed me aggressively before bending over and wiggling her giant jiggly bottom against my crotch in a perfect imitation of Melody. Russ bounced up too, doing this weird sort of shimmy, and I laughed and joined in. Kyle stood out for a second, his tanned arms crossed under his sleeveless T-shirt, then he jumped in and we all danced together like maniacs.

I was giddy with laughter. We formed a circle and took it in turns to dance around each other. Bodies swayed and moved around me. The beat always evolving. The firelight never waning. Mum tapped me on the shoulder, taking me by surprise, and gestured to join in. I nodded, and pulled her into our circle. She took both my hands and spun us as everyone else spun around outside of us – like we were the nucleus of a cell, if nucleus is the right word; I don't know, I can't remember GCSE science. We spun so fast that everything else became a blur, apart from her face. Her face that looked so much like my face, especially now her skin wasn't sallow and yellowish any more, and her eyes weren't red and watery like they used to be. Her sparkly eyes and her wild toothy grin were all I could see as we spun and spun and spun...and just a sliver of sadness found me, as I wished we were spinning back in time, back to before that day when she found Kevin and left me.

Situations that are destined to fail:

Me

+

American children

+

Discipline

Ten

It was arrival day.

The kids ran towards us like greased pigs shooting out the barrel of a cannon.

"I'm scared," I whispered to Russ. "Why are they screaming?"

"Brace yourself for impact," he replied as the wall of children got closer. I stood in my branded camp T-shirt and denim shorts, my hair bundled back into an already-frizzy ponytail. The instructions were simple enough. Get their names, check them off on the register, and then stand them in the appropriate zone until they'd all arrived.

So why did I feel like I was going into war?

The kids got closer. They ran with such energy, such a fighting look on their face, that it looked like one of those epic battle scenes in films – the slow motion ones where they all put their swords forward to charge, and the music gets all classical and they nobly run to their deaths. Except in those films, the soldiers aren't followed by enthusiastic parents cradling video cameras, yelling, "Gideon, Mommy's gonna miss you sooooooooooo much."

I turned to Kyle.

"Why do I feel we're about to fight to the death?" I asked. "That this is our precious home, and we have to protect it from the invasion?"

The corners of his wide mouth twitched up but he stared straight ahead.

"Just be careful of your genital area," he replied. "They tend to run straight into it."

Just as he finished his sentence, the first kid ran bang into Kyle's crotch. He bent over almost in two.

"KKKYYYYYYLLLLLLLLLLLLLLLLEEEEEEEEEEE," the kid screamed, unaware of the agony he'd caused. "D'ya remember me? D'ya? D'ya?"

Kyle straightened himself up but still clutched his groin.

"Hey, Elias," he said, in the most Disney voice I'd ever heard. "How could I forget you?"

More kids piled into him, like he was an electromagnet. Russ, on my other side, also had about eight children growing off him like benign tumours.

That's good, I thought. They were here last year, that's why they're being hugged. Nobody will hug me thankfully…

… Then I looked up and I saw hordes more children come through the forest from the car park – straight for me. I pushed aside panic, took one deep breath and bent my knees, ready to take the impact.

BAM BAM BAM BAM BAM BAM BAM

I had a million kids hanging off me.

"Who are you?" they demanded. "Why are you so tall?" "Why is your hair red?" "Where's my mom?" "Can I go on a jet ski? Can I? Can I?"

Why do American children sound infinitely more American than any other type of American thing?

"Wooooooah, everyone," I said, in the most fake cheery voice I could muster. "I'm Amber. And we have to get you all registered first."

Kyle already had a kid over his shoulder.

"Amber's come all the way from England to look after you this summer," he said.

"Wow, England?"

And eight million kids detached themselves from Russ and Kyle and electromagnetized themselves to me instead.

"OUCH," I yelled. A tiny child had run right into my vagina, their skull knocking into bits of it that should never be knocked into.

"I told you," I heard Kyle say. I looked up, trying to hold my injured bits without looking like a sex-offender, which is hard when your injured bit is your genital section and you have eight million children hanging off you. "Protect the nether-regions."

He smiled in a way that almost hurt my heart as much as my bruised vag.

* * *

"Okay, put down the scissors. No, I said 'put them down', not wave them near the eyeballs of your new friends."

Charlie Brown was already my new nemesis. He'd been at camp for a total of three hours and I wanted to throttle him.

He chucked the scissors onto the floor. "When can we go to the lake? When? When? Can I go on the jet ski? Can I? Can I?"

Considering I'd already answered his questions three times, I tried ignoring him. I bent down to the dusty floor of the rec hall and picked up his abandoned scissors.

They were making their name necklaces. As the Art Person, I'd been given the responsibility for getting them made. It was hard though. Energy vibrated off them. It hadn't helped that the first activity of the day had been giving them a tour of camp, i.e. showing them all the exciting things they weren't allowed to do yet.

I handed the scissors to a little girl called Rayanne, who still couldn't believe I was from England.

"Here, Rayanne," I said, copying Kyle's best Disney voice. "You still need to cut yours out."

She took the scissors in exchange for a bombardment of questions. "Where is England? Do you live in a castle? Do you eat little sandwiches? Mom says you all eat tiny sandwiches. Do you have a crown? Charlie Brown says you have a crown. Can I wear it?"

Deep breaths, deep breaths, deep breaths.

"Are we all almost done, guys?" I shouted. None of them listened. They were either preoccupied with their colouring, or laughing at Charlie Brown who was running up and down the hall with his T-shirt over his head.

Kyle came bursting through the doors, armed with two giant coolers.

"Hey, guys," he said, rescuing me. "Who wants juice?" he called.

"JUUUUUUUUUUUUUIIIIIICCCCCCCCCCEEEEEE." And they all abandoned their projects and ran at him to collect their pouches of orange squash. I noticed Kyle carefully cover his crotch and smile. He looked over, saw where my eyes were, smiled, and then went red.

"Gotta protect the boys," he said, sheepishly.

The boys? Did he mean his bollocks? Oh God, he did. I went deep red. Now I couldn't stop thinking about his bollocks. Which put me off him a bit. I mean, I'd never seen any, but from what Lottie had told me, I'd not missed much. "You know when obese people lose lots of weight and they have all that excess skin?" she'd told us. "Well imagine all that skin wrapped around two plums that smell slightly of cheese."

I turned my face so he wouldn't see my blushes and focused on tidying up the pencil pots.

"All right, guys," Kyle said in his Disney voice. "Take ten minutes, then we'll get your necklaces finished. But you're not to go outside yet, okay? We still haven't creamed you up."

The juice was glugged down in ten seconds, then the kids started running about like madmen. I took the brief respite to put my head on the table and close my eyes.

"Where's your mom?" Kyle sat on the tiny stool next to me. "Isn't she supposed to be helping you?"

I kept my eyes closed, wanting sleep, needing sleep. Yet it was only 3 p.m.

"She's having one of her lie-downs," I answered.

"Huh?"

I reluctantly sat back up again. "She gets these…umm… she needed to lie down, she said."

Kyle reached into his baggy pockets and pulled out two rescued juice pouches. He offered me one and I took it gratefully.

"I thought you weren't allowed to be left with the kids by yourself?"

I pierced my straw into the little hole and sucked so hard the juice was empty within three seconds.

"Man that is so good. And, no, I'm not. I'm only seventeen. She said it was only for an hour though…"

Kyle tried to keep his face neutral as he drained his drink. He eyed me curiously over the top of his straw.

"Well," he said, crumpling up the empty pouch with his hand. "For someone who's got no experience of working with kids, you're doing pretty well."

I looked round the carnage of the hall – the kids running around madly, bouncing and colliding like fireworks. "Are you kidding? They're behaving like savages."

He laughed and touched me briefly on the shoulder, making me sit up really straight.

"Not one of them is crying and you're not in the first-aid tent. That is incredible, believe me. It's first day of camp! They're too excited, all you can do is try and keep them alive. Russ is already freaking because one of his almost drowned."

"What?"

"The kid's okay. Russ lined them all up on the jetty to teach them The Rules of the Water and this one just got so excited he jumped right in. Even though he couldn't swim."

"Jesus. Is he okay? Russ, I mean?"

"Yeah. Sort of. He's just flipping out that the kid will tell his mom. He doesn't want to get sued."

I wrinkled my nose. "Why would Russ get sued?"

And Kyle touched my shoulder again, making each freckle there burst into flames.

"Oh, you innocent British person. I wish I had your naivety."

I smiled slightly. "Where's Whinnie?"

"Calming Russ down."

"Well now I feel like I've got off the hook," I said, gesturing towards all the intact children exploding about the hall.

Kyle furrowed his brow. "Your mom still shouldn't have left you."

"Mum shouldn't have done a lot of things…"

It came out without thinking – my voice was tight and bitter and choked. How the hell was I going to keep them all entertained until she'd decided she was rested enough? Maybe I could sing them Queen songs? That was British?

Kyle pulled his tiny stool in closer, making a screeching sound as it grazed the floor.

"Well, this was my last juice stop. You want me to stay and help out?"

Relief pooled in my stomach. "You sure? You don't need to be anywhere?"

"I think I need to be here," he said, just as two children collided head first and started crying.

Half an hour later and they were all wearing beautifully decorated necklaces, singing Freddie Mercury and dancing madly. Kyle and I were at the front of the hall, conducting them ferociously with our arms. Kyle'd made a quick dash to his cabin to pick up his old iPod and speakers.

"Who knew Queen was such a good pacifier for children?" Kyle said, watching them twirl.

I nodded with pride. "I have the younger stepbrother from Hell. I worked this out the hard way."

He pulled a face. "Ergh, is there any worse word in the world than 'step-something'?"

"I know." I nodded again, sadly this time. "It just means – the first attempt failed, doesn't it?"

Mum walked through the door, sunglasses on her face, and a pashmina draped over her shoulders. I leaned back off the wall and stood up straight. Kyle didn't.

She took in the music, and the dancing children, came over and rested a hand on my shoulder.

"Amber, what's going on here?"

I stood up straighter.

"Their name badges are all done. Kyle and I have just got them dancing to get rid of any excess energy."

She patted me. "You've done great, Amber. You know what my migraines are like when they hit. I really needed that lie-down."

I did know…

The headaches started soon after that day they got back from the hospital. I'd hear crashes in the kitchen at night, the shrill sound of glasses clattering.

Then Mum wouldn't get out of bed.

First Dad was okay with it.

"It's okay, Amber," he'd say. "Your mum is just grieving. Give her some time. We need to be patient."

"Grieving for what?"

Though I think I knew. They'd told me once I was going to be a big sister. They'd told me once I was going to get to choose its name.

But then they went to hospital and they never talked about it again.

"Just…just…we need to be patient."

A year later, when it was still happening, at least four days a week, he began to lose it.

He threw back the curtains and light burst into the

stinky room, bouncing off the mirrored cupboards. Mum – a cowering lump under the duvet – whimpered from beneath the blankets.

"No, Brian, please. I've got a migraine."

He ignored her, picking up her piles of discarded clothes and hanging them over his arms.

"You're taking Amber to school," he instructed, all businesslike. "I need to be in a meeting in half an hour. I told you I needed you to take her in today. Enough is enough, come on."

More whimpering.

"But, I'm ill. I've got one of my headaches."

He raised his voice, knowing it would hurt her head. "And we all know why!"

"It's a migraine. I'm too sick. I can't drive, YOU CAN'T MAKE ME!"

"Shh, Amber will hear you."

"I'm here." I'd been standing behind him the whole time – watching. Knowing my world was falling apart, but not sure why or how. He looked up, twitchy. I saw the pain seep through his face.

"Amber?"

I stepped out warily, and pushed my bush of hair down with my hand.

"Yes?"

"Your mum's having one of her migraines so she can't drive you to school. I can take you in, but that means you'll be early. Can you be ready in five minutes?"

The lump under the duvet was still. I looked down at my pyjamas. She'd once taken me to school in my pyjamas. They'd sent a letter home with me.

"I…I guess."

Another pain-ridden smile.

"That's my girl."

The lump said nothing…

"You feeling better now, right?" I asked her.

"Oh yeah. I just needed to lie down. I think the music may bring on a relapse though." She grinned. "You've done great," she repeated.

Kyle stepped forward with narrowed eyes.

"I thought Amber wasn't able to be left alone with the kids?"

I almost reached out my hand to stop him.

The only visible reaction she gave that she'd heard him was a small tight smile. I tried to give him warning looks with my eyebrows but Kyle ignored me, staring straight at Mum.

You don't question Mum. That's the rule. She's never wrong; it's never her fault.

"I mean, there's thirty of them. And Amber's only seventeen… It was lucky I turned up. And—"

She interrupted him.

"I thought you were on juice duty, Kyle?" Her voice was so cold, her smile still so tight.

I ached for him then – for that smile, for what it meant. The and-now-you've-asked-things-I-don't-want-to-answer-I'm-going-to-aggressively-deflect smile.

"I was." He struggled to hold eye-contact. I wanted to tell him it was okay. That she always turned on anyone who didn't support her...which is why I always swallowed my objections. "This was my last stop."

"I thought then you were supposed to go help Melody set up the campfire for tonight?"

"I was. But Amber needed my help here."

"So you ignored my orders?"

She was still smiling. Kyle wasn't. The easy effortlessness of his face was crumpled with expressions I knew so well – with disbelief, with that niggling feeling she shouldn't be able to get away with it...yet, she could, because it wasn't her fault.

It's never her fault.

You can't blame me, she'd said, when I'd cried. Because she was leaving. Because she was leaving broken bits of me, of us, of our family behind. It's not my fault. It's a disease. A horrible disease. I'm sick. Nobody can help getting sick. Anyway, you have a new family now...well your dad does...

"I didn't ignore them." Kyle's voice was losing its calm. "It was just obvious Amber needed a little help here."

I took a step forward, using his bravery to give me my own.

"He really did rescue me," I admitted.

Mum opened her mouth to say something but the music

stopped, the last *la la las* from Freddy Mercury echoing out. The children stopped running about and turned to us all at the same time, like in a zombie apocalypse.

Mum's tight smile melted into a genuine one.

"Aren't you all amazing?" She clapped her hands together. "Now, who wants to go see the lake?"

They jumped up and down on the dusty floor, and I remembered hearing once how if everyone in China jumped at the same time, it would cause an earthquake. "ME ME ME, I DO I DO I DO."

"Okay then, now buddy up. Don't forget your name tags."

In a buzz, the kids ran to collect their things. Kyle was clenching and unclenching his fists. I attempted to tidy up – not sure where to look. I scraped stray bits of dried PVA off the table and stacked the glue pots neatly. When I looked up, the children had formed an orderly crocodile.

Mum stood at the front, looking like someone who'd never had a headache before in their life.

And Kyle had gone.

Situations that are destined to fail:

Working a fifteen-hour day

+

Difficult conversations about your childhood

Eleven

For the second night in a row, I was in front of a campfire, watching Melody stroke her crotch.

"Don't cha," she hissed, jerking her butt back towards the flames. "Don't cha."

It turns out Bumface Kevin wasn't just a mother-stealing loser, he was a pervy loser. And therefore he'd asked Melody and her other Pussycat Dolls to re-perform last night's show "*so the kids can see it*". Because, you know, it's not summer camp without s'mores and mild stripping.

Whinnie leaned in and whispered: "She's rubbing her crotch so much, I'm scared she'll get a friction burn."

I was almost too exhausted to giggle. Almost...

I'd never worked so hard. We'd taken all one hundred kids to the lake, and then we'd had to get them all into their swimming costumes – which they seemed incapable of putting on themselves. Then, in the blazing sunshine, we'd had to see how well they could swim, grading them, putting them into relevant groups, marking who would be allowed to play each water sport safely. Then they'd all had to eat lunch. Spaghetti – great choice. I'd hardly had any time to eat as I dashed from smeared face to smeared face, frantically dabbing at them with a damp cloth, trying to make sure they didn't get sauce on their clothes. Then we'd taken ALL the children on a long walk around ALL the camp. Again. I'd trekked in the heat to the paintballing field, around every single cabin, to the sports section, down to the lake, and then up to the go-karting circuit, which was right near the road. All in all, we'd walked at least five miles.

But still the children weren't tired.

They'd demonstrated as much at dinner – burgers – squirting each other with ketchup, constantly changing their seats to make new friends. I'd dolloped baked beans into my mouth, almost too tired to chew. We still weren't done yet.

Now we were at the campfire. We'd painted their faces. We'd sung "You Can't Step In The Same River Twice" and "She'll Be Comin' Round The Mountain". And, once Melody had stopped rubbing herself, we would be sorted into our camp teams – splitting the kids and staff members into four groups.

If Mum put me in the same team as Melody…

The music stopped. Everyone clapped. Bumface Kevin the hardest. Mum put two fingers in her mouth and whistled. It annoyed me that I hadn't inherited her ability to do that. It annoyed me she was wolf-whistling Melody.

About eight hands pawed at my long legs.

"You ask her," a whisper said, loudly.

"No, you ask her."

I looked down at the children wedged beneath my feet, their faces decorated and all glowing and cute in the firelight.

"What is it?" I asked, half-clapping.

A girl with s'more chocolate all round her mouth, straightened up.

"If you're from England," she asked, "have you met the Queen?"

I closed my eyes for a little longer than I should. It was the eighth time I'd been asked that day.

"No." Their little faces dropped. "No, I haven't."

"I TOLD YOU," one of them yelled. "I told you she wasn't English."

I held my hands up. "Whoa, whoa, whoa. I am English," I explained. "Not everyone in England has met the Queen."

Their little heads looked up at me, their eyes all wide.

"What do you do, then?" Chocolate-smeared girl asked.

Whinnie nudged me to show she was trying not to laugh. Russ, on the other side of me, withheld a snigger.

"I don't know. The same as you guys, I guess. We live our lives."

"Is that ALL?" she demanded.

"Isn't that all any of us do?"

"Not me," she announced. "I'm going to Disneyland."

There isn't much you can say to that.

* * *

Kevin stepped into the circle, still applauding Melody and her mates – oh, and Kyle, who'd been asked to be a "backing dancer" again – as they climbed over the logs back to their places. Kyle shuffled in between Russ and me.

"Dude, I'm so jealous, I could kill you," Russ said. "Melody is fiiiiiine."

Kyle shifted uncomfortably and I stared ahead, pretending to listen to Kevin moan on about the ceremony of The Sorting. Kyle nudged the chocolate girl with his foot and she turned around. "Hey, Jenna, you like the dancing?" he asked.

She shrugged. "It was okay, I guess," she said. "You looked kind of creepy up there though."

Whinnie and I burst into hysterical giggles.

"Creepy? Right… That's, erm, not good."

Kevin clapped his hands, sensing he didn't have our undivided attention. "And without further ado," he said, "let's start The Sorting. Now, we don't like to group you by age at Mountain Hideaway Camp, as we feel you can learn so much from people both older and younger than you. So we'll be sorting you into teams based on the questionnaires we sent out." He beckoned to Mum. "Rosie, if you will?"

Mum walked out into the circle, carrying a big oversized hat.

"No way," I whispered. "That actually isn't a…"

"A sorting hat?" Russ answered, grinning at my reaction. "Oh, yeah, they use an actual sorting hat. I better not get put in Ravenclaw this year."

"What?" I felt my eyes bulge. "They even use the Harry Potter houses?"

Russ nodded. "Yeah, the kids love it."

I looked down at the children congregating on my feet. I could almost hear the vibrations of excitement chill through their bodies.

"As always," Kevin said, "we'll sort the staff first."

I instantly panicked and grabbed Whinnie and Kyle on either side of me. "They're sorting…us? Too? They're using the sorting hat on us now?!"

Kyle answered. "Yeah, we all get put into four groups. It makes the timetable easier to sort out."

"But – I never got a questionnaire! How do they know where to sort us? We're going to get sorted like, right NOW?"

Kyle gave me a weird look. "Yes…why are you freaking out?"

Two kids on my ankles looked up at me. I lowered my voice to a whisper.

"You don't understand. I…I…don't want to get sorted. I'm too scared. I've never even joined Pottermore for this very reason." Also, it wouldn't have felt right, being sorted on my own, without Mum doing it too…

Another weird look – this time from Kyle, and Whinnie *and* Russ.

"Why not?"

"Because." I threw my hands up, not knowing how it wasn't obvious to everyone else. "Because…what if I don't get into Gryffindor?"

They all cracked up.

"It's not funny. It's always been a genuine anxiety of mine."

Kevin pulled out a list and called a name loudly: "WAYNE?"

It was Watersports. He was called Wayne? He bashed knuckles with the guy next to him, pushed back his bleach-blond curtains and walked into the circle. The buzz from the kids thrummed harder, almost like they were generating their own electricity. Mum lifted up the battered hat and ceremoniously plopped it onto his head.

"Hufflepuff," she yelled. Just the word "Hufflepuff" sparked the children off. They clapped and cheered and generally freaked out from the thrill of it all. Wayne – obviously unbothered by the fact that he'd now never get to share a dorm with The Harry Potter – shuffled to where Mum pointed.

Kevin looked down at his list. "Russ?" he called.

"Ahh, man." Russ levered himself up off the log. He grinned down at the children under him. "I hope you get into my house y'all."

He stepped over them and approached the circle. I was worried for him. I was terrified for myself. Mum would put me into Gryffindor, surely? She'll remember…she must remember. One of my hands grabbed Whinnie, the other grabbed Kyle's T-shirt. He looked down at my hand but I didn't care. Russ looked pretty gorgeous in the dark, his black hair absorbing all the light from the fire. He waved at Mum before she dropped the hat onto him.

She was quiet for a moment, all dramatic.

"Dumbledore's Army!" she yelled.

Everyone cheered… Apart from me who yelled: "What the actual fuck?"

I covered my mouth the moment I said it, but there was a hiss of giggles below me and Kyle threw me a desperate look.

"She cussed! Amber cussed!"

"Ummmmmmmmmm," one said, their little American accent changing more octaves than Mariah Carey.

"I didn't cuss," I said, frantically wracking my brains for an excuse. "I said…umm…FECK, I said 'feck'. It's an English word. You don't have it here."

It seemed to work, they settled, and all started saying "feck".

Russ was siphoned off to another bit of the circle and another camp counsellor walked up to meet their fate.

"Gryffindor," Mum called. It got the biggest cheer. I wondered how many distraught kids would be crying tonight, gutted they didn't make it into Gryffindor. I would probably be one of them.

"What the hell is Dumbledore's Army?" I hissed at Kyle, as someone was announced Ravenclaw. "That's not a Harry Potter house."

"I know," he hissed back. "Your mum changed it after last year. She got rid of Slytherin and replaced it because none of the kids wanted to be in there."

At that moment, I hated her. Irrational? YES OF COURSE.

But, but...Harry Potter was our thing! Why wasn't she being true to the books? We'd loved them so dearly together. What was she playing at?

"What?" My outraged whisper wasn't very whispery. "What's wrong with Slytherin?"

"Umm... Well, nobody good belonged there, did they?"

"Are you stupid? Loads of good people were in Slytherin. Snape was in Slytherin, and he was a hero!"

How could Mum do this? She'd got me into the Harry Potter books in the first place. She'd tuck me up, smooth back my hair and tell me it was like Hermione's, and read a chapter aloud to me every night. We'd queued together at midnight when the last one came out. Yes, she'd been swaying and tripped over and dented my wizard hat, but she'd still done it. We were obsessed, the both of us. Christ, the very existence of the drunken house-elf Winky had explained more to me about what was going on at home than anything else. How could she change it?

And what the actual FECK was Dumbledore's Army for a replacement? It didn't even make sense.

Melody's name was called. She gently pushed off the grasping hands of children fawning on her after her performance, and stood in the middle of the circle without a hint of self-consciousness.

Mum lowered the hat onto Melody's head.

"Gryffindor," she shouted.

"Are you fecking kidding me?" I muttered. Well, I thought I muttered, but lots of people turned in my direction. Melody shrugged and smiled, as everyone but me cheered. My blood, which was already hot from a long day in the sun, bubbled over like when you boil pasta too hard in a pan. How could she? How could Mum put someone like Melody in Gryffindor? Melody didn't deserve to be in Gryffindor. She wasn't BRAVE – and no, wearing hotpants that hotpanty does not classify as "brave". She wouldn't have even *got into* Hogwarts. She would've been a Squib – a very pretty Squib or something.

I felt Kyle looking at me. "Are you okay?" he asked quietly.

"No I'm not okay. There are so many things about me that are not okay."

Just as he opened his mouth to say something back, my own name was called.

"Amber," Kevin yelled, before giving me a little smile and a "cooey" wave. I scowled back at him and dodged over the kids like it was a minefield.

No good could come of the next five minutes. Whatever happened, all of my childhood dreams would be ruined.

If I didn't get into Gryffindor, then, well, I would probably need to cry quietly somewhere without anyone seeing. If I *did* get in, then I'd be stuck working alongside Melody for the rest of the summer – listening to her drone on about how many people she'd slept with at college, which she'd already done, twice so far. Mum gave me a big beaming smile but I scowled again. I was aware of the whole circle watching, and felt my face glow red.

I hated people looking, they always looked.

The drab hat hovered over my head.

I closed my eyes, just like Harry Potter did, waiting…

"Dumbledore's Army," Mum yelled.

My eyes flicked open to everyone clapping politely. So many little branches inside of me died right there.

She hadn't put me in Gryffindor.

My *own mother* hadn't sorted me into Gryffindor.

This was even worse than removing Slytherin as a team.

The tightness caught in my throat and I blinked several times, fighting the tears that had been hiding so well in my soul, waiting for this summer with Mum to come out.

I couldn't even turn back to look at her cheering behind me. I was scared – if I did, I would turn her to stone.

Russ's loud whooping pulled me out of my sob-spiral.

"Woooooo, Amber! You're with me!" He held out his hand and dragged me over. His genuine excitement about spending the summer with me filled the hole a tiny bit. I launched myself at him, wrapping him into a fierce hug – not letting go until it was beyond appropriate.

"We're the dream team," he yelled into my ear, hugging me back. I'd never really hugged a boy before, and Russ was definitely a good place to start.

We broke apart.

"Dumbledore's Army, eh?" I said.

He raised an eyebrow. "I know, stupid, isn't it? What's wrong with Slytherin? Snape was the bravest one of all."

And, just for that, I hugged him again.

Another boy, a mate of Wayne's, had been sorted by the

time we broke apart. He strode into Ravenclaw, saying: "What the heck is a Ravenclaw?"

I saw Whinnie in the crowd – she waved, before pulling her lips down into a sad face. Getting it. Only my friend for three days and yet totally getting it. Kyle watched too and I waved, but he didn't wave back. He had that weird look on his face that I'd noticed before – all grim and determined. To be fair, I had spent most of the evening swearing under my breath next to him. Maybe my bad mood had jumped off me and onto him, like nits?

We watched as more of the team got sorted. They kept it quick, knowing the kids would be impatient for their turn. You could feel them thrumming with anticipation, quivering in their places on the forest floor, waiting for their turn in the spotlight.

Whinnie was up next. She struggled to get over the logs with her short legs. Though, just like Melody, she walked without self-consciousness.

"Dumbledore's Army!"

"Yes!!!! Go, Whinnie," we yelled, pulling her in for a hug. We jumped up and down, pulling in the two others who'd been allocated into our group. Some blond guy called Damien who wore an actual WWJD bracelet. And another girl, Bryony, who'd been in Melody's Pussycat Dolls dance. She was a brunette version of Melody – all legs and shiny hair. And I was about to judge her, when she said: "I'm so mad they got rid of Slytherin, I mean, Snape was, like, the best one," as she walked over, and I learned a lesson about not judging people until you've found out whether or not they've read Harry Potter.

Kyle was the second-last to be called and my breath caught in my throat. He threw us an anxious smile but glided down towards the fire. I got the sense that Kyle would get put into whatever group he wanted – that's just how his life worked. I wondered what group he wanted to be in.

I wanted him to be in our group. I guess I liked torturing myself like that.

Mum lowered the hat once more. "Dumbledore's Army," she called and Kyle breathed a real, genuine smile – one that crinkled up the corners of his wide brown eyes.

"Yayyyyyyyyyyyyyyyyyy," we called.

"Welcome to the winning team, brother." Russ high-fived Kyle as he scuttled over. He high-fived back and then grinned at Whinnie and me. "So here we are. The only not-real house at Hogwarts."

"When the kids get annoying, can we shove them into the Room of Requirement?" I joked, and they all laughed.

The excitement built as the children began their sorting. They practically hovered off the logs, waiting for their turn. At least two cried when they didn't get into Gryffindor.

"You should've seen it last year when we still had Slytherin," Russ told me. "Utter freakin' carnage."

"That is still no excuse for erasing it as a house."

"I know. Jeez, I know."

It was cute though, seeing the kids cheer when they got into our team. We started making an arch with our hands whenever someone got in, getting them to run under it as we chanted their name. We were already the "fun team", even when the others began copying. Kyle stood opposite me, so we had to hold hands each time we got a new arrival. It made my fingers tingle and my palms sweat. And sometimes we locked eyes when a kid ran beneath us and I didn't want to look away.

He started talking to me in snatches, whenever we leaned together to welcome in a new recruit.

"Your mom," he said. "She gave me a strike for helping you today."

I widened my eyes. At training we'd been told staff discipline operated on a three-strikes-and-you're-out policy, and they seemed pretty hard to get in the first place. "Seriously? But I, like, really needed you."

The chocolate girl – Jenna – ran under our arms, screaming with utter joy – her little legs almost going too fast for her body to catch up. We broke apart and jumped up and down, whooping like Indians (Russ said it was okay to use the word "Indians" when you were whooping like the ones in Peter Pan. He was our lecturer in Native American political correctness), getting the kids riled up. We waited for another recruit to be announced before we spoke again.

"Hank, Dumbledore's Army!"

A tall, scrawny boy with thick-rimmed glasses beamed at us and ran over. Kyle grabbed for my hand, quickly, so we could form the arch before Hank reached us. Once again, my entire body lit up like electricity.

"Is there...something wrong with her?" Kyle asked. I accidentally squeezed his hand to steady myself.

"Isn't there something wrong with everyone?"

"That's a philosophical answer to a pretty straightforward question."

"I've been hanging out with Whinnie all day. She is teaching me the philosophy of Pooh."

"Ahh."

Hank ran under us and Kyle let go of my hands, just as quickly as he'd taken them. Whinnie had started a new celebration, where we put each new recruit into our circle and galloped around them – the circle getting bigger and bigger as we acquired more campers. So I danced around Hank, my bare feet smushing into the cool dusty earth of the forest floor.

There were two more Hufflepuffs, then another Gryffindor. Then, "Dumbledore's Army!"

Kyle's hands found my hands. Kyle's eyes found my eyes.

"Do you not want to talk about it?" he asked.

"I'll never want to talk about it."

A child ran under our arms.

"You know, sometimes it helps, talking about it?"

"Don't get all American on me."

"I *am* American."

We dropped hands once more, my body entirely unhappy about this.

"Yes, well, rein it in, Prom King. British people have been successfully repressing our emotions since before your country was even a thing."

We were split up by children galloping around us.

The group of unsorted was dwindling. There were only about ten children left. I calculated that meant a maximum of ten times I would get to hold Kyle's hands again. Half of me wanted them all to get sorted into Dumbledore's Army so I could touch him. Because something weird inside of me really wanted to touch him. But the other half didn't.

I don't like questions about my mum. Mainly because I don't know any of the answers to all of the "whys?" no matter how I've tried to figure her out.

The other groups had copied our whooping and circle dancing.

"Everyone is copying us," I huffed at Whinnie, who was struggling from the physical exertion. Her face was wet, her glasses a little misted from the sweat behind them.

"Because we're the most fun."

Two children were left, looking sad and embarrassed and left-out. One was so clinically obese he could be in a documentary.

"Calvin?"

The boy wobbled up to Mum, pulling his stretched T-shirt down over his vast expanse of stomach.

"I hope he doesn't get into our group," Hank whispered loudly. All the kids laughed.

"Shh." Kyle's voice was so sharp I almost didn't recognize it. "If you talk like that again, I'll get you transferred straight out of Dumbledore's Army."

Our group did a sharp intake of breath, and Hank's face dropped in horror. Kyle glared at him, and then glared at the rest of us.

Calvin was oblivious to the whispers, or maybe he'd just learned to block them out. Suddenly I really wanted him to get into our group. So I could look after him, make his summer the best it could be. I'd been that kid – the one everyone looked at and whispered about. But I'd learned to deal with it, so I could teach him.

Mum hung the hat over his head.

Please please please please please.

"Dumbledore's Army."

And I found myself jumping and screaming, "Go, Calvin!"

I was so excited I grabbed Kyle's hands first to make the arch. He gave me a look involving a lot of his eyebrow.

"We got Calvin," I said, breathless with excitement.

"Yes," he replied slowly. "We did."

Russ and Whinnie drummed up cheers as he lurched towards our arch, beaming at our reaction. I bet nobody had ever cheered for Calvin his entire life. I cheered louder.

"You have a lot of emotions," Kyle said to me underneath the arch. "They change all the time, I can see it. But you like pretending they're not there."

"Whaaat?" I stuttered. "You've only known me three days!" The force of what he'd said had a two-second delay as I computed. Calvin was almost at our arch, his slow run not much more than a walk.

"What's going on with your mom? Why is she living in America and not in Britain with you?"

"I thought I asked you to rein it in, Mr Therapy? I don't want to talk about it."

Calvin ran under us and I cheered the hardest I had all evening, before dropping Kyle's hands. "I don't get why you want to talk about it."

Kyle gave a half-shrug. "Because you seem sad, I guess."

Did I seem sad? How? I'd been laughing and cheering and dancing and doing all the things I never usually do.

Was I sad?

I was knackered – the most tired I'd ever been. But it was summer, and I was in a forest with new friends, and the sun was hotter than anything in the UK...and Mum was here. Finally we were together again.

... And, yes, I was sad. I was so sad that I barely had room left in my lungs to let oxygen in.

Mum wasn't the fantasy version I'd been so excited to see on the plane over. She wasn't letting me in, she wasn't giving me answers. She wasn't even the good bits of Mum I distantly remembered from before the day she came back from the hospital crying and clutching her stomach. This woman was still the shitty replacement that woke up the morning after that day. The one who ran away from what happened, and shut you out if you tried to talk about it, and made Dad…go to Penny, and then left me with them once Kevin and his supersonic bumchin rescued her from herself… abandoning me.

I stopped dancing and wilted, staggering to the edge of our circle. Everyone was oblivious, and continued celebrating without me.

Everyone but Kyle. He gently put his arm around me and steered me away a little.

"I'm sorry," he said. "Now you look REALLY sad."

"I'm fine." But my voice choked.

"I shouldn't have pushed you. I guess I just got really angry on your behalf today, in the art room. It didn't help I got a strike."

"She's…she's…complicated."

"I can see that."

"I…I…" I looked up at him, into his eyes that I'd never seen until the other day, but that already felt familiar. *Every girl feels a connection with Kyle*… "I'm exhausted," I admitted.

I was. I really was.

Kyle broke into a grin. "First day with the kids is a killer. And yet, here I am, pressing you about your private life. Just what you need when you're exhausted."

I gave him a small smile. "In England we call it knackered."

"Knackered?"

"Yeah, for exhausted. We say knackered."

"I like that."

I really was tired, now I'd let myself think it. Kyle steadied me on my feet. I tried to find the strength to stay upright, but leaned back into him. He was so tall, he made me feel almost dainty.

"Yeah, me too. It's one of my favourites."

Over his shoulder, I caught Mum's eye. She was staring right at us – her face unreadable, but noticing. Definitely noticing.

My knackeredness evaporated. I felt myself bristle under Kyle's arms.

"Whoa, Amber. What is it?"

She hadn't put me in Gryffindor. My own mother… She'd put Melody in Gryffindor. And she'd given Kyle a strike when he was only helping me because she had left me.

She had left me again.

Because that's what she does.

But it's never her fault.

Only everyone else's but hers.

The anger slammed through my bloodstream, reaching peaks and crescendos.

"When is it bedtime?" I asked.

I so needed it to be bedtime.

So I could yell at her.

So I could tell her what I thought.

About her.

About that dipshit photo of me not in the main room.

He lowered his face so our eyes were level, which is not something short boys were ever able to do – not that they'd ever wanted to.

"After this. It will take an age to get them to sleep though. You're helping Whinnie, right? First night. Homesickness, the excitement of it all. I'll be on midnight feast watch all night."

I smiled weakly as a passing, whooping child nudged into me mid-gallop. Kyle and I were the only two not moving, not celebrating. "Why oh why did I come here again?"

He searched my eyes again. "That's what I've been trying to ask you all evening."

Bumface Kevin yanked out his megaphone and announced it was "OFFICIALLY THE START OF CAMP". The excitement levels broke and everyone ran towards the fire, merging with each other again, and showing off about who got put in Gryffindor. I jogged feebly behind them – so tired, so angry.

"You okay?" Whinnie was right next to me. There was so much sweat on her fringe that it was plastered to her forehead.

"Just tired."

"Jeez, I know. And we still have to get them to bed. You're helping in my cabin, right?"

I nodded.

I reached the fire and saw Calvin flagging, his face even sweatier than Whinnie's.

"How are you? Calvin, is it?" I asked him.

He smiled and used his pudgy hand to wipe away the sweat.

"Man, am I BEAT," he said, all American. I decided then that I loved him.

"Bedtime soon. But we have one last dance."

He stuffed his hands deep into his shorts pockets. "No one will dance with me," he mumbled towards the ground.

I was angry already – this didn't help. Why were kids so cruel? Everyone always moaned on about "the innocence of children", whereas, from what I remembered on the playground, children were mostly dickheads to each other. If you were fat, if you were tall, if you had red hair, if you had a weird mum who always dragged you in late, smelling a bit…well, there was no "innocence" in what I had shouted at me.

"That's because I asked everyone if I could have the first dance with you." I took Calvin's hand and twirled him around the campfire, glaring at anyone staring at us. He lost his self-consciousness pretty quickly and soon he was spinning me round uncontrollably, giggling…

"Oww…Calvin…I'll be sick."

He laughed harder and we spun and spun and spun.

The campfire blurred past me, snatches of people whizzing by as I got dizzier and dizzier.

The fire…Whinnie galloping in a circle with some of Dumbledore's Army…the darkness of the edge of the forest… the fire…Mum staring at me again, this time smiling…the forest…the fire…Melody approaching Kyle and starting her usual gyrating-dance against him…the forest…the fire… Kyle smiling…

"Whoa, I think it's time to stop." I let go of Calvin's hands. My feet turned under me, my knees buckled.

"Thank you for the dance," I said. "It was very…umm… spinny."

Then Bumface Kevin blew hard on his whistle, signalling bedtime.

Situations that are destined to fail:

Childhood memories

+

A mother who can't remember them

Twelve

As predicted, it took for ever to get Whinnie's cabin to go to sleep.

"But I miss my mommy," one whined, sitting up for the eighth time in ten minutes.

I took a deep breath. My temper was fraying, all my energy reserves had gone.

"It's good to get used to missing your mommy," I said. "When you're older, you'll have to spend lots of time away from your mother."

Especially if she emigrates, and doesn't take you with her.

"But I don't WANT to do that," the kid protested, sitting up further.

I firmly pushed her back into her pillow. "Yes, well, life is all about doing things you don't want to do."

I saw the moment on her face when she decided to cry, but Whinnie came barrelling over, just in time.

"Hey, do you want the special camp teddy tonight?" she

whispered, so as not to wake the children who had managed to get to sleep. Whinnie was already in her baggy Winnie the Pooh pyjamas, whereas I was still in camp uniform.

I stank of bonfire. Ever since I'd gotten to this camp, I'd stank of bonfire.

The girl nodded and Whinnie pulled out a moth-eaten Winnie the Pooh bear. She handed it to the girl carefully.

"This is our very special cabin Pooh Bear. Now, he's a bit homesick too, so will you look after him tonight and let him know everything is okay?"

"Yes."

"Brilliant. Now, try and get some sleep."

Whinnie and I tiptoed away and we heard the girl muttering to the teddy bear. "Now, Pooh Bear, there's no need to be scared. I miss home too. But we're at camp. And Whinnie is so nice, isn't she? She'll take care of us." Her voice got sleepier until it faded to nothing. All I could hear were the snorts and snuffles of sleeping children.

Whinnie beckoned to me to leave the cabin, and I crept out after her. The air had cooled – it goosebumped my arms. It felt nice. Whinnie was already perched on the steps. I closed the door as slowly as I could so it didn't squeak.

"Thanks for that," I said. My voice seemed loud in the quiet of the forest. I joined her on the step.

"It's okay."

We both fell quiet and listened to the sounds of the forest – the buzzing of the insects I still didn't know the name of, the giggles of a cabin next door that hadn't succeeded in getting its inhabitants to bed. My eyes closed, my head hung.

"You okay, Amber?"

I jerked up. "Yep. Why? Why is everyone asking me that today?"

"Whoa, calm down. It's just, it's your first day of camp. It's madness. Last year, I fell asleep on the first night before the children. They trashed the place while I slept, decorating it with toothpaste."

I looked back at her. "Sorry. Just Kyle was on my case earlier."

"You mean when you guys were talking at the campfire?"

I nodded. "It's like he's trying to win some award for the world's nicest guy or something..."

Whinnie rolled her eyes. "I know, right? What a jerk."

I laughed.

"He is just that bit too perfect, isn't he?" Whinnie continued. "I wonder why he tries so hard..."

Most of the cabins around us were dark now. Melody's was only next door. Hers had been dark for ages.

"I don't like people asking me about my personal life," I admitted.

"I've noticed. You do know it's in our culture though, to ask such things."

I smiled into the blackness. "I'm beginning to figure that out."

More comfortable silence. Whinnie just had a calming way about her. I barely knew her, and yet I felt just...okay sitting with her next to me, kind of like how it felt with the girls back home.

"When you were dancing with Calvin," Whinnie said, "I overheard Melody asking Kyle to sneak out and meet her tonight. She said they should 'mark the official start of camp together'."

I turned to look at her. "Seriously?"

Whinnie nodded.

"What did he say?"

"He said he didn't think his children would sleep tonight."

"What does that mean?"

"I dunno."

I thought of Kyle's arms guiding me through the dark as he steered me home my first night. I thought of his arms around Melody as they danced together.

Friendship. Sex.

One for me. One for Melody.

I let it sink in – feeling angry at how much I cared. Confused by it. It's not like I knew either of them, not really.

"You should go to bed," Whinnie said. "We have canoeing tomorrow."

I groaned. "Don't remind me. There's no way my legs will fit into a bloody canoe."

"And there's no way my butt will fit into a canoe. It's going to be like that Winnie the Pooh story where he eats too much honey and gets stuck in that hole."

"Shall we go in the same one and just drown ourselves?" I asked.

"Sounds like a plan."

I got up, brushing the dust off my bum. "I'll let you get some sleep."

"Cool. See you tomorrow...and Amber?"

I turned round on my heels in the dust. "Yep?"

"I'm glad we've been put in the same group."

Her words broke my anger a bit. I smiled.

"Me too."

The lights in Kevin's cabin were still on and I made my way towards them reluctantly, wishing they were both asleep.

I peered through the window before I opened the door. They weren't both asleep.

They looked like love personified, cuddled up on the dingy sofa – Mum's feet in his hands as he massaged them.

I stepped in and slammed the door – they both jumped and Mum's feet pulled away from Kevin. He stood up, all grinny grinnington, which made his bumchin stretch out wider.

"Hey, Amber. Did the kids go to bed okay?" he asked.

I shrugged, ignoring him, glaring at Mum.

"You didn't put me in Gryffindor."

Mum did her confused-victim face and stood up.

"What?"

I grabbed a glass from the countertop, filled it at the sink, drained it, and then slammed it down without washing it.

"Your own daughter. You didn't put your own daughter in Gryffindor?"

It sounded SO pathetic, but...but...

Kevin and Mum looked at each other conspiratorially, all *aren't-teens crazy?*

"I put you with your friends. I thought you'd be happy."

"Plus," Kevin butted in. "Your mum didn't choose it. The sorting hat did."

I gave him my very best *you're-an-idiot* face.

"Happy? You didn't even sort me into a real house! What the fucking fuck is Dumbledore's Army anyway?"

"Language," Kevin warned but I ignored him. Again.

Mum looked confused, then sad, then cross, then confused again.

"I thought you'd like Dumbledore's Army? That's the best one! Harry and his friends made that group themselves; it's even more special than an actual Hogwarts House."

If I'd been less angry and less tired, I could maybe have taken myself out of the situation and heard how crazy it sounded. And maybe, yes maybe, she really did think Dumbledore's Army was better... But I *was* angry, and I *was* tired, and my OWN MOTHER hadn't sorted me into the same house as Harry Potter.

I started towards my room but remembered something and stopped.

"PLUS," I said, my voice even louder. "You got RID of Slytherin?! I mean, what kind of person are you?!"

Mum cowered. Kevin answered. His face was red, his smile totally gone.

"We had to get rid of Slytherin," he told me. "There were so many complaints last year when kids got sorted into there. And, Amber, you are NOT to talk to us like that. Do you hear me?" I was breaking him down again… I felt triumphant and disgusted.

I gave him my death-glare then. "A," I said, "I wasn't talking to you. And, B, why didn't you tell those stupid fucking Americans to read the damn books and realize what idiots their kids are?"

"AMBER!" he yelled. "Don't make me call your father. If you don't respect us and the camp rules, we'll have to discuss sending you home."

Dad. He'd emailed to check I'd arrived okay, but I was deliberately not answering. I was still angry about the scene at the airport, about him not sticking up for me. And I was angry at Kevin, and Mum, and myself for being so stupid for thinking my trip could've turned out any better than this.

I turned once more, looking at Mum, pleading with her to realize why I was so upset (knowing Kevin would never dare call Dad anyway). My voice caught. "You knew," I whispered. "You knew how much it meant to me…"

Her eyes darted to and fro.

"Knew how much *what* meant to you?"

I couldn't bring myself to say the word "Gryffindor" again; it would sound so stupid. But she should've known.

We read them every night. We queued with our cloaks on at midnight. And I'd asked her, night after night, "*Mummy, what house would I be sorted into?*" And she'd tickled me and said, "*Amber, I've already said! Of course you'd be in the same house as Hermione.*" Then she'd pull one of my frizzy curls, unwinding it, then letting it go so it sprang back up. "*With hair like this.*" And I'd laughed, but waited for the second half. "*And because you're brave, Amber, aren't you? You're a fighter. You never cry, do you, big girl? My big strong girl. Of course you'd be in Gryffindor…*"

I looked at her, over the tiny kitchen table – wearing her wholesome chequered shirt, smelling of wholesome bonfire. She looked so confused.

I got it.

"You don't remember…"

And the tiredness I'd been fighting all day hit me like a cartoon tonne falling from the sky.

Of course she didn't remember. Every childhood moment that meant anything to me was lost to her. She'd stopped making memories the day she came back from the hospital. Ten years ago…

I'd shared my childhood with a ghost, a ghost with amnesia.

"Remember what, hon?"

"Amber, you've got to stop losing your temper like this!" Kevin had regained some control in his voice but his face was still red.

"I'm going to bed." I could hardly get the words out.

"Don't you think you should apologize?" Mum asked. On Kevin's side, always on his side.

If I didn't want to sleep with every inch of my body, there would've been so many comebacks.

Shouldn't you be the one apologizing? (the best)
I apologize for ever coming here (childish)
I'm sorry you're such a fuck-up (hurtful)
Sorry for ever being born! (most childish)

But I was too tired to be brave, brave like a Gryffindor.

"Sorry."

And I slumped onto my bed and ripped up the sketch I'd made of Mum and me on the aeroplane until it made the most delicate of confetti.

Situations that are destined to fail:

Hating another girl

+

Trying to get your feminist friends to bitch about her with you

Thirteen

The computer screen was completely black, apart from one scary night-vision eye.

"Lottie." I sighed. "Can you not get your camera working? All I can see is your eyeliner."

Her green eye blinked.

"Is it not working?"

"Nope."

"Hang on." Evie's voice floated from the speakers of Kevin's computer. There was a flash and my friends came into focus. Lottie was right up in the camera, so much so I could see a booger up her nostril. Evie was further back.

They both smiled and waved. I waved back, my heart hurting for them.

"I can see you now."

"Good," said Lottie. "Because I put eyeliner on, just for you."

I touched my chest. "I'm touched."

"Yes, well you're worth it, my transatlantic pal."

"How are you guys anyway? What time is it over there?"

Evie looked at the clock behind her. I could tell they were in Evie's room by the general cleanliness.

"Just coming up to eight. And we're good. Though it would be better if you were here of course..." Lottie interrupted her. "Who were those fit guys we saw?" she demanded.

But Evie interrupted *her*. "BECHDEL TEST," she yelled. "Seriously, Lottie? We're going to start by asking Amber about hot boys?"

Lottie, to be fair, pretended to look vaguely ashamed of herself. "Sorry, I got excited. Amber, tell me about your hopes and dreams and thoughts and feelings, before we get onto the boys."

I giggled, so did Evie.

"Umm – I *hope* that's not the only reason you're talking to me. I *dream* about someone finally combining cheese and chocolate into one incredible snack food. I *think* you're not listening properly because you're a horrific feminist and general pervert. I *feel* you're not even going to apologize for it, because you're grinning right now!"

Lottie was sniggering. "Brilliant. Bechdel passed. NOW – who were those fit guys we saw?"

Evie objected again, while I said, "Who?" innocently, though I knew who she was talking about.

"Those guys," she continued, ignoring Evie. "The ones we saw on the webcam. Amber, I'm so jealous! They looked like

GODS, all tanned and with accents. And both of them were taller than you!"

"Oh? Russ and Kyle? Yeah, we're just working in the same team."

"YOU LOVE THEM!"

"What?"

"How can you not? One looks like he just walked out of an Abercrombie & Fitch advert, and the other looks like Jacob Black's hotter and less *weird-falling-in-love-with-children-inclined* brother."

"Russ lives on a reservation," I explained.

"Oh, be still my beating loins," Lottie said, fanning herself.

"You're turned on by guys who live on reservations?"

"I'm turned on by TANNED guys who can probably build their own fires and tell me hot stories about the history of willow trees looking all sexy by the fire they built."

Evie and I raised our eyebrows at each other.

"I'm pretty sure Russ said he spends most of his time inside, playing his video games…"

"Oh, screw him then. Go for the Adonis."

"Kyle?"

I tucked my hair back to stop it sticking to my neck in the midday heat. I was on my lunch hour, cramming in time with the girls before the dreaded canoeing later. I'd hardly slept, despite being so tired. I'd already spent the morning playing gross "trust" exercises, involving the children launching themselves into the air with their eyes closed, relying on us to catch them. As a result of my tiredness, I couldn't control my facial expressions.

"Amber, you're blushing!" Lottie screeched, pointing at the screen. "You're blushing AND nervously biting your lip. You fancy the Adonis guy!"

"I don't," I protested, sounding like someone who'd farted trying to pretend it wasn't them. "We just work together."

Evie's face got closer to the screen. "You really are red, Amber."

"Yes, well, it's ten million degrees out here."

"Jealous! It's rained here all week... Do you like him, Amber?"

Was there any point pretending I didn't?

"Everyone likes him," I admitted. "He looks like...well... that. He was bloody Prom King. He's won a scholarship for smartness. He cares about everyone and oozes joy and loveliness wherever he goes. He's like a litmus test for sex drive." I thought about it. "Male and female sex drive, basically."

"But do you like him like him?" Lottie pressed. "And since when the hell have you known what a litmus test is?"

I looked away from the webcam and mumbled.

"What was that, mumbly?" Evie asked.

I sighed and looked back up.

"I said, I don't really know him. And there's no point even if I do like him. He likes someone else."

My friends, bless them, gasped in outrage.

"Who is this cretin?" Lottie demanded.

"What makes it worse is she's, like, everything I hate about girls – all rolled into one girl."

Lottie narrowed her eye-linered eyes. "What do you mean everything you hate about girls?"

"Chill out, let me explain. She's like – well – she's a cheerleader, for one."

Evie's mouth opened. "A real one? You mean, they're, like, real?"

Lottie nudged her. "Of course they're real. Did you think they weren't?"

"I thought maybe they only lived in movies about high school. I mean, think about it, if they are real, that's pretty damn weird, right? Like, they're a group of girls who exist in every American school, whose sole purpose is to wear tiny clothes and cheer the achievements of men. That. Is. Screwed. Up."

"Exactly!" I said, pointing at the screen. "And she is one. Her name's Melody, and she always goes on about how 'sexual' she is."

Evie pulled a face while Lottie furrowed her eyebrows.

"And what's wrong with being sexual?"

"Oh, CALM DOWN, Simone de Beauvoir. I'm just trying to paint a picture."

Lottie was "sexual" too, I guess. Well, she liked sex. But it didn't bother me the way it bothered me in Melody. I stumbled on my words, trying to figure out why.

"I wish you'd stop telling me to calm down. You know how I feel about that phrase."

"God, I'm getting all my feminism wrong today," I moaned.

Evie smiled. "Go on...you were complaining about her sexualness...?" Lottie scowled again.

"Stop stink-eyeing me, Lottie!" I said. "I know girls are allowed to like sex. But Melody deliberately shoves it in everyone's faces..." She didn't look convinced, so I galloped on. "Like, the other night, at dinner, before the kids arrived, she said, really loudly, 'Oh, I know I'm just going to get so horny this summer, stuck in the middle of a forest.' I mean, who says that?! And then, of course, all the guys looked round and she pretended to be embarrassed."

Evie nodded. Lottie looked a tiny bit won over.

"And I know you'll probably yell at me for this too – but she wears actually no clothes. Like, well, minimal amounts of clothes, showing off her insane figure. And, yeah, it's hot. But it's not THAT hot. She actually wore a bra the other day instead of a top – again, before the children arrived."

I thought about Kyle, the way he'd danced with her by the fire – the way his hands held and rocked her hips.

"And then we had to do this campfire performance thing – where we all put on a show. My group and I did Monty Python—"

"Which one? Which bit?" Evie butted in, the film queen.

"The Knights who say Ni? Holy Grail?"

"Nice one."

"I know...and totally non-sexual – because, well, because it's CAMP. But Melody and her friends did a strip show to the Pussycat Dolls, and then brought boys up to lapdance them."

Lottie held her hands up to the webcam. "Wait wait wait wait wait wait. You say she lapdanced to the Pussycat Dolls?"

"Yes."

"In public?"

"Yes. In the middle of a circle of twenty plus people."

Lottie let out a long sigh. "Christ, she sounds like a NIGHTMARE."

Finally! Finally she was getting it.

"I told you!" I punched the air and accidentally knocked the old webcam off its perch. "Whoops." I bent down to get it.

Lottie's voice was still banging out of the speakers.

"I've literally just finished reading a book about girls like Melody. It's amazing…" I got the webcam back up. There was hardly any Evie visible – Lottie had got all close up in her excitement. "Basically," she continued, "Melody is what this book calls a Female Chauvinist Pig."

"A what?" Evie's voice said from behind her.

"A Female Chauvinist Pig. Like a male one, but female."

"I got that much," said Evie. "But what does it mean?"

"Right, I'll explain… Hang on, I need cheesy snacks. I cannot lecture on women's equality without a stash of cheesy snacks…"

God I wanted cheesy snacks. For the eightieth time I wished I could climb through my screen.

Lottie disappeared and then reappeared with a coating of neon orange around her mouth. She was still crunching cheesy Wotsits as she started talking.

"Right," she said. "This Melody sounds like a Female Chauvinist Pig."

"She's too stick thin to be a pig," I butted in.

"Shh, I'm in intelligent mode."

"You're always in intelligent mode," Evie pointed out. She had a slight orange tinge around her mouth that made my heart happy – because she never would have been able to have that and not notice it a year ago.

"That's because I'm very intelligent. Now, I've been learning about this thing called 'raunch culture'. It's basically this very clever thing that's happened which makes women strip off all their clothes and make men happy by shagging them all the time, in the misguided belief that this behaviour is liberated."

"Huh?"

Lottie always used words that were too long. She sighed, as she often did whenever she tried to explain stuff to us. "Okay, so there was the female sexual revolution right? The pill got invented and women could boff anyone they wanted without getting pregnant. It was all free love and sharey sharey sex, and AIDs hadn't happened yet. And finally, women weren't forced to only have crappy boring missionary sex with the guy they married when they were seventeen—"

"I can't believe you just said 'boff'," I interrupted again. "Evie is rubbing off on you."

Evie giggled behind Lottie's face.

"Shh… Boff, sex, shag, fuck, whatever. We started doing it and it was a feminist triumph. Whoop de doo for girls finally being allowed to have sex. And oh my God, we might even ENJOY it too."

"What has this got to do with Melody though?"

Lottie shot me another look. "You KNOW I'm getting there, it just takes me a while. Anyway, now after this revolution this book argues that things have gone a bit too far. Women, like, HAVE to be sexual now. To the point where our 'sexiness' is making us into, like, a sexiness product. I mean, look at the gross porn all the guys at college watch, for one. Or any advert where a woman washes her hair and gets an orgasm from her shampoo. Or the way you can't buy a pair of denim shorts now that cover your butt cheeks. Or how in adverts for anything, women's bodies aren't shown as a whole – we're just disjointed legs, or cleavages, or hands – just our sexual bits cut off and shoved onto a page to sell a watch or something. Women are 'supposed' to be sexy now – otherwise we're prudes, or one of those hairy feminists nobody wants to sleep with. You see how we're judged all the time? How awful it is to be described as no one wanting to shag you? We have to be 'hot' now, otherwise we've failed at life. And if we achieve stuff and we're *not* hot – it's the first thing people lob at us to undermine everything we've achieved."

We let Lottie stop for breath.

"Riiiight," Evie said, in her slow voice which meant she was getting it. I was sort of getting it.

"So something that was supposed to liberate us has essentially become a way of controlling us again?" I asked, shyly.

Lottie pointed and beamed at the camera. "Yes, exactly!"

I always felt so proud when she did that. She was like our teacher sometimes. She was so going to kick butt when she got to Cambridge. I couldn't wait for her to be the next female prime minister and point and squeal whenever I saw her on the telly.

"And this makes Melody a pig how?"

"Well, this is the thing I've been learning about…" How did she have time to teach herself such things? She was already doing five A levels, needing an A in each. "… We used to be able to blame men for everything. They were the baddies, they were the ones telling us what to do, they were the ones keeping us down, and they were the ones responsible. But in this raunch culture, the sticking point is that it's GIRLS TOO who are contributing to this bullshit. They're complicit in their own oppression…"

"In English, please," Evie said.

Lottie sighed and thought about it. "Okay, sexy girls like Melody have teamed up with male chauvinist arseholes. They're adding to this bullshit that it's better to be sexy than smart or strong. Does that make it clearer?"

Evie smiled. "A bit… I think."

"So now girls are all in on this big quest to be 'The Hottest One'. Whether that's by showing off our butt cheeks in those fucking annoying shorts, going to strip clubs for 'fun' or pole-dancing classes for 'exercise' but really just so we can tell men that's what we do. Or we're pushing our boobs together whenever we take a photo, or talking loudly about our orgasms so everyone can hear how sexualized and hot we are. It's all a big competition. Who's the hottest? Who's the sexiest? Who's winning the most against other women? Me me me me me. This is the problem. They think they're being all liberated, but actually they're competing against other women to see who can be sexier to men."

I digested what she'd said. "And think who benefits from all this the most?" I said, sadly, thinking yet again of Kyle's hands on Melody's hips. "Guys."

"EXACTLY!" Lottie gave me a triumphant point. "How is this good for feminism? How is this our 'liberation'? It's backfired. Men are doing really really well out of this raunch culture. Instead of girls burning their bras and fighting to be paid equally, we're all worried we're not sexy enough and are competing with all the women we should be fighting alongside – not against – over who has the nicest tits."

Evie ducked away and came back with another handful of crisps. I watched her eat them with her hands and felt another beam of pride. Her OCD symptoms were getting so much better.

"So," Evie asked, through a mouthful. "Why is Melody a pig then?"

And, even though I hadn't read any of Lottie's posh books, I found I knew the answer. "Because girls like her are just as bad as Male Chauvinist Pigs when it comes to how girls are oppressed?"

Lottie looked like she was going to explode with joy.

"Yes! We've become both the victim of raunch culture, and the perpetrators of it."

"ENGLISH," Evie and I demanded at the same time.

Lottie sighed once more. "Okay, umm, the do-ers of it?"

I let out a small smile. "So we can hate her then?"

"NO, Amber! Remember, hating other girls is never the answer."

I pouted. "But she's a cheerleader."

Evie finished her mouthful of snacks. "I hate the sound of her."

"Thank you!" I gave Lottie a look.

"No hating!" she repeated. "She's still a victim. A very annoying victim, granted, but still a victim of the patriarchy."

I stuck my lip out. "She doesn't act like a victim."

"Okay, fair enough," Lottie said. "She does sound like a nightmare. And you say she's all over Adonis 101?"

"Kyle? Yes…"

"Stop looking at the floor all mopey, O American one. I've not finished talking. We're supposed to fight this stuff, remember? I need to equip you to fight Melody."

"Please don't say we have to jelly wrestle?"

More smiling. "No… But you can counter her by setting an example. Stop being so hung up on how sexy you are or aren't, that's just the raunch culture talking. Being hot is not the ultimate aim – getting equality is. And you're not going to get respect or equality if you're too busy worrying that your arse isn't as toned as someone else's."

My tummy hummed with love for them. I looked at the big clock on Kevin's kitchen wall. Only ten minutes to get to the lake.

"I have to go in a min," I told them. "They're trying to put me in a canoe."

"NO!" said Evie. "We've not even heard all your news yet. I want to know if any of the kids are actually called Randy."

"Just the one."

"Seriously?"

I nodded. "Seriously."

Evie sat back, so she was almost in darkness. "Well, I'll be darned."

Lottie and I glanced at each other, sharing the secret face we used whenever Evie talked like a grandma.

"You want my advice?" Evie asked, all knowingly.

"About what?"

"Everything."

"Oh, you know the meaning of life, do you? You've kept that quiet this whole conversation."

"Yes, well it's hard competing for airtime with Lottie. But, okay, this advice is not about everything. But about Kyle, and Melody. I can see how it's making you feel."

She could see how it was making me feel, even though I was just a collection of pixels on her monitor… She wasn't blood, she didn't grow up with me, but yet she could see it all…

"Go on then." My voice caught.

"Just be yourself. Just be happy being you. The best way to fight girls like Melody is to not buy into all their crap. Be strong, be outspoken, be respected for the right stuff. You naturally do all that, Amber. That's why we're friends." All sorts of bubbles caught in my throat. It was like hiccuping backwards. "How's stuff going with your mum anyway? You settling into spending time together?" Evie's eyes were all big and concerned.

"I…umm…" I looked at the big ticking clock. Five minutes. I didn't have time to tell them. I didn't have time to let it all out if there was no time to clean myself up again afterwards. Where would I start anyway? We'd spent no time alone since I'd got here… She left me on my own with thirty kids then got mad when someone dared help me… She didn't sort me into Gryffindor…

"It's…er…complicated," I compromised. "Too complicated to get into now. When I'm too busy worrying how my arse is going to fit into a narrow boat made of plastic."

They both instantly saw through my cover.

"You're all right though?"

"Umm…"

They both got nearer the screen.

"Don't get into a bloody canoe," Evie said. "Stay here. Tell us about it."

"I will. Just not now."

They turned to look at each other, silently communicating.

"We're always here," Evie said. "You know that, right?"

"I know. What you guys up to tonight anyway?"

"Going out," Lottie answered. "The Admiral apparently doesn't ID since it got a new owner. We're going to go try our luck. Jane and Joel might be coming."

"Yikes, those two are like furniture now."

"Indeedy."

"Well," I stood up to turn off my webcam, so not wanting to turn it off. "I better get going."

"Remember," Lottie said, as we waved goodbye. "Be you. It's all you can ever be anyway. But own being you. It's a fab thing to own."

"I love you guys."

"We love you too."

And, just as the screen went dark, I heard them singing the end of "American Pie".

Situations that are destined to fail:

A tall girl

+

A chubby girl

+

An obese boy

+

A canoe

Fourteen

"I can't get my stupid legs into this stupid canoe."

I pushed around with my feet, hoping they'd find an extra alcove to fold my limbs into.

"Well I can't get my stupid torso into this stupid canoe." Whinnie's voice came from behind me.

"Me neither," wailed Calvin, behind her. "In fact, I think I might be stuck."

I twisted round uncomfortably to take in the scene. Calvin was indeed wedged right in the back seat, his fat spilling over the red plastic, looking like melted drips of ice cream running down the side of the canoe. Whinnie wasn't faring much better. She wiggled her body about, but it was like trying to get a square peg into a round hole.

We caught each other's eyes and both started giggling.

"This was the worst idea."

"Absolute worst. We didn't have these stupid boats last year. If I'd known, I wouldn't have come back."

"Why is everyone else finding it so easy?" I asked.

If you ignored us, the scene was practically idyllic. We'd joined teams with Gryffindor for canoeing, and primary-coloured boats dotted the lake everywhere. The sun beat down on us, the water reflecting slivers of light onto our faces. It was pig hot, but the lake somehow generated its own breeze, lifting my curls, fanning them around my face. I heard distant calls of joy from other boats, the steady sloshing noise of oars piercing through water.

Whinnie and I laughed so hard the boat rocked dangerously.

"Don't!" Calvin squealed. "If this capsizes, I won't be able to get out."

I tried not to laugh harder. It wasn't fair on him. We weren't even supposed to be sharing canoes with other counsellors, but when we'd asked the kids to buddy-up, unsurprisingly no one would go with Calvin. Just as his bottom lip began to wobble, Whinnie and I had both jumped in at the same time, offering to be in his boat.

Kevin had agreed, giving me an *I'm-proud-of-you* wink that instantly made me want to withdraw my kind offer.

I heard him call across the water from his gold canoe. Yep, his was gold, the only one. That's the thing about Kevin. He acts all *Hey-champ-I'm-such-a-great-guy-counsellor-type* – but then he gives himself a gold canoe and preys on vulnerable women in rehab.

"You guys okay over there?" His voice echoed around the vast expanse of the lake.

"We're managing," I called back as haughtily as I could, considering I was yelling through both hands.

"You've not left the pier yet!"

"We're just taking our time," I called again. "We're fine." I looked at Whinnie. "You okay in there?"

She gave a small smile. "I feel like I'm wearing a corset made out of canoe, but I am in."

"Let me just try my legs one more time."

I changed the way I bent them and just about made it – though I would have cramp until Christmas probably.

"I think I'm in."

"It's a miracle!"

"You ready, Calvin?" I was now wedged in such a way that I couldn't look behind me any more.

"I...guess...so," his small voice answered. "Just... please...can we not rock the boat?"

"We would all drown," I agreed. "Now, who knows how the hell to row?"

The answer was: none of us. It took a good twenty minutes of giggling and calls of "*One, two, three, GO*" to even put ten metres between us and the pier. We drifted in circles and splashed water all over ourselves as we put the oars in wrong.

"We've hardly left the pier!" Calvin whined. "Everyone else has rowed for miles, and we've hardly left the pier!"

"We're trying our best, Calvin."

"You guys can't row!"

"We are aware of that, Calvin." I pulled a face because he couldn't see me. Children were so ungrateful in real life. In stories, if you do a good deed for a kid, they're all beamy, covered in chimney smoke and say stuff like "Why, thank you, Mister Scrooge, God bless ya". But, in real life, they just whinged and nothing you did was ever enough.

Calvin's humiliation at not having a partner was forgotten. "This is stoopid." I felt him drop the oar into its holder.

I remembered my camp pledge to be Disney at all times.

"Now, we can't do this without you, Calvin. We need you to row."

I ploughed my oar into the water again, pulling it backwards. It hurt my arm, the pain aching all the way up to my elbow. The boat only spun us about twenty degrees, so we looked directly back at the pier, and at the pitiful distance we'd put between us and it.

"I wanna go over there," Calvin whined.

"I can't see where you're pointing. But if it's any further away than ten metres, I think you need to lower your expectations."

"Ahhhh MAN." The boat starting rocking and vibrating.

"Is he crying?" I whispered back at Whinnie, desperately trying to move the boat forward at the same time.

"I think so. I can't turn around. My stomach hurts."

"I have cramp of the entire body."

And the boat shook harder as we both dissolved into silent laughter.

"You're LAUGHING." A wail echoed out of him and around the lake.

"Shh, it's okay, Calvin," I said. "Whinnie and I are trying our hardest. Whinnie, ready on the count of three?"

"Ready for what?"

"Rowing."

"Oh yeah. What do we do on the count of three?"

"I'm still trying to figure that out."

"Umm – how about you go backwards and I go backwards. Then we'll move...backwards?" she asked.

"That sounds like a plan. You joining us, Calvin?"

He wailed his answer. I saw two boats heading towards us – one was Kevin's, the gold canoe slicing through the water effortlessly. The other was a standard red boat.

No, I wouldn't let Kevin rescue me. I'd rather get blisters all over my hands that bled. Popped. And then bled again.

"One, two, three, GO!" I pulled back my oar, dipped it down into the water, spun the blade and then yanked it back, using all my strength. Whinnie's oar did the same thing...we were getting it...we were totally getting the hang of it....hang on...the boat just circled again...

Calvin cried harder. "You two are the worst."

I ignored him. "Whinnie?"

"Yep."

"The boat is broken. That is what I've decided."

"That is a most excellent decision."

"So, when Kevin gets here to rescue us, our line is the boat is broken."

"The boat is SO broken."

"I know. You hear that, Calvin?"

"The boat's not broken, you're just both LAME."

We attempted two more pathetic oar strokes, but the boat still twisted aimlessly in the water.

Kevin was almost with us. He was grinning, I could see it from here. The red boat was almost with us too, I sighed. It was Kyle's boat. He was also grinning.

"We have rescuers," I deadpanned.

"Really? Why?" Whinnie asked. "I could probably wade to the beach from here."

"YOU GUYS OKAY?" Kevin called.

"OUR BOAT IS BROKEN," Whinnie and I called back in unison.

"THEY'RE JUST LAME," Calvin added.

"Shh, Calvin, that's not the official line."

Kevin and Kyle arrived at the same time. I tried not to look at Kyle's arms as he worked the oars. I didn't try very hard. He had Jenna in the back, as well as my hyperactive nemesis – Charlie Brown.

"What's going on here?" Kyle expertly brought his boat up against ours.

"Our boat is broken," I repeated.

Kevin pulled up on the other side so we were in a superior rower sandwich.

"Hey, guys, looks like you've got into some trouble."

"The boat is broken."

"Umm," Kyle looked down at the oar in my hands.

"You're holding your paddle wrong."

I looked down with him. "This is a perfectly acceptable way to be holding an oar."

"Yeah, if it *was* an oar and you were in a rowing boat."

"I *am* in a rowing boat. That's what a canoe is."

"Well, that's not quite true. And also, this isn't a canoe anyway. It's a kayak."

I shrugged. "So?"

"So...have you considered what that massive flat plastic thing is on the end of your 'oar'?"

"That's the annoying bit."

"No. That's supposed to be in the water too...like this." He pushed our boat away so his was floating freely again, and then pulled out his oar, holding his hands at both ends with his arms wide. He dipped one end over one side of the boat, and then the other end over the other side of the boat, like a rocking motion. His canoe, or kayak or whatever, glided forward a good metre or two.

"Oh..." I said.

"Oh..." Whinnie said.

Charlie Brown looked at both of us in disbelief.

"You guys are TOTALLY lame."

Calvin had stopped crying. "I know, right?"

Bumface Kevin let out a huge thundery laugh. "Well, I guess I forgot to tell you guys how to paddle a kayak. I'd say right now you're rowing that boat like it's out of *Wind in the Willows*."

"We'll be fine now, thank you," I said sternly.

"Let's mix things up a bit, get Calvin to see the lake a little."

"No, thank you. We know what we're doing now."

Kevin stroked his bumchin as he thought about it. "I know." He pointed at me. "Amber, you swap with Charlie Brown. He's a good paddler, aren't you, Charlie B? You can help Whinnie and Calvin?"

Charlie Brown started scrabbling out of the boat.

"Hang on," I yelled, as he jumped down, practically on top of me. "I'm not ready yet." How would my legs get out of this canoe? They'd barely made it in! I turned to Whinnie, but she just shrugged, still holding her paddle wrong.

"Careful, Amber," Kevin said. I gave him my best glare and tried to free my feet so I could stand.

"Charlie, seriously, you're in my way." He rolled his eyes. A bloody ten-year-old rolled his eyes at me, but he wiggled to give me room. I tentatively stood up and the boat rocked. I threw my hands out to steady myself.

"Careful," Kyle said. It didn't annoy me when he said it. He was watching me closely, his eyes squinting against the sun. I looked at the small hole Charlie Brown had left. Then I took a deep breath and stepped one foot in. Kyle's boat lurched away from the impact, making me almost do the splits.

"Hang on." Kyle pushed his paddle down to steady the boat.

"I just ripped my crotch in two," I howled.

"Just move your other foot in quickly."

"I'm scared!"

"It's all right, I've got you." Kyle reached out his hand and I took it, still surprised by how nice his skin felt, even though I should've been immune by now. He gripped it and pulled me towards him, coaxing my other foot off Whinnie's boat. My centre of gravity shifted and I grabbed him tighter as I stepped down.

Everyone applauded.

"You go, Amber!" Kevin whooped.

Another glare.

Charlie Brown had already slotted himself into my old space and grabbed my paddle. "I'm the captain!" he yelled. And, before Whinnie and Calvin knew what was happening, their boat had taken off, powered by the strength and sheer egotism of a ten-year-old American who is good at sports.

I wedged myself down into a new hole of humiliation, which gave me a view of the back of Kyle's head. Some of his hair had grown long, curling around his ears. I looked back, towards Jenna.

"Hey, Jenna," I said, smiling. "I'm your new boat roomie."

She gave me a stern look. "You're not very good at paddling, you know that, right?"

I wiggled in, turning my back to her.

"I don't consider paddling a very important life skill. When will I ever need to paddle?"

"Umm…right now?"

"Well aren't you clever?" I muttered under my breath.

The boat rocked as Kyle laughed and craned round to us both.

"Now, Amber, are we ready to go? Do you think you know what you're doing with the paddle?"

I gave him a big fake grin. "Putting it in the water?"

"And not just one end...but?"

"Both ends?" I rolled my eyes.

"Good job," he said, as only Americans can. "On the count of three, ready, Jenna? One, two, three..."

...The boat turned in a circle as I deliberately shoved only one end of my paddle into the water.

"What the...?" Kyle craned round again, I smiled even more sweetly, holding my paddle up in admission.

"That..." I said, "was payment, for all the patronizing."

Once I got the hang of rowing and/or paddling – whatever the hell it was – it started to get quite nice.

Okay, so the paddle was already forming two hefty blisters between my thumb and finger, but Kyle, Jenna and I hit a rhythm and the canoe/kayak glided through the lake like it was being pushed by the gods.

Soon the pier was a tiny speck, and the other kayaks were too.

The water spread out in all directions, the trees lining it looking tinier and tinier. I pulled my baseball cap lower to shade my eyes from the harsh sun, looking around me in humbled awe as we dipped our paddles in the water

– the steady splish-splosh uniting us like a common heartbeat.

"How long till we reach the other side?" I asked, embarrassed by how far we'd gotten in the time it had taken Whinnie and I to move five metres away from the pier.

"If we paddle hard for five more minutes, we'll make it," Kyle called back.

"And what's at the other side of the lake?"

"More trees," Jenna replied.

"Oh." I was disappointed. "I thought there would be, like, something different."

"We're doing it for the achievement, Amber." Jenna's voice was so authoritative. "We're doing it because we can."

I pulled a face I thought that neither of them could see, but Kyle turned round and caught it.

"I was telling her about the first person to ever climb Mount Everest," he said, by way of explanation. "I read a biography about him. When he came down from the mountain, everyone asked him, why did you do it? And his famous answer was, 'Because it was there'."

I sighed. "He sounds like a douche."

"Ummmmmm, you just cursed!" Jenna sing-songed behind me.

"No I didn't."

"Yes you did."

"Didn't."

"Did."

"Douche is not a curse word."

"UMMMMM, YOU JUST DID IT AGAIN." She cackled with giggles, a weird hiccuping sound. I deliberately splashed her with my paddle and she squealed. "HEY, YOU SPLASHED ME." She splashed me back.

"Oi."

"Can't get me."

"Yes, I ruddy well can."

And we both dolloped water onto each other.

Kyle called behind him. "Amber? Can I remind you you're supposed to be a responsible adult?"

"When have adults ever behaved responsibly?" I twisted and grinned at Jenna. We both nodded and simultaneously aimed our paddles at Kyle, dowsing him too.

"You stinkers!"

He aimed back, and by the time we'd all calmed down we were totally soaked through. I laughed myself out, feeling good. About how the sun was already drying my clothes, about how it looked bouncing off the ripples, about the way the trees were so dense and old that they seemed to whisper secrets, about how Kyle had looked at me when I soaked him.

"Come on," Kyle straightened his paddle. "We're almost at the other side."

We pushed on, the trees getting nearer, the whoosh of our paddles stronger. Then, with an unceremonious thud, our kayak hit the bank of the lake.

"We did it," I cheered, and Kyle and Jenna whooped with me.

Kyle turned round again. "Whoever would've thought it was possible?"

"Oi, I just wasn't trained properly," I replied. "And kayaking isn't a key life skill. I'm good at useful things, like making a roux."

"A what?"

"A roux. It's the base of any white sauce, or soup. It's when you cook flour and butter together, a roux."

"I have no idea what you're talking about. I'm starting to realize this is quite common."

I stuck my tongue out. "Roux are more useful than kayaks, I promise you."

"You're a good cook then?"

I nodded. "Do you know what a roux is?" I called behind to Jenna, not breaking eye-contact with Kyle.

"Of course," she answered solemnly. "You need a good roux for macaroni and cheese."

"See," I said, triumphantly. "I bet the guy who climbed Mount Everest didn't know how to make a roux."

Kyle held a smile and then turned to paddle the kayak back the opposite way.

"Right, ready to head back? We've got swimming soon, in the lake to cool off."

"Yay!" Jenna yelled. "Can I show you my dive? Can I? Can I? I can dive REALLY good."

"Sure," we both replied.

We got back into the flow of paddling – the pier unbecoming a dot, and growing into a blob, then a bigger blob. Other kayaks joined us, all heading in the same direction. I spotted Russ, his feet up on the front of his boat, his arms crossed behind his head, relaxing as two kids paddled frantically behind him.

"That's it," Russ called, half-asleep. "You're doing great." The kids seemed to find it funny.

"Hey," I yelled, over the water. "Child labour is illegal in the States, you know?"

Russ jerked up and almost fell out. He saw it was me and covered his eyes with his hands to shield them from the sun. "From what I've seen today," he called back, "you are in no position to give lectures on the art of paddling."

Whinnie's boat was just in front of us. Charlie Brown was still paddling madly, like a wind-up toy on MDMA. The boats began to thump together, forming a disorderly queue up to the pier. Bumface Kevin was already there, reaching down with his big strong arms to yank children out, lavishing them with praise.

"*You go, well done you, you are so smart, what a team!*"

I turned round to Jenna. "You have fun?"

She nodded. "It was adequate."

And both Kyle and I shook the boat with our laughter.

We waited to dock our kayak. It was only when we'd stopped paddling that I realized my hands were red raw, but I didn't care. I felt all light – from chatting to the girls, from them helping me understand Melody, from learning how to kayak...

Speaking of Melody, she seemed to be waiting for Kyle on the dock. She'd rolled up her camp T-shirt into a minitop and rested against the wooden poles, one tanned leg cocked perfectly to accentuate her lean angular muscles.

We lifted Jenna from the boat first, and she ran in the direction of the beach. Then Kevin pulled me up onto the dock, then Kyle.

I hung back, waiting for Whinnie. Trying not to watch Kyle and Melody together. But not really trying.

She manoeuvred Kyle away down the length of the pier. I watched them stop, and she tucked a stray piece of his golden hair behind his ear.

I didn't hear it all, but I did hear her say...

..."I had such a good time last night."

And my stupid heart hurt, and all the good-feeling went again.

Like it always does. When you mistakenly let people in.

Situations that are destined to fail:

Trying to talk to your friends about boys

\+

A past record of not being very understanding about that topic

Fifteen

From: LongTallAmber
To: EvieFilmGal
Subject: Death to cheerleaders

Hello again you sexy gorgeous friends of mine.

How's the British summer going? I looked on the BBC site here (it's so weird, guys, there are ADVERTS on it in America) and...well...yes...sorry about the rain? I feel most smug here in the burning sunshine while you're being pissed on from grand heights.

Thanks so much for the last Spinster Meeting! It really cheered me up. The FCP girl is so much easier to handle now I have an academic-but-essentially-cruel word for her in my head. She's inevitably got together with the Prom King guy, because life is so ridiculously clichéd sometimes I wonder why we bother living it when nothing is ever a surprise any more... NOT BITTER. Definitely not bitter.

Love you all, miss you loads

Ax

PS Lottie, no, I won't send you photos of my sunburn. I told you, it's gone down!

PPS Did you know that canoes and kayaks aren't the same thing?

From: EvieFilmGal
To: LongTallAmber
Subject: RE Death to cheerleaders

Hello tall one,

How did you fit in a canoe? Are there photos? Please say there are photos.

I'm sorry about the whole cheerleader/Prom King debacle. Do you have any way of watching films out there? If so, I prescribe The Breakfast Club. And another film called Heathers. Honestly though, it's not worth it. Don't waste time mooning after guys who can't see how great you are. Do you not remember my whole first term of college with Guy?

How are things with your mum anyway? You went all stiff on us when we asked last. LET IT OUT. Again, remember my whole first term at college?

Learn from my mistakes, lovey.

We're all okay over here in Blighty, though the rain is crazy. Crazier than me even. We should totally section this rain.

Evie x

From: LongTallAmber
To: EvieFilmGal
Subject: RE RE Death to cheerleaders

Thanks for your email, love. Sorry it's taken a few days ~to get back to you. I've been knee-deep in all sorts of forced-fun unpleasantries. If I have to see another campfire again after this summer, I may have to MAKE THE WHOLE WORLD INTO A CAMPFIRE AND BURN EVERYTHING.

Sorry – that was unnecessary.

I can't believe the kids have been here for almost ten days. I'm so SO exhausted. And things with Mum??? Yep. I'm very stiff. Just writing this I can feel myself getting stiff. But okay, I'll let it out. Here's essentially my life in camp, day in, day out:

6 a.m. – Wake up. I KNOW!
6.30 a.m. – Try and talk to Mum over breakfast, but instead have to put up with Bumface Kevin poking his bumchinny bumchin in and never leaving us to ourselves.
7 a.m. – Feed the kids breakfast. Fight urge to tip oatmeal over the kids.
8 a.m. – ACTIVITIES i.e. how can we torture Amber some more?
10 a.m. – Break. Try to get some time alone with Mum. Blocked by eight million children, well, my group of about twenty, all wanting me to draw Harry Potter tattoos on their arms with biro.
10.30-1 p.m. – MORE ACTIVITIES. Spend most of the time trying not to look at Kyle...and then get annoyed at myself for realizing I do really quite fancy him.
1 p.m. – Lunch. Otherwise known as "Melody shares a sex story when the kids are too busy eating hamburgers to hear" time. Mum and Kevin go and eat lunch by themselves in the cabin, while I have to help in the canteen.
2-4 p.m. – Run my art class. To be fair, I do get to spend time with Mum here. But we're too busy trying to stop

the kids painting their entire hands with PVA glue so they can peel it off (don't blame them – most satisfying thing EVER).

4-5 p.m. – Chill out time. This is where I tend to hang with my new amazing pal, Whinnie, and discuss women's rights – while also trying not to look at Kyle, who keeps coming over to listen.

5-6 p.m. – Dinner time. I never want to eat macaroni and cheese ever again.

6-9 p.m. – Some sort of organized chaos, involving fire and singing.

9-10 p.m. – Try to get the frickin' runts to go to sleep.

10 p.m. onward – Try and talk to Mum, try and hang out with Mum, but always, always, the Bumface is lurking and she doesn't seem to care.

11 p.m. – Sketch in my room, try not to cry…go to sleep…

I wish I could watch those movies, Evie, – but alas! No such technology exists in the mountains. Prom King is SO confusing though! If he wasn't so darn NICE, I would put him down on the head-fuck list, along with Guy and others. Like, he's always walking me back to my cabin in the dark. Or sitting next to me at dinner. Or coming and sitting with me when I can't handle the sports section of the day because I'm so unfit and declare myself a political abstainer. (Note: American football is even worse and more boring than British football.)

Why do I have to fancy someone? I'm so mad at myself. I'm not here for that. And, look, I've just written a whole email to you about it, like some totally basic female fuckwit, when I should be asking you about your life… or, you know, fighting the patriarchy or whatever.

TELL ME ABOUT YOUR LIFE. I DO CARE!

Amber x

From: LottieIsAlwaysRight
To: LongTallAmber
Subject: Welcome to Headfuck Land

It's both Lottie AND EVIE here.
But it's me, Lottie, who is doing all the hard work of typing.

And can I just say: AHAHAHAHAHAHAHAHAHAHAHAHA HAHAHAHAHAHAHAHAHAHA

WELCOME TO THE HEADFUCK LAND OF BOYS, YOU WONDERFUL LITTLE HYPOCRITE, YOU!

Do you not remember THE LECTURES you gave us last year? About how much we were whinging about the complex and compulsive-worrying behaviour of men?

And DIDN'T WE TELL YOU how hard it is to maintain one's dignity and ability to think of useful things when boys we like behave all boy-like?

Welcome to karma, Amber…

Mwhahahaha.

Sorry – I just needed to get that out. We love you. We're here for you. It's just quite strange, seeing you crumple under the pressure, when you've always been so noble. To be fair, I have seen the arms on that guy, and if he was walking me ANYWHERE, I'd be thinking about it. A lot. Alone.

Just remember our advice. Be you. You are kick-ass and amazing.

Sorry things are tough with your mum. Do you need to talk about it some more? Remember she's just probably got a really set "routine" that she needs to stay healthy or something, and maybe it's taking her a while to adjust. As for Kevin, that's not fair that he won't let you have alone time. I can see how annoying that is, especially as you hate him so much. She loves you though. Who couldn't love you, you frizzy wonder?

Oh yeah, that reminds me, I bumped into your dad and

Penny in Sainsbury's the other day (how exciting is my life?) and they asked me to ask you why you're not replying to their emails. Amber, why aren't you replying to their emails? Now, I've done it...I'm just going to back away with my hands up in the air because I know what you get like when Penny is involved... Maybe just send the one though?

We have no news. It's rained here too much for anyone to do anything that makes news.

Keep us updated on you.

Lots of love,

Lottie and Evie (and cheesy snacks)
xxxxxxxxxxxxxxxxxxxxxxxxxxxxx

Situations that are destined to fail:

Drawing straws

+

Bad tempers

Sixteen

Russ carefully hid three long straws among the bundle of short ones in his hand.

We had only a moment's peace, while the kids were still smearing chocolate pudding down themselves, to decide this.

"I don't trust you, man." Kyle made to grab the straws. "I know how much you want this."

Russ twisted his hand behind his back. "We all want this. I swear, if I don't have a break from Martin's screaming and get a good night's sleep soon, I'm gonna go mad."

After fourteen days of solid work, The Weekend Cover were arriving. High school students who came and did our jobs for us for two days so we could sleep, and rest, and leave the actual confines of the camp. But only a few of us could go… We had to alternate weekends.

"Martin still having bad dreams?" I asked. Russ had been complaining about Martin since day one. Apparently he woke up every night, screaming the cabin down, waking everyone else up.

Russ nodded grimly. "Every night... Man, I hate that kid."

"RUSS!" Whinnie and I scolded.

"He *is* really bad," Kyle said. "I can hear him from my cabin sometimes."

"Well, what's wrong with him? Surely he must be disturbed or something?"

Russ shook his head. "Nah, he's just a wimp."

"Hey," Whinnie and I said at the same time.

"Okay, whatever," Russ said. "Can we just pick a straw already?"

He arranged them carefully in his gripped hand, making them all line up at exactly the right height. "How do we decide who picks first?"

"We draw straws?" I joked, but Russ looked confused by that. "Never mind...it was just a joke."

"It doesn't matter –" Kyle went to grab one – "statistically it makes no difference at all."

"Actually..." Whinnie said. "It does make a huge difference." She pointed at herself. "Maths major..."

They started bickering and I sighed and lunged towards Russ. "Just give me a straw already."

I felt guilty I was even in the draw. I had my own room in a private cabin, I didn't need a break as bad as they did. But I was also desperate to have a weekend off so I could go on a trip with my mum. Finally, after three evenings in a row of my careful hinting, she'd promised we could go sightseeing together – anywhere I wanted – if I got the weekend off. Just us two. Not a bummy chin in sight.

Russ leaned over and I plucked a straw from him. It was long.

"Ahhhh, lucky!" Russ pulled a face at me.

"See!" Whinnie said. "Now the rest of us statistically have a lesser chance of getting one."

"That means I'm next!" Russ plunged into his own palm and pulled out a short straw.

"DAMNIT!"

We had to stop him from dropping them all over the floor.

"Go offer them to the others," I said. Russ gave me a resentful look and went to present the straws to Bryony and the rest of Dumbledore's Army. Two of them drew short straws, cursing under their breath. Bryony delicately plucked out a long straw. "Awesome!"

The kids were rousing behind us. Pudding was finished. The clattering sound of empty plastic bowls filled the hall.

"Quick," I said. "We don't have long. The sugar rush from dessert is about to kick in."

Everyone laughed but I wasn't trying to be funny. I'd learned to dread sugar. American food seemed to be laden with it, even the healthy stuff. Like "raisin bran" – each raisin came in a crystallized winter coat of silvery refined sugar. One moment the kids would be okay – I could get them sitting quietly in the rec hall, painting or whatever.

Then they'd have a snack and suddenly it was like being in a Roy Lichtenstein painting – all KABAAM and WALLOP, as they ricocheted off the walls, running about and fighting with each other.

There were two straws left – one for Whinnie, one for Kyle. They both reached for the same one, and Kyle made a gentlemanly gesture.

"Okay then, you take it."

Whinnie did. It was a short straw. "Damnit!" she yelled as Kyle triumphantly grabbed the last long straw from Russ's hand.

"That's what you get when you're a gentleman!" He picked Whinnie up and whirled her around.

"You are not a gentleman."

"Oh yeah?" And he put his arms around her back and started ballroom dancing her about the hall. The kids – the sugar from pudding well and truly lodged in now – came running up behind us. "We wanna go, we wanna go."

Calvin grabbed me, his pudgy hands forcing me to turn with authority. "Dance with me."

"Calvin, you just can't go around grabbing girls like that."

He didn't listen, but dragged me caveman-like into the centre of the room and started twirling me with a determined look on his face. The other kids paired up too, and soon we were all swirling to no music, a silent ball, as Kevin and Mum laughed from the sides and took photos.

I slipped on a spaghetti hoop that had fallen to the floor.

"Woooooah," I shot into Kyle and Whinnie.

"Swap partners," Kyle called, expertly swapping me and Whinnie and kicking the treacherous spaghetti hoop to the side of the hall. He leaned in and whispered in my ear, making my curly hair tickle. "Consider yourself rescued."

I looked over his shoulder at Whinnie. Calvin was spinning her into circle after circle after circle.

"He is one determined child," I said. "Thank you… I think I have whiplash of the whole body."

We twirled, skidding a bit on some chocolate pudding. Russ had two small girls riding on his feet, and groaned whenever he had to take a step. Bryony and Melody and their group were teaching some of the girls to shimmy in the corner.

"I think he has a crush on you." Kyle spun me again so we could see Calvin staring at both of us. He was scowling a bit…

"Great," I said. "The first guy ever to have a crush on me, and he's an overweight ten year old in the first thrusts of puberty."

"I'm sure that's not true."

"What? You think he's still a while away from puberty?"

Kyle dipped me, but slid on some spilled juice. We collapsed onto the floor. Him on top of me.

"OUCH!" I said, as everyone stopped dancing.

"AHHHH YOU FELL OVER. DO IT AGAIN. YOU FELL OVER. OHMYGODTHAT'SSOFUNNYDOITAGAINAHA HAHAHAA." The children forgot the dancing and the hall of ballroom dancers all started deliberately skidding on leftover food, throwing themselves to the floor. Mum (sensing a lawsuit) clapped her hands in that loud way that made everyone stop.

"Time for campfire, everyone." They cheered and started lining up in their groups by the door. Kyle scrambled up and held out his hand to help me off the ground.

"I think I've got alphabetti spaghetti in my hair," I whinged. "And concussion of the butt area."

Kyle laughed a wide open laugh and steered me towards Dumbledore's Army.

"I was talking about the crush," he said. "I don't think it's true that Calvin is the first guy to have a crush on you."

And he was helping the children get into pairs before my mouth had even fallen open…

Situations that are destined to fail:

Sleep

+

A cup of hot chocolate

Seventeen

From: LongTallAmber
To: EvieFilmGal; LottieIsAlwaysRight
Subject: TIME OFF!!!!!

I'm getting time off!!!!!!!!!!

They're actually letting me leave the camp. And Mum's coming too! I've got an entire weekend with my mum AND NO ONE ELSE. She's driving us to Los Angeles and I want to take the obligatory photo of myself by the Hollywood Sign and wander about the place, hoping to bump into Joseph Gordon-Levitt so he can fall violently in love with me. I'm soooooooooo looking forward to chilling, just us two. I can never get her away from Bumface Kevin – I think his bumchin may have its own gravitational pull and you need some kind of rocket launcher to break Mum away from his atmosphere?

Thank you so much, as well, for your VERY SYMPATHETIC attitude towards my boy woe…not.

Okay, so I definitely had it coming… He's still being all confusing. Yesterday he said something about this chubby kid at camp who's developed a worrying crush on me. Kyle said: "I bet he's not the first guy to have a crush on you."

WHAT DOES THAT EVEN MEAN?

Anyway, that's tomorrow so I'll be offline for two days. Let me know all your news.

Lots of love

Amber

I putzed about on the internet a bit longer before bedtime, looking up things to do in LA. Did I want to go and see famous people's houses? Or go to Universal Studios? There was lots of tourist stuff about Wine Country – a part of California that looked really pretty. But I couldn't really suggest Mum and I went there…

An email pinged in just as I was about to log off.

From: LottieIsAlwaysRight
To: LongTallAmber
Subject: You do know you'll need to bleach your bum-hole, right?

That's what EVERYONE does in LA. It is one big anal bleaching EPIDEMIC.

And they don't give you normal omelettes, but ones made with only the white of the egg which everyone knows is the shit bit of egg.

Seriously, though, I am SO jealous. Have a great time with your mum! I am ALL alone this weekend. Evie is buggering off on a "Mindfulness Weekend" with Oli. I KNOW?! Maybe a bit of meditation will finally get those two together. We all went for a drink the other night and they kept looking at each other and pretending not to. It was so cute I almost vommed with happiness and banged their heads together. Things have got so desperate here that I've actually agreed to go drinking with Jane and Joel tomorrow night. WISH ME LUCK.

Oodles of love

Lottie

xxx

PS Don't let this guy mess your head around with his bulgy arms. If he has chosen Melody as his streetlight to piss on, he can't go around saying that sort of thing to you. Just close your eyes whenever you talk to him, so you're not pulled in by his arms (both literally and metaphorically).

I pottered to the kitchen quietly, smiling to myself as I filled up my water glass. Those girls… I was so lucky to have those girls. All I could hear was the steady buzz of cicadas – *I finally learned what they were called!* – as I ran the tap. I thought of everyone in the cabins surrounding us. Whinnie tucking the last of the children in, Russ trying to get to sleep quickly before Martin had another nightmare… Kyle sneaking out to meet Melody probably…

"Hey, sweetie."

I jumped, splashing water all down myself. It seeped into my strappy night-top, making my tummy lurch back in shock.

"Mum, jeez. You scared me. I thought you were asleep?"

"Kevin is. I was reading."

I grabbed a kitchen towel and dabbed myself dry. Mum looked like a Renaissance painting, all Pre-Raphaelite, her auburn hair streaming down her back, her pale skin all cushiony and glowing.

"Do you want a cup of hot chocolate?" she asked. "I was going to make one for myself."

"Sounds great."

Mum warmed up some milk on the tatty cabin stove while I sat on the countertop and watched her. I would never get tired of watching her. I couldn't even think about the end of camp, the end of this summer, when the simple act of watching my mother would be snatched away again.

"I can't wait to go to LA," I said, swinging my legs under the countertop.

Mum looked distracted as she poured the hot milk on top of the cocoa powder and stirred.

"Uh hur…"

"Can we go to Hollywood Boulevard and put our hands in the prints of famous people?"

Mum handed me a cup and grimaced. "Er, no. Hollywood is a horrid place. I thought we could take a hike."

"A hike?"

"Yes. Some of the LA mountains are beautiful."

"But we're on a mountain right now. We could hike, like, right now."

She walked away to the couch and perched on the edge. Mum never sat, she always perched, waiting to dart off again. Somewhere else. Somewhere I wasn't.

"I guess we'll see," she said. In that way. That way I remembered her using whenever she knew she wasn't going to do what I wanted.

We'll have to see, darling. Mummy doesn't feel very well this evening. I don't know if I'll be better to chaperone your school trip to London. Go to bed. We'll see in the morning.

"That was funny in the rec hall today" – she slurped her milk – "everyone bursting into ballroom dancing. The children loved it."

I sat across from her, perching myself, on the poufy footrest. My knees hunched up over my body, warming the cold bit where I'd spilled the water.

"They love everything," I said. "Apart from bedtime."

"You're great with them, Amber. You'll make a brilliant mother one day."

Anyone would in comparison to you. I felt guilty the moment I'd thought it.

"I saw you dancing with Kyle."

Why did she *always* bring him up?

I shrugged. "He only rescued me from Calvin. I think he was about to grab my butt."

"Remember what I said about him. Last year I saw so many hearts break over that boy."

"I know."

"He's friendly to everyone…and he looks like that…girls think they're special…"

"Jeez, Mum, I know, all right!?"

I knew he wouldn't fancy me. I knew he was just that way. I knew he would always go for girls like Melody because that's just what happens. I didn't need my mum to remind me he wasn't going to fall in love with me. I had daily reminders of that myself – from Mum… "I think he's with Melody anyway," I said helplessly. "Well, I think they hooked up."

"I just don't want to see you get hurt."

So rich coming from her. So SO rich coming from her. And yet I could sense she sensed my anger, and I didn't want to ruin our Hollywood movie moment. I guessed I could hike in LA, I mean Joseph Gordon-Levitt wouldn't fall in love with me anyway, even if we did bump into him.

"Thank you." I'd drunk all my drink already, but I sipped at my cup, so she wouldn't know. "I won't get hurt though. We're just friends."

"Uh hurr."

Mum seemed relaxed and, again, so many questions tumbled around my head, wanting to launch themselves off my tongue.

"Do you..." I started. "Do you ever miss home?" Thinking it was an easy one to lead into more.

"Of course," Mum said. She stood up, and I could see her drink wasn't finished. There was still half left. She was standing up anyway.

"The weekend staff arrive tomorrow," she said, like the question I'd asked before wasn't totally loaded, wasn't so totally a question with more questions behind it. "That's always a fun campfire. All that new energy..."

I winced at the word "energy" – feeling spent. Like all my optimism had bungee-jumped right out the small cabin window. All I wanted was a few answers...that wasn't too much, was it?

For her it was.

"Sleep well, poppet."

She rubbed my hair, making it frizz, and padded in her embroidered nightgown back to her bedroom.

I stared at the door for a while, playing with my empty cup. The sugar from the cocoa had woken me up.

I went back to my cramped little room and got out my sketchpad, doodling and pencilling and shading until all the bad thoughts quietened down enough so I could finally fall asleep.

Situations that are destined to fail:

Whiskey + Family history of drinking

\+

Whiskey + Cancelled trips to LA

\+

Whiskey + Repressed emotions of several years

\+

Whiskey

Eighteen

Mum was right. The weekend relief staff did bring new energy.

They arrived in jeeps, each cradling a rucksack, picking up the children for hugs and brimming over with the enthusiasm we'd all got too tired to muster. At campfire that night, us regulars just relaxed and let them do all the work.

They were desperate to make the kids love them in the time they'd missed. They started games and sang stupid loud songs, and basically did everything for us, so we could take it in turns to sneak into the fringes of the woods and knock back shots of Russ's whiskey.

"I love the weekend staff," I declared, to Russ, Kyle, Whinnie and Bryony, as I took my second shot and peered at the celebratory madness happening around the fire. "I love the weekend staff, and I really like that it's the weekend."

Russ took the whiskey bottle from me. "I'm so jealous! I don't think my body can handle another game of paintball."

We all laughed as Russ showed us his epic bruises. We'd been paintballing in the forest that day. Always looking for attention, Russ had been screaming "CAN'T GET ME" at all of the children. So, of course, it became a massive game of Get Russ.

I'd managed to only receive one direct hit – from Calvin – who stalked me through the woods, huffing and puffing behind me.

"Well I got two bruises, one on each butt cheek." Bryony took the bottle off Russ. "I swear Calvin is such a perv." She took a drink and passed it to Kyle. "You still on for LA tomorrow?"

I looked up.

"Hang on," I said. "You guys are going to LA too?"

Kyle nodded and drank. "You want to join us, Amber?"

"I can't," I said. "I'm going to LA with my mum…we're going hiking."

The whiskey felt warm inside me, which, combined with the heat of the fire, led to extra warmness.

"Hiking?" Bryony pulled a face. "With our boss?"

"Well, she's my mum."

"You're going to miss out. Let me know if you wanna ditch her. We're going to get so wasted. It will be amazing." Bryony peered out at the fire. "Right, I better get back there. They're attacking the weekenders."

We all followed her gaze and – true enough – loads of Dumbledore's Army had started to leap on our relief staff. They looked like they were covered in barnacles –

kid-shaped barnacles. A high school girl with blonde hair down to her bottom looked like she was about to buckle under the weight…then she did…falling forward, with twelve kids on top of her.

I felt Kyle stand just to the side of me.

"Why does it sometimes feel like we're babysitting a zombie apocalypse?" I asked him.

"Ouch! That was fun. Can you get off me, please…like now, please? Ouch!" The blonde girl was trying to keep her voice as Disney as possible but you could tell she was hurting and annoyed. Bryony wove through the madness and helped pull her out.

"Be careful of our new staff now, please. Calvin, I saw you jump on her!" He gave her a defiant chubby grin full of chins. Bryony turned back to our gap in the woods and mouthed the word "*help*".

"We better go," I said.

"We better."

Russ passed out breath mints so Mum and Bumface Kevin wouldn't smell the whiskey and we took it in turns to innocently return to the campfire.

Whinnie went first.

"Who's going to LA then?" I asked Kyle, as we watched Whinnie's backside wobble into the circle…she'd had a lot of whiskey already.

Kyle let out a big sigh. "Umm, well me and Bryony. Wayne, Jessie, Jude, and, er, Melody."

Melody, of course Melody was going. They'd probably

have attractive-person sex in the grubby nightclub toilets, just so they could juxtapose with something.

"You looking forward to spending time with your mum?"

I smiled and looked out for her by the fire. "Yes… Yes, I really am."

It was Kyle's turn. He crunched up his mint, releasing mentholy vapours on his breath that made my nose tingle. "See you in there."

I leaned against the prickly bark of a tree and watched him weave through the crowd. The children mobbed him and Melody came up and ruffled his hair playfully. They shared a secret smile… Well it would've been a secret smile if I hadn't been skulking about and watching them from the darkness like a creepy person.

I wondered what it must feel like to be him – Kyle. To be so popular. For every entrance anywhere to feel ceremonial.

It was my turn.

I made my way back into the clearing and picked through the children to sit down next to Mum. Bumface Kevin had his guitar out.

Oh no – *Kum ba ya* time. He bloody loved that song.

Mum smiled warmly and put her arm around me, cuddling me into her.

"Where did you go?" she asked. I didn't answer at first, just burrowed myself further into her. Not caring if it looked childish or unprofessional.

"I had to pee," I lied. "I've just about got the hang of

doing it in the woods now." Another lie. Eight times I'd tried and eight times I'd got significant amounts of urine down my leg.

Kevin strummed his guitar and the circle fell quiet. Everyone settled down on their logs, sensing the beginning of a sing-song. Another camp counsellor, Susan, whose frizzy hair rivalled mine, came and joined Kevin with her guitar. The fire crackled and everyone's faces looked still and peaceful. There was just something about this song that made everyone calm down.

"Kum ba ya, my Lord, kum ba ya," they sang smoothly, and we all joined in. The innocence of the children's voices sang pure and clean. "Kum ba ya, my Lord, kum ba ya."

I sang as quietly as I could, so as not to ruin it. Everyone always says they "can't sing" to be modest, but in my case it was the utter truth. I sounded like a toad being trod on by a stiletto.

"Someone's singing, my Lord, kum ba ya."

"Someone's singing, my Lord, kum ba ya."

Mum pulled away from me.

"Oh, Amber," she said. "I forgot to tell you."

My heart instantly started hurting. She was whispering, but she was using the voice. The breezy *I'm-about-to-let-you-down-but-I-have-a-good-reason* voice.

"What is it?" I asked, a lump already in my throat.

"About LA. Can we reschedule, honey? The centre called this afternoon. They're completely flooded with people and they need my help. That's okay if I go, right? I mean, they really need me there."

"But..." I knew she volunteered to help other addicts. And, I knew it was awful, but I wished she didn't. All of those people would've hurt others as much as she'd hurt me – why did they deserve my mum? Especially over me.

Tears. They couldn't come. Not now. Not in front of everyone.

"The weekend is always so busy there," she continued. Oblivious to my heartbreak, or maybe just very practised at shutting it out. "You can come, of course. But it won't be very fun."

"It's my only weekend off." I choked.

"Shh, yes. But you're off in another two weeks."

"Exactly. Our only chance to spend time together for at least two weeks."

Mum's voice sharpened. "Amber, don't make me feel bad. I made a commitment to help that shelter. I can't exactly let them down because my teenage daughter wants to look at the Hollywood Sign."

"Someone's crying, my Lord, kum ba ya," the camp sang. "Someone's crying, my Lord, kum ba ya."

"Anyway," she said. "We're seeing loads of each other. You're living with me. We had a lovely hot chocolate last night, didn't we?"

"For about two minutes." My voice verged on the cusp of an emotional eruption.

"Come on, Amber." She put her arm around me, and I

hated myself for softening into her touch. "Isn't there a group of them all going to LA? You can tag along with them. I know you're disappointed, but that shelter means a lot to me…I need it…I need to help."

"Someone's praying, my Lord, kum ba ya."

The light melody of the children's voices combined with the scratchy soulful plucking of Kevin's guitar was too much. Mum joined in with the singing again, like that was the end of it. But I couldn't. If I even opened my mouth for a second, a sob would break loose.

Everyone around me looked warm and cosy and at peace. It took all my physical strength to keep my bottom jaw from wobbling. Waves of grief and anger and guilt and hurt crashed and thrashed inside of me as I sat on that log, my mother's arm still around me.

As my face scanned the scene, I caught Kyle's eye.

He was watching me. He wasn't singing either.

"Are you okay?" he mouthed.

I didn't even have the energy to lie, or pretend it was fine, that I wasn't on the verge of breaking in a way that was utterly irrevocably Humpty Dumpty.

I gave a slight shake of my head. He stood instantly, to make his way over.

I stood too, shaking Mum's arm off.

"I need a wee." Even though my voice was full of crying she didn't stop me, or ask if I was okay.

"Again?"

"Yep."

I ran back into the safety of the trees, not knowing if Kyle was following, not particularly caring.

I needed more whiskey.

Just another shot or two, to make it go away, to make me feel like I had some warmth left.

Russ had hidden the bottle under a pile of pine needles. I untwisted the top and, without even wincing, downed a quarter of the bottle in one go. It burned my throat, scorching down into my stomach, curdling it instantly. That's what I wanted. It felt good that it hurt. That there was simple physical pain with a simple physical explanation – rather than this twisted unexplainable wrench of an ache in my guts that I knew came from a place that therapists like to find.

I coughed. Leaned back, and tipped another quarter to the back of my throat. It felt terrible and brilliant at the same time. A rush tingled through my body as the alcohol soaked into my blood system.

"Amber?" Kyle called, and I quickly hid the bottle again.

"Here."

He appeared through the pine trees, the fire behind him, lighting him all up.

"What's happened?" he asked, getting closer. Not too close. Not touching close. His long arms flagged uselessly at his sides, like he didn't know what to do with them.

"My…" I started, then turned back to the campfire. The calm atmosphere had broken. Kevin had put his guitar away and Melody and Bryony dragged the old iPod and speakers into the centre of the circle, getting ready to start the disco. The kids jumped on the weekend staff and yanked at their clothes with excitement.

I couldn't hold it in any more. "It's my mum…" I bent over on myself, like a folded piece of paper and dropped onto the dusty floor. "She…she…"

Kyle dropped too so he was balancing on the balls of his feet. He awkwardly put his hand on my shoulder. "She what?"

An echoing sob broke loose, I covered my mouth to try and contain it. It echoed around the forest, bouncing about the trees – my misery echoing around and reflecting itself back to me.

I was so alone.

I was in a strange stupid country, in a strange stupid camp, with no real friends, and why? Why was I doing this? To see my mother who didn't want to see me? To force her to love me? Force her to care when it should be something that comes naturally?

I wanted Evie, and Lottie, and my dad even. He left Mum and married that nightmare bitch, and broke Mum and it was awful, but he never left me. But she did…

Dad was asleep in bed probably, five thousand miles away and I was here. In the strange forest, with a boy I hardly knew, uncomfortably patting my shoulder and saying "*hush*".

I stood up so quickly my head spun and I turned on my ankle. "She's not taking me to LA any more."

Eight small words. One teeny sentence. To almost everyone, it would mean nothing. A minor disappointment. A last minute, *can't-be-helped* change of plans.

Not to me.

"Oh..." I could hear the hesitation in his voice, as he struggled to match this information to my sobbing. "I guess you were really looking forward to it, huh?"

I wiped my eyes with the back of my hand. My tummy really hurt. The alcohol already hitting me. The strong bassline of a Katy Perry song thrummed through the trees. The dancing had begun.

"We should go back," I said.

"You still seem upset."

"I am." I rooted around in the pine needles and got out the bottle again. I took three deep swigs.

"Want some?" I asked.

"I'm okay... Amber?"

I was already walking back into the circle.

"Teenage Dreams" blared out the stereo and the kids whizzed in circles, yelling along to some of the lyrics.

I was drunk by then. Already very drunk.

"WHINNIE!" I yelled, swinging my arms around her when I found her in the circle.

"Whoa, ouch." Her face got buried into my shoulder with the blunt force of my hug.

"HEY, KIDS!" I let go of Whinnie and picked up the

hands of two little girls and spun them round. "LET'S SEE HOW FAST WE CAN GO."

I spun them and spun them. They shrieked and giggled. I stumbled over my foot and fell to the dusty ground, bringing the two girls on top of me.

"Oomph." The two little girls were laughing. "We fell, we fell." I was about to laugh too but Russ's firm hand gripped me and pulled me up.

"What the holy Moses are you doing, Amber?" he whispered angrily in my ear.

I rolled my eyes at him. "It was an ACCIDENT," I hiccuped.

"You stink! Have you been drinking more whiskey?"

I shrugged, but covered my mouth with my hand. "I have insurance."

I wasn't sure if that was true, but I'd heard other Americans say it before.

"You need to sober up. At the very least, chew some gum."

"I don't need...to do...anything."

I looked over his shoulder. Whinnie was helping the girls up, who, to be fair, were totally unharmed. The song changed, to "Gangnam Style", and the children screamed and started galloping on the spot. Kyle appeared, gently pushing kids out the way, trying to get to me.

Oh no...not a lecture. I wanted to have FUN.

I galloped over to Bryony and Melody.

"Hey, guys," I said, jumping madly on the spot.

"Hey," Bryony replied.

Melody looked a little unfriendly. Though, this was like the only time I'd really spoken to her since that first night at the bonfire.

"Shall we slut drop then?" And, before they could say anything, I was in the dirt, falling over in the dust, cackling madly.

"Ooooo, I'm so sexy," I said. "Look at me and how sexy I am. Because being sexy is SO important, isn't it, Melody?"

Melody ducked down to pull me up. She wasn't smiling. "What the hell is your problem?" she asked.

I fell back down again when she let go too soon.

"You know what you are…" I said, suddenly angry. I was gonna tell her. Tell her how she was failing the sisterhood… tell her how there were academic books that condemned her behaviour….tell her that ACTUALLY I could see that she had brown roots…because that is a totally feminist thing to say. People were looking. Why was everyone looking? The music was still playing but there was less dancing. I looked about… Mum was heading straight for me, her eyebrows arched together with anger. Kevin was following her. No… No… I couldn't be told off, not now. I needed to run away. God, my head was spinning. Spinning so fast. Spin spin spin. Hang on? What was I going to say to Melody? I was gonna tell her! My stomach hurt. Mum was almost here.

"You know what you are…" I tried again. Melody wasn't even there any more. She'd left me in the dust and was dancing with her back to me. She and Bryony had their arms around each other and were doing deliberate sexy dance moves, all stroking each other… Show-offs…such show-offs… I never showed off… Maybe that's why Mum didn't notice me. Why she never talked about me… Maybe that's why… She didn't even care…my own mum…didn't even care.

A sob escaped, just as I felt a sharp tug under my armpit.

"Amber, let's get out of here." It was Whinnie's voice. But the grip was too strong to be Whinnie's.

"Whinnie?" I slid to my feet, like Bambi on the ice.

"Quick." Kyle's voice. He was the one touching me. God, he was strong. So strong. "Her mum's almost here. Up you get, Amber, come on."

I started crying. Children looked.

"Amber's not feeling well," I heard Whinnie tell someone. My mum? My mum was there now, but Whinnie was blocking her. "Kyle and I can look after her. I've got the weekend staff, so they can put my cabin to bed."

"You okay, Amber, honey?" Mum didn't look worried. Well, I couldn't tell. I couldn't really see much. All a blurry blur. Blur…

"Can't go to LA…" I muttered, stumbling on nothing, being righted by Kyle.

"Yep," he said, all loudly. "Too ill to go to LA with us, what a shame. Was it the hot dogs we had for dinner, Amber?"

He steered me away, through the circles of kids. Why were there always kids here? They were everywhere, like oxygen – but more annoying than oxygen. I didn't want to see another child for a very long time.

Walking... Walking... Out of the fire circle, into the forest.

Not going to LA...

It's okay... We may spend some time together in two weeks.

Not seen her for two years.

Tummy hurt.

Tummy really hurt.

I let go of Kyle and Whinnie and ran away from them, into the pitch darkness.

"AMBER," they called frantically. Ten metres, twenty metres. Couldn't see. So dark. Tummy really hurt. Too much whiskey.

Tummy...

I doubled over and was violently sick all over the forest floor. Crying and being sick. Sobbing and being sick. Whenever a new sob came out, more sick came out with it.

"MUM!" I screamed into the darkness. The word that causes me the most pain. The word that, to everyone else, brings the opposite. Brings them warmth, and love, and light and understanding and stability and security...

More sobbing, more sick. Everything hurt. My throat was on fire. My stomach felt like it had been shredded in a cheese grater.

Someone was holding my hair back. Someone was rubbing my back.

It was dark, so dark. In all the different ways – literally, metaphorically...

"Do you think she's done?"

It was Whinnie's voice. Whinnie's lovely American voice.

"Mum," I whimpered, coughing up something else.

More patting on my back. "Your mum thinks you've got food poisoning." Kyle's voice. Kyle's all-American golden boy voice of honey and niceness. "We couldn't let her smell the whiskey on you. We'd all get fired."

"She'd just be jealous," I wailed. "Because she wants it… all the time she wants it…that's why she's such a bitch."

I flinched as I said it. But it was true.

"Amber, why don't we move over here?" Whinnie asked. "Away from…umm…your puddle. And there's more light."

"What puddle? Oh…"

I looked down – I'd made such a mess. I wasn't even embarrassed. They manoeuvred me through the darkness, leaning me gently against a pine tree. I slumped to the floor, the bark scratching up my back as I did.

"I want to go home," I sobbed. Then I sobbed harder, because I didn't know where home was. It certainly wasn't here. But it wasn't really with Dad either, with my cow of a stepmum and my devilspawn of a stepbrother, and all of them secretly counting down the days until I left for Art College.

Whinnie kept rubbing my back, and said nice cooing things. I think Kyle just stared at me. I wasn't sure. I ran back to my puddle to be sick once more, then collapsed again.

I was sobering up already. The whiskey had spent such a brief time in my body, it hadn't had the chance to make much of an impact. It was grief keeping me on the floor now more than anything. All my hopes and fantasies for this summer melted inside of me, dripping out of my eyes, and merging into a puddle in the pine needles.

Whinnie stood up. "I need to find her mum."

"Why?" Kyle asked.

"She needs to see this. She needs to look after her."

"NO!" Kyle and I yelled at the same time.

"Please no." I tried getting up but my legs collapsed under me. Kyle bent down to steady me and I sort of collapsed sideways onto him, my head resting on his shoulder.

"Her mum's the reason she's so upset," he said, like I wasn't there. "I don't trust her to be helpful right now."

Even in my sicky fuggy haze, the truth of Kyle's words burned into me. He was so right. There was no way Mum would care for me when I was like this. No way she'd have an epiphany about her behaviour and rub my back and say it would all be different now. She'd dodge the blame. She'd bury down the guilt till it was six foot under. She'd yell at me. Tell me I was selfish. Irresponsible. Stupid. All the adjectives you use about teenagers whose parents have let them down and fucked them up and left them screaming inside, trying to get on with the shitty business of growing up when there's a gaping chasm of a hole where your feeling of solid roots was supposed to be.

"I'm all right..." I said, hesitantly, as I blatantly wasn't. "I just need some time...before...seeing her again... It was a shock."

Whinnie looked torn – the whites of her eyes were so bright against the rest of her face.

"She'll wonder where you are. I can't get fired, Amber. I really can't..."

I made to stand up. The last thing I wanted was for them to get into trouble. But Kyle pushed me back into him again.

"You go find her," he told Whinnie. "Say we've got her in the rec hall toilets because they're flushable. Say she's got food poisoning because she didn't cook her hot dog properly. Say Melody and Bryony are looking after her, not me. She hates me."

Whinnie hovered on one leg. "What if she comes to see her?"

"She won't," I said.

Clutching my stomach, I padded to their bedroom door, and knocked lightly.

No answer.

I whimpered, hoping they'd hear and wake up. Too embarrassed to call. I mean, I was fourteen, but I was sick...so sick...I needed them.

Nothing. I knocked louder.

"Mum? Dad?"

The door creaked open. Dad came out in his dressing gown.

"Dad, I've been sick. Like really sick."

"Amber, you poor thing! Where?!"

"All over my bed. I'm sorry. I didn't get to the bathroom in time. It hurts..."

It had hit me again, and I vomited all over him, all over myself, all over the corridor carpet.

He didn't get angry. He didn't even look grossed-out. He just kept stroking the hair back off my sweaty face and ran me a bath. He scrubbed the carpet while I washed, and he cleaned my sheets, and put new ones on. Then tucked me in when he was sure I'd stopped being sick. He curled up on the carpet next to my bed with a blanket.

I'd woken up crying. Been sick again. And again. And again.

"Where's Mum?"

That look came over his face. The one he used when he was about to lie.

"Mum's sick too," he said. "She was sick earlier. You must've got the same bug."

Mum slept through the whole thing.

I didn't stop being sick. I vomited for two days straight and ended up in hospital.

Salmonella. From the half-cooked chicken Mum had given me for dinner. The chicken I'd thought tasted funny but, when I questioned her, she'd flown off the handle and started screaming and ranting and I ate it just to shut her up, to try and calm her down before Dad got home.

She'd been too drunk to eat hers of course.

The day they discharged me from hospital was the day Dad took us to Penny's house.

Kyle and I didn't talk for some time.

There was almost no light, no noise, just us and the forest. Kyle didn't rush me to talk, but he kept holding me.

Eventually, I said, "She's an alcoholic."

My head sank on his shoulder as he breathed out heavily. "I'd figured out as much."

"She's been sober for over two years, after she went to this rehab place. We're all so proud of her." I could hear how hollow it sounded in my own voice.

He didn't say anything. I shuffled back so I was supported more by the tree. I wondered why he was here. Why he was always here. Why he was always trying to help me.

"Why are you always here?" I asked. The leftover whiskey made my thoughts tumble out of my mouth.

Kyle didn't reply for a moment. All I could hear was the rustle of the pine needles on the slight breeze.

"I'm...not sure," he admitted.

"I'm glad you're here." More words tumbled out with the whiskey. "I'm very far away from home and it's nice that you're here."

I coughed, my throat hurting. I must stink...

"You going to come with us to LA tomorrow?" Kyle asked. "A bunch of us have rented a van."

"I...I don't know."

I didn't want to go, not now. But if I stayed, then what? Just wander about the camp watching the weekend staff do my job? Trying not to cry about Mum? Or follow her to San Francisco and wait about in the city, seeing the sights I'd already seen, until she was ready to spend time with me? "I don't want to. But I don't know where else to go. I wish I could drive."

"Where would you go?"

I closed my eyes and pictured where I was on a map of the world. "Somewhere beautiful," I finally said. "Somewhere that isn't full of maniac children. Somewhere that would make me want to sketch. Somewhere that would put everything in perspective."

Kyle laughed. "Well, you're in the right place. America is full of big views."

"But I can't get to them... Maybe LA will be fun."

"Won't you be too hungover?" he asked, reminding me of what I'd just done. What he'd just seen. I was glad the darkness hid my blushing.

"I'll be fine. If I'm sick, I'm always totally fine the next day."

Was it bad that I knew that about myself? Was it bad I'd been sick enough times from drinking to figure this out?

Kyle was, evidently, thinking the same thing.

"Why do you drink so much? Hasn't it all...put you off it?"

I let out a big sigh, and let the remaining alcohol in my blood answer the question honestly.

"Out of spite, I think," I admitted. "Because I know she wants to do it, and she can't. Even if I'm five thousand miles away and she has no idea, I can do it, and she can't."

"You do know how fucked up that sounds, right?"

"Have you got an alcoholic parent?"

He didn't answer for a while. Then, "Nope. I don't think anything that's a big deal has ever happened to me."

I turned to him, keeping my mouth at a respectable distance so he couldn't smell the vomit on my breath. "Oh poor Golden Boy, you almost sound wistful."

He did one short laugh. "Maybe I am."

"Everyone who's never had drama always wants drama. I think they think it makes them more important, or deep, or something. That they'd write better diary entries or some bullshit like that. You know what? All I want to do is hand back my drama and say '*A boring life, please. Anything for a boring life*'."

"That's me told."

"Good."

"And now can I tell you that it's not wise to drink a lot if your parent is an alcoholic?"

I prickled, my skin actually standing on end. "I know the stats," I replied. "I know alcoholism can be in your genes." I stopped. "But I'll never be like her…I'd rather die than be like her."

"You won't be like her if you stop drinking," he offered.

A small patch of moonlight had found its way through the dense overhang of trees and landed right on Kyle's face, highlighting all the good bits. I wondered once more why he was here, why he was so confusing, what he wanted, why he kept making me think there was…something… and yet, Mum had warned me so clearly that that was just his way.

"Why does my mum hate you so much?" I asked, and he turned to me with a grim smile on his face.

"She's not my biggest fan this summer. I didn't think she would hire me again – but Kevin loves me."

"What happened?"

He shuffled his weight, reshifting himself against the rough bark of the tree. Already I dreaded what he was going to say. My heart went all fluttery, and my mouth got even dryer.

"I don't want to upset you."

"I think it's fair to say that I'm already pretty upset."

Another small grin. "Well, we got on really well last summer. I do, did, like your mum. I think she took a liking to me, she called me 'Golden Boy', like you do, and did little things like bring our group ice cream sometimes, just our group. Then, one night, a kid in my cabin got really sick – like projectile vomiting sick. I woke up Russ so he could look after him and then I ran to get your mum from her cabin as she's the main first-aider. I thought she'd be asleep. But when I got there, I saw the light on. Your mum was in the kitchen…" He stopped.

"Go on," I said. I was already crying again, silent tears dropping down my face.

"She was holding a tumbler glass of what looked like whiskey…and she was sobbing…like uncontrollably sobbing. Her hands were shaking, she was hysterical. I didn't know what to do, so I just stood and watched. And then, she screamed and threw the glass against the wall. It smashed everywhere, glass flew all over the kitchen. Even though I was outside, I ducked. Kevin came running in, and she was making this weird noise, like '*nooooo, nooooo*'. He hugged her while she cried on him…and then, she looked out the window and saw me. Just standing there, staring…"

I was holding my breath. Had she drunk any of the whiskey? Had she fallen off the wagon again? Or did she stop herself?

And Kyle, I was scared for him. Even though it was in the past, and he was right there, next to me in the woods, safe and sound, I was scared for him.

"What happened?" I almost didn't want to know.

"When she saw me, she must've stiffened or something because then Kevin turned and saw me. I was like a rabbit caught in headlights. I even waved! Kevin whispered something to her and then he was outside. I was so scared. I mean, I really need this job! I started babbling, saying, '*One of the kids is sick, I need a first-aider. I'm sorry. I didn't mean to… I just need someone to come and help.*' The whole time your mum was just looking at me out the window. I could see her so clearly with the kitchen lights on. I'll never forget the look on her face." He paused. "The whole thing was dark, Amber, really dark."

I stilled. I could picture it now, as if it was playing like a film in the front of my brain. I could see her expression; I'd seen it so many times before. The *who-can-I-blame-that-isn't-me?* face. I thought that face had died when she went to the rehab place. When she started her journey of getting better but leaving me behind. But the face had been here all summer. She was sober, yeah, but she still blamed everyone but herself.

"Anyway," Kyle continued, "Kevin helped me. He didn't say anything as we walked back to my cabin. It was the most awkward walk of my life. Just before we arrived he said, '*You know already it's not a good idea to tell anyone about this*', and that was it. Your mum...well I wasn't Golden Boy after that, that's for sure. Everything I did the rest of the summer was wrong. I kept getting shouted at for the tiniest things. I really didn't think I'd get the job again. I didn't tell anyone, I kept my promise. I've not told anyone until now... I guess it doesn't count if it's you."

I hurt. My throat was still raw. The tears did nothing to dull the pain – they only made it worse. My heart was in pieces, bits of it scattered over the campfire, lumps of my flesh left all over the forest floor.

The one thing that had got me through up till now, the one thing that helped, was knowing that – despite everything – she was sober. She was dry. And if that meant sacrificing me, if that meant her coming here, and having her healthy life in the mountains with Kevin and her never seeing me, if that was what she needed to stay dry, to not be that monster I lived with – well…that meant it was just about bearable. But if she relapsed…then why? If it was still hard here – why couldn't she just come home to me?

I really was crying now. Kyle awkwardly patted my back, in that *oh-God-I-really-don't-know-what-to-do* way all boys adopt when a girl is crying. It reached a crescendo whenever I pictured the scene, or whenever I remembered that we weren't going to LA the next day after all. And then, slowly, the tears ran out. Maybe I was too dehydrated to make any more.

"Should I have told you?" he asked, nervously. "I've been wondering since I met you. I wondered how much you knew. Why we'd never really heard of you until this summer…"

"I'm glad you told me." I looked up at him through my hazy tear-stained vision. The moon still caught all his best bits. In this light he looked like an All-American-Dream-Ghost – like if Casper won Prom King. He looked right back at me. We were so close. Our noses almost touching, his hand still on my back… I wondered if this was how close he'd been to Melody before they got together and did whatever they did… That thought hurt. I backed away, leaning against the tree again.

Noise. Noises in the wood.

"Guuuuuuys?"

It was Whinnie.

"Guuuuuys, you out here?"

Kyle took one last look at me and then turned in the direction of her voice.

"Whinnie?" he called.

"Where are you?" The uncertain wobble of torchlight came out from behind a tree, making both of us squint. I tried to stand, but struggled, and Kyle took my hand to pull me up. Whinnie's torch found us like a spotlight, and I turned my face from it, as it scorched into my eyes.

"Oh, thank God. I thought I was going to get eaten by a coyote before I found you." She ran over and hugged me. "How are you feeling? You look like the last survivor from a horror movie. Everyone else has gone to bed, but your mum is going frantic and Russ is pissed at you for drinking all the whiskey..."

"I bet he is," Kyle muttered.

"Well, he wasn't to know...everything," Whinnie said.

My stomach blobbed with yet more guilt. "I'll pay him back. I'll get some in LA tomorrow. If I can get served."

"You coming to LA?" Kyle and Whinnie both asked at the same time.

I shrugged. "What choice do I have? Where else do I go?"

"Do you want to go to LA?" Kyle asked. I shook my head instinctively.

"Honestly? No. But I don't want to hang around here in Kevin's cabin, feeling guilty that I'm not working. And I don't particularly feel like wandering around San Francisco, waiting for my mum to give a shit about me. I don't drive yet, and you can't walk anywhere in this bloody country. So yeah...LA. Great..."

Kyle gave me another big searching look. I swear he got searching looks on special offer at the emotion store or something. 2-4-1.

I stretched my legs, my heart feeling numb. Probably because half of it was still burning on the campfire. "Let's go."

We all walked back through the darkness, past the smoking corpse of the spent campfire, and along the twisted path towards the centre of camp.

"Thanks, guys." I was sobering up enough to feel very very embarrassed about the last two hours. "I'm not usually so drama."

Whinnie smiled and squeezed my hand.

"Yeah," she said. "What's up with that? I thought you guys were supposed to repress everything with a stiff upper lip until you're constipated."

"America is wearing off on you," Kyle added.

We all laughed. And I never thought I'd laugh on that evening. Not without Lottie and Evie anyway. All sorts of American sentimental gushes flooded through me – with added emotional gushes of something else that I felt for Kyle… Something that I was certainly going to repress, as I'd been hurt and rejected enough for one summer thank you very much.

Whinnie handed me some gum. "Here,". she said. "So you don't smell like Jack Daniels."

"Thanks, Whinnie, for you know, helping."

She gave me a sad *feeling-sorry-for-you* smile. "Well the word 'counsellor' is in the job title."

Eventually we stepped out of the dense forest overhang, the moonlight almost as bright as the sun. It hung all big and proud of itself in the sky.

"Why don't I take you back to the cabin?" Whinnie suggested. She gave Kyle a knowing look. "It might be better if it's just me."

Kyle nodded. "Cool, well I better go see if the weekenders have managed to get my clan to sleep. See you tomorrow, Amber. For LA?"

LA. I really didn't want to go to LA…

"Yeah, sure." I wanted to say so much more but Whinnie was there. I didn't know how to thank him. "Thanks again, and tell Russ I'll try and replace the drink."

"Don't worry about that. Night."

"Night."

Whinnie steered me to my cabin without asking what had happened while she'd been gone. She didn't even ask why I'd gotten so wasted and I loved her for that. Maybe she was just doing what Winnie the Pooh would've done.

Mum flung the door open and her arms around me. I was so shocked by the intensity of her affection I almost fell over.

"Amber, you poor thing. How are you feeling?" she gasped into my shoulder. "Was it the hot dogs? Aww, you poor munchkin. Have you been sick? You smell quite sick."

Despite everything that had happened I dissolved into her, hugging her back so hard – like a diver gasping for oxygen, not knowing when they'd get any more.

Kevin stepped out, stopping halfway through the door, so he was all highlighted from the lamp inside.

"Thanks for looking after her, Whinnie. We've got her from here."

I waved as Mum took me inside, her arm still round me. "My poor little baby. You just vanished! We didn't know where you were. I was so worried. It's horrible being sick, poor thing. What can I get you? Let's tuck you up on the sofa, hmm? Kevin? Will you get Amber some water?"

Water came. I drank it. More came. I drank more.

I wasn't even the slightest bit drunk any more, just drained.

Mum was stroking my hair, singing softly, one of my favourite Peter Alsop songs, the one she used to sing at bedtime – if she wasn't passed out before me.

"*Go to sleep, you little creep,*" she sang softly, her husky voice warming each word like a microwave. "*It's time to get undressed.*"

I was being carried to my room. My sicky T-shirt was raised over my head, I was put on my side. My pillow was fluffed. She kept stroking my hair. Everything was warm, so warm. Mum was being the mum I remembered from way back. The one that I knew was in there, somewhere…

I was so very tired.

"*We love you when you're wide awake, but when you sleep we love you best.*"

And the last thing I heard was Mum giggling at the funniest line as I slumped into a happy but confused unconsciousness.

Situations that are destined to fail:

Woken before 5 a.m.

+

With a hangover

+

By a boy you really quite like

Nineteen

I woke.

It hit me.

It all hit me.

I wasn't going to LA with Mum. She'd chosen a rehab centre over spending time with me. I'd gotten *so* drunk. I'd drunk all of Russ's whiskey. I'd been sick – oh God! In front of Kyle! And Whinnie! I'd cried, I'd told Kyle everything.

Why why why why why why why why? WHY?

I sat bolt upright, the uncomfortable yanking twist of humiliation wrenching my stomach. Such an idiot. Why was I such an idiot? Why was I just like her?

All the sadness came too – she wasn't coming with me today. She cancelled.

Just like that.

Just like that.

There was a gentle knocking at my window. What? I was still half asleep. Did I really hear that?

Another knock.

I leaned over and opened it.

Kyle's face was in my window, smiling in a way that could make you hand over all your money and worldly belongings. My eyes widened, in total shock.

"It's you," I said. So shocked I couldn't think of anything else to say.

"Good morning." He was smiling so hard now.

"You're in my window."

"I am."

I rubbed my sleepy eyes. "But why?"

I noticed something was wrong. Different. The forest was very quiet. The sun wasn't out yet… Hang on…it was still dark.

"I'm taking you away," he said.

"What?"

"I've got my jeep. It's got a full tank of gas. I'm taking us away for the weekend."

I rubbed my eyes again, to check he was really there.

"What time is it?"

"Four a.m. Don't you want to know where we're going?"

"FOUR A.M.? I've only been asleep four hours."

"You can sleep in the jeep."

What was happening? Why was he here? Why was a Prom King in the window? That doesn't happen to people, especially to people like me.

"I thought you'd be more excited."

"I'm still trying to work out if you're real." I folded my

arms over myself to hide my not-in-bra boobs. I was wearing practically nothing – just a tiny pair of shorts and a vest.

"I'm real."

"What about LA?" I asked, starting to wake up now.

"You don't need LA today. I'm taking you somewhere much better." He really couldn't stop smiling. I hadn't seen someone look more proud since Craig did a poo so big it blocked the toilet and he made Dad take a photo of it. Yep, that happened.

Slowly, realizing what was going on, I smiled.

"So where's better than LA?"

"It's a surprise."

"What do I bring then?"

"Good climbing shoes, sunscreen, lots of water. Your sketchbook."

"Hang on. I won't be long."

I closed the curtains and cobbled some stuff together. Smiling the whole time.

Within half an hour we were in Kyle's jeep, careering through the winding mountain roads, the sun just about to rise. There was a dark red scorch mark in the sky where it was due to go up, but other than that, it was just an inky blue sky, and the sound of nothing but our engine.

I'd scribbled Mum a quick note:

Gone to LA. Back tomorrow. Have fun at the centre.

If she knew where I was, and who I was with, she would

go mental. Or maybe she wouldn't care. Either way, yesterday's pain had matured overnight into a simmering pot of anger. But I put it on the backburner so I could enjoy the wind blowing my hair, and the sight of Kyle driving confidently, one arm slung casually on the ledge of the open car window.

There were some questions I deliberately wasn't asking myself. Why was Kyle here? Why was he doing this? Where was he taking me? What does this mean? I mean, one, I hardly knew him and, two, I seemed to be his charity project for the summer or something. He'd been with Melody and probably was still with Melody, and I didn't know how she felt about any of this. But I was fed up with questions. That's all my life had been for years. Why? How? But? Why? Please? Why? Why? Asking them constantly – of my mother, of the universe, of myself. I wasn't getting any answers, so I reckoned I'd try being one of those smug people who live in The Now for a weekend.

Kyle reached down by his long legs and pulled out a flask, handing it over to me. "Here," he said. "Have some coffee."

I unscrewed the top, and took a sniff. It smelled so good, steam rising up from the narrow funnel of the flask. "How did you have time to make this? How do you even own a flask?"

He kept his eyes on the road. "I'm American. I live in the mountains. I know how to do long car journeys."

"And how long will this car journey be?"

"It will be approximately as long as it needs to be."

"Since when did you become Yoda?" I took a sip of my coffee, it was still super hot. And nice, very nice.

"Is that helping your headache?"

I took another sip. "I don't have a headache. I never get one if I…" Puke. But I didn't want to say that, I didn't want to remind him of all the vastly unattractive puking I'd done in front of him the night before. "… Drink water before bed," I finished meekly.

I handed the flask back to him and he took a deep swig. It was so hard to look at him without looking like I was looking at him. He handed it back so I could screw the top back on, then nestled it down under his legs again.

"Well then, if you don't have a headache, you won't mind listening to some music." He smiled slyly, pressed play on his beat-up stereo system, and Peter Alsop came blaring out the speakers.

I sat up in my car seat.

"Oh my God. You have the Peter Alsop CDs? I've literally not listened to these in years!" The opening song of the *Wha' D'ya Wanna Do?* CD started playing and I almost felt like crying. Those guitar chords, his voice, the funny-for-kids lyrics, "No one ever plays with me, I'm bored, bored, bored!"

I was back there, in the car with my mum, singing along at the tops of our voices, giggling at all the jokes we knew so well.

We both started singing along. Kyle's singing voice was as crap as mine – his voice too deep, too flat. But he knew every line, just as I did. We sang the first two songs all the way through, as the roads got less windy and downhill, and more straight and more uphill again.

"I still can't believe you have these in your car."

"I only play them when it's just me driving. If there's anyone with me, I play rap. Or anything else that's supposed to be cool."

"Other than me?"

He looked away from the windscreen then, to study my face, and I grew all hot. "Other than you," he confirmed.

The first curve of the sun sneaked up on the edge of the horizon, casting arrowshots of yellow light into the blue of the dying night. Everywhere around us was so vast and empty. We hadn't driven past another car for over half an hour. It was just us. It could be the apocalypse and you wouldn't know. Not here. With just the trees and the bears for company.

A few songs passed.

"Are we there yet?" I asked, as the jeep inched its way around a steep mountain curve.

Kyle concentrated on steering. "As a matter of fact, we are."

"Am I allowed to know where we're going now?"

"We'll see the sign soon."

"There's a sign?"

"Oh yeah."

"And what else?"

He smiled to himself. "You'll see."

Two more twists and then the road widened. Two sleepy-looking cabins sat next to a large sign. My mouth fell open as I read it.

"Yosemite National Park!" I yelled at the top of my voice. So excited, so very excited.

Kyle smiled even more. "You said you wanted mountains."

"I have no idea why you're being so nice to me, but I'm very glad."

A park. A national park. With woods, and trees, and bears, and no alcoholic mothers and screaming children. I was happy then, full to the brim with surprise and excitement and all the good feelings and none of the bad which NEVER happens. We pulled up alongside the cabin and a man dressed as Yogi Bear leaned out of the window.

"One-day pass, please." Kyle handed over some dollars.

"Ya'll here early," Yogi Bear man replied, tipping his hat like a real-life park ranger.

"We're doing the Mist Trail before the crowds hit."

Mist Trail? What's the Mist Trail?

"Well that's a mighty fine idea." He handed Kyle a small sticker which he put in the front of his windscreen.

"Thank you, sir."

And, before I had time to ask for a picture of the man, we drove right into the sunrise. Our surroundings had been pretty awesome just on the drive here, but it was like the car knew we'd just passed a "Welcome to a National Park" sign and upped the scenic ante. We curved around the bottom of rock faces, drove in and out of the dappled sunlight through a thousand pine trees.

"We're almost at the falls, wait for it," Kyle said.

We emerged into the most stunning meadow, with yellow and orange wild flowers peeking out of the tall grasses. And there, in a backdrop so pretty it was like someone had painted it on, was a massive waterfall. The water cascading from seemingly nowhere – like the cliff needed a wee, but something much more profound and artsy sounding than that.

"That's Yosemite Falls," Kyle said, his voice taking on an edge of tour guide. "You should see it when it's at full strength."

We drove past, and I craned my neck to try and hold the view longer.

"Aren't we getting out?" I asked, desperate to get out and be in it. So glad that I had my sketchpad with me.

"In a second, we need to park and get the bus."

"The bus?"

"Yeah. I think the first one is at six."

He steered us past more eye-bulgingly beautiful sights, rapping out names for them with the kind of *bored-but-excited-for-you* voice I used whenever I took someone to London and they were excited at seeing Big Ben for the first time.

"Half Dome," he said, as I pointed towards a rock reigning at the top of the canyon. It looked like it had been sheared right in half with a posh kitchen knife. The sunrise turned the flat rock face orange; I'd literally never seen anything on that scale before.

"Mirror Lake is down that path," he said, pointing to a hole in the forest. "Maybe we'll get time to see it later. It's incredible. Like, well, looking in a mirror."

We drove through another meadow of wild flowers. There were photographers everywhere, crouching down with their tripods in the long grasses.

"Uh oh – the tourists are coming. The tripods are the first warning sign," Kyle said. "We better get there quick."

"Get WHERE?"

Just as I yelled it, we came to a built-up bit. Wooden huts sprung up everywhere. And parking spaces. Lots of parking spaces. Most of them were still empty, but the concrete in amongst all that natural wilderness jarred. Kyle parked effortlessly, with just one hand on the wheel. He turned off the ignition and grinned at me.

"To the best bit. Now, do you have hiking shoes?"

Situations that are destined to fail:

Me

+

Surprises

+

Self-preservation instinct

Twenty

Kyle still wouldn't tell me where we were going as I scrambled into my trainers. Nor would he when we boarded the cute little shuttle bus that drove us around the park. Only when the intercom on the bus said, "*Stop sixteen, Happy Isles!*" did he say, "We're here."

He took my hand to help me down.

Two other tourists got off the bus with us, taking photos instantly. It made me sad that their first memory of this would be through the eye of a lens.

There was a sign – *The Mist Trail – trailhead starts here*.

"What's the Mist Trail then?" I asked.

"It's my favourite part of the park," Kyle said. "But you have to do it before all the tourists arrive. You need to have the trail to yourself to really appreciate it." He started on the trail. "You'll soon see why," he called behind him.

I sighed and followed him.

Initially I wasn't that impressed. There was just a lot of

uphill going on. I mean, it was pretty. There was a raging river to the right of us, and lots of big fat rocks to look at.

But mainly there was a lot of uphill.

Kyle, thankfully, stopped for a short break. I lay back against a rock and caught my breath as attractively as I could.

"I love these big boulders," he said, pointing to a massive rock next to us. "I love thinking that they were just rolling down the cliff one day, rolling rolling, and then, for whatever reason, they lost momentum and stopped right here, and this is where they'll stay now for hundreds or thousands of years."

I liked what he'd said. So much so, that I patted the rock for want of something to do.

"Don't people say it's bad to just be a still rock?" I asked. "Aren't we all supposed to keep rolling so we don't gather any moss or whatever?"

Kyle looked at the boulder. "I like moss," he said. "I like staying still… I guess that's why I'm so boring."

I let go of the rock. "What the hell do you mean?" I asked. "You're not boring!" How could someone like him even think he was boring? He was, like, the main character in every teen movie. Which is what I told him. It just made him look sadder.

"That's the point," he said. "Everything I do is just walking a really clichéd set path, doing what everyone expects of me… I can't see myself doing anything remarkable."

I pulled a face. "What does remarkable even mean?"

"I dunno…" He wouldn't look at me. "…Like you, I guess."

WHAT!?

I perched on a fence protecting us from the river, resting my legs, staring at him in shock. "I'm the least remarkable person ever," I said. "If we're all living in a teen movie, I'm the helpful sidekick friend who never gets their own storyline. I'm the one watching everyone else getting asked to dance at the prom. I'm the one whose sole existence in any story is to help people like *you* find your way..."

I shouldn't have said it, it came out so bitter. I *was* bitter though, much as I didn't want to be. I mean, who wants to be bitter?

Kyle wouldn't look at me for ages, and I watched the tourists overtake us, lugging their camera gear in backpacks. Eventually he spoke. "I don't think you see yourself how I do. How anyone sees you. I don't think you're capable of being a supporting character in any story. It would be impossible."

I felt like crying. Why was he saying this? Why were we even here?

"... I mean, you're so strong..."

"I'm not," I interrupted. "I'm the least strong person ever. I can't even row a bloody canoe and I vomited all down myself last night because my mum wouldn't take me to Hollywood."

Kyle didn't laugh. He just scrunched and unscrunched his fists, and brought the conversation back to him again.

"I don't do anything. I don't believe in anything. I just do what everyone expects..."

I pushed myself up so I was standing again.

"I didn't expect you to turn up outside my window at four a.m. this morning and drive me to a national park," I pointed out. "And I'm really glad you did. Though my aching calves aren't so pleased."

He laughed then, his laughter shooting down the air pockets of awkwardness that had descended around us.

"Your calves don't know what's coming," he said. "I'm sorry, I'm just rambling. I'll shut up now. Poor Prom King, eh? I told you I was a cliché."

"You're not," I said… Though maybe he was. Maybe I was lying. He looked and talked like all the Prom Kings I'd ever seen in American movies. And my inkling that he'd got with Melody kind of proved that he acted like one too. Though he was here with me now…and I didn't know what that meant.

"Come on," he said, adjusting his backpack. "Let's keep going before I start crying about my childhood or something."

"Well I've already done that on you."

We walked through the dappled sunlight between the trees. The sun was rising higher, but it was still chilly, like when you're waiting for an oven to heat up. Soon I heard the unmistakable roar of a waterfall. We turned a corner and came out on a cute wooden bridge that looked up to the most impressive waterfall I'd ever seen. It was even bigger than the Yosemite Falls we'd passed in Kyle's car. We almost couldn't hear ourselves over the noise of the churning water.

"This is beautiful," I said, shouting the obvious.

"Good," he yelled back. "Because we're about to climb up it."

Kyle pointed to a small pathway with some steps. Not some steps... All the steps in the universe. They wound up and up till they disappeared into mist – like the top of the Magic Faraway Tree.

"We're climbing up the waterfall?"

"Yep."

"I don't know how I feel about that."

A massive huge Homecoming grin.

"You will love it, I promise."

As we began to climb, I quickly discovered why it was called the Mist Trail. The spray from the waterfall covered the path – making the steps slippery, my hair drenched, my T-shirt soaked through. We were, actually, literally climbing up the side of a waterfall and I'd never seen anything so beautiful in my life.

"This is awesome," I yelled backwards at Kyle, so he could hear me over the roar of the water.

"Just wait till we hit the sunlight." He pointed to an even steeper bit of the trail above us. My calves ached and I could barely talk I was puffing so hard. We climbed in a comfortable silence, stopping occasionally to catch our breath, or just to look down at how far we'd climbed.

"Almost there," Kyle called, "only ten more yards."

"That's actually pretty far when you're going up vertically."

"Wait for it."

We emerged from a tree-covered part of the trail into the

brightest sunlight. There was another stone staircase to climb, carved right out of the rock. It ran up right next to the gushing water.

I stopped so suddenly Kyle bumped into the back of me in a comedy way.

"Oh my God, Kyle," I whispered. "It's...it's... Is this heaven?"

There were rainbows everywhere – dozens of them. As the sunlight hit the mist, it flung them out in every direction. It was like standing in a paintbox. The steps led right through them, so you climbed through rainbow after rainbow to get to the summit. I'd never seen anything like it. My brain went quiet, like it needed all the mental space necessary to commit something so magical to memory. I wondered if I could paint it. If I'd ever be able to translate this onto paper with my watercolours.

"Pretty cool, huh?" I heard a click. I turned away from the view, to see Kyle holding up his phone. "Sorry," he said, "I couldn't resist taking a photo."

Was I in it? Had he taken a photo of me? I really wanted a photo of him. He was three steps lower than me, right where a rainbow ended. There was no pot of gold, just this guy, this really nice guy, who had taken me to a land of rainbows. I wanted to kiss him so much right then that I almost couldn't stand. I couldn't stop looking at him. The way his face was lit up by colour, how his toned arms were painted red, orange, yellow. That. Bloody. Smile. Why wasn't he mine? Why wasn't I a Melody?

He stared right back. And I dared myself to hope…to hope he'd take a step up…to make me a main character in a book, rather than a secondary one, the sort who gets kissed in rainbows.

But he just coughed and put his phone back in his pocket. "Come on, we've still got a lot of climbing to go."

My heart sank with disappointment – but when you're me, you get quite used to boys not kissing you when you want them to. The view helped heal the wound. I stepped onto a slippery stone and walked into more rainbows.

I could see why Kyle had wanted us to come here alone. Every other step provided a different viewpoint, a different explosion of colour. It was lovely to stop and drink it all in, without having to queue in a line of tourists to get your photo taken on the prettiest rock. It felt like ours, like it was created for us.

I'd even forgotten to be upset that this was obviously a charity trip, rather than a romantic one. I was just filled with gratitude that I was alive, that I could see this, that the world allowed such beautiful things to exist. And I thought, *Why would anyone get drunk? Why does anyone need anything like that to escape the world, when the world is its own antidote?*

When my calves and eyeballs couldn't take much more, the path turned off into a forest, and the rainbows faded into nothing. I sat down on a log to rest my aching legs, and twisted my T-shirt to drain out the water.

"You like it?" Kyle asked, sitting next to me. His wet arm

touched mine; I saw goosebumps erupt instantly, my ginger arm hairs springing to attention.

"That was incredible."

"We're almost at the top."

"Good. I don't think I can go much further."

One last staircase took us to the top of Vernal Falls. I leaned over the guard rail and my stomach flipped on itself as I stared down at the sheer drop and the roaring tirade of water disappearing over it. I handed my phone to Kyle and asked him to take my photo, which he did. Then he pulled out his phone and took another of me, in one of his confusing acts, which I was getting used to. I found it too churny, being at the top, so we walked along to "Emerald Lake" – a gorgeous calm body of water that glowed like a gemstone, and sunned ourselves dry on the warm stones baking in the sun.

I used my soaking wet hoody as a pillow and leaned back onto it – closing my eyes and enjoying looking at the pink of the inside of my eyelids and how the heat felt on my face.

It was then that Kyle kissed me.

He leaned over and gently put his lips on my lips, casting my face into shadow. I kept my eyes closed, hardly moving.

My first kiss, my first kiss, my first kiss.

Hang on, what was going on? Why was Kyle kissing me? I opened my eyes, just as he pulled away, staying close enough so our noses were touching. He delicately drew a line from the top of my forehead, down my cheek, and under my chin. My face tingled at his touch. I looked up at him, so confused…

Do I say something? Does he say something? What happens after you randomly kiss someone? I didn't know the etiquette. I went to touch my own lips, to check they were real, to check they'd been kissed. As I did, I brushed hands with his…and, oh, the electricity. We were touching hands, and it wasn't because we were doing some stupid dance at camp, but because he was choosing to touch my hand and I was choosing to touch it back…and…and…

…we were kissing again.

Every worry I'd ever had about kissing – *Would I be good at it? Would it be awful*? – vanished the moment Kyle's mouth fell on mine. Instinct and just a hunger for him guided me. I found myself wrapping my arms around him, stroking the back of his neck with my fingers just so I could touch as much of him as possible. All I could hear was the distant roar of the waterfall below us, all I could taste was him. The sun warmed the bits of my body which weren't shadowed by Kyle, creating a prickly heat as it dried. All I could think was how good it felt…

… Until I thought, *Why?*

I clumsily broke off the kiss, turning my head to one side.

Kyle kept kissing me, showering kisses on my arm, my neck… I closed my eyes, trying to enjoy it but thinking…

Why why why why why?

"Kyle?"

He kissed just under my chin.

"Yes?" he half-murmured.

"Why are you kissing me?"

He stopped, his mouth hovering in mid-air.

"I…I…"

He pulled away and sat back, so he was next to me. There was a gap between us, and I suddenly felt really sick. I was ruining it. I shouldn't have said anything. I just…just… I didn't understand. "Because I wanted to, I guess," he said. "Why? Do you not want me to kiss you?"

I ran my fingers through my damp hair, fluffing it out. Not sure if I could look at him.

"Yes, I do… But…but…I'm not sure what's going on?"

"I really like you, Amber," he said.

The words sank in slowly, like sugar dissolving in a mug of hot tea. He really liked me? What? But he was a boy. Boys didn't like me. They liked my friends, or other girls in my class, or girls who looked like Melody. Never me. It was never me. Especially boys who looked like Kyle.

I felt like smiling so hard my face would fall apart.

I also didn't trust it.

This was a good thing. Good things didn't happen. Not to me, never to me.

"You do?" I asked, not trusting, not believing.

He picked up my hand so our fingers were entwined.

"I've wanted to kiss you since that first night, when I walked you home."

What? When I was drunk? And complaining? And unfriendly?

"You did?" Not trusting, not believing.

"I thought I was being really obvious." He clenched my hand tight. His fingers felt so right in mine, and yet none of it made any sense.

"But...you..." And it tumbled out. "You got with Melody."

He opened his mouth, surprised I'd said it. Surprised I knew maybe. He let go of me and sighed.

I knew it was true then, my worst suspicions, made true. I felt sick. All the good from the kiss evaporated, like the mist coming off the waterfall.

"I only kissed Melody because..." He paused. "Because, well, I'm not sure, I just do what I'm expected to do. I told you... It didn't mean anything."

I moved away a little, making the gap between us wider.

"What do you mean? You're expected to?"

He threw his hands up. "I was trying to tell you earlier. I'm boring, I'm obvious. Everyone sees me and expects me to behave a certain way, and I just, I don't know, go along with it sometimes. Because I'm not sure what else to do."

I shook my head.

"Be yourself, perhaps?"

"I don't know who myself is. I'm so dull. I'm just, like, the most obvious person who does the most obvious things." He picked up a small rock and threw it across the lake. Even in my emotional state, I had to stop and pause a moment and appreciate just how far he'd thrown the rock.

"You're not saying anything," he said.

I picked at nothing on the rock face below me. "I don't

do talking about emotions very well, remember? British? Repressed?"

He smiled at that, but it was a small one.

"You're *so* not repressed at all. That's what I like about you. You're all fire and passion. You really care about stuff, you really do stuff. Like you came out here for a whole summer, to a new country, and you don't even know anyone? I've never even left America. I don't even have a passport. And you, you're always making comments, but in a good way, you don't just let things pass. You're just…you… You can't be anyone other than you. And I really like the you you are, Amber."

We were kissing again. Rougher. I couldn't work out what was happening. It felt so so nice, but he'd kissed Melody… Had he kissed her like this? Why would he kiss someone he didn't even like that much?

I remembered Mum's words: *Every girl feels they have a connection with Kyle…*

I broke off again.

"What is it?"

"I'm just…confused," I said. "About the Melody thing."

"I told you, I wasn't thinking. I just did it!"

"I get that. But I don't just kiss people. I've never just kissed someone. I don't understand. Plus, won't Melody be hurt by this?" It's weird, how I was suddenly on Melody's side. Maybe that's what girls need in order to like each other – a guy in common to confuse us and make us turn all solidarity. "I mean, what if you kiss someone else next week?"

"I won't, I really won't."

"I don't even know you," I said.

The moment the words came out of my mouth, I knew they were true.

I didn't know him, not at all.

I didn't know what he liked, what he didn't. I hardly knew anything about his family. He'd asked me about myself loads, but never really revealed much of him. He was just a great guy, a nice-looking guy, a smart guy. But what else? What did I really like about him? What he stood for? As a Prom King, a basketball player? Was I just into the idea of him? Also, I was only here a few more weeks. Would I ever get to know him? There wasn't any time to…

I stood up, just for wanting something to do. It was already busier. Tourists streamed up the last staircase, loads in anoraks, some with special walking sticks – all with cameras. A queue had already formed to get your photo taken at the top of the waterfall. They'd finally caught us up.

Kyle stood up too.

"Amber?"

"I don't know what to do." It was true.

"Be with me," he said, simply, clasping at my hand. The words melted in the hot air around me. A boy was standing on top of a waterfall, saying he wanted to be with me… Why was I closing him off?

"I don't know who you are."

I watched my words break him. His gorgeous face fell, his smile disintegrated. Yet I kept on talking. It was true,

I had no idea who he was – not really. "I live in England. You kissed Melody." They both seemed equally important. "I guess I'm just shocked."

"Shocked?"

"I didn't see any of this coming," I said.

He went to take my hand again but didn't.

"How could you not?"

He asked it so genuinely and I didn't have the answer. It hadn't really occurred to me that Kyle would like me, not really. Yeah, I'd fantasized about it – got confused by his signs, maybe entertained the thought – but that's different from believing it. I was struggling to take in how everything had changed so quickly. My brain was in full-on compute mode, trying to slot everything into place like a jigsaw, but none of the pieces fitted together.

Why would he like me anyway?

Why did he get with Melody?

What did I do now?

Would it just be a summer thing?

Is this real?

And why the hell did he get with Melody?

"I thought maybe I was a charity project…"

It was hard to talk about my feelings. I'd never known how unnaturally it came until I'd come here, to this strange country, where they talk the same language but vomit up so many honest feelings all day that it was a totally different tongue. The other day Whinnie had asked Russ, "Good morning, all good with you?" And rather than answering like every British person would – "Fine, how are you?" – even if half your leg had come off in the night and you were oozing blood all over the floor… No, Russ answered honestly. "I slept like crap. My back hurts, I think I pulled it." And Whinnie didn't look at him like he was breaking a secret code or something, like you would in England.

Kyle pulled a face.

"Why would you be a charity project?" he asked.

"Because of my mum. Because I'm in a new country. Because I would never in a million years ever be Homecoming Queen."

Kyle made this grunt of anger and stepped away from me. "Have you not been listening? I really, really like you, Amber. I love that you'd never be Homecoming Queen. I love that you'd never want to be Homecoming Queen…"

Well that wasn't true. Every girl, secretly, wanted to be Homecoming Queen. Even if we didn't even have them at home.

"Don't you hear what I'm saying, none of it means anything? I hate that I live a life that doesn't mean anything. But this –" he took my hand – "my feelings for you mean something. I know we've only known each other a few weeks but, like I said…straight away, on that first night… I just needed to know you."

My hand glowed hot at his touch, like it was agreeing with him.

I laughed. I don't know why.

"This is all very dramatic," I said, trying to break the atmosphere. "Can't we just go explore the rest of the park or something?"

I was pushing him away. I didn't know why, but I was pushing him away. Hard.

His eyes dropped to where our hands were entwined. He let go.

"Yeah, sure, whatever." He faked a laugh. "Sorry, I had it all planned in my head… I didn't mean to ambush you. I thought…" He trailed off.

Oh the awkward, so much of the awkward. Why wasn't I kissing him? Why wasn't I telling him how I felt? Was it because I was scared? Did I even know how I felt? I needed the girls here. Lottie would just tell me to "mount him" and worry about it afterwards. Evie could give me all her hand-me-down therapy. We could work it out together. I didn't trust me to work it out. I just messed everything up, like I had now.

It was getting so busy. The streams of tourists had become rivers. An unyielding tide of them huffed past the summit, sitting all around us with selfie sticks, cracking open plastic boxes stuffed with sandwiches, handing them out to each other. This was not the place to make any decisions… There was no space for us, and all the emotions catapulting between us right now. I looked once more at Kyle – GOD, he was good-looking, even with the pained expression on his face that made me feel guilty. I couldn't believe I had kissed him only moments ago.

I spoke. "At the risk of sounding very American indeed, can I have some time to process all this? And, in the meantime, can we just have a very nice day?"

Another sad smile. A determined-not-to-look-sad smile.

"Of course."

"I'm really, really happy you brought me here. You have no idea…"

"You just weren't expecting to get sexually harassed at the top of the waterfall." It was his turn to awkwardly laugh. He started walking away from me.

God I hated him walking away from me.

"That wasn't sexual harassment," I called after him, and a few groups of tourists looked round. I caught up with Kyle, glowing red. We burst out laughing.

"And now everyone is looking at us," he said.

"Yeah, I do that a lot. Say the wrong thing."

"I've noticed." He very carefully tucked a stray piece of hair behind my ear. It sprang back right away.

"My hair doesn't care that you're trying to be romantic right now," I said. Kyle let out a proper belly laugh at that.

"It's got your spirit."

"It's got itself into a humid environment. No amount of lovely, romantic hair-tucking will overcome its need to respond to a humid environment."

"Are we still talking about your hair?" His eyes were laughing, dancing. I wanted to kiss him. Why did I keep not kissing him? WHY!?

"God knows. Now, how do we get off this waterfall?"

Situations that are destined to fail:

Awkward silences

+

Rafting with just one other person

Twenty-one

We had to descend against a mad flow of tourists to get down off Vernal Falls. Like salmon going upstream, but, like…down a waterfall. We stumbled through, saying "excuse me" a lot to groups of people clutching trail mix, our knees aching as we got all wet in the mist again. I didn't look back to see the rainbows on the way down. I wanted to remember this place as we'd had it, when it was ours.

Eventually we got to the bottom and queued to get the shuttle bus.

"Where now?" I asked, thinking *youkissedmeyoukissedme youkissedmeyoukissedme.*

"How are you at rafting?"

"What did you say, please?"

"Rafting? Like, paddling a raft down a river. They hire them out here, and you can take the river right through the park."

"Kyle, you have seen me try to do water sports. I had to get rescued. By you, in fact."

"Rafting's easier."

"Hmm."

We got the now-crammed shuttle bus into the centre of the park, and Kyle expertly navigated us to the hire shop.

"How do you know this place so well?"

"I live in a small town not too far from Yosemite," Kyle said. "Everyone in my town works here. I'd go call on Mom, but they're in Florida for two weeks."

Some guys who looked just like Wayne equipped us with life jackets and gave us a quick course in how to paddle. ("See, this is what I needed before, basic instructions," I said.) Soon we were dragging the raft into the coldest river water the world has ever known.

I had lots of anti-feminism thoughts as Kyle got us all sorted and paddling along. Thoughts like, *It's so nice having a guy to carry most of the weight of this raft*. And, *It's actually really sexy how masculine he looks when he paddles*. And, *Oh those arms, why aren't you frickin' kissing someone back who has arms like that, AMBER?*

But, as we got into the swing of paddling, the sheer magnificence of our surroundings made my busy brain quieten right down. Everything we floated past blew my mind – its scale, as well as its beauty. We drifted past Half Dome again, the sun now shining on it full force, making the flat face glint almost silver. We paddled through bits of the park inaccessible on foot and all I could hear were the sounds of our isolated surroundings. It was like one of those nature CDs you buy in hippy shops to help you sleep.

The back of Kyle's head was also, well, a pretty gorgeous thing to look at. How could I fancy the back of someone's head? I watched his strong arms work the paddles, and tried to guess what he was thinking, how he was feeling. I still couldn't believe he liked me like that… That he'd been feeling like that about me. The thought was intoxicating.

He'd seen me last night, covered in sick and crying, and he still wanted me…

"Amber, Jeez, paddle, we're about to hit the leg of that bridge."

After about forty minutes, Kyle stopped us at a tiny pebbled beach that jutted into the river. We dragged the raft up, and he got out some sandwiches he'd made, passing me one. We ate in semi-contented, semi-awkward silence, watching other rafts float past us – some filled with giggling kids that made me sort of miss camp, some filled with families, a few couples, like us. It was like being on the most beautiful and calm theme park ride ever.

"I'm beat," Kyle said. "Can we just lie here for a bit? The early morning's catching up with me."

He put his big bare feet up on the cushiony side of the raft, pulled his baseball cap over his eyes and just kinda zonked out.

I watched the rise and fall of his chest as he sank into a deep nap, wanting so much to touch him. My skin prickled with the first hints of sunburn, so I took my pale self away from direct sunlight and sat under a pine tree, trying to figure out my feelings. I tried to draw for a bit, pulling my sketchpad out of the waterproof bag we'd been given, but I couldn't concentrate.

I had a few inclinations about why I may not be kissing Kyle back.

The first, he had kissed Melody. Yes, get over it, Amber. He said it meant nothing, but that kind of made it worse… And, like, why was he all down on himself? Saying he was generic and clichéd and whatever? What did that even mean? Did he just like me because I'm not an obvious girl for someone like him to fancy?

Mainly though, I was only here for a month.

And then what? Even in the happiest of scenarios, we'd fall for each other and have a month of kisses… God that sounded nice actually… But then I'd still have to go back to England. Wouldn't that hurt, like, a lot? It's not like we'd start a long-distance relationship. I was only seventeen, he lived in America, we were too young for that probably…

Also wouldn't he go off me if he got to know me? Like my actual mum – giver of my birth – had gone off me. What chance did I have with Mr Prom King?

Basically, I figured it out. This situation – kissing Kyle, letting him in. Whatever happened, it was destined to fail. It was doomed. The only possible outcome would be *Amber gets hurt*. I didn't do getting hurt very well… Why get myself involved in something that would break me?

It hurt already. It hurt not to go over and kiss him,

knowing that's what we both wanted. It would hurt putting my feelings to one side but I'd be protecting myself from stronger, worse feelings a few weeks down the line. The knot in my stomach would be like a lead ball of…umm… lead if one more thing happened between us.

Kyle could get over it, look how he'd gotten over Melody already.

I knew I couldn't.

When Kyle snorted himself awake, half an hour later, my mind was made up.

Protect me protect me protect me.

He looked over the top of the raft, his eyes so wide and earnest that I knew he was asking me a silent question.

I looked back at him, hurting so much more than I should be, and gave him my silent reply.

He looked down, and coughed.

We hadn't said a word, and yet we both knew it was over. Over before it really began. It was the only way really – unless I was a masochist.

I clambered back into the raft and we wordlessly paddled ourselves out into the steady swell of the river. I stared and stared at the back of his head as we floated past beautiful view followed by beautiful view, and tried to swallow down the tears that were wedged in my throat.

No reason to cry, Amber. Nothing has been lost. You're just being smart. Less hurt now to avoid more hurt later.

It's weird how the inside of your head can ruin such stunning exterior moments of your life. As we passed the Yosemite Falls, my head didn't take it all in and think, *Wow, this is so awesome, be humbled, Amber, be humbled.* Nope, it was whirring and churning about Kyle, about my mum, about me. Introspection, self-loathing, thinking, whinging, upset, all the time time time. I may as well have been looking at the view from Bognor Regis train station.

The river got quieter, smoother, even the views calmed down a bit. I could tell we'd been through the golden bit of the raft tour. We still didn't talk. Not even when I got us stuck under another bridge. Not when we came to the end of the rafting zone of the river, greeted by tanned topless boys who waved and helped us drag the raft up onto the beach. Not when we waited for the shuttle bus to return us to the top of the river again.

Kyle kept looking at me, like he wanted to say something, but he didn't.

"Wanna go see Yosemite Falls one last time?" he asked, finally.

I nodded.

We walked to the wild-flower meadow I'd seen when we first drove into the park. It seemed so long ago. So much had happened since sunrise.

"It really is pretty." My words sounded empty and forced.

"Yep." So did his.

"Can we get any closer?"

"Yeah, there's a trail."

The "trail" was a walkway made of wooden platforms and rammed full of people. The entire world appeared to be there to have their photo taken. We had to dodge and weave like we were on the London Underground in rush hour.

"Why is it so busy?" I asked, as we waited for a couple to finish taking photos of each other so we didn't walk in front of their shot. They thanked us and we walked past.

"It's American law that the national parks are for the people, they belong to us, they can't limit how many people come in," Kyle explained. "Good idea in theory. In reality it means they're all too busy to enjoy properly."

I could hear the thrash of the waterfall. A few more metres and a right-hand turn and we were right at the bottom of it. The water hit the rocks, spraying everyone on the cute viewing bridge with water.

I leaned over the railing, closing my eyes so I could feel the spray hit my face better. It felt good on the heat of my skin. There were no rainbows here though…

"That's interesting," I said. "That America sort of protects them, and then ruins them like that."

"Amber?"

I opened my eyes. "Yes?"

"Why are we talking like we're at a bad dinner party?"

I turned my head, and he looked so pained. He gripped the railings so hard he had white bumps on his fists.

"We are?" I played dumb.

"We really are. You just walked past an entire group of

cheerleaders on tour, all wearing matching hot pants with sexy nicknames monogrammed across their butt cheeks and you didn't launch into a rant."

"There was?"

How did I not see that? That definitely would've annoyed me!

"Yep. They got off a coach. They're right behind us on the trail. They were taking so many selfies we overtook them."

I tried to smile. "I thought Melody and her friends were in LA?"

"Stop changing the subject."

"I'm not..."

"You are. Look..." He ran his hands over his face. "I know I've messed up, okay? I shouldn't have kissed you..."

He shouldn't?!

"... It wasn't fair of me to just maul you like that. I just thought it was...mutual..."

It IS mutual! But...

"But it's been so much fun just to be your friend these last few weeks. I would be majorly bummed if I messed that up. So, can we just forget this morning ever happened?"

I could never forget that morning had ever happened – the mist, the rainbows, the way Kyle's mouth tasted, the way a big frozen part of me melted when we kissed again, a part of me that had frozen right back up the moment I'd wrecked it all with my overthinking.

"Amber, please? Can you just talk to me? You're never not talking!"

I whipped around. "Hey!"

We both smiled.

"Yay, I got words out of you."

"I…"

I opened my mouth to explain my thinking. All I wanted to do was just grab him and bury myself into him and say, *I really like you, and even though I don't know you very well, I think I want to be with you, but you're a fucking Prom King and you live in America and I fly away in less than a month and your heart will heal but mine really really won't.*

But he held out his hand to stop me.

"You don't have to say anything, or explain anything. Can we just go back to how it was? Like, six hours ago?"

It couldn't, both of us knew that. But when has denial ever been ignored as a very useful coping mechanism?

"In that case," I said, smiling, "can we go find these cheerleaders? I want to take photos to show Lottie and Evie."

Just as I said it, they appeared over the slope. We watched as they all bent over to spell a word that was formed by the letters sewn onto their bums – posing so long, as all of them wanted a photo taken on their phone, that they caused a queue for the waterfall.

I laughed so hard, Kyle had to hold me up. Then I told him all about Female Chauvinist Pigs, and he listened and smiled and didn't touch me. We drove out of the park and went for dinner at this cute youth hostel up in the mountains called the Yosemite Bug, and he didn't touch me. And we drove out into the night, talking, but not touching, until eventually we pulled up at some dubious-looking motel and collapsed into separate beds, not touching.

There was no touching.

Situations that are destined to fail:

Prom Kings

+

Psychoanalysis

+

Long car journeys

Twenty-two

Kyle was already up when I woke.

Fully dressed. Reading another biography.

Why do boys look so sexy when they read? Somebody should really tell them that. I blinked a few times, the dank motel room coming into focus as my sleepy mind awoke to where I was, what had happened.

Kyle looked up from his book. "Morning, camper."

I rolled over onto my front, so my full-of-sleep face wasn't on show.

"Morning. How long you been up?"

"Not too long. You snore, you know?"

"I do?" The thought was so horrifying I actually covered my mouth. I'd never slept in the same room as a boy before. I hadn't even really slept in the same room as many girls. The Spinster Club didn't have sleepovers as Evie found them too difficult and Lottie and I didn't want her to feel left out.

"Ha, only kidding." He smiled, and I thought how nice it was, to be smiled at like that, by a boy, in your own room, after waking up together.

Why wasn't I kissing him? Why wasn't I kissing him?

"Not funny," I grumbled. I kicked the covers off and quickly shimmied into a big sweater so he didn't see much of my body. "Is the shower here okay?"

"It's...umm... Well it works enough."

I stepped into the bathroom and saw what he meant. It didn't look like it had been redecorated since 1972. There was even wood panelling, with added spiderweb decorations in between the gaps of each panel. The shower was one of those small heads that dangles over the bath and it was covered in reddish rust. I sighed, and turned it on – waiting for the water to heat up, and using the sound of running water to cover the noise of me peeing in case Kyle could hear. After a vaguely unsatisfactory shower, I dressed best I could in the tiny bathroom and emerged to find him still reading.

"Who you learning about today?" I flopped down on my unmade bed. It was odd how comfortable I felt with him, even with all the kissing/no kissing yesterday. He just had this air of easiness, like a soluble heartburn tablet he could dissolve into the oxygen surrounding any social environment...or something.

He held up the cover of his book so I could see for myself.

"Al Pacino?"

"What's wrong with Al Pacino?" he asked, his eyes still on the page.

"It's just quite a leap from Van Gogh, that's all."

I hadn't brought anything to read in the rush to leave the previous morning, so I just lay back down and watched him, wanting to kiss him whenever he turned a page.

But not kissing him.

"Why do you like biographies so much?" I asked, deliberately interrupting him to get attention.

He put his book down.

"I like reading about people who've had interesting lives. Who've done something that wasn't expected..." He thought about it. "Who've broken the mould."

I stretched my foot up in the air, stretching the back of my thigh out. It was all cramped from the previous day's hike.

"Wouldn't you rather live an interesting life yourself than read about someone else's?"

His sad face came out again.

"I told you. I'm not like that. My life is just...blah."

I flopped my leg down and glared at him.

"You say it like you have no choice in the matter, like you're not in control of what you can do with your life."

"I know, I get that. I try... But as I said, I end up just doing exactly what's expected of me regardless."

Like kissing Melody...

I felt a small surge of anger. So what if he was stuck in this whole perfect predictable storyline, why was he whinging about it? It was better than my storyline. Screwed-up girl with alcoholic mother has screwed up life because she can't psychologically process her alcoholic mother...

At least I had the strength to know I could try and change that inevitability…maybe.

"You must've done one thing that isn't obvious. You must've done one thing that was just for you, because you wanted to do it, not because it was expected of you."

He picked up his book again, and started half-reading.

"I did," he said, practically into the book. "Yesterday. I kissed you."

The sides of my eyes stung as his words launched tears into them.

"… And look how that turned out."

He stared determinedly at his book, and I didn't know what to say or think or do. I just stayed still, on the bed, desperately processing, but none of it helping. I felt guilty, and confused, and all the adjectives you use in shit poetry you write in your diary when you're twelve and sad about something stupid at school. What did he expect to happen? Did he think he could just kiss me and then there'd be no consequences? When I live so far away, and I could so obviously and easily fall in love with him – if I ever got to understand who he truly was.

Finally, he looked up. "Sorry," he said, and I could tell he meant it. "That wasn't fair."

"No. It wasn't."

"I guess we've not really talked about yesterday, have we?"

"No." My voice was small.

"And I can tell you don't want to talk about it…" I went to protest but he held his hand up, making him lose his place in the book. "No, don't worry. I can see it all over your body language."

I let out a deep breath.

"How long till we have to check out?"

Kyle glanced at the time on his phone. "An hour. Then it's a bit of a drive back to camp."

Camp. Claustrophobic little camp. With no privacy, and no time, and no space, and my mum there to cloud my brain from thinking about anything else. I'd almost forgotten about it.

I really didn't want to go back. I wanted to stay here, with him. Even though I wasn't kissing him or touching him or doing all the things I really wanted to do and I didn't know why.

I tried to smile. "Plenty of time then."

He looked up. "Time for what?"

"For you to tell me who you are."

The tarmac slipped by under us – the road empty apart from Kyle's jeep.

"I still don't get what you mean," he said. "Who I am?" He adjusted his rear-view mirror.

"You were saying yesterday, you do things people expect of you. That means, if you think about it, that I don't really know who you are at all. And, considering you've seen me a) cry, b) projectile vomit, and c) you know just how ill my mum is, it seems only fair I get to know stuff."

"I told you, there's nothing to know!"

I rolled my eyes. "So, what? You're just a jock with a brain? That's all there is?"

He barely nodded, but his hands gripped tighter on the wheel.

"You must have beliefs, you must have passions!"

"I dunno. Be a good person?"

"*Everyone* wants to be a good person. Unless they're, like, the evil stepmother in a Disney movie."

"I TOLD YOU, I'm just really normal...boring, like everyone else." If he gripped any tighter, the steering wheel would come off in his fists.

I opened his glovebox and rifled around.

"What are you doing?" he asked, trying to keep his eyes on the road.

"Snooping."

It was pretty neat, considering what most people's gloveboxes are like.

"So, you're tidy," I concluded. "That's something... That's a personality quirk."

"Yeah, a boring one. When have tidy people been any fun?"

"They're very useful. You should see the state of my bedroom back home. I'm a pig! Honestly, you definitely wouldn't have kissed me if you'd ever seen it."

We fell silent at my attempt at a joke. Kyle looked genuinely stunned.

"British?" I tried to explain. "We make jokes about uncomfortable topics to feel less awkward about them?"

And, thankfully, Kyle did start genuinely laughing.

"But this is why I like you," he said, and his words melted further parts of me. He likes you! *He keeps saying he likes you!* "It makes sense that you're messy. You're creative, you're passionate! All the best people are messy."

"I'm not so sure about that. My friend Evie, back home, is all kinds of awesome, but she's like the neatest person ever… Anyway, being neat and tidy is still a thing, it's still a thing that makes you you."

"It makes me boring."

"God, shut up, will you? Why are you so insecure?" I carried on digging. At the back, was one of those old-fashioned CD cases. I hadn't noticed before that the jeep only had a CD player, it must've been as old as he said it was. I unzipped it and started flipping through, commenting aloud. "Rap, rap – English people don't really listen to rap…" I said, although maybe that was just my suburban hometown. I always used to call home a *leave-the-lost-glove-on-the-wall* town. You know? My town is the sort of place where people pick up a lost glove in the snow, dust it off, and leave it hanging in an easy-to-see spot in case the owner tried to retrace their steps and find it. When I went to London for the day once, an art trip to Brixton, right in the middle of winter, I saw, like three lost gloves trodden into the snow… I flipped through more CDs. "A-ha!" I said, just as Kyle spotted what I'd found and went to grab it. "The very best of Andrew Lloyd Webber?!"

"That's not mine!"

I held it out of reach and flipped over another CD. "Then why is the full *Phantom of the Opera* soundtrack here too?"

He'd gone so red I thought his head might explode. The car wobbled, almost going over the centre line.

I laughed, hard. "Oh my, you are actually Troy Bolton from *High School Musical,* aren't you? You secretly want to sing?"

"Shut it!"

He grabbed the CD case off me and stuffed it into the side compartment. "I don't want to sing, okay? I can't even sing. I never have been able to…I…I…" He sighed, and stared hard out the windscreen, slowly turning the wheel as we slid round a curve. "I just like music with stories in it, okay?"

I smiled harder.

"Stories?"

"Yes, like epic stories. But in song. I know it's not cool, but I like musicals, all right? And, like, modern music is all 'I wanna smack you, hoe' or 'I love you now I hate you, I hate how much I love you and I love to hate you more'." He sang all this in a weird falsetto voice, and I knew he wasn't lying about not planning to become a singer. "Where's the narrative in that? And…" he continued. "I don't, like, only listen to musicals, I listen to other stuff too. I just want it to have a story. Like, have you ever listened to The Mars Volta?"

"Mars whotta?"

"Volta. They're a band. They do concept albums."

"Concept what now?"

Kyle was finally smiling, his face all lit up like someone had put solar panels in his hair. "A concept album. It's, like, not just a collection of songs. The whole album is a piece of art that you're meant to listen to as a whole. The Mars Volta do incredible ones. But even albums by, like, The Beatles and the Rolling Stones, they tell stories, you know? You're not supposed to listen to random tracks in *Let It Bleed*. You're supposed to sit down properly, get the vinyl out, pour yourself a glass of something, and then really concentrate on the whole record – start to finish – and listen to the story they're trying to tell you."

Another curve in the road; Kyle confidently steered us around it. We'd gone from mountains, into highway interstate tarmacness, through long straight stretches of parched desert, and now we were back to driving into mountains again. Camp felt so far away, though it must be getting closer. I didn't want it to get closer.

"So you like stories, huh?"

"Yeah, I guess."

"Is that because you don't think you have a story yourself? Or the one you do have is so overtold or something, that somehow it doesn't count?"

Kyle took his eyes off the screen and really looked at me, his face all soft.

"Are you trying to psychoanalyse me, Amber?"

"Oh, yeah. Of course. I mean, I'm a seventeen-year-old art student. I'm so very qualified."

He laughed. "And what kind of stories do you like, Amber?"

I thought about it, thinking through books I've read, books I've discarded – films I'd borrowed that made me happy, or annoyed.

"I think I like the stories that don't try and sugar-coat the truth, you know? So, no fairy tales. I like the grim stories, where nothing really happens. At least they're honest…" I trailed off.

"That's funny…" Kyle said. "Because my favourite stories are the ones where everything comes good in the end, against all the odds."

"You like a happy ending?"

He snorted. "Oh yeah, I'm an American. You know they reshoot bits of English films sometimes, to make them happier, and show us that version over here?"

"No way!"

"Oh yeah. Remember that Keira Knightley film of *Pride and Prejudice?* Well, I read somewhere that in your British version, they didn't kiss at the end or anything. Whereas, in the USA version, it was a right-on happily-ever-after snog-fest. 'Snog'? That's a British word, right?"

I couldn't stop smiling. Little bits of the smart guy who'd got an academic scholarship to college were beginning to shine through. I was starting to get him, even in just a day. The only problem was it was made me want to kiss him more.

"Do you think maybe the Keira Knightley version of

Pride and Prejudice is a microcosm of the differences between us?"

Kyle laughed. "God that would be depressing."

"Evie, my friend back home, she would probably know that fact. She's a massive film buff."

The automatic car clunked into a lower gear as we wound up a sharp incline in the road.

"Your face goes all glowy, you know?" Kyle said. "Whenever you talk about your friends back home. Tell me about them."

And I could feel my face glow, the muscles around my cheeks twitching, as I pictured Lottie and Evie – what they'd say if I told them about this weekend, how much they'd care.

"Well, the most important thing I guess, is that we've started a feminism grass roots campaign group called The Spinster Club."

As the car climbed upwards, through clouds, past expanses of forest, I filled him in on the bits of my life that weren't all just the crap between me and my mum. I told him about Evie's relapse last year, about the constant academic bashings Lottie gave us at every Spinster Club meeting, teaching us all the big and important ideas she'd read about. I dug into my purse and pulled out my Spinster Club membership card – I'd made one for each of us, and Kyle even stopped the car on the side of the road so he could admire it properly. I told him how the college wanted to start it up as a proper club the next school year, inviting other students to join… They'd found out about us after we protested against a rape pop song being on the canteen's jukebox. Kyle seemed almost proud of it all as I spoke. The way he looked at me made me want to freeze time so I would always be looked at like that for ever. And when I went off on one of my many rants about women's issues, he didn't try and get pedantic about the facts I was using, or say stuff like "Well, it's hard for men too, you know?" and all the other crap I get thrown at me by guys whenever I dare bring up girl rights.

"It's just so great you're doing this," he said, instead. "I have two younger sisters. I don't want them growing up in a world where they're leered at, or put down all the time."

"You shouldn't only care about feminism because you have sisters."

"I get that. You should just care about feminism because it's the right thing to do."

And again, I asked myself why I wasn't kissing him. Honestly, why the HELL wasn't I kissing him? Instead, I said: "You didn't seem very feminist when Melody was dancing like a stripper around the campfire."

It came out just as bitter as it was.

But, surprisingly, Kyle didn't look ashamed. He just rolled his eyes.

"She pulled me out the crowd, Amber. What was I supposed to do? Humiliate her? Tell her I didn't agree with why she was doing this? Tell her she was letting women's rights down?" The car lurched into an even lower gear. "I know you're pissed that I kissed her, I get it. I'm annoyed I did too, as it's so obviously screwed things up between us. But, like, have you ever considered *why* Melody feels she has to do what she does?"

I didn't answer at first. Initially because I was angry. Then hurt. Then angry at myself that he might be right…

I wasn't very good at admitting I was wrong; my mother was my mother after all. So, when enough silence had passed to show I'd probably taken in what he'd said and understood it, I changed the topic of conversation.

"So what about you? What about your life?"

"I told you – what else is there to say?"

"That Andrew Lloyd Webber CD suggests there's something."

Another laugh.

"What's your life like at Brown? What's your family like?"

And it was his turn to talk. I learned how tough he found it to keep basketball up alongside getting the grades he needed to keep his scholarship. He told me about this creepy room-mate in his first year of college, Robbo, who looked like Gollum and essentially never left the room during the day, then would disappear at night. How he used to worry Robbo was out killing people or something. "Honestly, he was the type of guy you can imagine making a coat out of someone's skin." He liked how pretty the trees turned around campus in fall. He'd taken a photography class to try and capture the colours and then, "Discovered, sometimes, it's best just to stick to basketball." He had four siblings. He felt guilty every moment he wasn't at home helping out his ma. His favourite biography was about Winston Churchill – "Honestly, that guy, he got stuff done." Gradually, as I began to recognize the landscape, as I saw we were almost back at camp, the jigsaw pieces of Kyle assembled themselves next to me in the driving seat. He was warm, he was generous, he was insecure, he thought too much, he lived most of his life out of obligation, he liked the colour orange, he fancied Jennifer Lawrence, he wanted to grow his hair long one day, he always saw the best in everyone.

The sign for camp came up ahead – first a dot, then it was readable, then we turned into the forest and the sign was behind us. And I wanted to kiss him. I wanted to know him. What I knew wasn't enough. It had only started some reaction in me – *who are you, Kyle? Tell me more, Kyle. I want to be near you, Kyle. I want you to want to be near me.*

We slowed to a crawl as we got to the camp car park. I felt like crying. All I'd ever done since I came to camp was feel like crying. If I reached out and touched his face, would he take my hand? Would he kiss me, right here? If I let him know I wanted it?

I thought maybe he would.

But then what? That sign we'd just driven past, I'd be driving past it again in a few weeks. For ever. And putting an ocean between me and him, him and me, and everything we may or may not be.

And I would crumble…

"We're here," I said, hollowly, as he parked.

"We are."

I was about to say something else, but I saw trouble on the horizon.

"And so are the kids."

A collection of them were running at the car, hooting with excitement at our return. They began smacking on the windows, yelling, "You're back, you're back."

I looked at Kyle.

Kyle looked at me.

Our time alone was over.

Situations that are destined to fail:

Honesty about your feelings

+

Dishonesty about where you spent the weekend

Twenty-three

Mum hugged me so tight I thought she would break me when I got in.

"Amber, honey, how was LA? I missed you!"

I hugged her tight back – half loving it, half hating her.

"It was only two days."

And you didn't seem to miss me for two years.

She wouldn't let go. "Well it seemed much longer. Thanks again for being so understanding. We were SWAMPED at the centre, I swear I'm dead on my feet."

I released the hug, as I still had my bag in my arms and it was starting to hurt.

"I'm just putting this in my room."

"Okay, then you can tell me all about it. I want to see your pictures. Did the guys get one of you by the Hollywood sign? Isn't LA AWFUL? I knew you'd hate it. Are the others back yet? Would you be able to help with dinner in the hall later? I know you're supposed to be off until tomorrow morning, but it would be great if you could help out…"

Her voice faded away as I pushed into my bedroom and plonked my stuff on the bed. Shit! Pictures! I'd taken no photos. I'd barely even made any sketches. The only thing in my sketchpad was a drawing I'd done of Kyle the night before, in the motel, and, yes, I'm aware of how totally disturbing that is. He'd fallen asleep first, but I hadn't been able to. Just having his body so close to mine… It was like bursts of electricity were flying off me, onto him, like when you accidentally give someone a static electric shock on a trampoline. I gave up on sleeping. I couldn't resist drawing him – like that – the way he still looked sad, even in sleep, the way his tight jaw looked so stark against the softness of the pillow.

I couldn't show Mum that drawing, could I?

I could still hear her chatter through the walls, and I knew I was supposed to feel happy. She cared, she'd missed me, she wanted to hear all my gossip. But there was no space in my heart for her at that moment. It felt all trodden on, and ripped open, like someone had tried to wring the juice out of it. Kyle and I hadn't even said goodbye properly. I mean, why would we? We would see each other at dinner, with the kids all around us.

I'd just said thank you, and he'd said no problem, and that was that. But it wasn't, it wasn't, it wasn't. Everything had changed, everything was different.

I flopped face down on the bed, inhaling the foresty

smell of my bed linen, and let myself remember the previous day – climbing through the rainbows, the coldness of my face in shadow just before he kissed me.

I wanted to cry.

I was so lost.

I needed help.

I got out my mobile phone and switched it on for the first time since leaving England. It would cost at least three quid just to connect to an American server or whatever. I didn't care.

I messaged Lottie and Evie right away.

Videotime? SOS. America has broken me.

I checked the time as I hit send. It would be the middle of the night over there. They'd be asleep. But just knowing I'd spoken to them, even by text, helped.

I took a deep breath, picked myself up off the bed, and went to chat to Mum.

It was a mistake, to have not even thought about what I would've seen in LA.

"So, did you get the others to show you the movie stars' homes?" Mum asked, over a cup of herbal tea.

"Umm."

"Which one was your favourite?"

"Umm..." *Quick, think of a celebrity.* "Oprah's?"

"Oh, I never saw that one. Whereabouts does she live?"

"Umm..." *Quick, brain, think of a place in LA.* "Malibu?"

Mum nodded. "Of course."

Bumface Kevin joined us, sitting right next to me on the couch, which I didn't appreciate one bit.

"So, who all went?" He made this slurping sound with his tea.

Think, brain, think think think.

"Umm, Melody? Bryony? Wayne? And, er, loads of others."

"And what did you do in the evening? You guys didn't try and get into clubs, did you? You're underage."

I rolled my eyes. "Like I'd tell you if we did. I don't want you to fire all my friends."

"Don't take that tone with me." Kevin tried to use his nice voice, but undertones of pissed-off-ness shone right through.

"She has a point, Kevin," Mum said, stunning me. "We shouldn't know what the staff are up to in their time off."

Kevin bashed his tea down with just enough violence to make us both flinch. Immediately Mum began backtracking. "I mean, of course, you still wouldn't do anything like that, would you, Amber? And the staff know the rules, don't they? We can't have you breaking the law."

I looked from Mum, to Kevin, back to Mum again.

"Relax. We didn't drink or go anywhere we shouldn't."

Which I'm sure was a lie.

Mum had her pinched face on. I felt uneasy at what I'd

just seen. I didn't like Mum's franticness to placate him.

"So you're becoming friends with Melody and Bryony now? That's nice. I thought it was about time you branched out," Mum went on.

I crossed my arms. "Branch out from who?"

"Well, you know how I feel about Kyle... He's a manipulative boy. Lovely, yes. But there's a lot going on underneath."

I almost laughed. Mum, giving *me* a lecture on who was manipulative. Well, I could play that game.

"Yeah, Melody and Bryony are lovely. They really cheered me up about the fact you cancelled the weekend..."

Mum and Kevin looked up at each other at exactly the same time – I saw them silently unite.

Kevin defended her first. "Now, Amber, you know how important your mum's work in the centre is...an important part of recovery is giving back and—"

"I can't believe you're trying to make me feel bad," Mum interrupted. "For doing volunteer work! Honestly, Amber, I didn't raise you to be so selfish."

You didn't raise me at all...

I was stupid enough to say, "Really, you didn't?"

Kevin knocked his tea over as he stood up.

"You say sorry to your mother immediately."

"Honestly, Amber, why would you say that?"

"It's my house. You can't talk to us like that in my house."

"Are you trying to make me feel bad? Because, guess what, it's working. Happy now?"

As their yells rolled over me, I retreated into myself, blocking it out… Kyle understood. Kyle got why I was hurt. And yet I hurt him in return.

What's wrong with me? What's wrong with me?

I stood up too.

"I'm sorry, okay? I just wanted to spend the weekend with my mum. Is that so terrible? Aren't I allowed to be disappointed? Even if that makes me selfish?"

I went to the sink and picked up a dishcloth, wiping up Kevin's spillage.

They were both quiet. Mum started sniffling, but I knew she wouldn't cry. She never did. Not really.

Kevin regained his composure, pulling out his most patronizing *I've-had-professional-counselling-training* smile.

"I understand why you were disappointed," he said, all calm. "But do you think it's fair to make your mum feel bad? She's been so looking forward to having you stay. We've bent a lot of camp rules to have you here. I know you've travelled a long way, but we can't just stop our lives because you've come to visit."

I didn't know what to say. Not one word of that was fair. This was my first visit in TWO YEARS. I hadn't seen my mother in TWO YEARS. And, yet, I was SELFISH for wanting to spend just TWO DAYS with her…

Mum was nodding.

Of course she was nodding.

I didn't know how much hurt I could take. How much more twisting my heart could handle. I'd been broken the day I'd stepped on the aeroplane, and I'd thought this summer would mend me. But I felt more broken, if that were possible. At least the girl stepping onto that aeroplane had hope…

I couldn't be arsed to fight. There was no point.

"Isn't it time for dinner soon?"

Situations that are destined to fail:

Awkward reunions

+

Spaghetti

Twenty-four

Dinner, as normal, was chaos. The weekend staff had definitely lost their sheen. They all had big dark circles under their eyes and a tendency to flinch at anything.

I was so nervous about seeing Kyle. Okay, it had only been, like, two hours, but the dynamic was totally different now. And we had a secret, sort of. I mean, it needed to be a secret. If Mum found out I'd lied to her and run off with some boy, she would go mad. Especially if it was him.

Whinnie hugged me the moment I got in the hall.

"Amber, I'm jealous. You look so rested!"

Calvin spotted me from behind his stuffed jacket potato, and knocked over his chair to run over and hug me.

"Dooph," I said. "Did you miss me then, Calvin?"

He let go and shrugged, all trying to play it cool. "A little bit."

I ruffled his hair and he batted me off. "What did I miss?"

"I won a rosette for the painting you helped me with."

"That's amazing, go you!"

"And, did you hear we're having a dance? Right here in the hall? Next week?"

Whinnie nodded. "That's right. We're having a dance."

Calvin pulled at my T-shirt. "Will you dance with me, Amber? Will you? Will you?"

I nodded. "Of course… Now, go finish your tea."

He smiled. "It's so weird that you call it tea…"

"Go on."

Whinnie handed me an apron and I joined her behind the doling-out table, dispensing spaghetti hoops. I ladled out slop onto their plastic plates with dividing bits, deliberately saving the nice looking side of the spaghetti for myself.

"So, how was LA?" Whinnie asked, in a quiet lull in the queue. Most of the kids were already eating. The hall was packed, most of the seats taken, kids laughing and shovelling food down themselves. Mum and Kevin were already eating at the top of the hall. I caught Mum's eye and she gave me a sad sorry-for-herself smile. I smiled back weakly.

"It was great," I replied, in that high-pitch voice that always comes out when you're lying.

Charlie Brown came over for seconds.

"Not till everyone's had their firsts," Whinnie said. "Amber and I haven't even eaten yet."

He skulked off, kicking the floor in annoyance, and we were alone again.

"That's weird," she said. "Because the others aren't even

back yet… And on Saturday morning, they were all saying Kyle had disappeared."

I dropped my ladle into the spaghetti and the handle sank into the sauce. I swore and got my hands covered with neon red goop trying to pick it out.

"Oh, is that right?"

"And you weren't on the minibus with everyone else."

"I wasn't?"

"Amber. The minibus isn't even back yet, and you're here. You were quite obviously not on the minibus."

I looked down at myself.

"Oh yeah. I guess I'm not."

"Were you with Kyle?"

Just as I was stuttering, he was there. Back in his camp T-shirt, his sleeves rolled up to show off his arms. His usual massive grin stretched all over his face.

I want to kiss him. I want to kiss him.

"Kyle!" I dropped the ladle again.

"Hey, you want me to take over so you girls can eat?" He was talking to me all normally – like we hadn't kissed at the top of a waterfall, like I didn't know about his Andrew Lloyd Webber collection…

"Oh, hey, yeah, that would be…great…wouldn't it, Whinnie?"

Whinnie was looking at each of us in turn, not missing anything.

"Yeah, thanks, Kyle." She pushed her glasses up her nose. "Amber, you've got sauce all over the handle!"

He was behind the counter and budged me with his butt to move me out the way. The tiny physical contact made my whole body burn. He *really* was pretending nothing had happened. I felt our little world slip away, like trying to hold water in my hands… I didn't want to lose it… Even though it was all my fault, I didn't want to lose it.

"Oh, yeah, sorry."

Kyle fished it out and wiped it on the front of the apron he'd put on. *Why did he still look like that in an apron?* Whinnie and I grabbed some trays and helped ourselves to spaghetti hoops and a baked potato. We took a place right at the end of the table, away from most of the others. It took all my energy not to turn my head to look at Kyle…

"Are you going to tell me what's going on?" Whinnie whispered.

I took a bite of half-cold spaghetti.

"Nothing's going on."

"Okay. You're leaving me no choice but to guess. You and Kyle went somewhere?"

I tried not to move my face.

"Ahh, you blinked twice. That's a giveaway! Where did you go? Are you two, like, together?" She wasn't asking in a girly excited way, just a genuinely curious way.

I made a *shh* sign. "We're not together. But, yeah, he took me away. To Yosemite. Because I was upset about Mum."

Whinnie's eyebrows went all haywire beneath her glasses. "Wow. That's nice of him."

"What does that mean?"

"Just that. That it was nice."

I smiled at her and took another bite of my spaghetti. "Both of you were brilliant the other night. I really owe you."

She gave me a little affectionate nudge. "No probs. You can pay me back by telling me if you got together or not."

I looked up, to try and see if I could catch another look at Kyle. The kids were getting restless for pudding, the noise in the hall growing as they waited impatiently for their disgusting caramel whip I'd seen back in the kitchen.

"Umm, no," I said, half-heartedly. I caught my mum's eye again and waved, but she either didn't see or ignored me.

"Umm, no?" Whinnie repeated. "So you stayed the night in a motel together, I'm presuming? And all that happened was 'umm no'?"

"Basically." I pushed my tray away.

"Fair enough."

"Sorry it wasn't more exciting. What did I miss here anyway?"

"Oh, the usual. I want to get my ovaries tied the moment camp is finished. Charlie Brown shot some kid right near the eye with a paintball gun – so that was terrifying. Luckily the kid thought it was funny..." She trailed off. "I walked past the minibus on Saturday morning, you know. On the way to the first-aid tent to sort out the kid's eye. Melody seemed pretty upset that Kyle wasn't there..."

My tummy flip-flopped. I had no idea how I felt about Melody any more. She was like a stick that poked me in the gut, provoking all different kinds of emotions… Anger, jealousy, and now…a little bit of sympathy…

"Oh…well… I'm sure she found someone else to get over him with in LA."

Whinnie let out a bitchy giggle, but I didn't join in. I just smiled and then, when no one was looking, pulled out my phone and sent another overpriced message to Lottie and Evie.

Please wake up. I need you guys. Now… x

Situations that are destined to fail:

Defeatist attitudes

+

Lottie

+

Evie

Twenty-five

My phone went off at about midnight. Not that it woke me. I was lying on my back, staring at the ceiling. After spending the remainder of the evening staring at my sketch of Kyle like a proper psycho.

I leaped on it. It was Lottie's number.

We are both up at the CRACK OF DAWN. Get your ginger ass to a computer now.

Another text came in. From Evie's phone:

Lottie says sorry for the ginger ass comment. She's blaming it on her lack of coffee.

I kicked my sheet back and quickly crept into the sitting room, where the computer sat in the corner. I switched on the desktop and it made a loud excitable turning-on beep.

I actually put my finger to my lips to shh it.

Don't wake Mum and Kevin don't wake Mum and Kevin.

I listened. Silence.

And then a snore from Bumface Kevin.

If Mum were still a drunk, I could've relied on her staying asleep too. But she'd never slept well since she got dry. I'd just have to hope she was tired out from making me feel guilty.

I tapped my fingers impatiently as I waited for everything to load.

"Come on, come on..."

Just as the computer was figuring itself out, all *It's almost 1 a.m., what are you doing to me?* a little sign popped up in the right-hand corner.

Lottie would like to talk with you.

I double-clicked on the icon and then...there they were.

"HI, AMBER!" They both waved at the camera, big smiles on their make-up-free morning faces. The light of tomorrow's morning hitting them from the side, making them look like the saviour angels they were.

It was too much. I burst into tears.

"Christ," Lottie grumbled. "I'm not THAT scary without eyeliner on, am I?"

"Sorry, guys, I just..." I burst into a fresh heap of tears. They erupted from the very pit of my stomach, my ribs actually hurting from the effort of contracting out such physical grief. I missed them so much. I missed everything so much. I shouldn't have come here. I shouldn't have thought it would make things good, that my mum would want to see me, not really. I should be with them, without Kyle and Whinnie and Russ and Melody and all the other random Americans I'd never see again.

Evie – always the better of the two for emotional support – pushed herself closer to the camera.

"Amber? What's wrong?"

Another sob. I practically had to shove my fist into my mouth to stop myself from waking Mum and Kevin.

"Is it your mum? What's happened?"

I nodded. "It's sort of my mum, but also...also..."

Lottie pushed into the camera lens, shoving Evie to one side with her face.

"But also what...?"

The whole weekend flashed past me, seeping out of my brain and gushing confusion into my veins, pumping it around every part of me.

"Well...it's that boy..."

They made me go and get a glass of milk. Lottie did a wiggle dance to distract me out of crying and accidentally blocked the camera with her bottom. Within ten minutes, I was stuffing down cookies while they ate bowls of Cheerios, and we were laughing quietly.

I told them everything.

"Let's get this straight." Lottie's voice warped on the last word from the bad internet connection. "You're crying because a boy you really like, likes you back?"

I nodded, and crammed another Oreo into my mouth.

Evie nodded while Lottie shook her head.

"I don't get it. I mean, I've seen this boy with my own eyeballs. He is fit as. And you say he's a nice guy?"

"Of course he's nice," Evie butted in. "He looked after her when she was sick, and then took her to a dreamland full of rainbows...but that's not what it's about, is it, Amber?"

I swallowed – both the chewed-up black gunk of my cookie, and another lump that had wedged itself in my throat.

"Yes, no. I don't know what it is."

"Is it just because he kissed that Melody chauvinist pig girl?" Lottie asked. "Because if you're waiting for a guy to share all your firsts with, you really better pick someone less good-looking. He is bound to have kissed a lot of people. I mean, it's a waste of a sexual resource if he hasn't."

Evie turned to Lottie. "Are we referring to men as sexual resources now?"

"Blimey. No, you're right." Lottie slapped her own hand. "Sometimes I worry I'm a sexual predator."

"We all have that worry about you, Lottie," I said. And we all laughed.

"The Melody situation did wreck things a bit," I said. "Like, he was saying all this weird stuff about how he just does things because that's what's expected of him. And at first I thought I wasn't kissing him because I actually don't know him and I was scared I just liked him because he's so good-looking. But, then I got to know him better. And… well, he's a really interesting and nice guy. And he really seems to like me. God knows why…"

"AMBER," they both warned.

"Sorry… But, well, look at him, and look at me."

"I have," Evie said. "And you're being an idiot."

"I know." More tears threatened, and I rubbed my eyes with the back of my hand. "I don't know, girls. This summer, it's just been…hard. My mum has been…well…her. And I just feel a bit broken. And, what if I do get with him? Then what? I leave soon. I'll only get hurt. We're, like, only young, we wouldn't do long distance. And…I don't think I can get hurt… I feel, like, made of glass anyway. Why should I do something that will ultimately make me unhappy?" My voice broke on the last word.

Evie was nodding. But Lottie was determinedly shaking her head.

"Amber, you can't live your life like that," she said, all serious for a moment.

"I'm just being practical."

"When did being practical get anyone anywhere?" Lottie loomed at the webcam, her eyes all wide.

"So, what? I should just fall head first into situations that I know are destined to fail?"

"Yes!" Lottie said, just as Evie shook her head and said, "No!" Evie put her hand up. "Eves, you don't need to put your hand up to talk, you know?"

She gave Lottie a look. "Don't I?"

Lottie waved her hands. "Okay okay okay, I'll be less forceful in my delivery."

"Thank you," Evie said.

She pushed Lottie out the way to make more room for her face. "As someone who has been clinically diagnosed with a condition that makes you not want to put yourself at risk, I can kind of see where Amber's coming from. Why do something you know will end up hurting you?"

Lottie looked like she was going to explode. "Because it's the right thing to do! Because it's living. Because it's the only way you grow and change!"

Evie and I exchanged looks over Lottie's shoulder.

"I sense a lecture," I said.

"Too right," Lottie replied.

She began pacing in front of the camera, and if it wasn't for the distortion of the sound, or the occasional break-up in the picture, I could've been there with them, in Evie's super-clean bedroom, eating Cheerios and having another Spinster Meeting.

"What is this obsession with happiness?" Lottie threw her head back like she was surrendering to the gods.

"Umm, isn't happiness kind of the reason to be alive?"

"Is it? Look, I was reading this book..."

"Here we go again," Evie muttered, smiling.

"And in this book, they were analysing happiness levels in women – comparing them from now, back to when they sampled it in the seventies."

"And?" I prompted, wishing, sometimes, just sometimes, I could have a problem and it not have to lead into a Lottie TED talk.

"And, guess what? According to the sample, women were HAPPIER way back in the seventies. Back when their main purpose was usually to be a wife and squeeze out children. When the only career aspiration fed to them was to be a secretary and they'd get their arses grabbed by their drunken boss. It had only been legal to vote for fifty years, and the Equal Pay Act had only JUST been passed. So, of course, when this research came out, all the anti-feminist buttheads got massive men's rights boners. Loads of them came out saying, 'Well this just proves us right. Feminism makes women unhappy. Look at what you've achieved, you silly little things, and look how unhappy it's made you.'"

"That is really weird," Evie said. "It also has nothing to do with Amber…"

"Can you just, for once, let me build to a crescendo? This is good advice, I promise!"

I stuck my tongue out.

"So, we could go down the road of why this research is totally flawed in the first place. Which I will, a bit, but quickly. Firstly, why do girls and women need to be happy anyway? Why does society deem it utterly unacceptable for girls to be pissed off, or sad? No, we have to be meek little contented things with a bonny air of grace about us, otherwise we're labelled unhinged, or a bitch, or 'She's obviously not getting enough, is she?' or 'Is it that time of the month again, darling?' Whereas boys can behave like utter miserable arsewipes and it's all fine and cool like, I dunno, cool miserable people like Morrissey or whatever. ANYWAY...also, maybe just maybe, women in that first survey just...I dunno...LIED. Because women's lib was still pretty...new, and it takes a while for ideas to sink in... Ideas like, *You don't have to put up with this crap, and, did you know you can use your brain AND love your children, it could be better, you know?* And—"

"Shh," I whispered hard.

There was a cough from Kevin and Mum's room. I held my breath, and on the computer screen Lottie and Evie did the same thing...waiting... Another cough...then a long, long silence.

"I think they're still asleep," I said. "Sorry to interrupt your flow, Lottie."

She beamed at me. "We're getting to the point soon, I promise."

"Well, I look forward to it."

"Anyways, here's what I think... When you get your eyes opened up to what's wrong with the world, it does make you angrier. More bitter. More discontent. More, well, *sad*! Sometimes I think it would be so much easier if I wasn't a feminist. I could just concentrate on looking pretty, and turn on the TV and not feel sick with rage that there's hardly any female MPs on the news channel, and all the other women on TV don't have any clothes on. I could pick a boyfriend who's just such a macho douche, and think he's the bee's knees, and shower him with blowjobs and bake him cookies and think how lucky I am that he chose me… It could be nice. But it's not the right thing to do!" Lottie's face was red, and she punched the air. "It won't make the world change for the better! It won't make me change for the better. I won't grow, if I just accept what's what. *The world* won't grow. The same unfair shit will just keep happening, and yes it's easier to roll over and say, 'That's too hard and annoying, I just want to eat some pie' but it's not the right thing…"

Evie smiled slowly. "So you gotta fight for your right to be ruddy miserable?"

Lottie patted her shoulder. "Yes! Exactly. Because because because IT'S THE RIGHT THING TO DO."

It always took me a few more minutes to digest Lottie's lectures. I ate another cookie and watched them discuss it on the webcam, mulling it all over.

"So…?" I said quietly. "I'm still not sure how this relates to me and what to do about Kyle?"

Lottie turned her attention to me again.

"Do you like him?"

"Yes." I did. I really, really, did.

"I've seen him. So you obviously fancy him, because why wouldn't anyone?"

I nodded. "I confirm I fancy him."

"And he likes you?"

For some reason, just that thought made me want to cry.

"That's what he says."

"But you don't want to do anything about this serendipitous good fortune because you think geographically-wise, it's destined to fail, and you'll get hurt?"

"Umm...yeah, I guess."

"And yet you choose to be a feminist, even though it makes you angrier and sadder and feeling more helpless? God, do you remember last term at college, Amber? When the rugby lads fought against our jukebox rape song ban and *everyone* at college hated us?"

I could see where this was leading. My heart warmed up a bit. More than a bit.

"Yep, that's what I choose."

"Why?"

"Because it's the right thing... But how is snogging Kyle the same as getting a rape song banned from college?"

And it was Evie who answered, cottoning on to Lottie's point just about the same time as me.

"Because, Amber," she said. "Life doesn't always have to be about changing the world. Sometimes it's about living your life for you... Trying to find some happiness, completely selfishly, but just for you... And you should adopt the same lack of fear you have in your feminism to your search for happiness."

"But I won't be happy with Kyle! I mean, I'll be back on your side of the sea soon."

"Ocean," Lottie corrected. "But, think about it. Would you rather have everything stay the same, like those housewives in the seventies, feeling safe – but also stifled and numb? Or would you rather take a risk, fight for something, even though it may make you more unhappy in the end, but you'll grow, Amber. You'll be changing. You'll be living…"

I really did start to cry then.

"Lottie, you've made her cry again," I heard Evie say through the speakers.

"It's good crying though."

I sat up, showing them my red, tear-stained face. "Yeah, it's good crying." I cried harder.

My friends were right. I'm sure some expensive psychiatrist could say smart things about my drinking habits, and the fact I'm always angry, and that I tend to be sarcastic and nasty to new people as a way of pushing them away, and not wanting to get with Kyle, and they could easily pinpoint everything down to the shit with my mum, and abandonment issues, blah blah blah. And I could just roll over, and accept that's who I am, or I could fight…I could fight to change myself…to grow…even if it hurt, I would grow.

I kicked my chair back and stood up.

"Girls, I have to go somewhere," I said.

They began applauding.

"Go snog his face off!" Lottie saluted me.

Evie peered at the camera. "You have a booger on your cheek you may want to wipe off first."

"You know I love you girls?"

"We know."

"I miss you so much!"

"We miss you too," they chorused.

"Thank you. Honestly, thank you." I almost started crying again.

"Stop blubbing and go do the right thing," Lottie said. "And then, of course, tell us every single detail the moment you can."

I ran out into the darkness, my flip-flops kicking up scratchy pine needles. I could hardly remember where his cabin was, but something led me there. It was so dark. Probably so dangerous. There could be bears, or hyenas, or maybe not hyenas because this wasn't Africa, but other eaty type things.

What if I was too late? What if I'd missed my chance? What if this made my heart explode into so many pieces it was essentially vapour rather than a rather important organ needed for survival?

But I had to try… I might get hurt, but I had to try.

Scratched and scared, I flung myself out into the moonlight. I was here. In the clearing where his cabin was. Everything was so still. So stunning when lit by the moon. Two little cabins – one Russ's and one Kyle's. Full of sleeping kids, and maybe, just maybe, full of my future.

I paused.

I wasn't sure where Kyle would be sleeping. The weekenders were here until tomorrow, would they sleep in Kyle's bed? Was he sleeping elsewhere? Also, if I got caught, I would be in unimaginable trouble…

I tiptoed through the clearing. My heart thunk-thunking so noisily that I could actually feel it hitting my ribs. I got to the cabin door, stopping to take a deep breath. I was doing this. I was going to do this…

The door creaked open and I winced, waiting for stirring…but I was greeted with snores. Twelve humps of bodies dozed peacefully under their camp blankets – gentle grunting snore sounds echoed around the wooden walls. It smelled a bit, but I wasn't going to let something like that ruin my romantic moment. Kyle's bed was right next to the door. I crept up to it. Seeing his face, all covered in sleep, silenced any nerves. Instead I just felt light, giddy almost. And relieved that I'd found him.

This boy likes me. This sleeping boy actually likes me.

And…

… *You better wake him up now otherwise this will quickly feel creepy.*

I reached out and shook his shoulder, the warmth from his sleeping body seeping up my hand.

Kyle stirred.

Kyle opened his eyes.

"Am…?" And I covered his mouth with my finger, and said, "*Shh!*"

Oh, my heart, it was going bonkers. Every inch of my skin was covered in goosebumps.

"Is everything okay?" he whispered, his eyes all wide. He was panicking. He thought something was wrong. Of course he thought something was wrong. You only break into a cabin full of sleeping children in the middle of the woods and shake someone awake at 1 a.m. if somebody is sick or dead. I nodded frantically, as he rubbed sleep out of his eyes and sat up.

"Hang on... Why the hell are you here?"

I shushed him again, and pointed to the door.

"Outside." I tiptoed out before anyone else woke up.

It was a whole new level of dark outside – the moonlight had dipped behind a cloud and it was only just bright enough so I didn't trip over the log. I stood in the middle of the clearing, my arms wrapped around myself to keep warm in the night-time breeze, still in my pyjamas, waiting for him.

Kyle stumbled out into the night. He didn't have a top on, which made my stomach lurch. He wore pyjama bottoms though – chequered blue childlike ones.

"Amber?" He looked at me, in all my pyjamaed pale ginger-skin glory. "What's going on?"

I stepped forward – knowing that this was the stopping point, and I wasn't going to stop. I was ready to step over my imaginary line. I was ready to live. And get hurt. And maybe he wouldn't kiss me back. I mean, why would he kiss me back? I'd totally rejected him, and he was probably over it already, or had thought about the whole long distance thing and realized what a stupid idea it was.

"Amber?" he asked again, looking confused. Maybe worried. I'd still not reassured him no one was dying. "Is it your mum?"

I took another step, close enough to touch him. I reached

out and, unsure of myself, but also never surer, I stroked his tanned cheek with the back of my hand.

"Kyle...I..."

One more step. Our faces so close to touching.

I was over the line now. The line was a dot on the horizon behind me.

I put my other arm around his neck, and moved my head forward. Every part of me was alive and dancing. Kyle looked down at me – I loved how he was tall enough to look down on me. His eyes were wide, puzzled, uncertain. We stared at each other. Then I closed mine and leaned forward.

I brought my lips to his clumsily, holding down tears.

... Kyle kissed me back.

Situations that are destined to fail:

No time

+

No privacy

+

An insatiable desire to spend every second alone with each other

Twenty-six

Camp days became an exquisite torture, measuring the time I wasn't able to touch Kyle. It was a surprise how much it physically ached.

I lived for the tiny moments I hoped no one would notice. The knowing smile Kyle would give me over the paint pots, as I helped the kids blodge oils onto canvas during my art class. The shoot of electricity that ran through my body whenever he made an innocent-looking reason to touch me.

"Out of the way, Amber," he said, gently touching my back to move me to one side. "I need to get to the arrows." And my body sang with so much happy static, I missed every shot in archery, arrows flying up into the trees or skidding along the ground – the kids laughing at my ineptitude, Kyle giving me another secret smile, knowing he'd caused it.

Over the next week, we concocted all sorts of ludicrous

errands we needed to run, just so we could grab time together.

"Oh no," I'd say, during lunchtime, when the kids were sitting in a dusty circle somewhere, inhaling more sandwiches before more baseball. "I forgot the milk cartons. Can anyone help me carry them from the kitchen?"

"I'll go," Kyle shot up his hand. Russ studied us both, maybe figuring it out but I really hoped not.

"You sure?"

"Yeah."

"Okay, cool."

The moment we were swallowed by the forest, Kyle pushed me up against a tree, putting his hands either side of my face. We kissed like there was no tomorrow, which there wasn't really. Well, there were limited amounts of tomorrow… I couldn't believe I'd waited seventeen long years before doing something so great. The way he tasted, the way he caught his hands up in my mess of hair, the way he'd pull away from me, just to stare, before lowering his mouth again.

The milk was practically off by the time we'd managed to bring it back to the campers.

Yep – each day was torture. Having to talk about camp. Having to deal with runny noses, or grazed knees, or arguments over whose turn it was to have the special gold pen, and homesickness, or *I-don't-like-spaghetti*, when I could be learning Kyle's favourite book, or all his best and worst childhood memories, or what book-to-film adaptation made him the most angry, and where he kept his Prom King crown – and all the other tiny intricacies of a person that you only learn through time, when time was the one thing we didn't really have.

But the night-times... They were the opposite of whatever torture was.

I'd wait, every night, in my room – listening to Kevin and Mum's going to bed noises. I'd feign sleep until they went quiet. Which, for at least two nights in a row, took far too long. Mum had a mini insomnia patch, and I could hear her pacing around the living room, making cocoa, not realizing just how much she tortured me. I'd lie, waiting, staring at the wall, unable to keep still, my entire body anticipating Kyle...

When the cabin finally went quiet, I'd jump out of bed, shoving any bits of clothes on, before bolting through the door and running towards the small clearing outside Kyle's cabin.

He'd always be there, waiting for me. A smile already on his face, before he'd even seen me in the darkness.

"Amber."

And we'd mesh together, in a frenzy of kissing and touching and giggling. His fingers trailing all over my body. The weight of his body keeping me warm from the cool evening air. Touching each other's faces, tracing the details with our fingers to the backing vocals of cicadas.

We talked too, of course. Between all the kissing. There was nothing I didn't want to know about him.

"So, Mr Fan of Musical Theatre." I'd dragged some cushions out with me and we'd made a mini-camp under the trees. "What's your best bit of any musical, ever?"

Kyle absent-mindedly played with my hair. "Is this the point where I pretend to be all macho, and act like I don't have one?"

I kissed his cheek.

"This is the point where you tell me the truth. And, just so you know, that point always needs to be the point. I will have no macho posturing thank you very much. I'm not the kind of girl who likes all that nonsense."

More kissing. My insides melted in on themselves with happiness.

"Delay tactics won't work," I said, after a huge amount of kissing that led to one very long delay.

"Okay then." Kyle leaned back against the tree, picked up a stray pine cone and began expertly tossing it from one hand to another. "There's this bit, right at the start of *Phantom of the Opera*... It begins with this auction at the old opera house – everything is dusty and covered in sheets. All the actors and actresses are made up to look old... So you know we're at the end of the story, before it's even been told if that makes any sense? Anyway, the final lot is this gigantic chandelier. And then, all of a sudden, WHAM. The old chandelier turns on in a big blast of light, and all this crazy music starts, and the chandelier starts rising up above the audience. All the sheets are thrown off the set, and you're transported back into the opera house's glory days... Yeah –"

Kyle looked down, embarrassed – "whenever that bit happens, I basically almost piss my pants."

We both burst out laughing. "I'm such a loser."

"You're not. I know that bit – it's good! Anyway I get excited in any song with a key change."

"Key changes are so exciting!"

"Especially if boy bands do them, and all get off their stools at the same time."

"Do British boy bands do that too? Wow, who knew the key change stool stand was an international phenomenon?"

I pushed a cushion over my bare feet to keep them warm. "Have you ever read an Andrew Lloyd Webber biography then?"

"Does one even exist?"

"I'm not sure. But I do remember hearing this rumour… that he has a massive…umm…appendage." I was glad it was dark, as I'd started blushing.

Kyle cracked up laughing. "How could you POSSIBLY know that?"

I laughed too. "It's a well-known fact. It's a monster apparently."

"Jesus, this changes everything."

"What does it change?"

"I'm not sure… I need to digest this information for a while. Everything I thought I knew has been…drastically altered."

We laughed more.

"Amber?"

"Yes?"

More kisses.

"Why are we sitting in a wood, in the middle of the night, discussing the size of Andrew Lloyd Webber's schlong?"

"Do you not like it?"

"No, it's not that..."

I unravelled myself from his arm, so I could better look at his face. He was staring at me, really staring. It made me feel vulnerable, but in a really nice way.

"I've got a knack for bringing up inappropriate topics of conversation. The very first Spinster Club meeting I organized was about periods. I announced the agenda over lunch."

Kyle laughed and pulled me back under his arm. "You see. We've jumped from Andrew's tool to menstruation... What's next?"

I peeked up at him. Even the underside of his nostrils were attractive. It was overwhelming, how much... something...love, maybe? (No it was too soon for that...) But something was oozing off me in waves. All I wanted was to look at him, talk to him, be with him.

"I can totally ruin the whole evening and tell you all my bad childhood memories of my mother?" I joked.

Kyle's face dropped. "I want to hear all that too. And it would never ruin anything."

I clung to him tight.

"You say that..."

"I mean that..."

"Should we talk about periods instead?"

Kyle wiggled us both down, so our backs were on the ground, looking up at the sky through the trees. "You know what, Miss Inappropriate? We don't have to talk at all."

Situations that are destined to fail:

Hearing the romantic story of how your parents met

+

After their bitter divorce

Twenty-seven

From: LongTallAmber
To: LottieIsAlwaysRight, EvieFilmGal
Subject: Is there something wrong with me?

...I literally can't stop smiling. Like, at all. You know me. This is not usual. Have I got a disease?

From: LottieIsAlwaysRight
To: LongTallAmber
Subject: RE Is there something wrong with me?

Yes you have a disease. Hopefully by now a SEXUAL DISEASE.

From: EvieFilmGal
To: LongTallAmber

Subject: RE RE Is there something wrong with me?

It's okay. Lottie's calmed down now, and admits that romanticizing STIs isn't appropriate, or funny.

IT WAS A BIT FUNNY… That was Lottie taking over my computer. So, we take it you've kissed him then? Sounds like you're falling hard, girl. We're happy for you. Though, hasn't it only been like a week? That is falling both hard and fast.
IGNORE EVIE, SHE IS FAR TOO SENSIBLE. FALL IN LOVE AND USE A CONDOM.

From: LongTallAmber
To: LottieIsAlwaysRight, EvieFilmGal
Subject: RE RE RE Is there something wrong with me?

Okay, so totally can't stop laughing at your emails. Lottie, CALM DOWN, DEAR (uh-oh, patriarchy). I do like him. A lot. Thanks for all your advice. I think…

It had only been a week. How was that possible? I felt like I'd known him for ever. And, yet, I knew nothing. I felt sick at the short amount of time I had to commit his life to memory. To know every inch, every scar, every scratch, every hiccup. And kissing him already wasn't enough.

Last year, Evie got involved with this total-arsewipe we know called Guy and almost ended up losing her virginity to him. Afterwards she told me that she should've known it wasn't a good vibe because whenever Guy wanted to take things further her instincts had been *Noooooo, not yet!*

It was the opposite between Kyle and me. Maybe it's because we knew time was tight, but each moment in those stolen night-times was an exercise in self-restraint. His hands would drift into my bra, or up my shorts, and he'd have to stop himself and say sorry, and I'd say it was fine, when, really, I wanted his hands to be there, but I felt like I couldn't say that. Kissing wasn't doing it. I wanted to crawl into his skin. Every bit of his body that wasn't touching me seemed like a horrible waste.

I was drowning. And there was no one on this side of the Atlantic to stop me. Apart from me. And, well, Whinnie.

"I approve," she said, out of nowhere, as she helped me tidy up the paint pots.

"Huh?"

"Of you and Kyle," she said. "I approve."

"WHAT?" A paint pot clattered to the hall floor, echoing around the walls, making my protest even more obvious.

"Don't worry," she said, laughing over her glasses. "I won't tell anyone. And kudos, by the way, for not dropping me now you're in lurrrrve. I'm glad we're still hanging out, even though you and Kyle are together."

I pushed my hair back. "We're NOT together…" Then realized I'd already lost. "How the feck do you know?"

She rolled her eyes. "Come on, you guys are pretty obvious. You're always staring at each other. I would vomit if I didn't like you both so very much."

"I…er…we are? Shite, I hope Mum doesn't notice."

"Yeah, I was going to ask about that." Whinnie picked up another paint pot and tipped the chalky painty water down the sink. "Doesn't she hate him?"

I let out a big sigh. "I'm not entirely sure what I'm doing." Whinnie knowing made it seem more real, and more scary all of a sudden.

She sensed my upset, and put her pot down to hug me. I smushed into her – so glad I'd made a friend out here. We had already discussed her coming over to England to stay next summer… If I wasn't here visiting Mum again of course. Part of me still hoped Mum might be home by next summer… Stupid I know.

"Hey, I didn't mean to upset you. I was just curious."

"No, it's okay. It's just, well, I'm leaving soon…we only have a week left of camp…then I only have ten days after camp before my flight home…but Kyle won't be here for those ten days because camp will have finished…" I was all over the place. "It's all a bit strange," I added. I looked up at her and smiled. "What would Winnie the Pooh say?"

She smiled back. "He says a LOT about love, actually."

"Really? Hit me with it. I'll put my trust in you and Pooh."

"Well, he says, when people care too much, that's what you call love."

I nodded slowly. "Right, and what does that mean?"

Whinnie shrugged. "Just that. I told you – the beauty of Pooh is there's no depth to him."

I thought about Mum suddenly then, rather than Kyle. I cared too much. I really cared too much. It was definitely love – but was that good?

"What else does he say?" I asked, shaking my head a little to stop the bad thought seeping in deeper.

"Umm, well…" I could see her going through her Pooh library in her head. Her eyes shone. "This is more about friendship love, but there's this lovely bit where he's talking to Piglet. Pooh says the moment they met, he knew an adventure was going to happen."

"Riiiight. So love means caring too much and having an adventure? So what does that mean? What should I do?"

She grinned. "Jeez, Amber, I don't know. But you're smiling, like, ten million times more than the difficult drunk I met on the first night. So I reckon that's a good thing."

"I was difficult?" I picked up another paint pot and began laboriously cleaning it.

"You were SO difficult. And that's why we're friends."

The night before the big dance in the rec hall, Kyle and I agreed to meet at the pier at midnight. The atmosphere in camp was practically vibrating with the promise of slow dances and takeaway pizza. Calvin had yanked some daisies out of the field and asked if he could have the first dance, while Kyle wiggled his eyebrows in mock jealousy behind him. I was in charge of decorating the whole hall and Mum and I decamped there after dinner to work on it. Things were still tense from me guilt-tripping her; Mum knew how to hold a grudge, even against her own daughter. But, outwardly at least, we twirled long ribbons of coloured crepe paper in companionable semi-silence.

"You've been smiling a lot recently, Amber." She carefully cut some ribbon for the balloons we'd finished blowing up.

"It must be the Californian sun."

"Or getting to spend so much time with your mother?"

"That too."

I said it just to placate her, as we'd not sat alone together since drinking that hot chocolate. Apart from now, I guessed. I was starting to care less, feeling colder, and, of course, preoccupied by Kyle.

I searched the cluttered table for some Sellotape. I looked up and saw her staring at me, smiling. "You back at the centre this weekend?"

"Yes, it's going to be an exhausting shift after tomorrow's dance. The kids never go to bed afterwards, too high on drama and sweets. You're welcome to come join me?" She asked it nervously, but genuinely.

I shook my head.

"Thanks" – and I found I meant it – "but I'm not covered by weekend relief this week. It's Whinnie and Russ's turn."

Russ was so excited he'd made his watch bleep every

hour in countdown to the weekend. Whenever it went, he yelped with joy, and waved it at the kids' faces, going "Almost time, suckers." Luckily for him, they found it funny…

"Are they all going to LA too?"

"I think they're camping in Lake Tahoe."

I was so unbelievably jealous – the thought of being in a tent, with Kyle, with no kids, and no grown-ups.

"You've not spoken much about LA. Did you really hate it?"

I pulled a face to try and cover my *I'm-lying* face.

"It was…okay."

The only downside of a perfect week was the dread I felt whenever I thought of Mum finding out about last weekend. We had no one to cover us, especially after Melody went absolutely nuts at Kyle when he told her their kiss was a one-off thing.

"It's okay," Mum said. "I felt the exact same way when I first went. You get so excited because you've seen the Hollywood sign on the TV your whole life. Then you realize it's just a pretty gross and seedy place."

A flower of guilt blossomed in my stomach. "Yeah. It was pretty…um…seedy."

"Maybe go to a national park or something during your next time off?"

I dropped the Sellotape on the floor. "I'll hopefully be spending it with you," I squeaked.

Mum looked up at me. "Oh, yes, of course. It's in your last week of camp, right?"

How could I be thinking about my last week of camp? Camp was supposed to last a month – that's ages! How could it almost be done? How could it end when everything was just starting? And my heart did a little rip in two – I couldn't see Kyle in that time? It would be our last days together…but my mother, my blood and guts mother, I needed to see her too.

"I don't want to think about it," I said. Which was true.

Mum put her scissors down and came round to hug me tight. So I clung as hard as I could.

"I don't want to think about it either."

I started crying. Never in the history of my life had I cried more in a summer.

"Sorry," I said into the softness of her body, just above her breast, where my face was buried.

"It's okay. I know it's hard for you."

Wasn't it hard for her?

She let go of the hug. "So, you all set for this dance tomorrow? It's usually pretty dramatic. Lots of the kids seem to think they've fallen in love with someone already, can you believe it? Aged eleven? We try to minimize the amount of slow songs the DJ plays, to limit the collateral damage." She smiled, nudging me with her shoulder to make the joke funnier.

"Didn't you have a whirlwind romance with Dad?" I asked.

Mum went rigid.

"It was…quick…yes."

"You know, you guys never told me how you met."

Mum went back to twirling ribbon. "Do we really have to talk about your father? You know things are…strained between us."

"He's never told me. I can't ask him, he's always with that psycho bitch."

Mum laughed, then looked up, worried. "I shouldn't have laughed at that. Sorry."

"So… How did you meet?"

Mum put her scissors down again. "Amber!"

"Why can't I know?!"

"All right." Mum sat on her chair and looked off into nothing. I couldn't believe it – she was going to tell me. She was finally going to tell me something. I should call Penny a psycho bitch more often. "We met when we were both travelling. In India. We met on the same bus going to the Taj Mahal…talked the whole seven hours there. By the end of the seven-hour journey back, we thought we had this special connection. We spent the rest of our travels together. He proposed on our last night in India."

It was hard to imagine them like that, Dad more so. I could see Mum scurrying around the colours of India, taking photographs, bartering at stalls, making new friends in gross hostels. I couldn't see Dad there though. The dad I knew who wore proper trousers, even on the weekend. Who organized his ties into colour order. Who left Mum for someone like Penny, and trimmed the grass in that way that makes it have light green and dark green stripes.

I said it aloud. "I can't imagine Dad in India." Mum laughed again.

"I know. I don't think he was quite being himself. Maybe I wasn't quite being myself either – thus the problem..." She trailed off, and was quiet a moment. "It's easy to fall in love when you're young and the sun is shining and you feel like the world is just there to have an argument with, with someone you adore by your side. But then life happens, and you start fighting against them, rather than with them..." She picked up the scissors again. "You should always pick someone who's on your side, Amber. It's too hard to be fighting the world, *and* the person you love."

"Is Kevin on your side?"

Mum smiled slowly. "He is."

"And Dad wasn't?"

I didn't know if she would answer. I felt like I was tiptoeing on broken glass, getting this out of her.

"He wasn't on my side, no... Not when it mattered."

When you became an alcoholic mess...

I realized something... *I* wasn't on my mother's side. Maybe outwardly, yes. But inwardly, I was still so angry, so resentful.

"How do you know if someone is on your team, then?"

She picked up crepe paper and twirled it using one blade of the scissors. "You test it. You have to test it. Then see what side of the line they're on. Are they backing you up? Or are they shouting you down?"

I busied myself with tying some balloons together, the

squeak of the rubber drowning me out as I mumbled my next question.

"What was that, darling?"

I coughed and put the balloons down. Still in disbelief that she was opening up, hoping I wouldn't blow it. "I said, isn't it good to not have someone agree with you all the time? Aren't the best relationships supposed to test you?"

"Yes…" she admitted, slowly. "But there's a difference between pushing you somewhere gently because it's what's best for you, and throwing you off a cliff and saying 'Well, come on then, fly'."

She was trying to hide it, but for a moment, the bitterness was there. A hardening of her eyebrows, the setting of her jaw. I saw then how much Dad had hurt her. By leaving her, by meeting someone else. By taking himself and me away so she had nothing left to do but self-destruct to a point where she knew she needed help… I guess it was good in the long run. I mean, she wasn't dead. And there was that time we were told she'd be dead if she kept on drinking. But, still, for her, at the time, it must've hurt.

Mum tried to smile. "Now, can we please talk about something happier? And then, bedtime. I don't know about you, but I'm exhausted."

"Me too," I said, thinking, *But I won't be sleeping tonight.*

Kyle was already there when I got to the pier, laying out a blanket.

"Hey," I said shyly, still not sure how to be around him.

"Hey. You've been a while."

"I know. My mum… She wouldn't go to bed."

"Ha, it's like she knows."

"We'd know if she knew."

I'd gotten so used to navigating camp in the darkness, I no longer found it scary. I wondered if it would jar – the crammed-together streetlights of England, the night never really being yours – when I got back.

When I got back… I didn't want to think about that.

Kyle sat on the blanket and gestured for me to join him. I wanted to stop time, right at that moment. The way he looked, the open lazy smile on his face, the moonlight making his teeth look even more Hollywood white, the sound of the water lapping on the still lake…and the stars. I'd never seen so many stars. I didn't let myself think about all the rules we were breaking by being there. Anyway, we'd agreed it would only be for an hour or two.

I sat next to him as delicately as I could, which was always an effort when you're five foot eleven.

"Everyone asleep in the cabin?"

"Yes, and let's pray to everything it'll stay that way."

There was always an awkward moment when we initially met, the bit before we started kissing. I lay back first and stared up at the sky.

"Oh my fucking wow," I said. "The stars are, like, on steroids."

Kyle laughed, lay next to me and held my hand.

"Do you not ever see them like this?"

"Seriously, Kyle, we need to report these stars to some kind of committee. They're obviously on performance-enhancing drugs. We should check their urine."

"Why are you always talking about urine and periods when I'm about to kiss you?"

"Oh, that? That's my seduction act." I made myself turn away from the infinite gloriousness of the sea of stars above me to look at him. "Is it working?"

Kyle put on the worst British accent the world has ever known. "You can bloody bet it's working."

With a whoosh, he was on top of me, nuzzling me with his nose, kissing my neck. I groaned, it felt so good. I stared up at the sky, letting myself feel happy, if only in this moment. Letting myself stay just there, if only for a while.

After huge amounts of kisses, we broke apart, and just lay there, catching our breath. I rolled onto my side, curled my legs up, and nestled my face in the gap between his arm and chest. He moved his arm to snuggle me in tighter.

"I've been thinking," he said.

"Don't tell me Prom Kings are capable of such things?"

"Oh, you're hilarious. Seriously, I've been thinking... about myself."

I laughed. "Oh really, Mr Narcissist? You're not supposed to admit that. Everyone always and only, really, thinks of themselves, but you have to keep up this huge pretence you're interested in other people's boring existences. You're breaking the rules, Kyle."

"Yes, well, it's probably for the first time. But, ever since Yosemite...when you said you didn't know me..."

I reddened when I thought of what I'd said. "I was on the defensive...I'm not very comfortable with people liking me."

"Ha, I'd noticed." He kissed the top of my head. "But I was thinking, you're right. You don't really know me. So, I was thinking of stuff to tell you about me, and...well... there isn't anything. I don't really even know who I am..."

I rolled closer to him. "Come on, Kyle. This is getting dangerously existential."

"Hey, hear me out. Anyway, I went through everything I do, and put it into lists in my head – working out what I actually like, and what I do because it's what I think people want."

"And...?"

"And, I like basketball. But I don't like my major."

"What's your major?"

"Political science."

"Why don't you like politics?"

"I like it enough. But I don't love it. I don't feel the passion, you know? Like you do, whenever you start hating on the patriarchy."

"But politics changes things." I curled further into him, sleepily.

"Does it? Do you know anything about our political system at all?"

"I used to have a crush on Obama."

Kyle burst out laughing. "Who didn't? But he's a great example. Everyone thought he was going to change the world, there was so much hope pinned on him. But he couldn't really do much, because our system is so warped. All his decisions kept getting chucked out by Congress… I just spend most of my lessons feeling really pissed off, rather than intellectually enlightened."

I sat up and stroked his face, still feeling so lucky I was allowed to touch him.

"That's a common side effect of being intellectually enlightened," I said. "Has Whinnie not told you about her obsession with the *Tao of Pooh*? Basically, the more you know, the unhappier you are. That's why Winnie the Pooh is always happy – he doesn't get into politics."

"Maybe I should switch to a major that makes me happier?"

"I'm sure there is one…" I stopped, and thought of Lottie's speech. "Okay," I said. "I don't mean to go off on a tangent here, and I am more than happy to help facilitate this navel-gazing discussion about you we're having here."

"Oi." He dragged me back and distracted me with kisses. I laughed into his mouth.

"But…well…why are you measuring what you like and what you're passionate about by what makes you happy?" I paused and pushed my hair off my neck. "Have you thought about why I came to yours, the other night? What changed my mind?"

Kyle sat up and brushed his hand through my hair,

pulling it back to where it had been. "Not really. I'm just really enjoying that you did."

"I'm enjoying it too. But...well, it took a kick up the arse to get me there. I was chatting to my friends about the situation...I wasn't sure what was holding me back. And it was 'cause...well...I live in England, don't I? And you live in California and Brown, wherever the hell Brown is. I didn't see how I could get into a situation with you and come out without being hurt..."

Kyle's arm was instantly around me. "Hey, I'd never hurt you. You know that, right?"

I nodded, feeling sad, trying to get my words out. "I know. But, the situation, it's bound to hurt at some point, right? Even if we figure something out..." I felt dangerous even mentioning the future, daring to think he may want to figure something out, that this could mean more to him than a summer fling. "That's why I stopped things. But Lottie and Evie pointed out that being hurt or upset is no reason not to do something. In fact, sometimes the best things about people are the things that hurt them. Take my feminism for instance – sometimes I think it's not worth it. I get so angry, like you, at how unfair it all is and how hard it is to change things. I don't know how...happy it makes me, but it's one of my favourite things about me."

"It's one of my favourite things about you too."

"You, just saying that, is one of my favourite things about you."

"God, we're cute!" He grinned and pulled me in for

another kiss. I could sense him trying to plaster over something, to distract me with happiness, rather than think about what I was saying. But I was determined to finish.

"I'm just saying, maybe political science doesn't make you happy. But maybe that's a good thing? Every huge political movement has come from people feeling majorly pissed off. Anger is good sometimes, if you use it the right way."

Kyle went quiet, he looked out over the water. Then he turned, eyes sparkling.

"You know what? Now you've said that, I like that more. I'll put that in my *Kyle-likes-this* column."

"Why are you so hung up anyway? On *who you are*? For someone who had such an easy time in high school, you are a psychological anomaly with your low self-esteem."

Kyle stared out at the water again. It was so black, with just tiny hints of moonlight echoing off each ripple.

"I guess I just worry I'm boring… You know you're all about the feminism? Well, do you ever think it's possible for men to suffer from sexism too?"

I nodded. "It's definitely possible. Boys have to put up with crap gender roles too – feminism is about helping all of us. How come?"

Kyle picked at some rotten wood on the pier. "I just think there's this crap guys have to put up with, if they're nice men, I mean. The word 'nice' is almost an insult. I think there's like, a gender stereotype, *The Nice Guy*, you know? Girls are so judgemental about it. If you're a nice guy, you're basically bland, and boring, and they don't want to be with you… They say, 'I love bad boys', and then look really proud of themselves for falling for people they know are douches. Do you have any idea how many times a day people tell me I'm a nice guy?"

"You are a nice guy!"

"That means I'm boring!"

"And you're worried girls won't want to sleep with you?"

"No, it's not that."

"Because, anyway, girls definitely want to sleep with you."

He grinned, his happiness returning instantly. It was amazing how fast he ricocheted back to joyful, like it was his factory setting.

"Oh, do they?"

I went very red again.

"Kyle, you're not boring. You've just not figured it out yet…"

"Whereas, you know who you are…"

I screeched a laugh. "No I don't. I have no idea who I am. I'm just pissed off all the time. That's all I know about myself. I'm pissed off. And tall. How attractive is that?"

Kyle scooped me up in his arms and pulled me onto his lap. He kissed me right on the lips.

"You're very attractive."

"So are you."

We kissed gently, stopping here and there to stare at each other. His eyes were black in this light. He pulled away after a few minutes.

"I don't like thinking of you going away. I've not been letting myself think about it."

"It's not my favourite thing to think about either…but it's going to happen."

We were both quiet, contemplating it.

"How many days of camp left?"

"Not many."

"Seriously?" Kyle scratched the back of his head.

The night air soured around us at the cold hard truth of the situation. What were we supposed to say? It's not like we loved each other, not yet. It wasn't like that, I'm sure it wasn't. I always knew if I fell in love it would be like warming up a can of soup really slowly. So why was I doing this? I had just under two weeks left in America after camp finished, but Kyle would be driving to Brown, to try and get a job early. The thought of it being just me and my mum actually didn't appeal any more. It would just be her, me and Kevin – me gooseberrying my own mother, while she no doubt carried on living her life like I wasn't there.

"Hey, remember what Lottie said," I said hopelessly. "It's all about enjoying the moment."

"I guess…" Kyle still looked upset. "Wise friend you have there."

I nodded. "The wisest."

He pulled me into him and lay us down. The stars looked so close, like they'd been strung up on individual bits of see-through string. Easiness returned to us, as was so usual whenever Kyle was around. I told him what Mum had told me, about her and Dad. It seemed less sad and more romantic when looking at the stars.

"So they met abroad?" Kyle asked.

"In India, yes."

"Whirlwind romance?"

"Yep."

"And it went horribly wrong?"

"Yes, but, well, I think that was the alcoholism more than anything else."

He was still a moment. "Do you know why she even started drinking?"

I closed my eyes…said my guess out loud. "I'm not totally sure. I have these, like, bursts of memories of what she was like before. I just remember feeling really safe… but she's been a drunk for so long…" I paused. "I think they lost a baby… They told me I was going to be a sister… I remember Mum and Dad going away, and my grandma came over to stay. Mum came back – sobbing – and clutching her stomach."

"They've never talked to you about it?"

"No. And I'm too scared to ask them. You've seen what Mum's like. My memory is so muddled anyway. I can't remember if she drank before then, or if drinking maybe caused it…"

"So you have no real idea why she's an alcoholic?"

I shrugged. "Does anyone know why? Is addiction ever that simple?"

"I don't know…"

I smiled, just as a gentle breeze blew my hair.

"There were times when she dried herself out, you know?" I said, feeling warm in the memory of it. "She'd go weeks, months even, not touching a drop. She was so incredible to be around then – so creative. She taught me how to use paints. And she was so energized. She'd make just a trip to the park seem like the most amazing thing in the world – pointing out how pretty a cloud was, how beautiful just a regular meadow could be if the sun hit it right… She wore these amazing colourful clothes – all drapey fabrics that no one else's Mum had… It never lasted though. And I never saw Mum and Dad happy…not really. All I remember was fights and shouting and him pretending things were okay when they weren't… He had an affair eventually. With my stepmum. Forced me to go live with her and her evil kid… I've not been replying to any of his emails all summer. I'm mad at him…I'm mad at all of them."

I wasn't sure why this was spilling out of me. But something about Kyle's effortless ease made me want to share with him. I turned, and found myself just cupping his face.

He looked right into my eyes. "I'm sorry all this happened to you." His apology was so genuine, so heartfelt, it made me ache. Made parts of me crumble, like ancient ruins, leaving space where the pain had been. Space for where good things could grow instead.

"You have no reason to say sorry. And yet you're the only one who's ever apologized to me."

"Really? Not your mom? Your dad?"

I shook my head, shivered in the slight breeze. "Nope."

"Well sorry," he said again. "And sorry for bringing this all up, especially when I'm supposed to be being romantic." I felt him turn on his side.

I grinned, not wanting to be bogged down in it any more. Not tonight anyway.

"Who said this was romantic? I mean, all you've done is lay out a blanket. Which is also a bit presumptuous, isn't it?"

I turned over too, to see Kyle's teeth light up as he smiled.

"It's only to keep us warm. Now who's being presumptuous?"

We launched at each other, closing the gap between our bodies. As we kissed, all I wanted was more. More touching. More skin. More Kyle. It was the complete opposite to what Evie had said. The sand in the eggtimer was draining fast; I didn't want to build up to anything. I just wanted him. This moment. Kyle's tongue was in my mouth, doing brilliant things. His hands were up the back of my T-shirt. Every part of my body felt alive. I ran my hands over his body, over his arms, back down his torso…down…down… inside his shorts.

Kyle's eyes opened.

"Amber," he muttered into my mouth. "Are you sure?"

I nuzzled him, put my hand in further.

"I'm sure."

He adjusted his weight, manoeuvring himself so his arm was free. He carefully slid his finger down my stomach, a smooth delicate line, down into my own shorts.

I gasped.

I had one tiny worry… That he seemed to know what he was doing, and that meant he'd probably done it to someone else before. But the sensation was shortly replaced with just joy and longing. We kissed more, and touched each other, and without meaning to, we fell asleep under the stars.

Situations that are destined to fail:

Getting caught

+

The consequences

Twenty-eight

"Shit."

My eyes flickered open to early morning sunlight. The ripples on the lake glistened in the rising sun. Birds called out all loud and over the top.

I was half naked, my shorts abandoned at my feet, my head resting on Kyle's shoulder.

"Shit," he said louder. "Amber, wake up. We have to go."

The warmness in my stomach hardened. I sat up.

"Oh my God, Kyle. We fell asleep."

"I know. What's the time? I don't have a watch." He scanned the sun to see how high it was in the sky. "It looks earlyish… Shit… Amber, we have to go. Now."

"Got it." I burrowed under the blanket to shuffle into my shorts, while Kyle muttered and vibrated with stress.

"What if one of them woke up? No, they would've come looking for us. This is bad…this is so bad."

I hoped he wasn't meaning last night – which had been all the opposite of bad to me.

I zipped up my shorts and stood.

"Let's go."

Kyle took my hand, and gave it a reassuring squeeze. We ran off the pier faster than my dozy legs could really handle. I tried not to worry as we sprinted through the forest. If one of the kids had woken up and found Kyle missing, he was right, they would've come looking for us…wouldn't they? Would Mum and Kevin be awake? What would I say to them? When we came to the split in the path, we both stopped. I bent over to catch my breath. I looked up; Kyle was smiling.

"I'm sorry we're ruining what was a great night with all this running."

So he'd had a great night too? My head spun with happiness, an intense rush of just general goodness oozed through me.

"I had a great time too."

He pulled me in for one last kiss. Then another. Then another. Whenever I tried to pull away, he pulled me back, laughing, covering my lips with his.

"I'm really falling for you, you know that, right?" he said, serious all of a sudden.

My heart jumped up into the very depths of my throat.

"I…I am too." I was, I really was. "But we really need to go."

One last kiss. "See you tonight at the dance?"

I nodded. I wasn't with the rest of Dumbledore's Army today. Mum had made me organize a special arts committee – to finish decorating the hall.

"See you there."

"I can't wait."

Then Kyle was just a spot on the forest path, dashing back towards his cabin – where, hopefully, all the children inside would still be asleep.

I looked through the cabin window.

Mum sat at the breakfast counter, sipping her coffee.

Bollocks. Do I climb through the window? Or do I feign innocence? My bedroom window was tiny. It was highly doubtful my butt could get through without a park ranger being called in to rescue me like Winnie the Pooh.

I'd have to lie.

I barged through the door like the spirit of all the mornings in the world were singing inside me.

"Morning, Mum," I called, wiping my sweaty hair back from my face.

She put down her coffee in surprise.

"Amber? What are you doing up? It's not even six."

"I went for a run. Before it gets too hot."

Mum took a sip of her drink. "When have you ever willingly done any exercise?" She looked down at the flip-flops on my feet and narrowed her eyes.

"It's all this American food. I thought maybe I should try

jogging…wish I'd worn proper trainers though."

"I was going to say."

"Yeah, it wasn't my best plan."

I went to the sink and got myself a tall glass of water. Mum's eyes were still on me, like I was a maths problem she was trying to work out.

"Where's Kevin?" I asked. There was a distinct lack of bumchin in the cabin.

"Oh, something camp-related came up, he's just sorting it out."

"What's happened?"

Mum shrugged. "No biggy."

"Is it to do with the dance?"

"No. Honestly, everything's fine."

I was worrying over nothing, I had to be worrying over nothing. Just because I knew what happened last night, didn't mean the world did. That's how secrets worked, they were secret.

"I'm having a shower."

"Okay. I'll meet you in the hall soon."

The day dragged. Every minute seemed to mosey its way by, with no care for how much I wanted to see Kyle again. I smiled whenever I thought about the previous night. The parts of my body he touched still tingled and fizzed, like his touch was long-lasting popping candy. I had serene-like patience with the kids all day, as they pulled on my T-shirt, as they messed up my decorations, as they asked endless, endless questions about the evening.

What songs will they play?

Will there be cake?

Jenny said I copied her dress but how could I, I packed it before I even came to camp?

I've got paint on my outfit.

Jenny dared me to eat the paint and now I don't feel well.

I wondered what Kyle was up to. How Dumbledore's Army were doing, whether they were behaving. If it was too hot for the planned basketball and if they would just swim in the lake instead. Just the thought of the lake made me blush…

I'd never felt so…happy. So excited by the simple act of existing. So glad I was me.

Mum worked me hard in the harsh Californian heat. By the end of the day, sweat dripped into every gap of my body, but the hall looked fantastic. The DJ arrived, pulling some ancient-looking decks on a dusty wheel-along cart behind him.

"I drove all the way from LA," he told me, like he'd climbed Mount Everest or something.

"Umm, they really want you to play 'Gangnam Style'," I informed him.

He pulled a face.

"They're children." I called over to Mum. "Mum, can I go get ready now? The dance starts in half an hour."

"Okay, I think we're done."

I jogged back to the cabin, wishing I had more time to look nice. My stomach growled angrily, the usual dinner time had been moved to become a dance buffet instead. I let myself in and quickly showered, before unfolding my dress from my suitcase. Penny had made me pack it.

"Why would I need a dress?" I objected, trying to unpack it, but she'd firmly folded it in again. "Can you just leave my stuff alone, please? It's camp. It's in a mountain. I won't need it."

"A lady always needs a good dress," she'd said, her voice all annoying and wise. This was the only wisdom you'd ever get out of Penny... How to be a good woman, a good wife, a good anything-other-than-a-hardarse-feminist.

Now, reluctantly, I was glad she'd packed it. It was from my Year Eleven leavers ball, and it was deliberately very un-ball like, as I totally didn't understand why all the girls in my year were determined to spend three hundred quid on looking like a Disney Princess for one night. Unfortunately, because Evie and Lottie weren't at my secondary school and I hadn't met them yet, I was the only one who'd thought like this. I'd spent the evening feeling morally rigorous, but also very plain compared to all the shiny pastel taffetaed creations my school friends wore. The dress was simple. Dark green, very strappy, quite short, which was more a reflection of my general length than the dress's general length. It somehow made me look dainty, and my hair look more auburn than ginger, and it made my freckles look classy rather than unfortunate.

I moisturized my legs and shoved it over my head. I had ten minutes to blob on a dash of make-up. My face looked pretty weird in make-up after weeks of going barefaced at camp. Then I twisted up my curls, so they wouldn't misbehave, and piled them on top of my head.

I looked okay. My inner and outer smiles were definitely a brilliant wardrobe addition.

I wondered if Kyle would like how I looked…

I instantly got annoyed at myself for thinking that.

When I got to the hall, the music was on, the disco lights flashing, and Calvin was at my side.

"Amber, you said you would dance with me!"

"Calvin, you look very dashing."

He looked so cute I could have grabbed his cheeks and wobbled them. He'd squeezed himself into a white shirt with a red bow tie and used water to comb all his hair to one side.

"Shall we?"

We strode elegantly onto the dance floor, before he grabbed me and jumped me up and down which if all the other kids were an indicator was how ten-year-olds dance to Taylor Swift. I tried to find my friends, and mostly Kyle, in the hubbub.

Most of the boys weren't dancing – instead doing elaborate knee slides from one end of the hall to the other. The girls looked on, arms crossed, obviously pissed off the boys weren't being the gentlemen they'd imagined in their heads.

That said, Melody and Bryony had recruited a group of girls to do their own little dance routine in a circle. Whinnie was doling out pizza at the counter. She raised her hand and waved at me. I waved back, mid-jump.

I couldn't see Russ or Kyle anywhere.

Something felt…wrong in my stomach.

The music faded into a different song.

"Another dance," Calvin demanded. I tried to smile, and began jumping again, this time holding his hands so he could use me to jump higher. The children obviously thought this was a great idea, as they formed a queue to take a turn doing this with me. I scanned everywhere as child after child grabbed at my hands and swung themselves higher, using my body weight to support them. Mum had changed, into a long black dress; she looked nice. She was chatting with Melody and Bryony. My stomach twisted even more.

Where the hell were Kyle and Russ?

I only caught glimpses of Mum's face as Charlie Brown swung off my arm.

Mum looking curious.

Mum looking worried.

Mum's face sinking into that terrifying look of anger she gets when she's snapped.

Mum storming towards me, gently but forcibly pushing children to one side.

I let go of Charlie Brown.

"Hey," he yelled, looking like he wanted to stomp on my foot in anger.

"Sorry…I…I…"

Mum snatched my hand and pulled me away.

"What's up?" I asked, acting innocent. She pulled me into a dark corner, where the lights of the disco highlighted us every ten seconds or so.

"How was LA?" she asked.

I knew then I was busted.

"It was okay. I told you, why?"

Her mouth narrowed so much I couldn't see her lips. The look was so terrifying that I actively searched around the hall for help. And Russ was there. He'd just got through the door. He looked stressed, still wearing camp uniform, and searching the hall. He saw me and started making his way over, his face urgent.

Oh God, something had happened.

Mum pulled my arm to get my attention back.

"Bryony and Melody just told me you didn't go. They said they didn't see you the whole weekend."

Shit shit shit shit.

"Have you been checking up on me?"

Deflection; deflection was always a good idea.

"That's not an answer to my question."

"Well, technically, you didn't even ask me a question."

My fear was morphing into something new – anger. Why should she care where I was that weekend anyway?

She was the reason I'd had nothing to do, nowhere to go. Why did she think she could suddenly play the disciplinarian adult role now? I'd seen my mother piss herself on our living room sofa. I'd seen her clutching onto the sides of our family toilet as she retched up vomit that contained nothing but liquid. She had always been home later than me. She'd always broken more rules than me. Then she left and stopped even pretending to care. I wasn't going to let her start pretending now.

"Stop trying to be clever, Amber."

Russ waved, trying to get my attention, but when he saw I was with my mum, he halted.

"I'm not."

"Did you go to LA?"

A bright red disco light shone in my face, making me see stars.

"No."

Mum's face hardened. "Where did you go?"

"Somewhere that wasn't LA."

"Who with?"

"Why does that matter?"

She twisted my hand.

"Oww!"

"IT MATTERS." Her voice was so tight her vocal cords could snap. "Because you're my daughter and you disappeared for two days and I had no idea where you were."

I rolled my eyes, just to piss her off.

"Mum, you never have any idea where I am. When I'm

in England, and you're here, I could be doing ANYTHING and you wouldn't have a clue."

Her voice shook. "Don't you dare try and twist this on me. Tell me where you went, and who with."

I crossed my arms. "No."

Russ was practically jumping up and down to get my attention now.

"Hang on." I stepped away from her. What was wrong? Something was wrong… Where was Kyle?

"Amber, you can't just walk away when I'm talking to you…"

I ignored her and ran over to Russ.

"Russ, what's going on?"

"Amber!" His eyes were all wide. It was the first time I'd seen him upset since I'd met him. "They've fired Kyle."

No. No no no no no no no no.

"What?"

"He's packing now. He has to have left by the time the dance is over."

"Why? Why the fuck are they firing him?"

But I knew the answer…

"One of the kids in his cabin woke up early this morning with an earache. Kyle wasn't there. The kid flipped out and got everyone up. They all got in a right state. They woke me up, and I calmed everyone down. I thought we could keep it quiet, but the little kid told Kevin first thing this morning."

This wasn't real. This couldn't be happening.

"Why are you only just telling me this?"

Russ gave me a look, and I knew then that he knew. About Kyle and me. He looked pissed off but like he was trying hard not to be.

"It's been going on all day. Kevin's been interrogating Kyle all day, to find out what the hell he was doing. He won't say...so they've fired him."

My fault. It was all my fault.

"Where is he?" I asked with such urgency that any suspicion Russ had was instantly confirmed. "He's packing. He'll be gone in an hour. He... I think he wants to see you."

"Of course."

I could see how upset Russ was. They'd worked together two summers and now I'd messed everything up. I turned to run, but Mum was behind me, grabbing me again.

I turned back. Furious. She must've known this was going on all day, and she didn't tell me.

"What is it?"

"We've not finished our conversation."

I didn't have time for any conversation with anyone other than Kyle. He couldn't leave...he couldn't...it couldn't be the end. Right now couldn't be the end... We still had a week... My heart felt like someone had it in a vice grip and was squeezing it until all the juices ran dry.

Russ was hovering, waiting to see what I was going to do. This was my fault. If I told Mum, maybe I could change things?

"I went to Yosemite. With Kyle," I yelled at her so loud,

some children around us stopped pogoing. "Okay? It was my fault he wasn't in his cabin last night. He met me, because I asked him to... Because I told him I was upset about something. So you can't fire him. Promise me you won't fire him! It's all my fault. If you fire him, you have to fire me!"

Mum's face jerked back.

"You went away with Kyle?"

I nodded, frantic. "Yes. Nothing happened. Just as friends."

Though we weren't just friends now. So much more than friends.

"And you expect me to believe that?"

"I don't expect you to do anything. Other than NOT FIRE HIM, because last night was all my fault."

I yelled the last bit so loud I could be heard over the music.

A massive bumchin came into my line of vision. Kevin was at our side.

"Amber? Russ? What's going on?" His voice was still all breezy but I could hear the authority under it. We are not allowed to yell at camp. We are not allowed to express anything other than Mickey Mouse club personalities in front of the children.

But Kevin could help me.

I grabbed him instead. "Kevin! Kevin? You can't fire Kyle. You can't. Last night, it was all my idea. It was all my fault."

Kevin and Mum shared a look. One I didn't like.

Kevin's arm was around me – all faux sympathetic, because his grip on my shoulder was vicelike.

"Let's talk about this outside." He weaved me through the dancing and staring children. Russ followed. He was shaking.

I kept up a constant stream of gibberish. "I told him to leave the cabin. I needed his help… It's all my fault… Honestly, Kevin, you can't fire him. It's my fault. It's all my fault. You have to fire me, not him."

Mum stormed ahead. I could tell just from the back of her head that she was gunning for a fight.

I would fight…if I had to… I couldn't let Kyle leave.

The air outside was still sticky from the day's heat with absolutely no breeze.

"You can't fire him, you can't fire him."

"Shh, Amber, that's not your decision. And you have to keep it down! The children will get upset."

"No, Kevin. You don't understand. It's my fault."

"Amber. He left vulnerable children, alone, in a cabin. Anything could've happened. We have to let him go, we have no choice."

Maybe that was reasonable. It didn't sound reasonable to me.

"But it's my fault. I asked him to come!"

"But you're not responsible for sleeping in with the kids, Amber. Kyle is. He let us down in regard to that responsibility."

Mum stepped between us.

"And she's been seeing him! Tell Kevin, tell him that you

went to bloody Yosemite with him." She sounded so much more British when she was angry.

"That's not against the rules," I sobbed. Because I was sobbing now. In utter disbelief that things could unravel so quickly. "Please, Kevin, please. It won't happen again."

Russ stood at my side, his mouth wide open. I guess it was all news to him – Yosemite, Kyle sneaking out to meet me. Maybe he couldn't believe someone like Kyle would bother with someone like me. I used to not believe it either. But I did now. And I had to fight for him. No, I had to be with him… He could be leaving any second.

"You can't do this," I yelled into Mum's face.

I turned and I fled.

I was so used to the route in the pitch black, that my feet guided me along the forest path.

It took only seconds to lose their voices behind me.

I had to get to the cabin before he left. I had to. I had to.

What was I going to do when I got there? I didn't know. All I knew was that he couldn't leave. I wasn't ready for this – whatever it was – to finish. So I ran and ran and ran.

I bumped into trees, rocketed off stray branches and turned my ankle in my stupid disco shoes. When I wiped my forehead with the back of my hand it came back dripping. Yet I hobbled on, coughing up all sorts of crap from my lungs. So confused. So angry. So annoyed. Why did we fall asleep? Why did we even leave the kids in the first place?

My fault, all my fault. Everything is always my fault. I touch things and they crumple into shit, like the opposite of King Midas and his gold finger. If I was in a fairy tale, I would be called "PooFinger", and everyone would shun me and make me go live in some naff shack under a bridge, telling scary stories to all the children in the kingdom about the wench who turns everything to shit, just by touching it.

Running. More running. Why are forests so big?

Would I catch him? I couldn't miss him.

And then I was in the clearing…and the cabin light was on. He was there!

But soon…soon he wouldn't be.

"Kyle!"

I burst through the door, and there, there he was. He looked pale, even with his deep tan. He wasn't wearing camp uniform – just a baby blue long-sleeved T-shirt tucked into some belted jeans. The formality of how he looked… no baseball cap, no rolled-up T-shirt sleeves and baggy shorts. It made it real. This awfulness was happening.

"Amber!" He dropped the T-shirt he was folding in shock.

I leaned over on myself, huge ragged breaths heaving out of me.

"Amber? Are you okay?"

I held my hand up as I hacked up another cough.

"Just. A. Second. Ran. Here. From. The. Rec. Hall."

Three deep breaths and I was ready to look up. He was totally shell-shocked. My eyes went from him, beautiful gorgeous him, to the suitcase on his bed. It was packed so immaculately – everything folded neatly, all the corners of his clothes folded with sharp creases. It was so Kyle… so him…

I started crying and Kyle was right at my side.

"Hey, oh no, Amber, don't cry. It's going to be okay."

"They fired you," I wailed.

"They did. But it'll be okay. Kevin said if I leave quietly, he won't tell anyone. I'll still get a reference."

"They can't fire you."

He hugged me like I was a scared child. "Amber, they can. I left the children overnight. It was so stupid. And it's so illegal. What if something had happened? Like, if someone had come in? Or if there'd been a fire? They so have to fire me!"

"It's all my fault." I heaved another sob.

He cupped my face in his hands, not minding that snot and tears were rolling down onto them.

"Look, neither of us were thinking straight. It was stupid. Last night was so so stupid."

He regretted it. He wished it had never happened… My heart – already a ball of dust – re-exploded…

Kyle hadn't finished talking.

"But I wouldn't change last night for anything. Amber… Amber? I can't believe I'm leaving you." He looked like he was going to cry too. We just stared into each other's eyes, each in utter disbelief about the horror of the situation.

"When do you have to leave?"

"Within an hour."

He let go of my face and drop-kicked a T-shirt across the floor. "Within a fucking hour."

That was nothing. An hour was nothing.

I knew, when it started, we had no time. But this was too much no time.

I couldn't. No. Not just an hour.

He was back in my arms, hugging me, kissing the tears off my face. I didn't know I could feel pain like this, over someone I hardly knew. But all of me ached, all of me was broken. I grabbed at him, kissing his lips. Not believing his lips wouldn't be mine within an hour. That they'd be gone… for ever…unless…

"I could leave with you?"

The moment I said it, I knew that was what I had to do.

Kyle's eyebrows drew up in shock. "What? Amber? You can't leave with me."

"I can. I've got money! They paid me for my camp hours before I left the UK, just so America didn't get all weird about me working here."

"You can't leave your mum."

I nodded, realizing I could. I so could. There was the love in life you couldn't choose. The love you just felt, that you couldn't let go of, that tortured you and messed you up and made you sometimes too screwed up to let the other kind of love in. The other kind of love, was the love you did choose. The love you didn't have to give, but you gave anyway. Since I'd met Evie and Lottie, I'd begun to learn I was capable of that love. That I had some left to give to them. And now,

I realized, right in that moment, that I'd found a tiny bit left for Kyle too. I'd chosen to love him. And the great thing about the love you choose, is you don't choose abusive alcoholic narcissists who leave you in fucking England, by yourself, without a fucking mother, without even an explanation or an apology.

"Kyle, why would I stay with her? You've seen her. There's no point. There was no point in me coming here this summer…" As I said it, I knew it was true. My already-catatonic heart caved in from the pain of it. "But the reason why I'm here this summer has changed." Could I say it? I hardly knew him, would it hurt if I said it? Yes, probably. But the girls had said, hadn't they? It's worth hurting if you've living, if you're doing the right thing. And telling people you love that you love them is always the right thing. "You've changed everything, Kyle. I think… I think… You can't not take me with you…because if you did you'd be leaving someone who might love you behind… Please don't be someone else who I love who leaves me behind."

He was quiet, and I thought: *This is it. He's going to freak out. He's going to put his arms up and say "Woah, slow down, psycho lady. I don't love you. I just touched you up on the pier and find your politics make for good conversation."*

Then Kyle drew me towards him and kissed me so deeply that it was like the roof of the cabin had collapsed so I could see the stars.

"I'm not going to leave you behind," he said. "Come with me, Amber."

I laughed into his mouth, with the sheer delight of it all.

"Where are you even going?"

We were hugging now, squeezing each other so hard that my ribs hurt.

"Back to Brown. My parents will flip when they find out I've lost my job. If I don't sleep much, I can drive there in three or four days. It's quiet on campus in summer, I'll get a job in a coffee shop or something. Then when camp ends and they're back from Florida, I'll tell them what happened. They'll go less crazy if I can say I've already got another job."

"So you're driving across the whole of America?"

He let go so he could cradle my face in his hands again.

"*We're* driving across the whole of America."

"America isn't, like, big, or anything, is it?"

He proper laughed, and I did too. Despite everything, all the mess, this felt right.

"I have to go pack..." I said.

"You need to be quick. I promised Kevin I'd be gone by the time the dance is over."

"I need to tell my mum..."

"You do," he said quietly.

"She's found out about Yosemite."

"How did she take it?"

"She's furious."

"You've done nothing wrong, Amber. Remember that. Now, when you go tell her, remember that. Nothing between you is your fault, don't let her trick you into thinking otherwise."

Just those words, his words, confirmed I was doing the right thing. I kissed him again.

"Come on," he said, between kisses. "We don't have time."

"Is this crazy?" I asked him. "I hardly know you. I don't even know where Brown is. Are we totally and completely bonkers?"

Kyle kissed me again. Each kiss was newer, more urgent.

"I have no idea what 'bonkers' means, but yes. It is bonkers. And that's why I trust it."

"Isn't that a line from *Titanic*?" I asked, laughing. So scared, but laughing. "What is it with you and overly dramatic love stories with camp soundtracks?"

"Amber, we need to go now."

"I'll bring this up again in the car."

"I'll make you listen to the *Titanic* soundtrack in the car."

"Is it too late to back out?"

"Yes. Now go pack! I'll meet you by my jeep in half an hour… And, Amber," he called, just as I was halfway out the door.

"Yes?"

"Remember what I said. Don't let her make you think it's your fault."

Situations that are destined to fail:

Finally saying how you feel

+

After several years

+

A person who refuses to accept blame

+

It being really important to you

+

Because they're your mother

Twenty-nine

I could hear the disco music as I fled back through the woods. It reached out into the quietness of the forest, seeping into the silence, tainting the surroundings, making it feel like this beautiful wood was suddenly Butlins or something.

My mind raced with all the thoughts I needed to have at the same time. What do I pack? Should I leave a note for my mum? Or should I track her down and tell her at the dance? Was this illegal? How could I say goodbye to Whinnie? Could I leave her a note somehow? And the children, especially Calvin? But my head was also dancing with happiness, with excitement, with total pure joy. I was running away, with a boy I thought maybe I loved. It was destined to fall completely apart – I was sure of it – and yet I couldn't wait. I really couldn't wait.

The cabin was empty and I ran straight to my room, chucking all the contents of it into my suitcase. There was no time to fold anything. No time to think really. Just chuck chuck chuck. I sprinted to the bathroom and emptied my toiletries into a bag, and hunted about in the chest of drawers for my passport. I didn't even know how I was going to get back to England. My return flight was from San Francisco. I knew I wouldn't be taking it. Finally, carefully, I put my sketchpad and art supplies on top of all my stuff and zipped it up.

Mum was at the door.

"Amber?"

She stood in the threshold – her arms crossed tightly. The sheer anger in her voice unleashed something inside me, something that I'd been repressing for so long. It was my own rage, my own fermenting rage. And it was ready to have its say.

"Amber, what the hell are you doing?"

I picked up my bag.

"Leaving."

"Don't be ludicrous."

"I'm not. I'm leaving with Kyle. Tonight. Now, in fact."

"Stop being silly."

"I'M NOT BEING SILLY. I'm leaving! Now."

Mum's eyes darted from my face to the bag and back to my face again. Her own face drew in on itself when she realized I wasn't kidding.

"Amber, you can't leave," she said quietly but firmly. "You're working here this summer. You've made an obligation."

"And you've taught me that obligations mean shit."

"What's that supposed to mean?"

"You know precisely what it means."

"You can't leave with Kyle. I don't trust that boy. I never have. He's a bad influence."

"ARGH!" I chucked my bag on the floor just to let some of my anger out. "He's not," I yelled. "He's good. In fact he's probably one of the best things that's happened to me. Ever since you LEFT ME, Mum. Yes, you LEFT ME. All alone. Without my mother. My mother! It's not like you DIED, but you may as well have. I never hear from you. I travel all the way out here to spend summer with you and you can't even cancel a fucking shift at the centre. What about *your* obligation, Mum? To be my mother? Kyle doesn't *have* to care for me, but he *does*. And I'd rather choose someone right now who chooses to care, than stay here with someone who obviously doesn't."

Mum's face was frozen.

"Amber, you can't talk to me like that."

"Why not?" I screamed. "Because you're an addict? Because you're a useless alcoholic? Kyle told me why you hate him, he told me what he saw. And what? It's not his fault that he saw that. But you don't blame yourself, do you? You blame everyone else. Everyone else has the problem. The world is against you. You poor, vulnerable addict you. How dare I be hurt by you abandoning me? HOW DARE I even try to talk to you about it, in case it makes YOU feel bad? Well what about me, Mum? What about how I feel?

Have you EVER even considered it?"

Mum stepped forward. She wasn't crying, but she looked like she might. "Of course I've considered it…"

"But you left me anyway. But you didn't spend time with me this summer anyway. Because you're the most important one."

"Amber…I have a disease…"

The tears came with those words, but they were too late. And they weren't for me anyway, they were for her. Her tears were always for her.

"So fucking what." I shrugged, I actually shrugged. Because I was done with feeling sorry for her, I was done with making her excuses. "You can't just go to AA and have Kevin tell you you have a disease and that makes what you've done okay."

"Amber, come on. You can't leave!"

"Don't pretend you'll even miss me. I'm leaving in a few weeks anyway. You probably weren't planning to spend any time with me – I don't fit into your perfect life over here. Your perfect life without your daughter. That is not someone who's going to miss me. My own mum…" My tears came now, hot and angry. "…never even misses me. You swap me in for some patronizing git with a bum instead of a chin and dump me with Penny and Craig when you know what they're like and you don't even care, God forbid, because that might make *you* feel bad."

Sobbing now. We were both sobbing. Me sobbing about her. Her sobbing for her. No one sobbing for me. All the things I'd never said, lying on the floor between us, bleeding out into the carpet.

I picked my bag off the floor, and pushed past her to the front door.

"AMBER?"

I turned round one last time. She'd sunk to the floor, her knees up to her chest, her hands over her ears, rocking back and forth.

She didn't really try and stop me leaving.

Just as I knew she wouldn't.

Situations that are destined to fail:

Crying

+

More crying

+

More crying

+

Knowing crying can't make the pain go away

Thirty

We drove for hours into the blackness, Kyle steering his battered jeep along the ups, downs and infinite curves of the mountain roads.

I cried the whole time, staring out into the inky black sky – not even the stars able to warm my confused stupid heart. I kept replaying what I'd said to Mum, how her face had looked, how I'd left her.

What if she relapses? What if she drinks again? Because of me? She looked so broken…and yet, it's not like she'd said sorry.

She'd never once said sorry.

Kyle, either out of awkwardness or just a general psychic ability to know this was what I needed, let me cry. He drove us in silence – no music, no small talk. Every so often, on a straight patch of highway, he'd take one hand off the steering wheel and squeeze my knee. We stopped for gas once. I stayed in the car, still sobbing, worried if I went in to buy gum or whatever they'd take one look at me and arrest Kyle for kidnap.

I wasn't sad I was with him. But I was sad I'd left Mum. I was sad I'd had to say what I had, sad I had to let it out the way I did. I felt like maybe I'd failed somehow, if there was a test on *how to empathetically deal with addict parents*.

I wasn't sad I'd done it though. And now, finally, after all these years, I let myself cry for her. And more than that, I let myself cry for me too.

I cried for the child that saw what she did. I cried for the young teenager I was when she hopped on a plane and left me behind like a lost teddy. I cried for the two years I'd been forced to live through, feeling like a complete fucking stranger in my family home, having to put up with my idiot stepbrother, having no one in my family ever putting me first, not ever. And, as the darkened mountains whizzing past my passenger window morphed into a straight boring blur of American interstate, I realized I'd not really let myself cry at all, until now. Until this summer.

Maybe there in a set amount of crying your body needs to deal with any trauma. There's a certain water-level of tears you need to shed until you can find acceptance or move on or whatever. And, if you don't cry them out, they just catch up with you. I'd been on the cusp of crying since the day she didn't take me with her. And yet I'd never quite allowed myself to open the floodgates. I turned all the emotion into rage instead – at my dad, at my stepmum, at the patriarchy (*but, hey, at least that one's helpful*), and emotion kept bubbling up inside of me, like an underlying herpes virus, but something less gross and more poetic than that.

I whispered goodbye to the people I'd left behind at camp – knowing I'd never see them again, knowing they'd always wonder what happened to the two of us. Hoping, somehow, Whinnie and I would be able to find each other online.

But, other than Whinnie, I didn't really care. Not really.

I cared about the boy squeezing my knee. I cared about the road straight in front of me. I didn't care that I had not one holy clue where it led to.

In fact, that was what I liked about it.

Kyle eventually pulled up into this teeny town called "Lone Pine".

"It's got a great view of the mountains." He backed the jeep into a parking space outside a cute yellow motel that looked like it had been shrink-wrapped in 1959 and never once let the air in. "You'll see it in the morning."

I nodded. Crying.

"I'll go book us in."

I hiccuped. "Do you need any money?"

He gave me a sad smile. "I'll get this one. We'll sort out money tomorrow, when we've both slept."

I cried as he got us a room. I cried as we wheeled our stuff into it. It was cute – all wooden panelling and fake antlers sticking out everywhere. There was only one bed, which I lay face down on, and continued to sob. Kyle went out to explore, after asking if I was okay twenty million times first. I spread out on the bed – a big one, in total privacy, just for us. Last night, under the stars, this would've been our dream. Now the world had spun once on its axis and changed everything.

Kyle came back in, the hum of cicadas interrupting the steady hum of the motel's air con.

"There's a pizza place that's open till half eleven over the road," he said. "We have time to still go and order something."

Was it not even midnight yet? It felt like three o'clock in the morning.

"I don't think I'm hungry."

"I don't care. You're eating..." He perched on the edge of the bed, and stroked my hair – the gentle touch of his fingers on my scalp calming me. "But you really need to stop crying before we go in...otherwise I'm going to have to answer a lot of questions."

I hiccuped again. "I'm trying to stop but it just keeps coming out."

He laughed quietly. "It really is a rather impressive display. I wish I had a stopwatch. I would've started timing you the moment you started crying and entered you into some kind of record book."

It worked. I laughed. Then started crying again.

"Well that broke the sobbing for, what was it? Two seconds? I need to think of more jokes."

I laughed again and took his hand. He looked at my face, and I saw the hurt I was causing him. He really stared into my eyes, and slowly pushed back a tendril of my hair, tucking it behind my ear.

It sprang straight back to where it was.

"I warned you before, you can't do romantic shit with my hair," I said. "It's even more strong-willed than I am."

"Are you…" he began tentatively. "Are you upset you came? I can drive us back?"

I shook my head fiercely. "No. Don't. I just need… tonight… I think I'm grieving over something I should've grieved over a long time ago."

"You see?" he said. "These stiff upper lips only get you so far."

More laughter. A longer break from tears.

"Yeah, if it had been you," I said, "you would've had extensive therapy with a shrink, dealt with all of it within ten sessions, had a 'reconciliation service' with your mother, and both started up some kind of 'foundation' to mark all your 'emotional progress'."

"It makes my heart hurt, in a good way, to hear you make a joke…" Kyle tried tucking my hair back again. "Do you think you could eat something?"

I did one final sniff and sat up.

"That depends. Is American pizza as amazing as you all say it is?"

"You've flown all this way and not tried proper American pizza?"

"No. I've only had camp food. And one burger and some raw food in San Francisco."

“Oh, Amber.” Kyle picked me up off the bed and dragged me along the carpet towards the door, kissing my head as he did so. “No wonder you’ve been crying.”

Situations that are destined to fail:

Private sketchpads

+

Nosy sort-of boyfriends

Thirty-one

I woke up before Kyle the next morning.

It was the most glorious feeling – your consciousness returning with the heat from the guy you really, really like cuddling next to you. I'd managed to eat two slices of (admittedly amazing) pizza before the tears started again. Kyle immediately stood up, dropped a ten-dollar bill on the table and, with his arm around me, steered me back to the motel. I'd fallen asleep, crying onto his shoulder, as he held me – whispering that it was going to be okay, that we could always drive back, that he was proud of me, that everything was going to be fine.

On this new morning, I didn't feel like crying at all.

I felt light – like all those tears I'd been carrying around, unshed, for two years had weighed a tonne.

I wiggled around so I could stare at Kyle's face.

God, he was fit. I still couldn't believe it. That I got to touch him, got to kiss him… I wanted to touch him then.

The urge boiled low down inside me but it wasn't fair to wake him. He'd driven miles the previous night and we had Lord knows how many to cover today.

So I sneaked out of bed, quickly changed into my swimming costume, and stepped outside in my flip-flops to check out the motel swimming pool.

After a night of motel air con, the Californian heat hit me hard and my body warmed up instantly. The motel ran around on itself like a square, and the swimming pool lay in the middle. I flip-flopped over, stopping to admire the incredible mountain view – even in midsummer, the very tips of them were covered in snow. The pool area was empty, and I let myself in through the small gate and chucked my towel onto a white plastic sunlounger. Without giving myself time to think about how cold it would be, I dived right into the deep end, swimming an entire length before coming up for breath.

It felt amazing – the water, the lightness inside of me, the sun shining so strong that I could still feel its heat through the water. I swam length after length, smiling stupidly to myself. I realized I had no regrets. Not about leaving with Kyle. Not about what I'd said to Mum. For once, I'd made a decision based entirely on me, what I needed, what I wanted. The only regret I felt was that we had left the children in the cabin overnight, and that was wrong… But it was also an accident and nothing had happened to them.

After about thirty lengths, I dried myself in the sun for a while, then went to wake up Kyle.

The bed was made and he was lying on it – looking through my sketchpad.

"Well you look like a much happier version of the Amber I had with me last night."

I couldn't help but smile.

"I think I'm done crying. Thank you…for last night. You were amazing."

I wrapped my towel around myself further and shivered in the air con, suddenly unsure of my body.

"Don't worry about it. I was glad I could be there."

"And I'm still so sorry I got you fired."

Kyle beckoned for me to join him. I sat on the edge of the bed, my feet still on the floor.

"I got me fired, remember? And come closer, please. It felt entirely inappropriate to tell you last night, but you looked really beautiful. And you do this morning too."

I blushed, but scooted closer, leaving a damp trail across the bed. He put his arm around me and I nuzzled into his chest – kissing it through his T-shirt.

He turned a page of my sketchpad and I jerked up a bit.

"You're going through my art?"

I felt him nod, as his chin rubbed up and down on the top of my head.

"Shamelessly so. I've wanted to ever since I first saw you carrying your sketchpad around camp." He turned another page, to one of the lists I'd been working on with my special black fineliner pen. "Though I am intrigued by these pages."

I tried to shut the book, but he put his hand in the way. "I've already read them all."

I kicked him.

"You do realize looking at an artist's sketchbook is like reading their diary?"

He ignored me and pointed to another page. "Why are you so obsessed with situations that are destined to fail? You've, like, drawn the whole summer. And I LOVE that I'm in them, by the way."

I was SO embarrassed. I grabbed the book off him and hit him on the head with it.

"Oww."

"Good, you deserve it."

"You're, like, really talented. You know that, right?"

"Flattery will get you nowhere, you snoop."

"Seriously though, what's with everything that's destined to fail?"

I turned redder. I'd been doodling these cartoons all through camp… I never thought anyone would see them.

"I dunno… I've just been thinking about it as a concept over the summer, I guess," I said. "Did you know there's sometimes foreign words for really cool things that should totally have an English word? Like *schadenfreude* in German? It means 'getting pleasure from someone else's pain'. Like, the good you feel when you see someone else fall over or something."

Kyle's smile was so large, it made all bits of me goo.

"I LOVE those words!" he said. "Like, don't the French

have a word for that moment when you think of the PERFECT thing to say in an argument, but like, two days too late?"

"*L'esprit de l'escalier*," I said, grinning. "The wit of the staircase..."

"You know it?"

"I know lots of them. I really like them – these weird phrases. Like, do you know *voorpret*? It's Dutch and means 'the feeling of fun you have anticipating an event'. Or, there's this really beautiful one in Arabic *ya'aburnee* – it translates as 'you bury me'. It means hoping you'll die before the person you love, because the thought of living without them is so terrible."

Kyle picked up my hand, holding it so our fingers entwined. He pulled me in for a kiss, before grabbing my book out of my hand and pawing through it again.

"Stop!"

"No, they're good. And you've still not explained it all."

I twisted my hand in his... I didn't like talking about my art much, I was always scared I'd sound like a twat.

"Well, these foreign words that represent cool concepts. I once found this amazing artist's website where he makes digital art of what these words look like. It gave me an idea for my A level coursework next year – we have to pick a theme, and follow it the whole year. I think there are words that haven't been invented yet, and I want to invent them, and do my project on them. Situations or scenarios which language hasn't caught up with yet. Like, do you remember a time before the word 'selfie'? Someone invented that word, for a situation we all know. Well, so, for my project, I had this idea to come up with these types of situations, and make them into paintings and then invent words for them."

"God you're smart," Kyle almost whispered.

"Not really. Anyway, that's what this is." I jabbed at my ink drawing. "I was thinking about situations people get involved in where they know, without a doubt, that it's going to fail. But they do it anyway. There isn't a word for it, but there should be. Like…I dunno…going into a battle when you have no chance of winning. Or trying to argue a Christian out of believing in God. Or knowing you're not the prettiest by miles, but still entering the pageant. Or falling in love with someone who's dying… Or falling in love with an addict… I guess most of them probably relate to falling in love…"

Kyle let go of my hand so he could brush my hair with his fingers. His touch was so electric, my body automatically turned towards him.

"How about falling for a dude who lives in America and running away from camp with him? Does that count?"

I looked up, worried. Even though I knew what he meant. "You think this…us…is destined to fail?"

"No… I guess it depends what you mean by 'fail'. I mean, look at all these." He used his spare hand to gesture towards my sketches. "You've listed all these situations that were destined to fail, but what happened? Really? They all came out okay, didn't they? Like, you're still alive…"

"So failure is dying, everything else is okay?"

He dug me in the ribs for being difficult and I squealed. "I guess I'm just saying, yeah, these things are hard, but you did them anyway. And they all led up to us being here, in this very private motel room I might add..." It was my turn to dig him in the ribs. "You just...lived, Amber. You just did stuff and got through hard stuff and life happened to you, and you happened to life. And, I guess I'd be lying if I said I'm not a little freaked out by what you and me are doing here, and what's going to happen, and, well, I think I'm in danger of possibly falling hard for you..." My heart stopped then, it just stopped. But I let him finish, though I could hardly breathe. "And you could see that as a stupid thing to do, something that's destined to fail. I mean, whatever happens between you and your mum, you'll have to get back on a plane to England at some point this summer. America is not just going to let you stay here, we can be certain of that. And that thought makes me, like... Well...everything hurts. You're already proving to be practically the best person I've ever known..."

"What?" I interrupted. "Even with all the crying?"

I was crying again, silently, at his words.

"Of course. With everything that's gone down with your mum, it would be weird if you WEREN'T crying. In fact, I'm relieved you're crying, rather than chucking all of Russ's whiskey down your throat... Anyway, yeah, I'm falling for you. That may be something that's destined to fail, if failure means I'm going to get hurt. But you know what I think failure really is?"

I looked up and stroked his face.

"What is it, wise Prom King?"

He grinned. "Failure is never getting hurt. Because that means you've not done anything you cared about."

I thought back to my conversation with Whinnie, about Winnie the Pooh, and love being caring too much.

"That's very deep."

"I know. Don't tell the basketball team."

"So we're going to drive across America together? And maybe fall in love? And not worry about the fact it's inevitably going to be terrible when I have to get on a plane back to England?"

"Yes, we're going to do all of that. But right now…" Kyle turned over onto his side, and grabbed me, turning me so I faced him, so that the whole front of my body touched the whole front of his. It sent uncontrollable waves of lust through me, every teeny hair on my body stood on end. "We're going to make full use of this private motel room."

"Otherwise we're failures?" I said into his mouth.

"Otherwise we're total delinquents."

Situations that are **destined** to **fail**:

Running away

+

With someone you only met a month ago

+

The consequences

Thirty-two

We didn't have sex.

Not yet. But I knew it was coming, and not one part of me was worried about it.

But we did spend far longer in a motel room than you're supposed to if you're meant to be driving across an entire continent.

Eventually, we got dressed. Kyle went out to check the jeep. "I need to make sure the poor thing can make it across. I've not even checked the tyre pressure."

"Wow, you're one of those 'real men' who knows what to do with cars."

"Stop oppressing me with gender stereotypes."

And we'd fallen, laughing, onto each other's mouths and taken our clothes off again.

* * *

We went through our route together, using Kyle's phone to work out a basic plan of action.

"It doesn't look so far," I said, looking at the big squiggly line, marking one side of America to the other. "Will we be on Route 66? I've always wanted to do that."

"Umm, no. We're going a bit further north than that. But we'll go through Utah, and that's beautiful, I promise. So, I'll get the car sorted, and then we need to drive through Death Valley."

"Ooooh, sounds fun."

Kyle pulled a face. "It's beautiful. But it's a tough drive. We may need to turn the air con off to stop the jeep overheating. Don't wear many clothes today. In fact, what you're wearing now is just great. Wear that."

I was wearing just my bra and a pair of cut-off denim shorts. Kyle wiggled his eyebrows.

"Stop objectifying me."

"Never!"

We kissed more, until we both had to stop ourselves.

"So, what's after Death Valley?" I asked.

"Well, we *could* drive as far as we can, and pull up on the side of the road somewhere. But, I was going to ask you. We go right past Las Vegas. It's only a four or five hour drive there… How would you feel about…"

"GOING TO LAS VEGAS? LIKE TODAY?"

I stood on the bed and began jumping.

"Well, yes. You can get super cheap rooms there, in the huge hotels like Caesar's Palace. I thought maybe it would be worth actually seeing something. Because, after that, all we'll be driving through for the next few days will be desert and farmland."

I jumped higher. "We're going to LAS VEGAS?!"

"Yes, we are."

"Today?"

"We need to check out within the hour."

I borrowed Kyle's phone, as his got internet and mine didn't, and connected to the motel wi-fi while he checked oil levels or whatever.

I was dreading logging into my email, but I guess I had to acknowledge some kind of reality. I had run away from a summer camp with a near stranger after all – though that's only how it looked from the outside.

I had over twenty unread emails.

From: Management@MountainHideawayCamp
To: LongTallAmber
Subject: Where are you?

Amber, it's your mum. Where are you? Kevin and I are worried sick! Please, we promise you're not in trouble. Just come back to camp. Calvin misses you. So do I. Call me anytime and I'll come get you.
Please, Amber.

From: BrianB
To: LongTallAmber
Subject: Call your mum, now

Amber
Why haven't you responded to ANY of my emails? And what's going on? Your mum just called in the middle of the night, in total hysterics. She said you've run off with some guy you hardly know? Amber, I beg you to be reasonable. Ring her, now. We are all very worried about you.

From: LottieIsAlwaysRight
To: LongTallAmber
Subject: Can I come?

AMBER
Your dad just called in a right state. You've run off with the Prom King guy? That. Is. Amazing. I AM AROUSED JUST THINKING ABOUT IT...

Sorry, that was Lottie. It's Evie typing now. I've explained to Lottie that this can only start being arousing once you've told the parents where the hell you are so they stop worrying. Promise me you'll tell them, Amber! Your dad was a mess. What's happened over there? Did something happen with your mum? Is this Kyle okay?

Promise me you've made all your own decisions, and you've made them out of a place of strength, not to get back at your mum. I don't care if you're angry at me for saying that. This is serious.

SERIOUSLY AROUSING.

That was Lottie again. She keeps taking the keyboard. At the very least, let US know you're okay. We're worried. Well, I'm worried. Lottie is dancing around my bedroom and thinks they should make a movie out of this. Please reassure your very worried friend. I will play the OCD card if I have to!
TELL US EVERYTHING. ARE YOU GOING TO HAVE SEX WITH HIM? WILL YOU TAKE PHOTOS OF HIM TOPLESS WHILE HE'S SLEEPING????

Okay – it's Lottie still. I am worried too. But I trust you, tall one. I trust you to first, let us know you're all right so we can all calm down. But I also trust you to do what's best for you. We're behind you, all the way, you know that.

Seconded – Evie.

Lots of love
x x x x

To: Management@MountainHideawayCamp; BrianB
From: LongTallAmber
Subject: Don't worry, I'm fine

I'm fine, I'm safe. Don't worry about me. I've got money. Kyle is a good guy. I just can't be at camp any more. Mum, you can fill Dad in on why.
I'll get in touch when I've worked out flights home and stuff.
I do love you both.
A x

From: LongTallAmber
To: LottieIsAlwaysRight, EvieFilmGal
Subject: RE Can I come?

Hello girlies

Okay, firstly, I am FINE. In fact, I am BETTER than fine. I am sheer wonderful! Do not worry about me honestly.
Yes, I have run off with Kyle.
Yes, this is entirely of my own free will.
No, Lottie, I will not take photos of his bare chest while he sleeps. You are SO bad at objectifying guys sometimes.
Yes, stuff went down between me and Mum. But it was nothing new. I just actually told her how I feel about it for once. I'm okay though. I cried a LOT yesterday, but

I'm feeling better. I think I need to do this...

No, not slept with him...yet...

...I'm just leaving room here for Lottie to combust with excitement...

We're in a small motel in California now, but we leave in a moment for Las Vegas. I promise you I won't get married. We're just stopping there for the night at Caesar's Palace and then heading towards Brown uni, where Kyle goes. We've planned out a route, and places to stop and everything. It's all very thought through and legit. And I can't wait, guys.

I'm so...happy. Please be happy for me.

I love you both LOADS. I'll be home at the end of summer, safe and sound, I promise I promise I promise.

Keep me updated on what you're all up to. I'll email again when I can.

Lots of love

Amber

x x x

Situations that are destined to fail:

Sweat

+

No air con

+

More sweat

Thirty-three

The drive through Death Valley was deathly.

We left Lone Pine behind, with *The Very Best of Andrew Lloyd Webber* blasting from the stereo, and drove off into the wilderness with careless abandon. The first stretch of road was so straight Kyle basically steered with his knees as we shot through California – arguing whether or not the phantom from *The Phantom of the Opera* was fanciable or not.

"I saw it once," I said. "Dad took us all for Christmas because it's my stepmum's favourite. I have to say, I was… taken with him. I was only, like, fourteen, and SO angry because Dad had only just left my mum… But the phantom distracted me and I had all these dreams about him, and wished I was Christine."

Kyle shook his head, laughing. "HOW can you fancy the phantom? He's a) disfigured, b) a psychopathic killer, and c) he lives in this creepy little dungeon with a dummy version of the girl he fancies dressed up as a bride."

I shrugged. "I swear, sometimes, there's something about what you find sexually attractive as a girl that is very confusing, especially if you're supposed to be a feminist," I said. "Technically, I am against abusive stalkerish behaviour. Murder, of course, is a big no-no. And yet…when he does all that almost-touching stuff with Christine…and the way he's so, like, obsessed with her. Well, I kind of got off on it."

"You should be very ashamed of yourself. You know that, right?"

"Oh, I am, believe me." I laughed and looked out the window. There were loads of weird billboards alongside the main roads of America and I'd started trying to take photos of them to show the girls. Most of them were pretty tame stuff – giant posters of Jesus and the American flag emblazoned with "God Bless America". But we'd passed at least one sinister abortion one.

As the deserty nothingness of Death Valley approached, the billboards calmed down until it was just road, and nothingness, and more road.

"But I do think there's this weird double standard in what you're not supposed to find sexy being what you secretly really do find sexy," I continued. "Like, in all those romantic movies and books or whatever, the male characters we're supposed to fancy are all controlling and possessive, and us girls are all like PHWHOAR."

Kyle turned the CD down so we could talk better. He looked incredibly sexy driving in the heat: the sleeves of his

T-shirt rolled right up, the fact I couldn't see his face behind his mirrored sunglasses.

"You know what?" Kyle said. "I've always thought there's a reverse sexism thing going on with films like that. Essentially, you can only get away with doing 'romantic' but totally-freaky-stalkery gestures for a girl if you're considered conventionally good-looking. It's like girls only let you be abusive and strange if you have a six-pack and really good bone structure. I mean, like, I can obviously be as creepy as I like, because I'm so darn good-looking."

I pulled a face at him. "You are? Oh. Sorry. I totally hadn't noticed."

Kyle laughed. "You know what I mean! But, say Bella Swan moved to wherever the hell it is she moved to, and this dude with long greasy hair, acne, glasses and a penchant for wearing those shitty T-shirts with logos on them, you know? Well, imagine he rocked up in her bedroom and started watching her sleep, or staring at her insanely like a maniac during the science lessons. She would call the cops! He'd be considered a scary freak. But, oh no, as long as you're R-Patz, it's okay. As long as you have green eyes and a 'crooked grin' you can be as creepy as you like. Girls are totally double-standardy. You get all het up if we dare to judge you on appearances. But then you do *exactly* the same to us."

"How do you know about Bella Swan?"

He laughed. "I have two sisters!"

I reached out and put my hand on his knee, just because it felt wrong if I wasn't touching him.

"Other girls may be like that, but you're talking to the girl who had a crush on the Phantom of the Opera, remember? He's only got half a face, and I still liked him."

Kyle brought my hand up to his lips to kiss it.

"And that is why I'm driving you to Las Vegas."

We passed a sign that said "Welcome to Death Valley" and the landscape changed almost instantly. We really were in total and utter nothingness. The road spun and curved along twisted pathways through rock and nothing, and more nothing, and the occasional extra rock.

"Are we on a different planet?" I craned my neck out the window, just in case I was missing something.

"Eerie, isn't it? We're going to get, like, really below sea level soon. Jeez, look at the thermometer."

The little digits on Kyle's dashboard told us it was well into the hundreds outside.

"We're not going to break down, are we?" I asked nervously.

"Let's hope not."

As we got into the heart of the park, it got even hotter. Kyle's car made all these weird noises, just around the time signs everywhere told us to turn off the air con.

"This is what I warned you about," Kyle said. "You ready to strip to your bra?"

"I am not stripping to my bra."

But, as we turned the air con off to preserve the engine, I really did feel like it.

We turned the radio off too, to give the jeep its best chance at making it. We rode in silence, both of us too hot to chat. Sweat dripped from every part of me. I was sweating in places I didn't even know I had sweat glands, like my knee pits, and behind my ears. And, still, we drove through nothingness. It seemed utterly unimaginable that something as exciting and alive as Las Vegas was at the end of the road. The road seemed like it could spread out for ever – that your car would run out of gas and you'd just perish there, with no one passing to find you.

Eventually though, Kyle's car became more spritely and we put on the air con and the stereo again. He insisted I gave The Mars Volta a go, and I sat there, in bewilderment, as all this weird stuff blared out of his speakers.

According to the signs, we were out of Death Valley now and Vegas was coming up, which was a reassurance as we drove in a single line into the empty desert.

"What the heck is this music?" I demanded.

"Do you not like it?"

"I am not one of those girls who pretends to like music that the boy she likes likes."

"This is incredible stuff. Each song is like a story!"

"A really naff story."

The bickering continued as we drove into the horizon. I was just starting to think Vegas was a figment of everyone's imagination when there – shimmering in the distance – I saw it. Skyscrapers and towers and signs of life.

"We're almost in Vegas, baby." Kyle pushed his sunglasses up his nose.

"Before we get there, you have to promise that was the

one and only time you use the word 'baby' after the words 'Las Vegas'?"

He smiled. "Whatever you say, baby."

"In fact, let's just ban the word 'baby' in general."

"You can't ban anything, BABY. We're in Vegas now. There ain't nothing banned in The Vegas."

"You're not allowed to call it The Vegas either."

Situations that are destined to fail:

Taking things slow

+

A luxury hotel room

Thirty-four

The shimmering strip drew closer and I pressed my nose against the window to get a better view. My heart pounded with excitement. I mean, come on, Vegas! The Vegas! How had this summer led me here? I turned off Kyle's weirdo music and began singing "Viva Las Vegas" in my very best Elvis voice. When that was exhausted I switched to "Uptown Funk" which has nothing to do with Vegas, but seemed to fit appropriately.

After being the only car for so many hundreds of miles, we were now one of thousands, and slammed into an epic traffic jam.

"Kyle –" I pointed out the window as we waited for a never-changing red light – "why is there a massive naked lady outside my window?"

Kyle rolled his eyes. "Welcome to Vegas."

We were next to a gigantic travelling billboard of a completely naked woman with her legs spread, sucking her finger suggestively as her massive eyes stared blankly into the traffic. She was advertising *Hot Girlz Direct 2U.*

"This is never in the movies," I said, as the billboard turned left and another naked billboard pulled up alongside us.

"It *is* called Sin City."

"Is there more stuff like this in Vegas?"

Kyle took my hand and kissed it. "Oh, Amber, you have no idea what's coming for you."

We inched through traffic light after traffic light. I counted another ten naked lady billboards. And an entire hotel called *Hooters*, where Kyle informed me all the female staff had to have massive boobs.

"I'm starting to worry Las Vegas is just a place where the patriarchy took a massive dump in the desert," I said.

"Or just humanity."

"Why did you bring me here?"

Kyle smiled. "Because we're going to have fun."

We made it through to the main strip. It was so surreal, seeing all the hotels I'd seen so many times on TV in real life. We passed New York New York and Excalibur – this neon garish fairy-tale castle. We passed The Mirage, which Kyle informed me had a resident white tiger who lived there.

"What? Just padding along the corridors?"

"I don't think so, I think he's in a cage. But I wouldn't be surprised. This is The Vegas after all."

"I warned you not to call it that."

"And how are you going to punish me?"

He grinned, and it was there again. The insane sexual tension, quivering between us, taking off all its clothes.

"How long till we get to our hotel room?" I replied.

Kyle's face went serious, in this really intense sexy way that made me want to jump over the car and just start grappling him right then.

"Not soon enough."

Two more traffic lights and Kyle steered us left, right into Caesar's Palace. It was very tall. In fact, it was so tall, I wanted to stand next to it for the rest of my natural life, so I'd never feel tall again. Kyle pulled up in this huge circular driveway, before stopping in front of two men dressed in strange little outfits.

"Here we are," he said. "It's valet service, so we need to get our stuff out the car."

I nodded. "Right. What's a valet?"

He laughed and opened the door, saying hi to the weird outfit guys.

"It means they park the jeep for us."

"Oh."

I picked my bag off my feet and opened the passenger door. I was hit by the most intense heat of my life. My skin instantly broke out into a sweat; the air was so dry I wanted a drink. Like, straight away.

"It's so HOT," I announced. Kyle was at the boot, helping the guys take out our suitcases.

"It's Vegas."

"Is that going to be your answer to everything for the next twenty-four hours?"

"It's Vegas."

I chased him and hit him with my bag.

"That's not funny at all."

"Vegas."

"I'm going to run away and marry someone else at the Elvis chapel."

Kyle grinned. "How very Vegas."

"Stop saying Vegas!"

The dudes in the uniforms stunned us by both cheering "VEGAS" at the same time and giving us a thumbs-up.

I was so surprised and impressed I gave them double tip.

Kyle queued up to get us a room, telling me to hover rather than queue with him, just in case they twigged I was underage. I watched him flirt with the hotel receptionist, and saw the way she warmed instantly to him, the way everyone did with Kyle.

I remembered Mum's warning – *everyone falls in love with Kyle*... But I didn't want to think about her, not in this strange new adventure...

Anyway, not everyone has Kyle fall back in love with them.

He dragged his bag over, smiling with every bit of his face. "Good news," he said. "I got us an upgrade."

"What?" I squealed. "How?"

He picked up both our cases and steered us through to the elevator. It was just…nuts inside the hotel. Giant gold statues of Romans adorned everywhere, the sky was decorated with ornate gold everything, huge marble columns held up all the garishness. Even the lift, once we got in, was insane. There were so many buttons I felt like I was in Willy Wonka's Great Glass Elevator.

"It's quiet season because it's so hot in summer," he said. "So it's always worth trying your luck. I just told her I would try the other hotels if she couldn't offer me a deal. Instant upgrade. I read it was worth a try online. It worked."

The elevator pinged open and we emerged into a long corridor. It was more hotel-looking up here – just lots of doors and red carpet and parked cleaning trolleys. We walked and walked and walked until we found our room. Kyle jammed the card into the card reader and I pushed the door open.

"Oh my nuts," I said, walking in.

"Oh my nuts?"

"I got stuck between saying 'Oh my God' and 'this is nuts'."

The hotel room was the size of a country. Not one, but two beds, both bigger than my bedroom back home dominated the space. But there was a wall to ceiling window showing us a great view of the strip.

"Oh my nuts, the bathroom." I dropped my bags and ran inside. There was a jetpool bath that could fit my entire family in. And a rainforest shower thing.

I came out to find Kyle flopped backwards on one of the beds, his arms above his head. His eyes closed.

I climbed on top of him, kissing his face and neck.

"You tired from the driving?"

He opened his eyes, smiling, and put on his shit English accent. "I'm bloody knackered."

"I'll let you nap a while." I went to clamber off, but he made a noise of protest and dragged me back. I giggled and we started kissing, all the energy from the car going up an octave, filling the room with lust and longing and no way was touching each other doing anything to satisfy it.

"Don't we need to go see The Vegas?" I asked, between breathless kisses.

"You felt the temperature outside. No one goes out in Vegas until at least sunset. We'd melt."

"And how long until sunset?"

"An hour or two."

I kissed his ear, finding myself biting it – I wasn't sure where it came from, but Kyle seemed to like it anyway.

"What we going to do until then?" I teased.

Kyle flipped me so he was on top of me, and rained kisses down on my face and body. I closed my eyes and sighed – feeling like life couldn't feel any better than this, like my heart couldn't ever feel this full.

"Have you not met the bath, Amber? You must surely want to meet the bath?"

And I squealed as he hurled me over his shoulder, and carried me, yelling with faux protest, into the ginormous bathroom.

We lolled in big white towels afterwards, on one of the big beds and watched the hazy sunset. The city around us lit up like a pinball machine.

"When can we see the city then?" I shuffled through my things, wondering what to wear. I only had the one dress, the green one. It would have to do.

"Now, I guess. It will have cooled down some. What do you want to see?"

Umm, I tried to remember things I knew about Vegas. "Erm, those dancing water jet things I guess?"

"The Bellagio fountains?"

"What you said."

"Okay."

"And I'd like to see at least one real poker game. To try and work out who's bluffing."

Kyle stood up, took off his towel, and began to root around in his clothes too. His temporary toplessness rendered me all incapable.

"We're too young technically to be in the casinos. If they think we're underage, they'll move us on. But we can try."

"Bugger, we won't be able to drink, will we?"

He shook his head. "Nope."

I thought of the night with Russ's whiskey. "Probably just as well."

I locked myself in the bathroom to get ready and stared at my reflection a while, turning this way and that, to see if I looked any different now. If the outside world would notice what had happened in the last two hours. I twirled all my hair up on top of my head, letting a few loose pieces hang down. And I half-heartedly dabbed mascara on and a bit of lipgloss. I felt clown-like though, after a summer of not bothering. So I wiped the lipgloss off and just kept the mascara on.

When I emerged, I stopped, and stared. At Kyle. A posh proper shirt had arrived on his body out of nowhere, and he looked so yum that I forgave him for putting clothes on at all.

He stopped and looked at me.

"You're beautiful," he said, at the same time as I said, "You look nice."

We both laughed.

"God, we're disgusting," I said.

"Too cute for words. I hate us. You do though, look beautiful I mean. I like that dress."

We kissed, collapsing on the bed.

"Am I going to see any of America on this road trip?" I asked, between kisses. "Or just see the inside of motel rooms?"

"All right, all right, we'll go out."

We untangled our limbs, got my little handbag sorted, and veered out into the corridor.

When we closed our hotel door, we didn't see the red light on the phone flashing.

Situations that are destined to fail:

The Vegas

+

An academic understanding of "Raunch Culture"

Thirty-five

I, almost instantly, didn't like Vegas very much.

"Why are my hands full of porn?" I asked, as we waited on the steaming pavement to cross the road. The moment we'd left the hotel, we'd entered a gauntlet of roadside hustlers, all with stacks of porn phonecards. They shoved them into your hands before you even had a chance to say no.

"Do you not want hot girlz direct to you?" Kyle said. "Because they are plentiful."

We dropped the calling cards on the already-littered pavement.

The light turned green and we joined the throbbing crowd crossing the road. It was madder than London, the pavements were jammed. Fifty per cent of everyone was drunk, though it was only like eight o'clock. The other fifty per cent wielded massive cameras with lenses poking out almost into my eye.

We'd had a look in the shopping area of Caesar's Palace, where I'd marvelled at the spiral escalators and rode up and down them twice.

"I take her all the way to Vegas, and she's excited by some revolving stairs," Kyle'd said. But now I wanted to see The Venetian, hoping that maybe it would have a bit more class. We'd asked for directions and they'd said it was only a few hotels over. But I hadn't realized each hotel was the size of a continent. We'd been walking through the busy street and porn gauntlets for ages.

"Ahh, there it is." I pointed to an Italian looking tower. It took longer to get to it than we'd thought. Like a desert mirage, the tower kept seeming to get further and further away. Eventually though, we crossed the fake Rialto bridge and got into the guts of the hotel.

"Holy moly," I said, looking around. "It's almost like being in Venice. Well, what I think Venice is like."

There was a fake sky, painted to look just like a real one, like an Italian version of the enchanted ceiling of the Great Hall in Harry Potter. There was an actual real-life canal, with actual real-life gondoliers punting people along.

"It's so over-the-top," Kyle said.

"Let's at least pretend we're in Italy." I took his hand.

We walked along the canal, looking at the people who could afford a gondola ride and eat at the pricy hotel restaurants (we'd grabbed a McDonald's on the way there). Kyle's hand was warm in mine; the way our bodies linked, just with entwined fingers, made everything inside of me feel safe and nice. We stumbled into the casino and managed to loiter enough to catch a high roller poker game. It wasn't fun though. No one was laughing. There was no joy in the room. It was hardcore gambling. The air felt cold. The lighting was all off. It was impossible to know what time it was.

"Why are those grannies plugged into the slot machines?" I pointed at a row of old biddies who were all strapped into some bleeping machines.

"To keep them upright, so they don't fall asleep."

"That is quite a commitment to gambling."

"Yep."

"How much do people win?"

Kyle shrugged. "Sometimes hundreds of thousands."

"And how much do they lose?"

Another shrug. "The same."

We left The Venetian and crossed over the strip to check out some pirate ship hotel that Kyle said he'd heard about. But it was just the same as the other casinos, though maybe the staff here wore even less clothes.

From what I could tell from my short time in Vegas, everything had to ooze sex. And not the classy kind of sex ooze – like a deep slit in a posh evening dress, expensive perfume and good linen. No, it was the other side of sex. The blatant, in your face, thrusty thrusty, raw, caveman, belts-as-skirts, look-at-me-rub-myself kind of sex.

From the outside, these hotels were grand over-the-top marvels of human imagination. But, on the inside, they were all the same. Bleeping machines. Zombie-like gamblers. Waitresses in essentially their underwear carrying trays of drinks to encourage y'all to stay longer. I couldn't help but crinkle my nose a bit, but stayed quiet, in case Kyle thought I was un-fun.

We stepped back out into the beyond-balmy night.

"You want to see the volcano that erupts every hour?"

I couldn't help but pull a face.

"You don't like The Vegas," he said. "Do you?"

We were arm in arm, dodging more porn gauntlets.

"It's okay…" I said. "It's just very in your face."

Kyle burst out laughing. "That is one way to describe it, for sure." He put his arm around me, saying "no" firmly to a guy shoving another call card in my hand. "Come on, let's go to the Bellagio fountains, I think you'll like those at least."

My feet ached by the time we got to the enormous curvature of the Bellagio hotel. There was already a two-deep queue around the big swimming pool and fountain area.

"It goes off every fifteen minutes." Kyle pushed me in front, so he could hold me around the waist from behind again. "A different song each time."

"Great." I leaned back into his body, pondering if it was wrong that I'd rather be in a nondescript room with him, feeling his body against mine, than standing in front of an iconic tourist attraction.

"You know what?" he whispered in my ear, sneaking his arms tighter around me.

"What?" I whispered back, still in disbelief about the number of actual bumbags worn around me.

"You've passed a secret girlfriend test by disliking Las Vegas."

"I like it just fine," I said. Hang on, GIRLFRIEND??

"Amber, I can see you don't. And, as I said, I'm glad you don't. I only came here once before, as a kid. Even then I found it seedy and I was too young to even really understand what was going on. I thought you would want to see it. I mean, everyone wants to see Vegas. But, as I said, I like that you don't like it here. It makes me like you more."

Just then, the music started and the water began to dance. For the first time since we'd arrived, I found some beauty in Las Vegas.

The fountains were magical, the way they moved and twisted with the music – reaching insane heights as the song built to a finale. I gasped, and snuggled closer into Kyle. When it was over, everyone applauded and dispersed, making room for the next queue of people. I stayed put.

"You like it?"

"I love it. Can we watch another? Please? Please? How many different songs do they do?"

"Of course." We took the empty spaces of the tourists who'd left, and leaned against the wall to get the best view.

"You called me your girlfriend." I didn't dare look at him in case he said, "Whoops, my mistake".

"I did."

"Am I?"

"I don't think I'm the only one who gets to decide that."

Girlfriend... Despite all my feminist priorities I'd always wanted...always worried I'd never be anyone's...and yet, here, just like everything else, Kyle gave me something without effort.

"You're my gal." He put his arm around me. "You totally rock my world, Amber."

"That is another contender for the most American phrase of all time."

"So, am I your boy?"

"People don't belong to people," I said, teasing him by quoting *Breakfast at Tiffany's*.

"Riiiight. Is there any more feminism you'd like to get out the way before you can say I'm your boyfriend and we can make out before the fountains start again?"

"You know what, no. Not for now."

We watched five more water shows, each one totally dramatic and yet totally with its own personality. I reckoned it was worth coming back to Vegas, just for the fountains.

It was getting just about late enough to make up an excuse to go back to our hotel room. Anticipation hung in the air like heavy fog. Every part of my body fizzed.

Kyle kissed me in the elevator as we rode up to our floor.

"How about we get up at the crack of dawn tomorrow and drive off before sunrise?" He asked. "We're heading towards Utah. It's just mountains and rocks."

I closed my eyes as he moved to kiss my neck.

"Ooooh, keep saying mountains and rocks." We both laughed.

"No porn gauntlets in Utah, I promise."

We kissed as we waited for our floor. We kissed in the corridor. We kissed up against our room door before we'd even got in.

Then we tumbled onto the bed, Kyle on top of me, as we giggled into each other's mouths.

He opened his eyes and paused over me.

"What is it?" I followed his stare.

He looked at the phone.

He rolled off me.

"We have a message."

I rolled over and stared at the phone too.

"How? No one knows we're here."

My tummy dropped to my ankles, like I'd just swallowed five cannonballs in one.

"Maybe it's just reception, saying we left something down there," Kyle suggested.

"Maybe."

He reached over and pressed play.

Of course, of course, it was my mother's voice.

"Amber, I'm here. In Vegas. In the Caesar's Palace lobby in fact. I know you're here. Come down. We need to talk. I won't leave until you come down…"

Situations that are destined to fail:

Your mother

+

Alcoholism

+

Even though you're both trying your hardest

Thirty-six

My hand shook as I pressed the button of the elevator. So much that I accidentally pressed the wrong button, and had to detour to a different floor before the doors slid open to the lobby.

There was too much fun around me. People were stumbling around drunk, the *ching ching ching* of a winning fruit machine, the whoops of the winners…

This was not the time. This was not the place.

She had come anyway.

It wasn't hard to spot her in the expansive lobby. My hair. She had my hair. She sat, with a book, and a clear drink in front of her.

Mum didn't jump when I sat down across from her.

"Amber." She looked up. Her face unreadable, as it always is.

I pointed to the drink.

"I hope that's not a vodka."

Mum's eyebrows pulled together. I could tell there was

at least a little bit of "angry" hidden in there.

"It's a soda water. I've been here for hours... I did think about it... Out of all the places you picked to run away to, you would have to pick the most triggering place for a recovering alcoholic, wouldn't you?"

I blew out my breath and shook my head in disbelief.

"You are SO manipulative. How did you even know where I was anyway? It's not like I want you here."

She was tarnishing everything, like she always did. This was one place that was free from her, free from my guilt and pain and longing, and yet she'd just rocked up anyway.

"Your friends told your dad..."

My mouth fell open. Evie, it would've been Evie. Argh, she was always so sensible!

"They did the right thing. You can't just run away like that, Amber."

I crossed my arms.

"So what, I ran out on some stupid summer camp. You ran out on your only daughter..." I wasn't going to cry, I wasn't going to cry...

But Mum did start to cry. It was a small, hollow sob that she tried to cover with a sip of her drink. But that didn't hide the tears that streamed silently from her eyes, like long rushing rivers.

I still kept my arms crossed.

"I didn't have a choice, Amber," she said. "I'm an alcoholic."

"Oh, are you? I hadn't realized."

"I don't expect you to understand."

"No, that's where you're wrong. You expect me to understand all the time. Every day. Whenever you mess up. It's your trump card – 'Oh, I'm an alcoholic'." I took a deep breath. "And I get that it's hard. I do. But that doesn't take away all the hurt you cause…"

"It's not my fault," she said, crying harder. "I can't help it. It's a disease."

"I GET THAT!" I almost yelled. "But I'm allowed to be hurt by the disease, aren't I? You don't even let me talk to you about it… You don't even…" I trailed off. I wasn't even sure what I wanted to say.

Mum reached over and took my hand. Part of me wanted to shake it off, but I didn't.

"Amber, look, I know I wasn't as here for you this summer as you wanted me to be. I didn't mean to give you any…false expectations of what I could be for you. But I *am* a recovering addict. It's very important I stick to my routines – that I stick to what works for me. The addiction…it's bigger than me. It's bigger than you. Bigger than my love for you. My love for anyone… If it wasn't, don't you think I wouldn't have screwed up in the first place? I was such a terrible mother…" She trailed off and sobbed again. I held her hand, waited while she got it out. A small part of me in wonder that everyone around us was ignoring the scene we were making. "The addiction always comes first, Amber. It came first when I used to leave you as a child, alone in the house, while I went and drank by myself in the park. It came first when I destroyed my marriage, your dad's life. It still came first when the doctors said I'd be dead in two years if I didn't stop drinking. It came first all the time. Therefore I *have* to put tackling it first, all the time. Otherwise, I'll die, Amber… I'll die. It will kill me."

She really was sobbing now. I tried to steel myself against her tears. That freedom I'd felt that morning, in the swimming pool. I thought I'd somehow, finally, after all these years, managed to stop her getting to me.

"You have my photograph in the guest room!" I said, weeks after I'd first thought it.

She looked up. "Because it's too painful to look at you every day. It's too painful to remember what I had to leave behind to stay alive."

Mum was answering. She was finally answering. I'd had to run away from her, give up on her at last to make her follow. But she was here now and she was talking. It didn't seem real. And, now she was here, now she was sharing, I was scared of what her answers would be.

"Why did you have to move away to America though? It's so far, Mum," I said, my voice cracking. "And you never came to visit."

She tried to compose herself, sipped more water. Her hand was so tight in my hand.

"Because I couldn't bear to see the mess I'd made of our family. The hurt I saw in your face. It destroyed me, Amber. The way you looked at me…" Another sob bubbled. "It made me feel like such a failure, it made me want to drink. I had to move away, to have a fresh start. And Kevin, I know you hate him and blame him for me coming here, but he saved me. He believes in me. He loves me, despite all I've done. He lives a healthy life, he gives me a healthy life – one that doesn't make me want to drink. We go hiking, we help others, we run the camp, we live in the mountains… I'm a different person, I'm someone to be proud of. But I'm still an alcoholic, Amber. And I've found this summer so hard, because you still look at me like that. Like, if only I tried harder, I could be a better mum. But I'm trying my best, Amber, I really am."

When Mum left for America, Dad made me go to this one counselling session, where they handed over all these leaflets about alcoholics. The leaflets said that addicts were "manipulative" and that they could be "emotionally abusive". Right then, I could've chosen to interpret Mum like that. But she was my mum, and she was actually answering my questions for the first time ever. This was the first conversation we'd ever had about everything that had happened, beyond her just going on the defensive or changing the subject. It hurt so much, but I finally realized maybe I wasn't the reason she left, *she* was the reason she left. There was nothing I could've done to keep her at home, make her better myself. I listened to what she said, and I… believed it. If she hadn't met Kevin, if she hadn't moved here, she would probably be dead. It still ached, I still wished she'd never left me, but I knew now…

I could finally understand why.

"I'm really proud of you," I said. And I was.

I stared at her, her healthy skin, her glass not full of vodka.

I couldn't imagine the strength it must've taken for her to get to this place, to give up what she needed to get here. I never thought I'd feel proud of my mum. But now, now I did.

"And I'm so proud of you, I really am, honey," she said. "It's been…a blessing having you here this summer, seeing how strong and beautiful you are, despite all you've been through." She looked up into my eyes, and it was my eyes staring back at me. "Please come back, Amber." She held my hand tighter. "You won't get into any trouble. Kevin said so. He's really not the monster you think he is. If you need to blame someone for leaving, blame me. I'll try and make more time… We only have a few weeks, but we'll make them count."

Blame. She was finally accepting blame. She was finally saying everything that I'd wanted to hear.

Yet I let go of her hand.

"No."

Her eyes fell. "What?"

"I'm not going back. I'm driving to Brown. With Kyle."

As if on cue, Kyle appeared at the elevator doors. We'd agreed he'd give us half an hour then come down and check on me. The worry on his face made my heart truly, fully, give itself to him. I made a hand signal, telling him to wait. Mum saw, turned round and scowled.

"Amber, you can't drive off with him. How will you get back?"

"I'll figure it out."

"You're underage. I could stop you."

"You won't."

"But...but...what about our time together?" She looked like a child.

I sighed and pushed a stray tear back into my eye. So much of me wanted to go back – to have those fairy-tale weeks I'd imagined when I first booked my plane ticket.

"Mum, you said you need to put the addiction first, and I get that, I really do. And I'm so happy you've come here, and you've told me all this." My voice wobbled. "But I need to do something for me now. I need to put my own happiness first. And driving to Brown, with Kyle, who you've totally underestimated by the way, is part of that. I need to do this, Mum... For me... It's my turn to need to be selfish..."

Her head fell down, and I thought she was going to cry again. But when she looked back up, she was smiling. Sadly, but smiling.

"Then, go for it... And, Amber?"

"Yes?"

"I'm sorry..."

She said sorry...

The apology melted in the air between us.

And then, like all apologies, I realized I didn't need it.

"I love you, Mum. It's okay," I said.

Because it was okay now. As okay as it could be. And that's all you can ask for sometimes, when it comes to love.

We both cried, and hugged, and said goodbye. Because that was the last time I'd see her that summer. That year. Maybe even the next year after that.

And that was okay too.

Situations that won't fail if you don't let them:

You

+

Someone who loves you

+

Whatever the world throws at you

Thirty-seven

We woke well before dawn, like we said we would. Piled ourselves into the car and drove out of the city, leaving the still-glittering lights behind us.

Soon there was just desert. And a horizon. And us driving into it.

Kyle's hand stayed on my knee. Still checking I was all right.

I was all right.

The first twinges of sunlight inched their way up the sky, casting yellow light over the vast expanse of the desert stretching out in front of us.

We weren't driving off into the sunset.

We were driving into the sunrise.

Our journey hadn't even started yet.

Turn the page for an <u>exclusive</u> look at...

Kyle's love letter to Amber

+

Holly's top tips for the perfect American road-trip

Dear Amber,

So I just said goodbye to you at the airport. And, yes, I cried on the drive home, because men are allowed to cry too – FEMINISM, you know!

I can't believe this summer is over. I've had the most amazing time with you. I still can't get over how that sarcastic intimidating girl who kept referring to my town as "poo-dank" is now my girlfriend. I was so blown away by you that night, and I still just feel like the luckiest "bloke" (as you would say) alive that we got to have this summer together.

Your sketchbook showed me you're a fan of lists, so, as you jet through the sky away from me, I thought I'd write down my favourite memories from these amazing past few weeks:

Making us stop and stand next to EVERYTHING when we drove across Colorado while yelling, "I FINALLY don't feel too tall any more".

Forcing us to detour hundreds of miles, just so we could take the road to Amarillo because of some stupid song you wouldn't stop singing. Then, once there, volunteering for that 72-ounce steak challenge which you failed at miserably. Also, the look of utter wonder on your face for the next twenty-four hours, when you kept showing me your food baby and exclaiming, "I still haven't finished digesting!"

THAT kiss (you know which one) you made me pull over for in Kansas, because you were bored of looking at cows for 400 miles.

In Kansas, again, where you revealed that you didn't know tornadoes were "real" and were only from the WIZARD OF OZ.

Your astonishment at the melted-butter tap when we went to the cinema in Indiana. Who knew this only existed in US cinemas?

When you told me you loved me at exactly 6.05 p.m., on i70, just as we passed the state border of Ohio. You were wearing a yellow T-shirt and you put your hand on mine on the gear-shift, and I knew then, more than I've ever known anything, that my life is not going to be the same ever again.

Every single night we shared a motel room together... because...well...I'm a guy.

Your befuddlement that Brown "isn't that brown".

I know things won't be easy for us. I know everyone's going to say we're too young/live too far away/too different etc. etc. for this to work – but they're idiots. This will work. Because, from my point of view, this HAS to work. Because you're the most extraordinary girl I've ever met, or ever will meet. And, well, I'm a sexy Prom King – what else do you need?

Seriously though, I'm just writing this to let you know that, if you still want me – once you're back in England – I'm totally yours.

All my love,
Kyle x

Holly's American road-trip tips

When I was twenty-four, in an uncharacteristic bout of spontaneity, I quit my job to drive from one side of America to the other.

To anyone who likes my books, we owe America for them. It was over there that I decided to give this writing thing a shot. At the end of my 4,500-mile trip, I sat in Yosemite Park and watched the sun set over Half Dome, plunging the valley into steady darkness. I remember it so clearly. I was relaxed, I felt healthy for the first time in years, and I only had a week before I had to fly home and face reality again. A very clear voice came into my head, and said, "Holly, go back and finish that book you're writing." It was so strange and profound that I listened. And, less than two years later, I had a publishing contract that would change my life. So – thanks, America.

This book is a love story. Not just to nice boys who call themselves feminists. But also to America – a country that is full of such positive people, who really believe you can change the world.

I'm going to share my top ten travelling tips I learned from my epic journey:

1) Don't go to Texas if you're a vegetarian. They even put beef in the tomato soup.

2) Driving across America in a Toyota Yaris isn't the coolest of vehicles, but you will save hundreds of dollars in gas.

3) The Grand Canyon is absolutely something you have to see before you die. Go, just go. But make sure you get there before 5 a.m. in the morning.

4) You will never eat as well as you will in New Mexico. Also, there's a tiny town called Taos, which is pretty much the most perfect place I've ever been to. Go there and stay in an earth ship. Eat at Taos Diner and order the Copper John's eggs. If you go to Taos, and don't go to Taos Diner and don't order the Copper John's eggs, please never tell me you've done such an unforgivably stupid thing.

5) Don't go to Las Vegas if you only have $30 to spend. You won't have a great time.

6) If you're ever in New Orleans, make sure you check out the World War Two, 4D experience. I don't care how drunk you are, just do it.

7) Do the Mist Trail at Yosemite National Park before 7 a.m. Bring a camera. Realize your camera will never do that level of beauty justice.

8) Siesta Beach in Sarasota, Florida, has sunsets you can't even imagine. It also has a drum circle every Sunday night, an hour before sunset. Go, dance, feel more alive than you can possibly imagine.

9) Go spraypaint a buried Cadillac along Route 66, just outside Amarillo. Yeah, it's cliché. But the photos look great.

10) Get ice-cream at the Bi-Rite Creamery in San Francisco. It will fill the gasping hole in your stomach caused by all the raw food restaurants.

About Holly Bourne

Holly writes YA novels and blogs about feminist issues. Her favourite things to complain loudly about are: the stigma of mental health, women's rights and the under-appreciation of Keanu Reeves' acting ability.

Holly's first two books, *Soulmates* and *The Manifesto on How to be Interesting*, have been critically acclaimed and translated into six languages. The first book in the "Normal" series, *Am I Normal Yet?* has been chosen as a World Book Night book for 2016, and has inspired the formation of Spinster Clubs across the country.

 @holly_bourneYA

 hollybourneYA

www.hollybourne.co.uk

Acknowledgements

I've been very lucky in that I've never found love very hard. For that, I can only thank my brilliant family – for loving me and supporting me no matter how hard I am to love. So Mum, Dad, Eryn, Willow – thank you as always for being the glue that binds me back together again. Through writing this book and being in Amber's head I've understood how blessed I am. So, cheers.

Thank you to Connie, for letting me come and stay with you in California when I was a confused teenager who didn't know who she wanted to be. It breaks my heart that you will never get to read this book.

Thank you to Peter Alsop, for shaping my childhood. I still cannot believe I've got your songs into my books. I cannot tell you how much that means. Thank you in particular for "Rachel and the Moon", which played constantly in my head while I wrote this.

As always, I want to say thank you to my agent, Maddy, for continuing to be the best agent a gal could wish for. And Cara and Thérèse too. And Usborne – brilliant, wonderful Usborne – for letting me write this trilogy and getting it and making it so much better than it would be without you. Thank you, Rebecca, Anne, Becky, Sarah, Amy, Anna and Hannah especially. I will never stop hugging you all and gushing at you whenever we meet. Sorry about that. If you want me to stop, you're going to have to stop being so wonderful. Thank you so much to Neil and Kath for my continually-amazing covers.

This was supposed to be a road-trip book, until Amber and Kyle kept refusing to get in the car. I'd like to thank Christi and Alexia a LOT, for a year of listening to me panic over cocktails, wailing "WHY WON'T THEY GET INTO THE CAR?". You two have become such rocks and I am so grateful. In fact, there are infinite amounts of UKYA people that make me feel good about humans. Thanks to Mel, Holly S, Anna, Carina, Matt, Lara, Kelly, Lee, Lisa, Non, Lucy, Jim, Lucy P, Jess and SO MANY OTHERS for being such a supportive community full of goodness and prosecco.

Thank you to Rich, for driving from one side of America to another with me and not strangling me along the way.

Thanks as always to Owen, for holding my hand through this crazy year.

I'd like to thank my readers, who have taken such a shining to the Spinster Club since *Am I Normal Yet?* came out, especially to those of you who've started your own feminist rebellions. Honestly, I love you. Please keep sending me updates and photos. I cannot tell you how happy it makes me. We will kick this patriarchy – I have such faith in the future with brilliant feminists (male and female) like you out there.